ABOUT THE AUTHOR

When Janet O'Kane outgrew
moved on to what her Mum
And despite occasional dal
fiction, that's what she has ha
now she writes it too.

Her career before turning to writing fulltime included
selling underpants to Roger Moore in Harrods and
marketing nappies for Boots. It was when she worked for
a GP surgery that she decided a family doctor would make
an excellent main character for a crime novel.

Janet lives in the Scottish Borders with her stonemason
husband and two cats, two dogs and far too many
chickens. *Too Soon a* Death is her second novel and she is
now working on her third.

ISBN-13: 978-1519209184
ISBN-10: 1519209185

https://www.facebook.com/JanetOkaneAuthor

Janet O'Kane

TOO SOON A DEATH

ALSO BY JANET O'KANE
No Stranger to Death (Borders Mysteries Book 1)

AUTHOR'S NOTE
This book is a work of fiction. While many of the Scottish Borders locations I describe are real, the village of Westerlea is not. With the exception of the individuals who agreed to appear as themselves in this novel, any resemblance to actual people, living or dead, is coincidental.

To John

ONE

Now Zoe understood the police officer's reluctance to bring her here. He had wanted to save her from having to slither down this steep, pebbly slope, not from seeing what lay beyond it. She reluctantly took his arm and clung to him during their descent. Once the terrain became flat and even, she broke free and strode along the grassy path, spotting a protruding tree root just in time to avoid tripping over it.

The River Tweed came into view, as did about a dozen people wearing white coveralls. They milled around, their actions and interactions seemingly random, although Zoe knew each would be carrying out an assigned task. One of them, a short woman carrying a clipboard, broke away from the rest and approached Zoe to ask her name.

The constable who'd brought her here spoke before she had a chance to. 'This is Doctor Moreland from the Westerlea practice. I was told to fetch her.'

The woman noted Zoe's name and the time of her arrival, then stared at her stomach and the calf-length dress stretched across it, obviously struggling over whether to insist on her donning a coverall. In the end, she merely handed Zoe a pair of latex gloves then led her towards the river.

Erecting a pop-up tent had been impossible, so despite the efforts of the police officer watching over it, the body was overlaid with countless flies. As each flap of the officer's arms saw some off, yet more took their place. Abandoning all pretence of sure-footedness, Zoe accepted the help of another officer to cross the narrow channel of sandy mud and step onto the first of a series of overlapping flat stones which jutted out into the Tweed. Although it was only mid-morning, heat bled through the soles of her sensible shoes.

As she picked her way over the stones, someone called, 'Doctor's here,' and the officer standing guard over the body moved to give her more room. She stepped forward, batting away the flies which instantly swarmed around her. Bending over was already uncomfortable and would soon be impossible. Lucky, then, that most of her patients could sit, stand or lie on a couch to be examined. Unlike this poor individual.

The dead boy looked about fourteen. He was skinny with short black hair, and he lay on his side, arms outstretched in front of him as though reaching for something. His uppermost hand was swathed in a grubby bandage. The back of his blue tee-shirt had come untucked from a pair of faded jeans and both his shoes were missing, as was one sock.

A memory flashed into Zoe's mind of a scene in a film, a heavily pregnant police officer leaning over a dead body in the snow. Her throat constricted as she also recalled the occasion on which she'd watched it.

She swallowed hard. 'He's so young. Just a boy.' His mother was probably not much older than her.

'Chinese, do you reckon?' the constable said.

The boy's round face and the epicanthic fold in his left eye certainly suggested he was of Asian descent, but Zoe knew from working at a large city hospital that guessing a person's ethnicity in this way left a very high margin of error. 'Maybe,' she said.

The flesh surrounding the right eye was so swollen that he wouldn't have been able to open it when he was alive. The constable reached past Zoe to point at the inch-long gash which followed the line of the boy's cheekbone. 'Could've hit his head going in. Knocked himself out and drowned.'

'Maybe,' Zoe said again. 'Though that black eye needed a few hours to develop.'

'Morning, Doctor.' The voice sounded familiar, but before Zoe could turn around, the speaker stood beside her.

She had met Detective Sergeant Trent several times the previous winter, when he had always appeared badly affected by the cold weather, despite being swaddled in several layers of clothing. Now, during what was reputedly the hottest summer the Scottish Borders had experienced for more than fifty years, he appeared equally uncomfortable, his face ruddy and dripping with sweat.

'Hello, Sergeant. This is a pleasant surprise. I would have thought you had more important matters to deal with than a suicide. At least, that's what I was told it most likely is.'

Trent dabbed at his forehead with a handkerchief. 'I learned long ago to keep an open mind when it comes to dead bodies.'

'So why am I here? Is your usual doctor not available?'

'The constable was supposed to fetch one of your colleagues. Because of this.' Trent held up a small evidence bag.

Zoe squinted in the bright sunlight, struggling to make out what was inside the bag. '"This" being . . .?'

'A note of your practice's address and phone number. We found it in the dead boy's pocket and thought he might be one of your patients.'

'May I take a closer look?'

Trent handed the bag over and Zoe studied its contents. 'I don't recognise the writing, but that doesn't mean anything. I've seen this logo before, though. It belongs to a brand of painkiller that's only recently come out. This piece of paper has been torn from one of those promotional notepads drugs reps are always foisting on us.'

'So it definitely came from your surgery?'

'Not necessarily. Why would anyone at the health centre write down our contact details if the patient's already there? We have a practice booklet for new patients. Maybe he went to register at another practice and was told to come to us because he lives near Westerlea.'

'You don't recognise him?'

'I've definitely never seen him, but I'm not there all the time. I'd have to check with the others.'

'I expected the constable to come back with Doctor Ryder. I'm sorry he dragged you out here.'

'Paul was taking surgery and Walter's not around at present because he's had to go back to Wales to organise his mother's funeral. I offered to come, so please don't blame your constable.'

'It's good to see you again, Doctor. You're looking well.' Trent smiled. 'I think your baby's due about the same time as ours.'

Zoe obviously failed to keep the surprise from her face, because he added, 'I know what you're thinking and yes, I have left it a bit late.'

'Is it your first?'

Trent nodded, smiling even more broadly. His obvious pleasure at the prospect of being a father caused Zoe a momentary pang of regret at not having anyone to share the joy of her own pregnancy with. She turned her attention back to the corpse and pointed at the bandaged hand. 'This looks professional. Even if he's not registered with us, he may have come into the health centre for treatment.'

'We'll need to find out for sure.'

4

'I can check with our practice nurse when I get back to the health centre.'

'What's her name?' Trent took from his pocket one of the small data recorders which had superseded policemen's notebooks and pencils.

'*His* name is Colin Barclay. Tut tut, Sergeant.'

'I stand corrected.'

'I'm being a little unfair. Colin job-shares with a female colleague but she's on holiday at present. As I'm here, do you want me to examine this poor boy? I won't remove his clothes and I can't take his temperature, but things I notice now may at least help you know if he was dead or alive when he went in.'

Trent looked back towards the track Zoe had slithered down. 'There's still no sign of the duty doctor but I don't think I can let you touch the body. Can you tell me anything just by looking at him?'

'I'll try.' Zoe took a butterfly clip from her bag and used it to pin up her ponytail, then slowly lowered herself to her knees. 'Apart from his clothes being damp, it's hard to believe he's been in the water at all. There are none of the usual signs of immersion, like swelling and wrinkling of the skin.'

'Maceration, you mean?' The policeman saw her look of surprise and winked. 'I've seen a few floaters in my time, picked up the jargon.'

'Of course. So there's no maceration and the note you found in his pocket is still legible. He can't have been in the water for long. What time was he pulled out?'

'I've no idea. He was like this when we got here.'

'How did you know where to find him?'

'CrimeStoppers got a call at about seven o'clock this morning to report a body lying on the banks of the River Tweed near the Chain Bridge. The caller rang off without saying anything else. Most people try not to get involved with the police if they can help it, and we've no way of finding out who he is because calls coming in on the 0800 number can't be traced.'

Zoe twisted her neck to get a better view of the boy's unbandaged hand. 'This palm has a nasty-looking injury. It's probably safe to assume he has a similar one on the other hand. One of the bandages must have come off when he was being pulled out of the water.'

'Any indication what caused it?'

'It could be a burn but there's too much swelling to know exactly how it happened. It's badly infected, though. He would have been in a great deal of pain.'

'So that didn't happen today?'

'With this amount of swelling? Unlikely.'

Trent wiped his face again. 'Are you able to tell if he was dead or alive when he went into the water?'

'Diagnosing drowning can be hard, Sergeant, even with the benefit of a post mortem.' Zoe reached towards the boy's face but stopped herself in time. 'It's difficult without touching him but I can't see any white froth coming from his mouth or nostrils. That's one of the signs to look for.'

'Anything else?'

'In cases of drowning in a river like this you often find grass or weeds clutched in the hands. Even the bandage and the damage to his other hand wouldn't have prevented such an instinctive reflex.'

Trent exhaled loudly. 'So not a suicide?'

'I'm no expert, but it seems likely to me he was already dead when he hit the water.'

'Any indication what did kill him?'

'You'll have to wait for the post mortem to give you the answer to that question.'

'An answer which will lead to yet more questions, I expect.'

'Often the way in your line of work, I imagine.' Zoe's eye was caught by something sticking out of the waistband of the boy's jeans. 'What's that?'

Trent's gloved hand halted hers as she reached towards the scrap of green fabric. 'Let me,' he said, taking a plastic evidence bag from his pocket. As he gently pulled it free, she saw it wasn't fabric but something more rigid, with a dirty-brown underside and chipped edges.

'I think I know where this is from,' the policeman said. But before he could elaborate, he looked past Zoe and muttered, 'Here comes trouble.'

TWO

Zoe followed Trent's gaze to a tall, middle-aged man in a white shirt and grey trousers marching along the riverbank towards them. When approached by the constable in charge of recording the details of all visitors to the site, he pulled off his sunglasses and stood impatiently twirling them.

'I'm late already,' he said in a strident voice. 'Some idiot gave me the wrong postcode. Satnav took me miles out of my way.'

'Oh dear,' Trent said. 'Doc Ferguson's crabbit at the best of times. Having to venture this far east obviously hasn't improved his mood.'

'Doesn't he usually cover this side of the Borders?' Zoe asked.

'Only during the school holidays. Lives in Peebles and not a family man himself.'

They watched Doctor Ferguson put his sunglasses back on then snatch the white coveralls which were offered to him and thrust his long limbs inside them. No one else hindered his progress towards Zoe and Trent, but no one tried to help him either.

The stone ledge felt crowded when he joined them, causing Zoe to imagine it breaking off and plunging them all into the water. She took some deep breaths then pulled off a glove and held out her hand. 'Hello, I'm Doctor Zoe Moreland, from the Westerlea practice.'

A vein pulsed at Doctor Ferguson's temple and the large mirrored lenses of his sunglasses filled with Zoe's reflection as he stared at her before wordlessly responding with a handshake which was over before it began. He turned to Trent and demanded, 'Why is a GP here?'

'Doctor Moreland is helping with the identification of the deceased.'

'I hardly think gloves are necessary for that. She has neither the knowledge nor the equipment to undertake an examination.'

Trent's ears turned red. 'She kindly agreed, at my request, to make some initial observations while we were waiting for you to arrive.'

'That was totally out of order. She's not even wearing protective clothing.'

'I think you can see the reason for that, Doctor.'

Chest thrust out and nostrils flaring, Ferguson pushed past Zoe, forcing her to step perilously close to the edge of the stone. She bit back the protest she felt entitled to make and concentrated on getting safely back onto the riverbank, then made for a bench in the shade a short distance away. It felt blissful to sit down, although with no guarantee she would get them on again, she stopped short of kicking off her shoes.

The Tweed's silent progress towards the coast was barely discernible, only the passing of the occasional leaf or feather indicating it was moving at all, while birds flew low over the water, skimming its surface to scoop up insects. Zoe glanced at her watch. It wasn't yet eleven but the temperature, even given the slight breeze, already felt more Greek island than Scottish Borders. The heatwave had started in early May and still, in mid-July, showed no sign of abating.

A few minutes later, Trent came over and sat down on the bench beside her. 'Sorry about that. The Doc's not the most charming of men, but he does have a way with dead bodies. Which is why he's tolerated.'

'He was probably right to question my presence.'

'If there's any flack flying, I'll take it. The DCI will understand when I tell him what happened. And that it's you.'

'DCI Mather, you mean?'

'Aye. I've called him with the news that we've got a suspicious death. He'll be along himself, once he escapes the meeting he's at in Edinburgh.'

Zoe nodded, playing for time. Should she ask how Erskine Mather was, make out to his Sergeant she'd not seen him since they last officially met, just before Christmas? She was saved from having to make that decision by the arrival of a constable whose boyish face she recognised but whose name completely escaped her.

'Yes, Geddes, what is it?' Trent asked.

Constable Geddes. Of course. Although still looking too young to shave every day, he appeared more confident and less fazed by the presence of a corpse than he had at their first encounter.

'I found this in the bushes, sir.' Geddes held out an empty plastic sack which, judging by the pictures on it, had at one time contained feed for game birds.

Trent grasped the sack, stared inside it and looked up. 'Am I missing something?'

'The smell, sir.'

Wearing a puzzled expression, Trent positioned his face at the sack's opening and sniffed. 'Fish,' he said.

'Poachers use these sacks to carry their catch, so it won't leak in their cars. Scales can be used as evidence.'

'You're well informed.'

Geddes beamed. 'I spent a couple of days with the Wildlife Crime Coordinator earlier in the year.'

'So you think it may have been a poacher who reported seeing the body?'

'Would explain why he didn't want to leave his details, sir.'

'Good work, Constable.' Trent turned to Zoe. 'I need to speak to someone about this and then I'll drive you back. You're not pushed for time, are you?'

'No, I'm not taking surgery until tomorrow morning. I was only at the health centre trying to catch up with some paperwork.'

As she waited for Trent to return, she remembered an ex-army friend who reckoned he'd been trained to eat any food which became available, because in combat you never know where your next meal is coming from. Pregnant women soon learned to apply the same principle to visiting the loo. What a pity the surprise visit from a police officer had made her forget this before exchanging the comfort of the health centre for the middle of nowhere. She shifted on the bench in an attempt to get more comfortable and glanced at her phone. Sergeant Trent had been gone nearly twenty minutes.

He surprised her shortly afterwards by approaching from the opposite direction he'd walked off in, no longer wearing a coverall. 'Sorry to be so long. My car's parked up near the Chain Bridge. It may look further but it's actually less of a walk than the path you came down by, and there are steps which'll be easier to negotiate.'

'That's fine by me. I just wish my dog was here. He'd love it.'

'I remember him. Bit of a Heinz fifty-seven, isn't he?'

'Everyone we meet has their own theory as to his parentage. A greyhound crossed with a spaniel is one of the more outlandish ones.'

'My wife had a greyhound when we first met. It hated me.'

Zoe laughed. She and Trent walked along the side of the river, chatting about dogs and then, inevitably, babies. He and his wife knew the sex of theirs: it was a boy.

The bridge which had seemed so distant loomed in front of them surprisingly soon. It was smaller than Zoe expected, its deck suspended by a network of metal cables between two towers of pinkish stone. A police car drove across; it must be stronger than it appeared.

Trent took the stone steps two at a time, Zoe following at a more sedate pace but still feeling breathless before she reached the top.

'There's my car.' He offered her a set of keys from his trouser pocket. 'I have to go on to the bridge. It shouldn't take long.'

'I'll come with you, if that's alright. I've never been here before.'

'You'd have no reason to, living where you do.'

'What's on the other side?'

'That's England, Doctor. If the body had ended up on the opposite riverbank I wouldn't be here. Northumbria Police would be running the show.'

A pair of stone bollards guarded the entrance to the Chain Bridge, the scuffs of paint on them warning drivers of anything bigger than a family car to venture no further. As they emerged from under the arch, the breeze Zoe had enjoyed at the riverside felt stronger, causing the sides of latticed metal struts and cables to creak and rattle.

'A Crime Scene Examiner should be here soon, but I wanted to take a look myself,' Trent said, striding along one of the wooden walkways on either side of the tarmac deck. 'I'm sure I don't need to remind you not to touch anything.'

She peered down at the river, happy to keep her hands away from the painted cables which were stained with rust and bird droppings. A swan cruised directly below them, creating a V-shaped wake. Back where she and Trent had come from, even more white-shrouded figures now milled around the water's edge.

Trent pulled out the evidence bag containing the fragment of green material found on the dead boy and held it against a horizontal cable. 'Perfect match,' he said.

'So he was dropped into the water from here?'

'They wouldn't even have to lift him up over the top cable, because there's enough room to slide him between two of these lower ones. What they didn't realise — or probably didn't care about — was that some of the paint is so loose it got caught in his clothes.'

'Were they relying on him sinking or floating out to sea? Neither seems a reliable way to dispose of a body.'

'He wasn't weighted down and we're a good few miles from the coast. Seems like they didn't mind how soon he'd be found. They just wanted rid of him.'

'What on earth had someone so young done to deserve that?' Zoe said, unaware how plaintive she sounded until Trent put out a hand as if to pat her on the shoulder. At the last moment he must have thought better of it, and instead plunged his hand into a pocket to take out his handkerchief again.

'We'll do our best to find out what happened to him, Doctor, I promise.'

As they walked back, a car came up behind them from the English side, causing the bridge to move. Trent, seeing Zoe's surprised face, said, 'Feels like being on a boat, doesn't it? Don't worry, it's meant to. The bridge was designed by a naval captain.'

He turned to glare at the vehicle's driver, who'd brought his car to a halt and was looking out of the window. 'Didn't you see the diversion signs? This road is closed. You'll need to go back the way you came.'

'Did the victim jump from here?' the man asked. Not bothering to wait for an answer, he leaned out of his window, holding a large camera.

Press. Zoe turned away but too late to avoid making eye contact with him. The sound of his camera a second or so later took her back to the previous

November, when photographers and journalists had made her life a misery until a more sensational story came along.

'Leave her alone,' Trent said.

'Just doing my job. Keep your hair on.' The photographer raised his car window and sped away, narrowly avoiding a police officer who had emerged from the steps at the side of the bridge. Trent told the officer to turn back any further vehicles, then he and Zoe walked to his car.

They opened every window but the roads were too narrow to drive at any great speed and without the air-conditioning Zoe enjoyed in her Jeep, the temperature inside the car remained intolerably high. It was a toss-up which she felt more desperate to do: have a pee or take off the shoes clamped around her swollen feet.

The car swerved as Trent only just avoided hitting a hare running across the road in front of them, reminding Zoe that a full-to-bursting bladder had priority over everything. She closed her eyes and tried to ignore all the messages her body was sending, to concentrate on what she was planning for the rest of the day. Now the decorators had finished she no longer had any excuse to put off buying nursery furniture.

'Alright, Doctor?'

She opened her eyes in time to see the familiar sight of a row of five small wind turbines on the edge of a field. Unmoving today, when they turned, the single blades reminded her of batons being twirled by majorettes in a parade. Why was Trent taking her past Berrylaw Farm? Her heart began to beat faster. She knew why.

'I don't think we're going the right way,' she said.

He slowed the car down and glanced across at her. 'I thought you wanted to go home, not back to the health centre.'

'I still live at Keeper's Cottage.'

'You didn't move into the place you were converting last year?'

'I sold it.'

Trent's face turned an even deeper shade of red. 'Sorry.' He didn't ask why.

THREE

Sergeant Trent parked up outside Keeper's Cottage and Zoe undid her seatbelt with a sigh of relief. She had started to wear the lap strap under her bump, but it still felt uncomfortable, especially with an overfull bladder.

'As I'm so close I thought I'd go into the health centre and see if your practice nurse or any of the other staff remember seeing this laddie.' Trent held up his mobile, which he'd loaded with several head-and-shoulders photographs of the dead boy. 'What are you going to do about collecting your car?'

'I have a friend coming for lunch. She'll give me a lift.' Zoe scrambled out of the car then leaned back in to add, 'Thanks, anyway.' The amused look on Trent's face told her he'd guessed why she was in such a hurry to get indoors.

A few minutes later, she walked barefoot out of the bathroom, bladder emptied and feet soothed by the chill of the recently-laid slate tiles. She considered, not for the first time, taking down the hall mirror. Everything was swollen, even her face. And still nearly two months to go.

The cat lay in the airing cupboard as usual, which would have been unbearable had the plumber not removed the hot-water tank when he recently installed the cottage's new heating system. Zoe unlocked the French windows out of the kitchen — another timely home

16

improvement—and went out onto the patio, opening up the garden umbrella and lowering herself carefully onto the sun-lounger. Mac followed her outside and went to sit in his current favourite place, under an old holly tree.

She alternately sipped from a glass of iced water and held it against her face. A house martin swooped past on its way to the nest under the cottage's eaves which she had insisted must stay until the autumn, against the advice of the stonemason who'd been forced to work around it. In the distance, a chainsaw started up with a noise like a motorbike.

As if sensing she'd relaxed, the baby began to kick. Zoe smiled and patted her swollen abdomen. 'Don't give me a hard time. I'm not going to get many chances to put my feet up once you're here so I'm making the most of it now.'

The side gate creaked open, causing Mac to leap up and bark briefly until he recognised the figure dressed in a pink top and cut-off jeans picking her way through building debris towards them. He raced to greet her, tail wagging.

'I thought maybe you'd forgotten our date when there was no sign of your car,' Kate Mackenzie said, sitting down opposite Zoe in a chair not covered by the umbrella's shade. 'Then I saw you back here. What a pity your hedge had to come out. A fence with a few rose bushes behind it gives you no privacy.'

'It keeps Mac in, which is the most important thing. I'll get more trees planted once all the work's finished.' Zoe looked straight at her friend as she spoke, even though the sun made her squint. Kate's skill at lip-reading was remarkable, and many people chatted to her at length without realising she was deaf, but even she struggled with faces partly turned away from her. 'A man with a digger's coming soon to spread those piles of earth from when the new drains were put in, although the lawn can't be laid until autumn. Do you want a cold drink?'

Zoe swung a leg off her sun-lounger but Kate gestured to her to stay put. 'I'll get it. Remember, I know only too well the hassle of climbing out of a low seat once your bump's that big.'

Leaning back, Zoe said. 'Bring a jug, will you? With ice?'

Kate laughed. 'Being pregnant has definitely mellowed you. Not long ago there's no way you'd sit there asking someone — even me — to do that.'

'I know. I'm getting so lazy.'

'Zoe, no one could ever accuse you of being lazy. You're just more laid back. Which is a good thing, believe me.'

Kate disappeared into the house before Zoe could argue, coming back out a few minutes later. Ice cubes clattered against the side of the blue jug she carried, then splashed noisily as she poured water into her own glass and topped up Zoe's.

'Do you want to move your seat into the shade?' Zoe asked.

'No thanks, I love the heat. We'll probably never see another summer like this in my lifetime, so I'm making the most of it.' Kate ran her fingers through her cropped hair, which had recently changed from brick-red to white-blonde. 'I know we're not supposed to allow ourselves to tan these days, but peely-wally is only ever flattering on models, not normal people.'

'You're looking great,' Zoe said, aware Kate's recent weight-loss and bloom were more likely thanks to happiness than a suntan and the new swimming regime she'd adopted to help tackle a recently-diagnosed degenerative spine condition. Zoe lived in fear her friend's rekindled relationship with Erskine Mather might be snuffed out at any time, given his uncertain marital status, but she kept those thoughts to herself. She was hardly in a position to counsel anyone on how to run their lives.

'So are you. Pregnancy suits you, although

typically you've not put on weight all over like I always do.'

'Yes I have. Look at my face.'

Kate tilted her head and stared. 'No, can't see it myself. Maybe because your already splendid hair has become even thicker and shinier. Needless to say, mine got thin and greasy every time I was pregnant.' Her eyes travelled down Zoe's body. 'You're carrying high and to the front. You must be having a boy.'

'I know what you're doing, Kate.'

'What do you mean?'

'I can't tell you what sex it is because I truly don't know. Why won't you believe me?'

'It may have something to do with your refusal to admit you were pregnant until even Dad noticed.' Kate grinned. 'Remember how embarrassed he got when Mum said maybe you'd just put on weight and it was very rude of him to mention it? She was winding him up, of course, but even after nearly fifty years of marriage he still can't tell.'

'And I felt obliged to put him out of his misery and admit he was right. I still think you and Etta planned it.'

Kate took a long drink rather than answer. Anxious to move the conversation away from her pregnancy, Zoe said, 'I got called out by the police this morning. To see a dead body.'

This had the desired effect. Kate gasped and put down her glass. 'Who was it?' she asked.

'A young Asian boy, maybe sixteen at the most. He'd been thrown into the Tweed.'

'Thrown in? How awful. Does anyone know who he is?'

'No, that's why I was there. The police thought he might have visited the health centre recently.'

'Why did they think that?'

Zoe hesitated and Kate frowned. 'You're wearing

the shut-down look on your face I've become very familiar with. If he's not a patient, you can talk about it. This isn't like last time, you're not actually involved, are you? I mean . . .'

Kate's voice petered out and a flush spread across her face. 'Sorry. Thoughtless of me.'

Zoe absentmindedly plucked at some stray dog-hairs which had landed on her dress. After being friends for nearly a year, she ought to be used to Kate's tendency to say things which would be better left unsaid.

'Sorry,' Kate repeated.

Zoe raised her face and forced a smile. 'You're right, I'm not involved. And I don't wish to be. But you should have seen him lying there, so young and innocent-looking. What could he have done to make someone treat him like that?'

'Did he drown?'

'I don't think so. It's likely he was already dead when he hit the water. Sergeant Trent thinks someone drove him to the old bridge just up from Paxton and threw him off it.'

'The Chain Bridge, you mean?'

'That's the one.'

'Was Dave Trent in charge?' Kate asked.

'Don't you mean, was DCI Mather there?' Zoe said. Kate had her own weak spots. 'He's in Edinburgh this morning, though I would have expected you to know that.'

'Actually, I haven't seen Erskine for a few days. He's got a lot on at the moment.'

'But everything's okay between you?'

'He's suggested we all go to Crieff Hydro next half-term. I'd rather it was just me and him but I've looked at the website and they've got a pool and ponies and even a cinema so the kids'll be kept occupied.'

'Planning ahead's always a good sign.'

'A sign he doesn't intend going back to Glasgow, you mean?'

For Glasgow, read Mather's wife. Zoe had no intention of getting into a discussion about a woman she — and Kate, for that matter — had never met. 'I have a confession to make,' she said. 'Although I remembered you were coming round, I forgot to get anything in for lunch. So shall we nip into Duns? My treat.'

Kate raised her eyebrows but went along with this clumsy change of subject. 'That'll be good. If we're lucky, we may get a table outside.'

'And then you could drop me off at the health centre on the way back so I can collect my car.'

Kate nodded. 'Sounds like a plan. Do you need help getting up?'

All the tables outside were occupied, so Kate and Zoe sat inside the cafe, beneath the huge wooden clock on the wall and beside an electric fan which produced a welcome breeze. They both ordered gazpacho served with homemade oatcakes, which Zoe found a more pleasing combination than she expected. It also proved very filling, so when Kate said, 'I think I'll have a piece of chocolate cheesecake,' she opted for just a mug of tea.

'You didn't finish telling me about the dead boy in the river,' Kate said, digging her fork into her sweet. 'And why the police thought you might know him.'

'They found a piece of paper in his pocket with the health centre's address and phone number written on it. Sergeant Trent was expecting one of the partners to pitch up, but he got me instead.'

'His wife's pregnant too, you know.'

'So he said. Anyway, he's gone to see Paul himself as I was no help.'

'The Borders isn't exactly racially diverse, is it? A young Asian boy would have stood out. Someone will remember him.'

21

'I hope so. His family must be missing him, even if they don't know yet that he's dead.' To her horror, Zoe felt her eyes prickle as she thought again about the young life ended so prematurely. Damn these hormones. She found the physical changes due to pregnancy just about bearable, but hated how emotional she'd become. A patient's distress over a late miscarriage had nearly triggered a bout of crying last week, which would have been both humiliating and selfish.

Luckily, Kate was too intent on gathering up every remaining chocolate curl on her plate to notice. When she lifted her head again, Zoe asked how her latest contract was shaping up.

'I'm going across to Hawick to do some research at the Heritage Hub on Monday.'

'Who's your client this time?' Fascinated by Kate's job as a genealogist, Zoe enjoyed hearing her friend talk about what she called her history detective work.

Kate looked embarrassed. 'Strictly speaking, I'm not supposed to discuss it with anyone.'

'Oh. In which case you mustn't.'

'This client's a bit strange, to be honest, but things are slow at the moment so I can't afford to be choosy.'

Knowing she carried out most of her business using email and Skype, Zoe asked, 'You've actually met him?'

'Yes, last week when I was up in Edinburgh. Don't worry, he's perfectly harmless, just rather intense. Wouldn't stop talking, didn't listen to hear what I had to say. You know the type?'

'Only too well. Do many clients worry about confidentiality?'

'My contract's usually enough to cover the things that might concern them, like me discovering something scandalous about their ancestors and going to the press with it. I did once work for someone who thought he was more famous than he really was. He made me sign a confidentiality agreement.'

'Is that what you've had to do this time too?'

'No, it's nothing formal. He was just weirdly insistent I shouldn't talk to anyone else about it.'

'A pity.'

'If it's any consolation, the job doesn't sound very interesting anyway.' Kate put down her fork and pushed her plate away. 'I shouldn't have had that, but it was good. Are you ready to go? I've just remembered I said I'd collect Dad's prescription from the chemist.'

'I'll pay the bill and see you there,' Zoe said.

When she left the cafe a few minutes later, she wasn't surprised to find Kate's progress across Duns Square had been slow, most likely due to having stopped to chat with almost everyone she encountered. She caught up with her at the Mercat Cross, a symbol of the town's past trading status and, as Kate once gleefully informed her, where the severed heads of the vanquished were put on display in earlier times. These days, the red-stone column was mainly used as a gathering point by teenagers sharing fizzy drinks and cheap cigarettes.

An elderly man held the glass door open for them and Zoe went in search of deodorant while Kate approached the pharmacy counter. Having made her purchase, she joined Kate to wait for another month's worth of the medications which had thus far helped Ranald Mackenzie stave off another stroke. Kate swapped pleasantries with one of her mother's friends while Zoe watched a young woman wearing a white coat check a display of homeopathic medicines, occasionally jotting something down on a notepad.

A notepad.

She edged towards the woman to glance over her shoulder. The sheets were larger than the one found in the dead boy's pocket and the logo at the top wasn't the same, but the notepad was definitely a promotional freebie. GPs weren't the only recipients of drug companies' largesse. Why hadn't she thought of this before?

'Good afternoon, Doctor Moreland. How are you?'

George Romanes owned this pharmacy and several others in the Borders. Zoe had first met him when he invited her to see the state-of-the-art dispensing robot he was rightly proud of, and although she wasn't one of his regular customers, that would probably change once the baby arrived. She smiled a greeting and said, 'Can I ask you something?'

'Of course. Let's go somewhere a bit more private.' He led her into a room off the shop floor, and they sat down.

'I don't know if you've heard,' Zoe said, 'but a young man was found dead on the banks of the Tweed near Paxton this morning.'

'I've heard a rumour going about but there's been nothing on the news yet.'

'The police called me out because they thought he may have been a patient of ours. I didn't recognise him—which doesn't mean anything, of course—but I'm wondering if he came here. His hands had been bandaged by someone who knew what they were doing.'

'Was he Asian? Very young?'

'So you did see him.'

'It was me who bandaged his hands. They were both badly burnt, more seriously than I was comfortable treating, to be honest.'

'And you gave him a note with the health centre's address and phone number?'

'I told the man who brought him in he should go to see a doctor, but he was insistent we should just patch him up.'

'What did the boy himself say?'

'He couldn't speak English, not a word. I brought him in here, tried to explain how badly injured he was. All I managed to get was his name, by pointing to myself and repeating "George" then pointing at him.'

'What was it?'

'I think he said Ara.' Seeing the look on Zoe's face, George spelled out, 'A-R-A.'

'Ara,' Zoe said. It felt important to commit his name to memory.

'And you say he drowned?'

'Not necessarily, although he'd been in the water. So the man who was with him spoke English?'

'With a strong accent. Eastern European, if I had to guess. He'd been in the wars himself, kept playing with a nasty scar on the side of his head. Told me the boy was his cousin and he'd burnt himself on a saucepan.'

'I don't suppose he mentioned where they were living?'

'I didn't think to ask. My main concern was to get the boy the treatment he needed. He was in a lot of pain and when he pulled back one of the filthy bits of towel wrapped around his hands I could see why. They were a mess.'

'When was this?' Zoe frowned. 'I'm sorry for firing all these questions at you, George. I know I should leave it to the police, but I feel kind of involved, having seen him.'

'That's okay—I'd be the same. They came in late yesterday afternoon, although it was obvious the damage had been done a few days earlier.'

'And he was dead less than twenty-four hours later.'

They sat in silence for a few moments then George placed his hands on his thighs and pushed himself up. 'I'd better give the police a call,' he said. 'Do you know who I should speak to?'

'I dealt with Detective Sergeant Trent.'

'Ah, Dave. His wife's having a baby too.'

Everybody knows everybody round here. Zoe followed George back out to the shop floor, where she saw Kate still deep in conversation, though with a different person this time.

George turned and Zoe assumed he was going to say goodbye. Instead, he wore a pained expression on his normally cheerful face. 'I knew something was wrong,' he said. 'That boy wasn't only in pain. He was terrified.'

FOUR

'What was all that about?' Kate asked when she and Zoe got back to the car. 'One minute you were standing beside me, the next you'd disappeared into George's little room with him.'

'Just a pregnancy thing I needed his advice on.'

Kate snorted. 'Aye, right. All respect to George, but you're a woman and a doctor. You know more about it than he ever will.' Despite her uncompromising tone, she didn't press Zoe any further but put her ageing Volvo into gear and they sped off in the direction of Westerlea.

Used now to the silence while Kate drove, Zoe let her mind wander during the short journey. She imagined Ara — even if that wasn't his name, she would use it until she knew otherwise — walking into the chemist with strips of dirty towelling wrapped around his hands. In life, his face had been contorted with pain, unlike the repose death had brought to it. But George said he looked scared too, so what caused that? And where did he and his cousin go after getting Ara's hands bandaged? They couldn't have travelled far, because the boy turned up dead a few miles away so soon afterwards.

She looked down at her swollen stomach. Was this preoccupation with the fate of a boy she'd never met another consequence of the mothering instinct she could still hardly believe had been awakened in her?

The car drew to a halt at the health centre's front

27

door and Kate turned to face Zoe. 'Thanks for lunch. Do you want to come over to Mum and Dad's on Saturday? They're having a barbecue. Just a few friends and half a cow, you know the sort of thing.'

'I'd love to, but I'll be out for most of the day.'

'Oh.'

Zoe could tell her friend was itching to ask where she was going, but had no intention of telling her. 'I'll be back late in the afternoon. When does it start?'

'Not till about six.'

'Perfect. I'll have time to shower and change. See you then.'

The health centre's automatic front door sat open. Convinced those early days of non-stop sunshine would cease as soon as the practice spent money on the comfort of its staff and visitors, Walter Hopkins had fought the purchase of several electric fans but was overruled by Paul Ryder, the practice's senior partner. This hadn't prevented him from bagging the largest fan for his own office, but Zoe saw to her satisfaction that now he was absent, Walter's fan stood on the reception desk. She doubted he'd ever get it back.

Margaret Howie looked up and smiled, her hair fluttering around her plump face in the current of cool air. 'Hello, Doctor Zoe. I didn't expect you back today.' The lynchpin of the practice, Margaret had outlasted all the other staff Paul had employed over the years, and her knowledge of its patients went far beyond any computer records.

'I had to collect my car. Did Sergeant Trent get to see Paul?'

'Yes, then he asked us all if we'd seen that poor boy. And my Hector's phoned to say it's on the news now. They're calling him The Boy Under The Bridge.'

'Not strictly accurate but hardly surprising. I wonder if anyone will come forward to identify him?'

'Why did the police think he'd been here?'

'His hands had been bandaged by someone who knew what they were doing.'

Seemingly satisfied with this response, Margaret said, 'You had your fill of policemen last year. If I'd been on the desk, I wouldn't have let that laddie near you this morning. I've told Penny she should have made him wait for Doctor Paul. A dead body wasn't going anywhere.'

'I didn't mind.' Zoe's mobile rang. She pulled it out of her bag. 'Excuse me, I need to take this.'

She knew who was ringing her but still hadn't settled on what to call him. 'Hello.'

'Hello, Zoe. Can you speak?'

'Yes. I'm at the health centre but not taking surgery. How are you?'

'Well, thanks.'

'And Helen?'

'Oh, you know how it is. She has good days and bad. Today's not one of her good ones.'

'I'm sorry to hear that.'

'I was just calling to say I'll be later than planned tomorrow. Have to wait for the MacMillan nurse to arrive. Can we say twelve o'clock rather than eleven?'

'Of course, not a problem. We can make it even later, if you want.'

'No, I can be there for midday. Have a safe journey over.'

'Thanks. See you then.'

Margaret's head turned away just a little too quickly when Zoe looked over at her, but unless her lip-reading was even better than Kate's, she couldn't have known what Zoe was saying, let alone who she was speaking to.

Paul's consulting room door was wide open, signalling he didn't have a patient with him. Zoe gave a start as she entered the room and he looked up at her.

'Your beard's gone.'

'Hello, my dear.' He ran a hand down one side of

his face. 'Come and sit down. Yes, for the first time in about twenty years.'

'Did you get too hot?'

Paul cleared his throat. 'No, I just thought it was time for a change.'

Unconvinced this was the real reason but not wanting to pry, Zoe said, 'It suits you.'

'Thank you. I think I owe you an apology. It should have been me who went with the policeman this morning. I heard you had to clamber down a steep path to the river's edge, which couldn't have been easy, given . . .' His voice trailed away.

'Given I'm so huge now,' Zoe said, smiling. 'It wasn't easy but I managed. The annoying part was I couldn't help them once I got there. And I made myself unpopular with Doctor Ferguson, the police doctor.'

'I heard that too, but don't worry. We've all had spats with him.'

'Sergeant Trent suggested he isn't the easiest person to handle. Even so, I can't believe he managed to fall out with you.'

'We worked together years ago and he hated how I did things. Accused me of being a pushover, said I needed to be less familiar and more assertive with the staff. As if that was the secret to getting the most out of people.' Paul straightened his trademark tartan tie which, despite the heat, was still firmly knotted around his collar. 'I suppose we should make allowances for him. He's never been the same since his wife took off with her gym instructor.'

After allowing a moment's silence to signal her sympathy for Ferguson, Zoe asked, 'How much did Sergeant Trent tell you when he came here?'

'Only that the body of a young Asian boy has been found on the bank of the Tweed near the Chain Bridge and he had a piece of paper with our address and phone number in his back pocket. You didn't recognise him but his hands had been professionally bandaged, so the chances are he's been here for treatment.'

She shook her head. 'I've just come from speaking to George Romanes. He's the one who bandaged the boy's hands. He also gave him the note because the burns were so bad he thought a doctor should treat them. He'll have spoken to Sergeant Trent about it by now, so we're out of the loop.'

'What a pity you had to be dragged into the situation at all.'

'My only concern is that the police find out who the boy was and why someone killed him.'

'DCI Mather thinks it was murder, then?'

'He wasn't there.'

'Oh. I thought he ran things down here now.'

Zoe wondered where he had got that idea from. 'I believe there are a few layers of management above him, although he does seem to attend a lot of meetings.'

Paul coloured slightly. 'Was the boy dead before he hit the water?'

'I couldn't find any indications of drowning. And there's evidence he'd been pushed off the bridge rather than jumped from it of his own accord. But we'll have to wait for the post mortem to be sure.'

Paul sighed. 'He looked so young in the photograph Trent had on his phone. What a wicked world this is when a teenager taking his own life is the least bad alternative.'

'George said he spoke no English, and if he wasn't living around here, identifying him is going to be difficult. And without knowing who he is, how will the police find out who killed him?' Zoe paused, aware of the distress which had crept into her voice. She must control these emotions.

Paul reached out and patted her arm. 'Now we know we're not involved, let's talk about more cheerful things. How's your building work coming along? Will everything be done in time for the baby?'

'They've finished indoors already. This weather's helped—no days have been lost to rain at all. Outside's still a mess but that's hardly a priority.'

'It was a wise decision to stay there.'

'I was lucky Robbie Mackenzie let me have the cottage. Kate says he never usually sells any of his properties. I have her to thank for that.'

'It's not what you know but who you know round here. And didn't he fix you up with a good builder too?'

'Better than the one I had before, that's for sure.' Zoe's smile faded as she remembered the steading conversion she had planned to make her home. She was about to return their conversation to safer territory by asking after Paul's son when a knock sounded on the door and Colin Barclay entered the room. He stopped in his tracks when he saw Paul wasn't alone.

'Sorry for interrupting, Doctors. I'll come back later.'

'I was about to leave,' Zoe said, rising from her chair. 'He's all yours.'

'There's nothing you can't say in front of Zoe,' Paul said. 'You look worried. Is there a problem?'

Colin moved forward, stopping at Zoe's side and giving her a close-up of the tattoo on his forearm nearest her, an anchor entwined with rope which she knew was matched by a compass on the other arm. She remembered the first time Walter had spotted these and caused such a stooshie—her favourite of the Scots words she'd learnt in the past year—that Margaret had felt obliged to call her out of surgery to calm things down. All of Walter's prejudices, which had nearly succeeded in blocking Colin's recruitment, had come to a head and resulted in a ferocious verbal assault against the male practice nurse. Having herself been the subject of Walter's resentment for several months after joining the practice, Zoe had admired the dignity with which Colin handled the situation. An uneasy truce now existed between the two men, although this worked mainly because they avoided each other whenever possible.

'That dead boy the policeman showed us on his phone,' Colin said. 'When I was putting the signed prescriptions into an envelope to take to the chemist I remembered something.'

FIVE

Colin fidgeted with the pen tucked into the breast pocket of his tunic. 'I said I'd never seen the boy, but now I'm not so sure.'

'You need to tell Sergeant Trent,' Zoe said. 'People often don't remember things when they're asked. It isn't till later, when they've had a chance to think, that something comes to them.'

'I don't want to waste anyone's time. Or look an idiot.'

'Why do you think the police do appeals on the television?' Paul said. 'They know it jogs people's memories.'

'What exactly is it you've remembered?' Zoe asked.

'I think I did see the dead boy, yesterday at the chemist's when I dropped off the prescriptions.'

Paul and Zoe glanced at each other but said nothing.

'I was about to go in through the front door when this tall bloke with a crew cut barged out without even looking at me. Nearly knocked me over. I was conscious of someone behind him holding back to let me in but I was so annoyed I wasn't paying attention.'

'And you think it was the boy in the picture?' Paul asked.

'I'm pretty sure it was.' Colin sighed. 'Doesn't sound much, now I've told you. Hardly worth bothering the police with.'

'A policeman I know likes to compare an investigation to doing a jigsaw puzzle,' Zoe said. 'They have to put together lots of small pieces in order to see the big picture.'

'But what if I'm mistaken?'

'I don't think you are,' she said.

The next morning, Zoe was tempted to take Mac with her but knowing he couldn't safely be left in the car because of the heat, she took him for an extra-long walk. Aside from her obligation to the dog, she was determined to keep as active as possible for her own sake. The main challenge she faced was being able to reach her boots. She would struggle to tie them before long.

They got back just as the postie pulled up on the road outside Keeper's Cottage.

'Morning, Doctor!'

'Hi, Donald. How are you?' Zoe went to the red van's window and took the bundle of envelopes, fliers and catalogues he offered her.

'Doing away, Doctor. Doing away.' He gave a cheery smile and drove off towards Westerlea.

She sifted through her post as she walked round to the back door. The latest offers from the Co-op, a credit card company offering zero percent interest on balance transfers, two clothing catalogues and a postcard of the Grand Place in Brussels. She turned over the card; as usual there was no message. It joined the others in a kitchen drawer.

Choosing what to wear is easy when virtually nothing in your wardrobe fits any more. Zoe pulled on a pair of navy leggings and a sleeveless turquoise tee-shirt. Wanting to look her best though unsure why, she also put on a multi-coloured necklace and slipped its matching cuff onto her wrist.

She had first made this journey in January, and for several months the frequent, hammering rain which often became sleet the further west she travelled had meant driving was a chore rather than a pleasure. However, since April, she had been able to enjoy crossing into Dumfries and Galloway, which shared the Borders' empty roads and beautiful scenery. These outings felt less of a culture shock than the occasions when she travelled north to Edinburgh, despite her destination being further away.

As the A708 curved to the right on its approach to Moffat, Zoe's mouth went dry. She reached over for the bottle of water sticking out of her bag, feeling foolish for being so nervous. She and Andrew Balfour had met several times since he first approached her outside the health centre last December. On that occasion, she had stood rooted to the spot and listened to what he had to say, then asked him not to contact her again. He didn't argue, just stood staring at the ground as she got into the Jeep. She had sat for a moment, opened her window and asked him for a number she could call him on, then raced home, unable to get indoors before vomiting up her lunch. Of course she hadn't known then that she was pregnant.

Moffat was starting to look familiar. As usual, she smiled when she caught sight of the statue of a curly-horned ram on top of a mound of large stones. She found a shady spot in the hotel's car park but remained in the Jeep for a few minutes, trying to quell the butterflies in her stomach. Having once again made allowances for non-existent traffic jams — a throwback to her previous life in a city — she'd arrived twenty minutes early.

On the dot of midday, as she sat on a wooden seat in the beer garden, reading a book and swirling ice round the bottom of her glass, she heard someone say her name. She looked up, shading her eyes with a hand. Andrew came forward, hesitated then bent down and kissed her lightly on the cheek.

'Can I get you another drink?' he asked.

'Please. Lime and lemonade with lots of ice.'

By the time he returned, Zoe had put away her book and taken a few more deep breaths to calm her nerves.

Andrew set down their drinks. 'I assumed you wouldn't want to eat out here, so I've reserved a table in the dining room. We can go in whenever you want.'

'Great, thanks. I don't think these seats were designed for tall, pregnant women.'

'I'm sorry I couldn't be here earlier. Hope it doesn't mean you'll have to rush back.'

'There's no need to apologise. Really.' Zoe looked across the table at her father. His hair, streaked with grey, used to be the same colour as hers, and she could see now where she got her long, rather narrow nose from. She wondered if they shared any traits which were more than skin-deep.

'I do that rather a lot, don't I?'

'All the time. How's Helen today?'

His face fell. 'Since I spoke to you yesterday, I've realised she only has bad days now. The doctors say she probably won't last another month. They've asked me if I want them to find her a place in a hospice but as long as we can keep her comfortable at home, we'd rather she stayed there.'

'I can understand why. It must be so hard for you all, though.'

'Nina's taken over running the house. Her way of coping, I suppose. She never used to lift a finger but she's suddenly grown up. Ewan's only sixteen and not very mature anyway, but he's hardly helping the situation. We rarely see him. Says he's spending time with friends but I've no idea who they are.'

'People deal with things differently. Being a

teenager's difficult enough, but having to watch a parent die must feel like your world is ending, slowly and painfully.'

'How did you cope with losing your mother, Zoe? You said you were only twelve when it happened.'

'It was different for me. A road accident. She waved me off to school one day and in the afternoon my teacher told me she'd been killed. It was awful, brutal even. But not long and drawn out.'

'I should have been there,' he said.

'You're here for Nina and Ewan. That's what's important. I'm all grown-up, so you don't have to worry about me.'

'I never stopped thinking about you.'

'I don't blame you for what happened. And neither did Mum.'

'Finding you is helping me cope with losing Helen. I just wish you could meet her before it's too late.'

'But you said you didn't want her to know about me. That she would see what happened between you and Mum all those years ago as a betrayal.'

'She would. Your mother was the only secret I've ever kept from her.'

'Do you really think she'd care after all this time?'

'There's something else I haven't told you.'

Andrew stared at the glass in his hand without speaking for so long that Zoe eventually asked, 'What is it?'

'We adopted Nina and Ewan because Helen couldn't have children. We tried for years and it tore her apart. My having fathered you during a brief relationship with another woman was the worst thing I could possibly have done to her. I can't tell her. Maybe if she'd been well, but not now.' He gave a humourless laugh. 'This should be such a happy time. I've been reunited with my eldest daughter and soon I'll have my first grandchild. But in exchange, I lose my wife.'

He stood up. 'Let's go in and have lunch.'

Their meal was more enjoyable than Zoe expected. As usual, the food was excellent and Andrew made a big effort to be more cheerful, even getting out his phone to show Zoe a photograph of himself with his Border Collies. When she asked if he had any pictures of his family as well, he shook his head. 'Ewan took this one and set it to show when I turn my phone on. I prefer to use a real camera.' He tilted his head to one side and studied her. 'You've got the Balfour nose. Something else I should say sorry for, I guess.'

Zoe smiled. 'So I can expect my baby to have one too?'

'I suppose that depends on his or her father.' Andrew reddened as soon as his words were out.

Before he could apologise yet again, Zoe said, 'It's okay. I may not talk about him, but I can't deny he existed.'

'I hope you'll allow me to be part of the child's life.'

'He's got more family than I ever did. It'll be important for him to know them.'

'It's a boy, then?'

'No, I simply find it easier than keeping on saying him or her, he or she. My friend Kate is beside herself with curiosity, convinced I know but won't tell her. She can't believe I feel no need to find out before the birth.'

'That's Ranald Mackenzie's daughter?'

'I was forgetting you knew him. Yes it is. She got married, moved away for a few years then came back. She's divorced now.'

'Her father and I used to meet at Kelso races. Years ago, of course. I doubt if he'll remember me.'

'The whole family has been incredibly kind to me. I'm going there tonight for a barbecue.'

'I imagine the entire country will be having a barbecue this evening. You can't have expected this sort of weather when you moved up here.'

'That's true.'

They went their separate ways mid-afternoon without making any further arrangement to meet up. Andrew felt unable to commit himself, given the unpredictability of Helen's illness, and although it remained unsaid, Zoe knew she would only see him again after his wife had died.

As she drove past the turning to the inn which sat between St Mary's Loch and that other loch whose name she could never remember, she noticed an ancient, blue Ford Fiesta behind her. It kept a safe distance back, so all she could see of its driver were a baseball cap and big sunglasses. The same car was still there, two vehicles separating them now, when she stopped briefly at a junction in Selkirk. The next time she looked in her mirror, it had gone.

SIX

Zoe arrived at Tolbyres Farm at six-fifteen, accompanied by Mac who had sat on the passenger seat panting with excitement all the way there. The number of cars parked behind the farmhouse suggested a bigger occasion than Kate's spur-of-the-moment invitation had suggested, but it was too late to turn round and go home now.

As soon as Mac's feet hit the ground, a Border Terrier appeared from nowhere, scattering a group of brown hens pecking at the dry earth nearby. The dogs approached each other warily then ran off together towards the garden and quickly disappeared from view.

The path along the side of the house was dry and dusty, reflecting the lack of rain in over two months, in contrast to Etta Mackenzie's flower beds which teemed with colour and her husband's meticulously striped lawns. Zoe breathed in the scent of lavender and stopped briefly to admire a swathe of bright red poppies. Arriving in the front garden, she spotted several children crowded round Mac and his new friend, while scattered groups of adults stood on the lawn talking and laughing.

A boy in blue shorts and a bright red tee-shirt rushed over. 'Hello, Zoe. Mum said I was to take you to her as soon as you arrived.'

'Hi, Frankie. Just tell me where she is and I'll find her.'

'In the sitooterie.' Kate's eldest child pointed

41

towards the single-storey barn set at right angles to the farmhouse. A century ago it would have contained machinery but now its arches were too low to accommodate even the smallest tractor, so it was used as an extension to the house. 'She and Gran are bringing out the food while the barbecues heat up. We're having steak and beefburgers and sausages.'

'Sounds great. I'll see you later.'

After straightening the ruched material of her dress which clung to her bump, Zoe strolled across the wide lawn. Kate came into view, wearing pink pedal-pushers under a white, sleeveless blouse and carrying a tray piled high with baskets of bread rolls.

Zoe waited to speak until Kate looked up from placing the rolls on one of the trellis tables covered with red-and-white tablecloths. 'Hello. I made it, as you can see.'

Kate beamed. 'Come and get a drink then I'll introduce you to a few people. It's a pity you're off alcohol at the moment, because we have Pimms.' She led Zoe to the far corner of the barn nearest the house, where guests surrounded a table laden with bottles, jugs and glasses, proclaiming, 'Make way for the pregnant lady.'

Cheeks burning, Zoe forced a smile, but the temptation to flee subsided when she recognised most of the people who turned towards her.

'Zoe, how are you?' Robbie Mackenzie stepped forward and kissed her on the cheek. His year-round tan had darkened several shades since the last time they met. 'Sis tells me the work on Keeper's Cottage has gone well.'

'Yes, thanks to you. I can't believe how fast the builders have worked.'

'Good to hear. I—'

Robbie broke off as a young woman with the body and bearing of a dancer came forward and linked her arm through his.

'Aren't you going to introduce us?' Her southern English voice stood out from the clamour of soft Borders accents.

'Sorry, darling. This is Kate's friend, Zoe Moreland. She lives in a house I used to own. Zoe, meet my lovely wife, Ingrid.'

The women exchanged wary smiles. Ingrid's asymmetrical curtain of blonde hair shifted slightly as she looked Zoe up and down. 'I like your dress,' she said. 'Coral suits you.'

'Ingrid has an eye for colour, don't you, darling? She's an interior designer, does all my properties.'

'Thank you.' Zoe now knew why Kate rarely mentioned her sister-in-law. Robbie couldn't have married a woman more unlike the one he'd grown up with.

As if reading her mind, Kate reappeared bearing a tall glass of orange juice which she handed to Zoe. Ignoring her brother and his wife, she grasped Zoe's arm and pulled her aside.

'There's someone here I want you to look after.'

'Not another baby, I hope. It didn't go well last time, did it? She cried all the time until her mother came back.'

Kate rolled her eyes. 'No, it's a man. Here he is.'

Oh God.

A figure wearing camouflage-patterned shorts which were slightly too long for him was walking towards them, clutching a bottle of wine to his chest. Zoe recognised Patrick Dunin immediately, although she'd never seen him before so casually dressed or without a stethoscope around his neck.

Kate scurried across the grass to meet him. 'Hello, Patrick. Come and see who's here.'

The new arrival handed Kate his bottle and allowed her to lead him to Zoe. He nodded gravely. 'Good evening, Doctor Moreland. I'm glad to see your dog's fully recovered. He and mine have hit it off.'

Zoe followed his gaze. She could see no sign of the Border Terrier now but Mac was chasing a tiny brown dog down the garden towards the life-sized wire statues of a ram and a ewe which Kate and her three brothers had given their parents last Christmas. 'I hope they're okay. Mac's so much bigger than yours and can be very boisterous.'

'Peggy'll be fine. Dachshunds can stand up for themselves. If he gets too much, she'll let him know.'

'Zoe, will you show Patrick where the drinks are?' Kate said. 'I need to get back to helping Mum with the food.'

Powerless as usual to do anything but go along with her friend's wishes, Zoe walked with Patrick to the barn, wishing she hadn't worn heels which made her tower over him. It seemed like good manners to hang around while he poured himself a glass of orange juice. He was obviously acquainted with several other guests but just as Zoe had decided it wouldn't be too rude to leave him chatting with them, he rejoined her.

'Our dogs have disappeared. Shall we see if we can find them?' His smile came as a surprise. During all the visits she and Mac had made to his surgery back in February, the vet had never smiled once, not even when the test for canine pancreatitis had come back negative. In fact, his expression had been so serious before telling her the result that Zoe had steeled herself for bad news.

As they strolled down the garden, she asked how long he'd known the Mackenzies.

'Not long. I was over this morning, putting down an injured sheep, and Mrs Mackenzie invited me here tonight. It's not really my sort of thing but I didn't feel able to say no.'

'They're very persuasive, aren't they? Kate's a whirlwind, taking everyone with her. I find it easier not to argue unless she suggests something really outlandish.'

'Which is why you've ended up stuck with me.'

Patrick smiled again. 'I promise I won't hang around any longer than you want me to.'

'Oh no, I didn't mean that,' Zoe said hurriedly. 'I'm not much of a party animal myself either. I'd far rather talk to one person than flit between groups of people trying to be witty.'

'Look, there they are,' Patrick said, pointing. 'Peggy!'

Mac seemed keen to remain sniffing at the stone wall which marked the boundary between garden and field, but on seeing Peggy race away, he followed. Zoe looked at the tiny dog running towards them and for the first time noticed something unusual about her. As Peggy's owner scooped her up into his arms, she asked, 'What happened to her leg?'

'Someone trod on her when she was a pup and by the time they turned up at the surgery, it couldn't be saved. In fact, the owner wanted me to euthanise her but I refused. I could only get him to change his mind by offering to rehome her, although at the time I didn't realise it was my own home she was destined for.' The little dog started to squirm and he carefully lowered her back to the ground.

'Doesn't hold her back, does it?' Zoe said.

'Dogs and cats adjust remarkably well to the loss of a limb. I did wonder if having such a long body would make it more difficult for her to balance but as you can see, my concerns were unfounded.'

'She's adorable.' Zoe looked around and nodded towards a wooden bench under a tree. 'Do you mind if we sit down?'

Remembering Patrick had mentioned coming to Tolbyres earlier, when they were seated she asked, 'Do sheep often injure themselves? There were some in the field behind me for a while and they never seemed to do anything but eat.'

'Unfortunately this one had been attacked by something. A dog probably, larger and far less friendly than our two.'

'How horrible.'

'It happens more often than you'd think. In my opinion, some people aren't fit to keep dogs but there's no way to stop them. Better a sheep than a child, I suppose.' Patrick pulled a biscuit from his pocket, broke it in half and fed the pieces to Mac and Peggy who then ran off again. 'Sorry. I'll climb down from my soapbox any minute now.'

'No need to apologise for feeling passionate about something.' Zoe looked towards the house. 'I can see smoke billowing from the barbecues. The food must be on. We'd best be getting back.'

Rising, Patrick said, 'It's been nice chatting. I hope I haven't set too many tongues wagging by monopolising you.'

'I'm used to being the subject of gossip.'

'I suppose you are. Can't be easy, though, given what you went through last winter.'

Zoe froze. She'd hoped he was different, not pretending to be friendly in order to find out what had really happened.

'Here.' He offered his arm. When she didn't take it, he let it drop to his side. 'Sorry. I wasn't suggesting you couldn't get up on your own. I deal with lots of pregnant ladies but none of them human.'

He looked so genuinely contrite that Zoe said, 'Try again.' This time she took hold of his arm and used it to lever herself up. She was about to thank him when they were both distracted by loud shouts coming from near the farmhouse. One of the voices was Kate's.

'Sounds serious,' Patrick said. They set off up the garden. When they reached the lawn nearest the house, numerous other guests had congregated there. All eyes were on Kate and the man she was berating. He wore rimless spectacles which he kept pushing back onto his face and occasionally held up his hands in submission. This was obviously failing to allay Kate's anger.

'How dare you come here unannounced!'

'Please, Kate, can't we go somewhere and talk this over like adults?'

Kate took a step towards the man and jabbed a forefinger at him. 'You haven't wanted to talk for years. Why start now?'

'I've a right to see my kids.'

So this was Ken, the ex-husband Kate regularly spoke so disparagingly about.

As if on cue, Frankie appeared. 'Dad?'

His grandmother, hitherto hidden behind a group of guests, pushed forward and took him gently by the shoulders and led him away. As if suddenly aware they had an audience, Kate dropped her hand to her side. 'You've spoiled Mum and Dad's party,' she said more quietly. 'Go away and come back tomorrow. I'll see you at the cottage at eleven o'clock. Not a minute before.'

They both stood in silence as Ken seemed to consider if it was worth arguing further, then he turned on his heel and hurried away, nearly colliding with someone just arriving. Seeing who the latecomer was, Zoe wished Erskine Mather had turned up five minutes earlier. His presence might have prevented the confrontation.

She was surprised to see Mather here at all. Kate's father made no secret of his disapproval of his daughter going out with a man who appeared unwilling to sever links with one woman before moving on to the next. Etta Mackenzie, on the other hand, was one of Mather's staunchest defenders, giving him credit for being totally honest about the situation and saving her disapproval for the unknown wife who, despite not having provided him with any children, still felt she had a claim on him. As far as Zoe was concerned, she liked him and respected his abilities as a policeman, but having been instrumental in reintroducing the pair after they had spent many years apart, she hoped their relationship wouldn't go horribly wrong.

Characteristically, the extent to which Mather had embraced casual clothes for the evening didn't extend to the shorts worn by most of the other male guests aged under sixty. Instead, he had on crease-free cream chinos with a striped, short-sleeved shirt, but at least he'd forsaken his usual black patent-leather, lace-up brogues for a tan pair.

Far from having a pacifying effect, his arrival prompted Kate to protest noisily at her ex-husband's audacity in gate-crashing the party. Mather responded with the slight downwards gesture with his left hand Zoe often saw him use to tell Kate she should lower her voice. However, on this occasion it didn't work.

'What did he expect? That I'd hand him a glass of Pimms and a burger?'

'He may not have known there was a party going on,' Mather said.

'What about all the cars? Even Ken could have put them together with the fact it's a sunny Saturday evening and realised Mum and Dad were entertaining. He gave up his right to just turn up the day he walked out and left me with three bairns to raise on my own.'

Mather looked around him, possibly seeking Etta. If anyone could calm Kate it was her mother, but she hadn't returned from wherever she'd whisked Frankie away to. His eyes met and held Zoe's, compelling her to join them.

'Did you see what happened?' Kate demanded as Zoe arrived next to her.

'Yes,' Zoe said. 'Do you think you should find Frankie and the girls? They may be feeling a bit, well, confused.' She feared she'd overstepped the mark, given her own lack of parenting experience, but Kate's anger

48

dissolved in an instant and she started to walk towards the house.

Mather remained with Zoe. 'Thank you,' he said.

'Do you want to get a drink?' she asked him. Patrick was hanging around as if waiting for her to join him again now all the fuss was over. It might be no bad thing that their tête-a-tête had been curtailed.

Crossing the lawn with Mather towards the drinks table, she noticed how many people acknowledged his arrival with a nod or the raising of a hand, yet no one came over to greet him. She wondered if this was a response to his being a policeman or married. Or maybe no one else had her advantage of knowing him well enough to realise his uncompromising demeanour masked considerable kindness and patience. After all, she'd only discovered this herself by spending more time with him than she would have chosen to.

As if to prove there was still a lot she didn't know about him, Mather chose to drink Pimms. Zoe suppressed a smile as he led her to a table, carrying a glass with a straw and a sprig of mint poking out of it. They sat down, Mather considerately rejecting the upright chair in favour of a lower one she would have struggled to escape from when the time came to leave it.

'Sorry about the mix-up yesterday,' he said. 'Dave Trent's mortified you got caught up unnecessarily in the investigation.'

'As I told him, it really wasn't a problem. I'm a doctor, so I should be prepared for the occasional dead body.'

'Even so.' Mather took a sip from his glass. 'You know what I'm trying to say, Zoe.'

It still felt weird when he addressed her by her first name, though less so than when she tried to use his. 'Have you identified the dead boy yet?'

'No. Early days of course, but it's going to be a challenge, I think.'

'But you'll know now what killed him?'

The policeman gave her a look which could only have been sterner if he'd been peering over the rims of a pair of spectacles.

She spread her hands. 'You can't blame me for being interested.'

'Leave it alone, Zoe. You're not involved this time. I doubt anyone round here is.'

'At least satisfy my professional curiosity.'

He continued to stare at her, saying nothing. She hoped his silence meant he was inwardly debating what to do, so there was a chance he would give in.

'Because that's all it is. Professional curiosity.'

He sighed and leaned towards her. And Kate chose this moment to reappear, her face still flushed but a lot calmer than she had been earlier. She positioned a chair to face both Zoe and Mather, and sat down.

'Mum's told me I should apologise to everyone for creating a scene. Erskine, you weren't here to see it but, Zoe, I'm sorry I dragged you away from Patrick. You seemed to be getting on like a house on fire.'

'Were you watching us?'

'I couldn't read your lips, if that's what's worrying you. But his body language did all the talking.'

'You're imagining things.' Zoe patted her stomach. 'Look at me.'

Kate shook her head. 'Trust me, Patrick Dunin is looking past your bump. And it won't be there much longer, will it?'

'No, it'll soon be a baby and then I'll have all time in the world for a man in my life.' Zoe smiled to reassure her friend she was joking, while also trying to think of a way to change the subject. In the end, Mather did this for her, by tapping Kate's arm and rising from his seat.

'We'd better get a move on if you're going to say sorry to all your parents' guests before they go home,' he said.

'We can't leave Zoe sitting on her own.'

Despite a suspicion that his suggestion was more to do with avoiding further questioning from her than anything else, Zoe said, 'I'll be fine, really,' and waved the couple away. She watched as Kate linked her arm through Mather's and leaned into him as he led her towards a group of elderly ladies in floral dresses. Despite the difference in their heights, they looked like they belonged together.

The baby kicked. 'I hear you,' Zoe said. 'Let's go and get some food.'

The rest of the evening passed pleasantly enough, but just before ten o'clock, tired from driving to Moffat and back, and weary of endless baby talk from most of the people she chatted with, Zoe sought out Etta and Ranald Mackenzie to thank them for their hospitality. She found them in their enormous kitchen where, as usual, Kate's mother was surrounded by food she had lovingly prepared for others. Ranald sat at the dining table with a small child asleep on his knee. He looked frailer than she had ever seen him.

Etta gave Zoe a hug. 'I'm so glad you could make it. Kate said you were out all day so you must be tired.'

'I am, a little. I don't sleep well at the moment, what with this heat and being the size of a bus.'

'I remember that feeling all too well. You mustn't overdo things.' Etta lifted a cool-bag from the kitchen unit behind her. 'I made far too much food, so I've put a few bits and pieces in here for you. And half a dozen eggs.'

Zoe knew better than to protest. Losing her mother and being brought up by elderly, somewhat distant grandparents had made her self-reliant and unused to being fussed over. However, in the past few months her relationship with the older woman had developed in a way she would once have resisted: Etta treated her if not quite like a daughter, then a beloved niece. And Zoe took pleasure in this.

51

Clutching the cool-bag, she went back outside. The guests had thinned out now, the old and very young having departed for their beds, so she easily spotted Mac on the lawn curled up next to Peggy at Patrick's feet. Patrick introduced her to the couple he was with and offered her his seat.

'No thanks, I'm going home now.' As if on cue, Mac rose and came to her side. She slipped the lead over his head, glad her dog wasn't as low-slung as a dachshund.

'I'll walk you to your car,' Patrick said, picking up the cool-bag.

They were passing the row of lavender bushes when Zoe heard someone call her name. She turned and saw Robbie hurrying towards them.

'Can I visit you tomorrow morning before we go back to Edinburgh?' he asked. 'I'd be interested in seeing what's been done to the cottage, if that's alright with you.'

Zoe thought this a little strange but said, 'Of course it is.'

They agreed on eleven o'clock, the exact time Kate would be meeting with her ex-husband.

SEVEN

Zoe gave up trying to get back to sleep at four in the morning. It was Sunday after all, so she made herself a pot of tea and returned to bed, accompanied this time by Mac. No longer permitted to spend the night with her, the dog flopped down with a contented sigh. He was more than a year old now and she hoped he would accept the presence of a small human in their home when the time came. She should maybe ask Patrick what, if anything, could be done to minimise the dog's inevitable jealousy. This thought led to other, less welcome ones, like whether Kate was right about the vet's interest in her and if so, how to handle him. Should she tackle the issue head-on and give him the just-good-friends option, or simply ignore it and wait to see what happened? Instead of reaching a decision, she leaned over for the book on her bedside cabinet.

The previous night's weather forecast had promised a day even hotter than had been experienced thus far in the record-busting Scottish summer, so she got ready to take Mac out not long after six. Although never a fan of team sports, she had been active all her life and saw no reason to stop just because she was pregnant. She could still walk as far as ever, albeit more slowly; it was the getting ready that took time and effort. In addition to her mobile and Mac's biscuits, she must now carry water for them both and a fold-up drinking bowl for Mac as well as the usual lip-salve, tissues and mobile, necessitating the preparation of a small backpack before every outing. And what to wear was a constant challenge. Preferring to go off-road for all but the briefest of walks, she couldn't risk bare legs or do without sturdy footwear, but pulling on trousers and struggling to do up walking boots often left her overheated and exasperated.

After ensuring both house and garage were secure, she led Mac a short distance up the road then released him and watched him race along the grass track which went down one side of a field of barley. At the far corner, rather than keep going round the field he took a sharp right and vanished into a patch of woodland. Zoe called, 'Wait for me,' and he reappeared, tail wagging as though urging her to catch him up, but by the time she reached the trees, he was again nowhere to be seen. Unconcerned, she followed the path they often took, enjoying the shade.

She was about to walk back into the bright sunlight when she heard squeals and barking off to her left. Mac tore out from behind a group of conifers, followed by a huge, unfamiliar dog which passed her in a blur of mottled brown coat and flapping jowls. With just a few metres between the animals, the second dog terrified Zoe. If it caught Mac, he wouldn't stand a chance. She shouted, 'No!' and hurried after them.

The field ahead was planted with oilseed rape. Used to seeing the landscape swathed in yellow when the crop was flowering, she'd been surprised to witness recently how the straight, green stalks eventually became fibrous and tangled, creating impenetrable jungles which must surely be harvested any day now. She watched helplessly as Mac tunnelled into the rape in an effort to escape the bigger dog which, after a moment's hesitation, ploughed in after him. Calling wouldn't help; all she could do was wait and hope Mac's size gave him an advantage over his pursuer.

She forced herself to sit on a prone tree trunk in the shade for nearly half an hour. Her bottle of water was soon empty but she still felt thirsty. Noises coming from the rape field had long since died away; the only sound she could hear now was birdsong. She tried to force images from her mind of Mac stranded in the middle of the field, unable to find his way out or, worse, caught up in the undergrowth with the Hound of the Baskervilles bearing down on him. Finally, she pulled out her mobile. She didn't have his personal number but Patrick had told her last night that he was on call, with emergencies being transferred to him between midnight and ten this morning, when his colleague would take over for the rest of the weekend. She doubted he could offer any practical advice, but she needed to talk to someone, to share her anxiety. Had it been later in the day she would have texted Kate, but she was unlikely to be up and about at this time.

Despite the early hour, Zoe had to shade her mobile's screen with her free hand. It showed three missed calls, all from blocked numbers, all coming in just after one in the morning, but no message had been left. Distracted by her concern for Mac, she wrote these off as drunken misdials, and scrolled through her contacts until she found the vet's number. She had just hit the green handset symbol when a noise made her look up.

Mac stood a few feet away. He whined again. The garland of stalks and seed pods trailing from his head would have been comical had his right eye not been closed and a cut on his nose dripped blood. Cancelling the call and abandoning her mobile on the tree trunk, Zoe rushed over and dropped to her knees, simultaneously hugging and checking him for serious injury. As she fussed over him, constantly asking, 'Are you alright, boy?' Mac's tail started to wag, although his eye remained closed. Not wanting to risk another encounter with the other dog, which might emerge from the undergrowth at any moment, she attached the lead to Mac's collar and steered him towards home, remembering just in time to pick up her mobile.

Her first priority on getting back to Keeper's Cottage was to tend to Mac's poorly eye, bathing it with cotton wool dipped in warm water. It gradually opened, then the dog passed with flying colours the only sight test she could think of, catching the biscuit she threw to him. As she wiped the blood from his scratched nose and brushed his coat to remove all traces of oilseed rape, she wondered if she should inform anyone there was a dangerous dog on the loose. Then again, it must surely be the same animal which had attacked the Mackenzies' sheep, so it would already have been reported.

She glanced at her mobile to check the time. It was only just after eight but felt much later after such an eventful walk. Robbie Mackenzie wasn't due until eleven, which gave her enough time to eat a leisurely breakfast, take a shower and put her feet up for a while. She looked again at the phone, remembering those calls she'd missed during the night. They were logged as having come in at one-ten, one-thirteen and one-twenty. Because the caller identification had been blocked, she had no way of knowing if they were from the same person, although it seemed likely. This alone was strange, as her personalised message, albeit brief, would have told the caller the first time that they had reached the wrong number. It crossed her mind that the photographer she'd encountered on the Chain Bridge last week may have recognised her and somehow obtained her mobile number, but she swiftly dismissed this idea as paranoia.

Mac started to bark just after eleven, rousing his owner from a nap she'd had no intention of taking when she put up the umbrella and lay down on the sun-lounger an hour earlier. Unlike his sister, Robbie didn't come round to the garden, choosing instead to ring the bell and wait for Zoe to let him in. He was on his mobile when she opened the door, an apparently important conversation because he nodded to her and stepped inside without stopping talking. Zoe might have taken offence, had he not given her the broadest of grins, reminding her of Kate, when he did eventually end the call.

'Sorry,' he said, keeping his mobile in his hand.

'No problem. Can I get you a drink of something?'

They agreed on tea, and while the kettle was boiling, Zoe led Robbie around the house, showing him the work which had been done since she bought it from him at the start of the year. Seeing Keeper's Cottage through someone else's eyes, she appreciated for the first time what a major undertaking the extension and remodelling had been, and what a difference this had made. The single-storey house now had a proper bathroom and a separate loo, a decent-sized kitchen and a second bedroom which she refused to call the nursery, despite everyone else doing so.

'They've made a good job,' Robbie said as he scrutinised the bathroom tiling.

'I gather some of your work was delayed in order to fit me in so quickly. I hope that didn't cause you any problems. Time's money in your business, I imagine.'

'My deadlines aren't as pressing as the one you're working to.'

Zoe smiled politely at this first pregnancy reference of the day and made her way to the kitchen.

Although she expected her visitor to prefer to stay indoors while he drank his tea, he carried his mug through the new French doors and repositioned a chair to face the garden. 'What are your plans for out here?'

'Something low maintenance. Lawn and a few shrubs are about the extent of my green fingers.'

'It's not very big. Children need more space than you'd think, once they start running around.'

'I'm not thinking that far ahead, to be honest.'

'How do you feel about having livestock at the end of your garden?'

57

'I liked looking out on sheep earlier in the year and quite miss them now. You grew up surrounded by animals but I wasn't even allowed a goldfish.'

'Unfortunately they won't be coming back, because my tenant has given notice. He's retiring.' Robbie kept his tone casual but his right knee had started to jiggle. 'So . . . I was wondering if you'd like to buy the field from me.'

'Won't you find someone else to rent it?'

'I've been looking at my portfolio, with a view to rebalancing it away from rural to urban.'

'How much do you want for it?'

'I'd not be looking for the full market value, as it's you.' Robbie named a sum which even to Zoe, who knew nothing about land prices, sounded a trifling amount for such a big field. 'You'd substantially increase the value of the cottage if it came with a bit of land.'

'Can I give it some thought?'

'I'll call you in a couple of days, yes? I'd prefer to get this sorted quickly.'

Like his sister, when Robbie decided on something he was obviously single-minded about seeing it happen; there was little use in arguing with him, so Zoe didn't try. Of course she wouldn't agree to something which wasn't to her advantage, but on the surface his proposition seemed reasonable, generous even. She could afford it, after all, but would still sound out her solicitor, who also ran a successful estate agency, tomorrow.

She studied the field which surrounded Keeper's Cottage on three sides with more interest than usual. There would be nothing to stop her renting it out herself, until she made long-term plans for it.

Having got the business part of his visit over, Robbie's leg ceased to jiggle and he started to tell Zoe how worried his parents were at the reappearance of Kate's ex-husband.

'You don't think she'll have him back, do you?' Zoe asked. 'Especially now Erskine Mather's around.'

'No, but Ken's always been trouble. When he left, it affected Sis badly, whatever she might claim. The children were all too young to realise what was going on. Now, though, they've already started asking questions, like why he's here, are they going to have to go and live with him. Mhairi was in tears over breakfast and she didn't even see him last night.'

'Oh dear. Let's hope his meeting with Kate this morning will be the end of the matter.'

'Now he's back he'll not be easy to get rid of, trust me. He's after something — money, probably.'

'Surely that was all sorted out when they divorced?'

'Maybe he thinks Dad'll pay him to go away. Again.' His mobile, sitting on the table between them, chose that moment to ring. He lifted a hand to shade its screen and said, 'I'll have to take this.'

Zoe thought about what he'd just said, oblivious to the one-sided conversation going on next to her. Did she misinterpret him, or did he let slip that Ranald Mackenzie had paid his son-in-law to walk out on Kate and their children?

After ending the call with an abrupt 'Yes', Robbie said, 'I have to go. Thanks for the tea. I'll ring for your answer about the field on Tuesday.'

A few minutes after Robbie left, Zoe put aside the tuna salad roll she was preparing in order to answer a call on her mobile. Curious to hear how Kate had got on with Ken, it wasn't until she held the phone to her ear that she remembered Kate only ever texted.

'Hello, Zoe, it's Patrick Dunin. I know this is probably a daft question, but did you call us earlier today?'

'Yes, I dialled the surgery number but I didn't think the call connected.'

'Is everything okay? Did you have a problem with Mac?'

'You could say that.' She briefly explained what happened on their early morning walk.

'That must have been terrifying. How is he now?'

'His eye's still not fully open but his sight doesn't seem to be affected.' She paused, then asked, 'How did you know it was me?'

Patrick cleared his throat. 'A sequence of one-two-three-four in the middle of a mobile number is pretty memorable. I've come into work to do some paperwork and your contact details on Mac's records jumped out at me. When I compared the number that called with yours, I found they were the same. I hope you don't mind me following it up.'

Zoe couldn't help smiling at the suggestion he just happened to be looking at Mac's records on a Sunday morning. He had obviously planned to ring her anyway, but she'd provided him with the perfect excuse. 'It's me who should apologise for wasting your time. I can't have ended the call properly because I was so pleased to see Mac reappear.'

'Do you plan on bringing him in to be checked over?'

'There's no need at the moment but I'll call you if it turns out the damage is worse than I thought.'

'Good. Well, I'm pleased to hear it.'

Zoe waited for the vet to say more, although she had no idea how to react if he suggested they meet up socially. However, it didn't come to that. He simply said goodbye and she responded likewise. Maybe Kate was wrong after all.

After sharing her roll with Mac, she opened the laptop, checked her bank account then turned her attention to nursery furniture. She soon felt overwhelmed by the choices to be made. Dark wood, pale wood, or white? Cot, Moses basket or crib? And how could a tiny baby possibly need a wardrobe?

She heaved a sigh and went to make a cup of tea. This part of imminent parenthood was fun, or so everyone told her. But any concerns she had about giving birth then enduring months of sleepless nights were far outweighed by the need to acquire furniture, bedding, clothes and everything else deemed essential for a new baby. It wasn't the money involved, although she was shocked by how much she could easily spend, but the inescapable fact was that however much she wanted the child she was carrying, the arrival of nursery paraphernalia would confirm once and for all she was going to be a mother, entirely responsible for another human being. This terrified her.

A text came in from Kate mid-afternoon: *Want a visitor? Promise not to go on about exes!*

Eager for a distraction, Zoe texted back then closed down her laptop. Unlikely though it was that Kate would be able to keep her promise, she sounded upbeat, suggesting her meeting with Ken had gone well. Once again, Zoe thought back to what Robbie had said, still unsure if he had been telling her that Ken took money from the Mackenzies to end his marriage to Kate. Telling herself this was none of her business, she got up and attempted to put it out of her mind by emptying the dishwasher.

'What a lovely dress,' she said on opening the front door a few minutes later.

'It's Sunday.' Kate struck a pose to show off her pink frock with white embroidered flowers. 'I like to wear something special, even if I don't go to church.' She bounded in, nearly knocking over the hall table.

'How did you get on with Ken?'

Kate's grin became a pout. 'Let's sit down and I'll tell you about it.'

Once they were outside with their glasses of iced orange juice, Kate launched into an account of her discussions with her ex-husband, which had centred around the news that Ken had recently remarried and his new wife was expecting a baby. 'This appears to have reminded him of the existence of the children he already has,' she said, her ability to sound sarcastic unhampered by her lack of hearing. 'Doubtless egged on by the new Mrs Simons, he's decided he wants us all to play happy families.'

'What would that entail?' Zoe asked.

'He wants to spend time with Frankie, Eva and Mhairi in order to "build relationships" with them.' Kate's exaggerated air quotes demonstrated what she thought of this idea. 'And then, when they're better acquainted, he expects me to pack them off to stay with him on a regular basis.'

'Won't that be difficult, as he's living in London?'

'Oh no, here's the best news of all. He's been offered a job in Newcastle and is planning to bring wifey and sprog up to live just over the Border in Northumberland. They're already house-hunting around Alnwick.'

'Oh.' Zoe had no idea how to respond. Had anyone else presented her with this development, she might have argued it could be good for all the parties involved, especially the children. However, she knew the strength of Kate's antagonism towards Ken precluded any chance of such an agreement being acceptable to her. 'What do your parents say?'

'They're as upset as I am. Don't forget they had to pick up the pieces when Ken walked out on us. I don't know what I'd've done without them. Mhairi wasn't two months old.'

'So how did you respond?'

'I was very calm. At first, anyway. I asked him if this meant he was going to start paying maintenance. Needless to say, he hadn't even considered *that* possibility. Things went downhill from there.'

'Did you manage to agree on anything?'

'Only that he's going to consult a solicitor, so I must spend money I don't have on doing the same.' Kate's glass thumped as she deposited it on the table. Seeing Zoe wince, she picked it up again to check for cracks, then set it down more carefully. 'Anyway, I'll do what I have to. He's not going to disrupt our lives again.'

'Have you told Mather? Sorry — Erskine.'

'Not yet. As you know, his job doesn't respect normal people's routines. And it's not his battle anyway.'

'True.'

'Can we talk about something else?' Kate asked. 'What have you been up to today?'

Zoe told her about Mac's early-morning adventure and Kate agreed the stray dog was most likely the one that attacked her father's sheep, even though the incidents were several miles apart. Ranald had informed the police and warned other farmers nearby to be on the alert.

'And I'll be going to see my solicitor too, following your brother's visit.'

Kate looked blank. 'Why?'

'Sorry, I assumed you knew. Robbie's offered to sell me all this.' Zoe extended an arm to indicate the field that surrounded them. 'I'm going to be a landowner.'

'Really? He almost never sells anything. I had to work on him about letting you buy the house.'

'I got the impression it's just a small part of a bigger plan, what he described as rebalancing his portfolio. I hope I haven't been indiscreet in mentioning it.'

'Of course not. Robbie's always far too busy these day to tell me what he's up to. I was surprised he found time to come down to Mum and Dad's barbecue, though he needn't have bothered, seeing as he ended up having a row with Dad.'

'Not a serious one, I hope.'

'I doubt it. Dad pretends to disapprove of Robbie's flashy lifestyle — especially all the holidays they take, and sending the girls to a private school—but secretly he's proud of how well he's done. Especially for someone who was thrown out of agricultural college.'

'So Robbie did try to go into the family business?'

'Only because it was expected of him. And although he had to face telling Mum and Dad about being asked not to go back to college, he was pleased really. They sent him to work with Uncle Bill, who at the time was doing up some old cottages to sell. It was meant as a sort of penance, but instead he got the property bug.'

'He's obviously good at it.'

'The money to be made in the Borders is paltry compared with Edinburgh, so that's where he mainly operates now. And lives. Because the lovely Ingrid wouldn't be seen dead in a pair of wellies.'

'I got that impression from our brief encounter last night.'

'He was never going to hook up with anyone normal. They met on a skiing holiday in Switzerland.'

'Ordinary people go skiing too, you know. I'm not very good, but I do enjoy it.'

'Is there any dangerous sport you haven't done?'

'They're not dangerous if you do them properly. And in answer to your question, hearing your dad enthuse about the Jim Clark Rally reminded me I haven't tried my hand at competitive driving. Yet.'

'You'll forget that idea when the baby arrives.'

'There's an expression you use when I say something outrageous like that.'

'What's that?'

'Aye, right.'

They both laughed, then Kate looked grave. 'I've been putting it off, but there's something I need to show you.' She lifted up her handbag and rummaged inside it, bringing out a folded sheet of A4 paper. 'First of all, I need to explain how we got this.'

'You're being very mysterious.' Zoe reached out her hand. 'Come on, show me.'

'No, it's important you know we've not been spying on you.'

'Now you've got me worried, Kate. What have you found out?'

'Frankie brought it to me. Last year, when all that unpleasantness was going on, he set up a Google alert for your name. I had no idea, honestly, but he was curious and a bit scared because no grown-up would talk to him about what was happening.' Kate paused but Zoe said nothing. 'Anyway, here we are, six months later, and he gets notification of this on that awful Scotland's News website. I'm so sorry.'

Zoe grabbed the paper and unfolded it. At the top was a photograph of her standing on the Chain Bridge, frowning.

EXCLUSIVE
Pregnant Borders GP with tragic past
involved in river death mystery.
Soon-to-be-single-mum, Doctor Zoe
Moreland, 38, is once again helping
the police with their enquiries just
months after narrowly escaping death
herself when ...

Not wanting to read any more of this rubbish, she held the sheet of paper out to Kate, who thrust it back into her bag. Neither woman spoke until Kate said, 'They got your age wrong.'

'They all did last year too.' Zoe swallowed hard and reached for her drink, but just the smell of the orange juice made her feel sick. She put the glass down again. 'Shit!'

'If it's any consolation, hardly anyone I know ever looks on that website. It was set up by some people who didn't like the BBC's coverage of the independence referendum. It reports on stories none of the proper news outlets is interested in.'

'I hope you're right. But it's still there, and will be forever more now. That's the trouble with the internet.'

'Did you know someone had taken the photograph?'

'Yes, but I told myself even if he was from the press he couldn't possibly have recognised me. I look rather different to how I did last November.'

'Aren't they supposed to identify themselves?'

This at least made Zoe smile. 'In my experience, they're not bound by any rules at all. He'll be an opportunistic freelancer hoping to get a picture of the police working a murder scene, who struck lucky finding me there too.'

'Can you try to get it taken down?'

'That'd be a waste of time. The best thing I can do is ignore it.' Zoe winced and rubbed her stomach.

'Baby kicking?' Kate asked. 'Amazing, isn't it, to think of a little person living inside you?'

Grabbing this opportunity to change the subject, Zoe said, 'I've been trying to choose nursery furniture for when that little person comes out, but I can't make up my mind what to get. Do you want to help me?'

'Where are you looking?'

'EBay and Amazon.' Seeing Kate's scandalised expression, she added, 'I'm not buying second-hand, don't worry.'

'You can't possibly buy those things online. We need to go to John Lewis.'

'I couldn't face shopping in this heat.'

'Nonsense. Haven't you heard of air-conditioning? A department store is probably the most comfortable place to be at present. And afterwards we can reward ourselves with cake.'

'But you're busy.'

'I'm never too busy to help someone else spend

money. And I have to visit the ScotlandsPeople Centre in Edinburgh to do some research this week. Would Wednesday suit you?'

'As long as I can get someone to take Mac for the day.'

'I'm sure Mum will. Which reminds me — I told her I'd only be gone for half an hour. I'll text you about it, okay?'

Recognising her friend's intervention was probably the kick up the backside she needed, Zoe agreed. Despite Kate's insistence that she should stay put, she pushed herself up from the chair. They had just gone back into the kitchen when the house phone rang. Zoe pointed at it to indicate what she was doing, and went to take the call.

'Hello.'

Silence.

'Hello.'

Expecting a click, signifying the automatic dialling system in a distant call centre had rung off, instead all she heard was the sound of someone breathing. She rammed the handset back into its stand. Once Kate was gone, she'd dial 1471 to find out who the caller had been, although probably all she'd get would be confirmation they had withheld their number.

Was this the work of the same person who rang her mobile three times during the night?

EIGHT

Although too fond of driving to be a fan of public transport, Zoe had allowed herself to be persuaded by Kate that taking the train to Edinburgh would be their best option, and as she stood on the platform at Berwick-upon-Tweed station, cooled by the sea breeze and sipping from her bottle of chilled water, she felt inclined to agree. Less than a week had passed since she had driven to Moffat to meet Andrew, yet every time she pulled a seatbelt across her body it felt more confining. If her father wanted to see her again before the baby arrived, she might have to insist on their meeting somewhere far closer to Westerlea. He would, after all, have to come to her once the baby arrived.

She turned round to Kate, who was staring at her mobile and shaking her head. When she looked up, Zoe asked, 'Problem?'

'I knew telling him I'm in Edinburgh today was a mistake.'

'Who?'

'The client I'm doing the research for. He says he's got a clear diary so we should meet up and I can give him a progress report.'

'If you can't come shopping with me, I'll understand.'

'You're joking, aren't you? I'd rather turn him down than miss that.' Kate undid the clasp on her oversized handbag and peered inside. 'I haven't got his complete file with me so I can't give him more than an

68

overview, which won't take long. We should be in Edinburgh by eleven, so I'll text him saying to meet me in the John Lewis restaurant on the fourth floor at eleven-thirty. If he proves too demanding, you can come and rescue me.'

Zoe followed Kate onto the train, letting her go ahead to claim an empty table. They sat down facing each other, and as soon as they had left Berwick, Kate pulled out the contents of her bag and started to sort them into piles. Zoe reached into her own handbag for her book but as she opened it, Kate said, 'You might find this interesting.'

'If it's to do with your work, I'm sure I will. But I didn't think your client wanted you to discuss what you'd found out about his family.'

'You're the least gossipy person I've ever met, so where's the harm? And anyway, he'll never know.'

'I'm not sure that's the point.'

Kate flapped a hand, dismissing Zoe's concern. 'I've managed to go back to when my client's great-great-grandfather and his parents were arrested in Jedburgh. Look at this.' She slid a piece of paper over the table.

Zoe studied the photocopied sheet. Although she struggled to read some of the handwriting, the typed headings of every column were clear: she was looking at an extract from something called the Roxburghshire Criminal Register, which recorded arrests made in one week in February 1861.

'This is fascinating. I love the details. Under education the choices are "neither reads nor writes", "reads and writes imperfectly", and "superior education". I wonder how they judged which category each prisoner fell into?'

'Delving into old records is the bit I enjoy most about my job,' Kate said. She indicated a series of columns on the Register. 'Because it was still the early days of photography, they had to make do with noting down things like height and eye colour to identify them. There's the chap I'm interested in.' She pointed halfway down the page. 'Adam Ainslie, aged fifteen. And below him, his parents Archibald and Grace, both in their late forties.'

'All arrested for theft,' Zoe said, 'although it doesn't say what they stole. Couldn't have been much. They got away with a fine.'

'There's a lot more I'd like to discover, but I've not managed to so far,' Kate said. 'But this is the sort of detail clients love. It makes their ancestors come alive.'

'So they don't mind you finding out they're descended from petty criminals?'

'As long as it's far enough in the past, they quite like me to drag up a scandal or two.'

Zoe stared down at the Criminal Register then met Kate's gaze. 'You do realise that if this information is accurate, Archibald and Grace are unlikely to have been Adam's biological parents?'

'You're kidding me.'

'No, I'm not. Archibald and Grace both have blue eyes while Adam's are brown. I've never studied genetics but I'm pretty certain that brown eyes are dominant. If one of his parents had passed on the brown-eye gene to him, they would have had brown eyes too.'

'Hell.' Kate scrabbled through her piles of paper, eventually pulling out an A3 sheet which Zoe recognised as one of the draft family trees on which she recorded her findings. A number of the small boxes had been filled in with names and dates, some in pencil, others in ink, all in Kate's neat handwriting. 'According to this, he was their only son, born in July 1845. I found the record of his birth, which is why he's inked in.'

'I'm not saying it's impossible, only unlikely.' Zoe started to wish she'd kept her mouth shut. 'Or maybe their details in the Register were written down wrongly. Take no notice of me.'

Kate pulled a face. 'I can't do that. My clients pay me good money to discover the truth about their ancestry.'

'I've made your job a lot more difficult, haven't I?'

'I'll just have to do a bit more digging to dispel the doubt you've raised. I've found a record of Archibald and Grace's marriage, proving they were together years before Adam came along. If he'd been born before they married, that would have increased the chance of him being the product of another liaison.'

'In which case, would your research reach a dead end?'

'Not necessarily. It might be possible to guess who the father was, based on other information.'

'Like what?'

'A census showing Grace had been in service at a big house nine months before her son was born, for example. Some lairds back then considered servants fair game.'

'But that would only be speculation, surely? Impossible to prove without DNA testing.'

'You're right. A couple of years ago I discovered an illegitimate child with a middle name which was the family name of the people his mother had worked for until she suddenly relocated several counties away just before giving birth. Not proof either but definitely significant.'

Without warning, goosebumps rose on Zoe's arms and she hugged herself.

'You've gone very pale. Are you okay?' Kate leaned forward, looking concerned. 'Is it the baby?'

Once again, Zoe recalled the December morning when Andrew had first approached her outside Westerlea Health Centre and asked what her middle initial stood for. Was this Kate's way of saying she knew about him? 'I'm feeling chilly. The air-conditioning's on a bit high, don't you think?'

'That's surely not possible at the moment. Do you want me to get a coffee to warm you up?'

Kate started to rise, her genuine concern quashing Zoe's paranoia and tempting her to confide in her friend about Andrew. She reminded herself she must respect his insistence that they tell no one at present and said, 'Thanks, but we'll be in Edinburgh before you get back with it. How much of your findings will you share with the client when you see him?'

'Not as much as I'd planned to, on account of your eye-colour bombshell.'

'Sorry if I've made things difficult for you.'

'Better to know now, than have someone else point it out after I think I've finished. Remember me telling Erskine I'm a kind of detective too? I'll have to consult you on all my cases in future.'

Still feeling guilty for giving her friend more work, Zoe sought to change the subject. 'Has Robbie told you I've agreed to buy his field?'

'No, but we'll probably go weeks without hearing from him again. So your solicitor thought it was a good deal?'

'Her exact words were, "Say yes before he changes his mind".'

'What will you do with it?'

'I have no idea. Maybe extend the garden a bit, plant some trees, that kind of thing. Then I'll find someone to rent the rest of it.'

'When the baby's older you could build a tennis court, or maybe keep a pony. My two girls are always on about learning to ride.' Kate frowned. 'You're lucky you got to see your solicitor so quickly. Mine's on holiday till next week.'

'Isn't there someone else there who can help?'

'My solicitor's like my hairdresser. He knows me and I trust him to give me the best advice. I'm not going to be rushed into things by my idiot of an ex-husband.'

They spent the remainder of their journey looking out of the window, Kate pointing out various landmarks, which included a castle, a nuclear power station and a cement works. When they arrived in Edinburgh, Zoe followed Kate up the series of short escalators which deposited them next to the Balmoral Hotel on Princes Street, where a porter was helping an elderly woman into a taxi. Although there were still several weeks to go before Edinburgh's festivals began, pedestrians crowded the pavement in a parade of brightly-coloured tee-shirts, frocks and shorts.

'Oh look,' Zoe said, grabbing Kate's arm then pointing a short distance down Princes Street. 'A tram.'

'I haven't travelled on one yet, though I've seen them a few times. Do you want to take a ride later? We could get one out to Haymarket and pick up our train from there.'

'That would be fun if we have enough time.'

They crossed Princes Street and Kate led Zoe past a statue of a horse and rider then pointed at the grand building of mustard-coloured stone which stood behind it. 'This is Register House, where the national archives are kept. If only you had Scottish ancestors, I could show you how to research them.'

Once again Zoe held her breath, certain Kate must be trying to provoke her into revealing she did indeed have Scottish ancestors. However, Kate strode on, obviously unaware of her throwaway remark's effect. 'Is it too early for an ice cream?' she asked as they entered the ugly shopping centre and passed a Thorntons shop.

'Yes.'

Their first port of call in the John Lewis department store was the ladies' loos, then they made their way up to the fourth floor restaurant, where Kate positioned herself not far from the entrance. They agreed Zoe would return at twelve-fifteen and look to see if Kate had placed her handbag on the table, code that she wanted her meeting to be interrupted.

Wondering how was it possible to spend so much money in less than an hour, Zoe returned to the restaurant at ten past twelve carrying several bags of maternity clothes and underwear. She dropped into a seat which had a clear view of Kate and her client's back. Ten minutes later, Kate casually lifted her handbag and placed it on the table beside her coffee cup. She put on an unconvincing look of surprise as Zoe approached.

'Hello. Is it that time already?'

'Sorry if I'm interrupting.'

'No you're not. We'd just finished, hadn't we, Simon?'

The man sitting opposite Kate could only be in his mid-twenties, far younger than Zoe had expected from the amount of grey flecks in his otherwise dark brown, curly hair. A thick neck, broad shoulders and forearms with muscles straining at the short sleeves of his shirt suggested he did more than watch rugby from the comfort of his sofa. This was corroborated by a nose which showed signs of having been broken at least once.

'Simon, this is Zoe Moreland, the friend I told you about. We're going shopping for nursery furniture now you and I have finished.'

Kate's client smiled at Zoe with his mouth but his eyes failed to convey a scintilla of warmth. He closed the notebook sitting on the table in front of him and tucked his pen down its spine. 'Thank you for your time, Kate. A fortnight, definitely, until you can give me a full report?'

'I hope so.'

Simon withdrew legs which were as substantial as the rest of him from under the table. He thrust his notebook into the saltire-adorned rucksack which hung on his chair and walked away.

Zoe sat down in his still-warm seat. 'He's not at all how I expected. You described him as intense, and for some reason that conjured up someone older and smaller. He looks like a rugby player.'

'That's because he is. He works for RBS, something in IT, but I get the impression rugby provides the passion in his life.'

'How did your meeting go? It lasted longer than you expected.'

'I've had to listen to yet another lecture about how brilliant his dad is and how alike they are.'

'Is he having his family tree traced for his father? I know a lot of your clients give them as gifts.'

'He hasn't said so. I'm not bothered, to be honest. As long as someone's not a pest and pays me for what I do, that's good enough for me.' Kate looked at her watch. 'We may as well have some lunch before we go in search of your nursery furniture.'

'Are you sure you've got time? Don't you have some research to do?'

'I've decided to come back up on Friday. The rest of the day is going to be all about spending your money. Though I see you've started without me.'

NINE

Zoe looked at herself standing sideways to the mirror and groaned. The maternity capri pants she'd bought the previous day were so comfortable, she felt tempted to go online and order several more pairs, but they made her look enormous. The middle of August couldn't come soon enough.

She returned to the kitchen and found Mac lying on the floor, pawing at his face. Etta had mentioned when Zoe picked him up from Tolbyres Farm yesterday that he seemed to be squinting, and now a greenish discharge was coming from his right eye. Despite her emergency first aid, she must have missed a piece of whatever had scratched him on Sunday morning and it had caused an infection. She decided to take him to the vet's afternoon surgery and wondered if Patrick would be there.

Opening up her laptop as she ate a piece of toast, she read on the BBC News website that Police Scotland had not yet identified the dead boy. In the hope of jogging someone's memory, further details about him had been released, including his arrival the day before he died at the Duns chemist with towels wrapped around his damaged hands, and his departure a few minutes later with both of them bandaged. An appeal was made for anyone who remembered seeing him or his companion to come forward, especially with information about the vehicle they had been traveling in.

The fact that so little intelligence had been received thus far didn't surprise Zoe. If a pair of strangers had arrived in Duns early in the morning, the town would have been bustling with tradesmen stocking up on rolls, pies and bottles of juice for the day ahead, and older citizens collecting their newspapers. However, at four-thirty on a Thursday afternoon, especially during the school holidays, Duns would often be deserted. If deliberate, the timing suggested a familiarity with the neighbourhood rather than someone who was simply passing through.

She put away her laptop and closed the curtains throughout the cottage in what was probably a vain attempt to keep it cool. The humidity, already uncomfortably high at seven o'clock when she walked Mac, was even worse now as she went out to the car, and her arms tickled as thunder-bugs landed on them. The weather forecast had warned of heavy storms in the west, but the southeast corner of Scotland was destined to stay dry and muggy all day. As if confirming this prediction, several of the fields she passed on her way into Westerlea were being irrigated, the plumes of water creating small rainbows.

Margaret greeted her with the broad smile she always wore when she knew something Zoe didn't. 'That nice Geordie policeman has been on the phone for you. I said you wouldn't be available until after surgery.'

'Do I have to call him back?'

'No. He said he'd pop in when you've finished seeing patients. I got his number in case it's not convenient.' Margaret offered Zoe a piece of paper which she automatically reached for, although Trent's number was already programmed into her mobile.

'Thanks. Have I got a busy morning ahead of me?'

'A full house. Your first patient's here already.'

'I'd better get a move on then.' Zoe set off towards her consulting room, slightly puzzled as to why Margaret was following. She knew the reason as soon as she walked through the door: an enormous bouquet of flowers lay on her desk.

Margaret came up behind her. 'Happy anniversary, Doctor Zoe.'

'Thank you, but I—'

'It's exactly a year since you joined us and I wanted to mark it in some way. Doctor Paul didn't think you'd remember.'

Zoe turned to hug the older woman then went to her desk and lifted the flowers, taking a deep breath of the lilies' scent. 'They're gorgeous, thank you. And Paul was right, I hadn't remembered.'

'You've got a lot on your mind. My Hector says he doubts anyone in the Borders has had such a year as you.'

'That's one way of putting it.' Zoe looked around her consulting room. She would need the sink to wash her hands. 'Could you stand them in some water in the kitchen for me?'

Margaret bustled out with the flowers, while Zoe sat down and switched on her computer. She supposed Margaret was right and it really had been a year since she moved to Scotland, but when she considered this, it felt like both five minutes and forever. As usual, Hector had hit the nail on the head. She swallowed some water then called up the details of her first patient and went in search of him in the waiting room.

Mr Griffiths was one of her regulars, a seventy-year-old whose asthma flared up with a frequency Zoe attributed to the habit which had also stained the fingers of his right hand yellow. He sat down, wheezing. 'Pollen count's that high, I cannae get my breath, Doctor.'

'Let's see how it compares with last time, shall we?' Zoe handed him a peak flow meter which he blew into, coughing noisily afterwards. The lack of improvement by his third puff confirmed her patient's lungs were working even more inefficiently than usual.

She fixed him with a stern look. 'Have you managed to reduce the number of cigarettes you get through?'

'I told you before, I only take the odd one to be sociable. My neighbour's garden's full of flowers, that's what's causing it.' A fit of coughing shook his entire body.

Zoe waited for the coughs to subside then said, 'I'm going to prescribe you a short course of steroids, which should help. Come back in a week, even if you're feeling better.'

'Will you still be here?'

'If I'm not, one of the other doctors will see you.'

'Can't imagine finding that boy's body last week would've been good for you. Not in your condition.'

Zoe hesitated before saying quietly, 'I didn't find him, Mr Griffiths. I was asked by the police to attend in case I could help identify him.'

With a grunt which Zoe had learned could signify disbelief, disapproval or simply a farewell, the old man took his prescription and left. She sighed. It was going to be another of those surgeries when she would have to correct assumptions and deflect questions about events she was only marginally connected with.

Both her next patients were in their late teens and consequently too wrapped up in their own lives to have any interest in that of their doctor, but then came a stream of older individuals with time on their hands and more curiosity about what went on in their neighbourhood. As Zoe examined the infected mosquito bites on Molly Lawton's arm, legacy of a recent visit to Corfu, her patient nodded towards the newspaper sticking out of her shopping bag. 'Says there his hands were bandaged. Was that why they wanted you to see him, because you were the one who'd patched him up?'

'I'd never seen him before,' Zoe said. 'You'd best brace yourself. This may sting a little.'

Several subsequent patients repeated a rumour which Zoe was already familiar with: a fish processing company in Eyemouth had reported one of its migrant employees missing. She disappointed them all with her lack of insider knowledge. After their eagerness to involve her in their speculation, it was a relief to show John Wilkie into her consulting room. This wasn't the first time they had met and she knew him to be a quiet and courteous man. About six months previously, when he was suffering from a bout of insomnia brought on by the stress of losing his job as a forklift-truck driver, she had prescribed him a short course of sleeping pills. He had made a return visit solely to let her know he felt a lot better and to thank her.

Today, John's hunched posture and shuffling gait suggested he was in physical pain. 'It's my back,' he said. 'It's been sore for a while but I could hardly get out of bed this morning.'

'When did this come on?' Zoe asked.

'It might have been while I was decorating my daughter's bedroom last week.'

'Did you lift something heavy or fall off a ladder?'

He took off his glasses and began cleaning them with his tee-shirt. 'I can't remember doing anything.'

'It's possibly just a strained muscle but I want to check there's no problem with your spine.'

John obeyed her instructions as she took him through a range of tests, observing as he stood as straight as possible, leaned forward and came back up slowly, then turned his head one way and then the other. It wasn't until he lay on the couch and she was taking him through a number of movements to check sensation and reflexes that he spoke again. 'Have they identified the laddie found down by the Chain Bridge yet?'

Saddened to discover he was like everyone else, Zoe replied more sharply than she intended. 'As I've been saying all morning, not that I've heard. Tell me if this hurts, will you?'

'I'm sorry, Doctor, you'll be sick of talking about it.' Despite still being horizontal on the couch, John removed his glasses and rubbed them again with the hem of his tee-shirt.

She gave him a rueful smile as she bent his right knee and then his left. 'I'm just frustrated at people assuming I know so much more than I actually do.'

'Please don't think badly of us. It's upsetting when something awful happens in your community. And this was a young person given a working-over then thrown off a bridge. Inhuman, I call it.'

Zoe had turned round to reach for her tendon hammer, not really listening to him. However, for some reason his words concerned her, so when she started testing his knee and heel reflexes, she asked, 'What did you say?'

'Throwing a boy off a bridge. I said it was inhuman.'

'Oh. Yes, I agree.'

Unable to find any evidence of damage to John's spine, she concluded he was suffering from muscle strain. He left clutching a prescription for anti-inflammatories after giving his specs a final polish.

Her last patient of the day demanded to know what nationality the dead boy had been, because she didn't believe the local Chinese takeaway owners' claim that their eldest son had left to stay with relatives in Inverness. Zoe advised her to think very carefully about what she was saying, but if she genuinely had cause for concern, she should tell the police about her suspicions.

A few minutes later, she made her way to the practice's small kitchen. As she entered, Sergeant Trent sprang back from smelling her flowers. 'They're gorgeous,' he said. 'Yours?'

'Yes.'

'Birthday or admirer?'

'Neither.'

'Oh.' Trent nodded in the way people do when the answer to a question leaves them none the wiser but they're too polite to enquire further. He accepted Zoe's offer of coffee. She put on the kettle and got out a pair of mugs advertising a new treatment for heartburn and, although the window was open, switched on the electric fan. Neither of them spoke until they sat down.

'The dead boy still hasn't been identified, I see,' Zoe said, before adding, in case she'd sounded disparaging, 'It must be very difficult when you have nothing to go on.'

'We've received a lot of tip-offs about who he might be. Most of them have turned out to be groundless. You always get those in a high-profile case like this, but we're obliged to look into them all.'

'I've been on the receiving end of several theories this morning. A migrant worker at a fish-processing factory seems to be the preferred outcome. But you're not here to discuss the progress or otherwise in your investigation, are you?'

Trent pulled at his collar and loosened his thin tie a little. 'I've come to share a piece of information with you which I shouldn't. But I'd never forgive myself if something happened.'

Zoe stiffened. 'What have you found out?'

'You're in no immediate danger. Not like . . . well, you know. But the boss tells me you've been asking questions and he's worried you'll try to get involved. Neither of us wants you to do that.'

'Did Mather tell you to talk to me?' Zoe suddenly felt even hotter than usual. How dare he send his sergeant to do his dirty work?

'He doesn't know I'm here,' Trent said. 'I'd be for the high jump if he did.' He waited briefly for Zoe to respond. When she didn't, he continued. 'Doctor Moreland, what that boy's post mortem revealed was shocking. I can't go into details, but it tells us we're dealing with cruel and ruthless people. You mustn't get involved.'

'Why on earth would I want to?'

'Forgive me for making assumptions, but I saw you with the body. You didn't treat him as a piece of evidence like Doc Ferguson. You responded emotionally, I could tell.'

'"Emotionally"? Ah, now I get it, Sergeant. Because your wife's pregnant, you assume you're an expert on all pregnant women and of course we're entirely ruled by our hormones.' Zoe rose to take her mug to the sink, even though she'd hardly touched the coffee in it.

Trent sighed. 'Now you know why I'm not the DCI. I'm useless at expressing myself. Sorry.'

His shoulders slumped and he looked so crestfallen that Zoe took pity on him. She gave a quick laugh and said, 'Well, if you did think like that, maybe I've just proved you right.'

'My wife accuses me of being over-protective towards her, so maybe the problem's mine. But if you'd seen what that boy had been put through, you'd understand why I'm here.'

'Did you attend the post mortem yourself?'

'It's one of the worst parts of the job. I can take the smells and the blood, but what's hard to bear is the suffering that's sometimes revealed.'

'The injuries on his face suggested he'd been beaten up a few hours before he died.'

'That was the least of it.'

Seeing the policeman's clenched fists, Zoe wondered if this was in response to the fate of the boy or if it indicated he was fighting the urge to tell her more. She knew from experience that silence often trumped questions when dealing with someone holding back, so she waited. Eventually, the words spilled out of him.

'He'd endured weeks, perhaps months, of physical abuse. What we couldn't see down at the riverside were cigarette burns all over his body, broken ribs and . . . worse.'

Still Zoe remained silent. The poor man needed to

speak about this; it was obviously eating him up. He could hardly go home and talk it through with his wife.

'The injuries to his palms were burns, and the pathologist found bruising on his wrists. That boy's hands had been put against something very hot, like a cooker hob, and held there.' Trent paused and took a deep breath. 'He'd been sexually assaulted too. Repeatedly.'

They stared wordlessly at each other, united in their horror, then Trent asked if Zoe wanted to sit down. She shook her head, not annoyed with his attentiveness but still trying to take in what he'd just told her.

'I think you should. You've gone very pale.'

She allowed him to take her arm and guide her back into a chair where she sat hugging her bump. Of all the things she'd become involved with over the past year, this felt the most shocking. Could Trent be right? Was it affecting her so badly because she was pregnant?

The policeman took out a handkerchief and mopped his brow. 'I knew I shouldn't have said anything.'

Zoe leaned back in her chair, trying to look more composed than she felt. 'I'm fine, really. If it's any consolation, you've managed to convey the seriousness of the situation far more effectively than DCI Mather's evasion ever could. You're dealing with sex-traffickers, aren't you? People think girls are the only victims but as I found out when I did some voluntary work before coming here, that's not always the case.'

'It's one possibility, yes. We're working with the Human Traffic and International Unit who know a lot more than we do on the subject.'

'Now you've told me this much, will you share how he died?'

'You're a bit of a chancer on the quiet, aren't you, Doctor?' Trent said, yet he must have realised he'd gone past the point of no return. 'They think he was electrocuted, although a specialist's coming over from

Glasgow to confirm it. And that's positively the last bit of information you're getting out of me. I must go.'

Zoe walked him to the health centre's front door. Just before leaving he said, 'We're making none of this public, except for the injuries to his hands.'

'I'm a doctor, Sergeant. None of it will go any further.'

Trent looked cheerful as he left, obviously believing his mission to curb her curiosity about the boy's death had been a success. And while common sense told Zoe he was right to warn her off, deep down she knew his only achievement—apart from revealing a sensitivity she hadn't seen before—had been to make her even more determined to find out what had happened to the dead boy.

Ara. His name was Ara.

TEN

Someone, she'd forgotten who, once told Zoe that now she was living in Scotland she should never let the weather put her off doing something, because if they all did this, the country would grind to a halt. Judging by Margaret's reaction to the news that she planned to visit a garden centre in Kelso on Thursday afternoon instead of going home and putting her feet up, this advice hadn't come from her.

'It's far too hot out there, Doctor Zoe.'

'If I overheat I promise to sit down for a while in the cafe with an iced drink.'

Margaret's face had gone red, as though she could feel the heat Zoe would be exposing herself to. 'Nothing will grow if you plant it now.'

'It's really just to get some ideas. I don't plan on buying anything except maybe a couple of books.' Zoe smiled to let Margaret know she appreciated her concern. 'I'll be fine, honestly.'

However, when she opened the Jeep and felt the temperature inside it, she almost changed her mind. Resisting the urge to open all its windows, she waited for the air-conditioning to take effect then set off. A few minutes later, driving slowly through the village, she noticed a blue Fiesta in her rear view mirror. It was some way back, also keeping to the speed limit, and maintained the space between them as she slowed down to let the postie's van out of a side road. Then it fell back and disappeared from view.

As her car gained speed, Zoe turned the music up loud and tried not to think about the dead boy and how he must have suffered. She failed miserably. Having attended post mortems herself, she could imagine only too well the scene in the mortuary as the pathologist went about his work, pointing out evidence of abuse to the police and other observers. The cigarette burns, the cracked ribs, the burnt hands. And worse. The bruising on the boy's face was rendered almost irrelevant by the sadistic nature of the treatment which must have caused his other injuries, yet for some reason she had a strange feeling it was important. She just couldn't work out why.

The satisfaction she'd experienced at extracting information from Sergeant Trent had vanished. He should never have told her so much. He probably realised this too by now, and she felt burdened by having to keep the knowledge to herself. Last year, her friendship with Kate had nearly been destroyed by what Kate viewed as Zoe's secretiveness, and since then she had tried to be more trusting. In this instance, though, there was someone else's reputation to consider.

As she neared Kelso, a blue Fiesta came up behind her. It looked like the one that had followed her through Westerlea a little earlier and, now she came to think of it, had trailed behind her on the way back from Moffat on Saturday. She'd taken nothing in about the driver then, so couldn't tell if the person wearing a baseball hat and dark glasses today was the same one.

On impulse, she indicated right and immediately took the minor road that ran round the back of Kelso Racecourse. In her hurry to escape the other car, although she had no idea if it was following, she came close to losing control of the Jeep as she took a tight bend much too quickly. Shocked into recognising she was endangering not only herself and her baby but anyone unfortunate enough to be coming in the opposite direction, she slowed right down. As she passed the racecourse entrance, she allowed herself a brief glance in the mirror. No Fiesta, no other vehicle at all.

By the time she'd passed the Golf Club and Kelso Ice Rink, rejoining her original route at a mini roundabout, she felt foolish. 'Sorry. I was being silly, wasn't I?' she said, patting her bump. 'But we're going to the garden centre now. Nothing sinister ever happens in one of those.'

Forty minutes later, having wandered around the tempting displays of shrubs and trees and treated herself to a beautiful hardback book on garden design by the Royal Horticultural Society, Zoe drove out of the garden centre's car park. As she set off in the direction of Kelso Abbey, she noticed a blue Fiesta parked at the side of the road, a hand hanging out of the driver's window with a cigarette clamped between its fingers. She checked out the sole occupant as she went past. He wore a baseball cap and aviator sunglasses.

She pulled into an empty space up ahead and got out.

By the time she reached the passenger side of the Fiesta, the little car was already indicating to pull away, but a succession of vehicles coming from behind it prevented this manoeuvre. Even with his face turned from her, the driver, in a faded red tee-shirt and ripped jeans, looked unlike any journalist or freelance photographer she'd been hassled by in the past. And he seemed desperate to get away, not confront her.

'Why are you following me?' Zoe shouted. The driver kept his face averted. She went to grab the door handle and at that moment, the Fiesta jerked forward and pulled away in a cloud of diesel fumes. She stumbled back against the hedge which lined the pavement.

A middle-aged woman rushed up to her. 'Are you alright, hen? You need to take care of yersel, y'know.'

'Thank you, I'm fine.'

For much of the way home, Zoe berated herself for not having had the presence of mind to take the Fiesta's registration number, but by the time she arrived back at Keeper's Cottage she realised that information would only be useful if she intended to involve the police, which she definitely didn't want to do. Mather would insist on making it official and she couldn't bear getting caught up in yet another investigation.

For the first time in months, she locked her front door as soon as she got inside. Mac's greeting was more subdued than usual, probably because his inflamed eye was troubling him. Although reluctant to go out again, she couldn't ignore it and called the vet for an appointment. Only the last one of the day was left and it became obvious as soon as they entered the crowded waiting area that Patrick and his colleagues were behind schedule. The smell of disinfectant hung in the air and a wet-floor sign stood in the passageway leading to the consulting rooms. A young woman dressed in a tiny pair of shorts and balancing a cat basket on her knees slid along the bench seat to make room for Zoe to sit down. Mac lay at her feet, his tail wagging slowly as he sized up the other dogs.

Patrick appeared beside an elderly man with red-rimmed eyes who carried a small dog-collar. He nodded at Zoe and as the man produced his wallet with a shaking hand, took his arm and escorted him past the reception desk, murmuring, 'Don't worry about that now.' The waiting pet owners looked on in sympathy and several reached for their own pets. Zoe got out her book.

Forty minutes after their appointed time, Patrick ushered them into his room.

'Sorry to keep you waiting so long. It's been a hectic afternoon.'

'Don't worry. I often find it impossible to stick to a schedule too. You can't just throw patients out of the door when their time's up.'

He bent down to look at Mac's eye. 'So this has come on since his adventure at the weekend?'

'I thought there was no lasting damage but a couple of days later he started rubbing his head on the carpet then he developed a squint in that eye. Now there's a discharge coming from it.'

Mac was on his best behaviour as Zoe held him and Patrick cleaned out his eye then put a warm compress over it for a few minutes. Apart from reassuring the dog this wouldn't take long and praising him for his patience, neither of them spoke.

After administering the first dose of antibiotic drops and rewarding Mac with a biscuit, Patrick stood up, stretched his back and looked at Zoe. 'You'll need to clean his eye morning and evening before putting the drops in. I don't have to tell you to wear gloves, do I? Especially at the moment.'

'No you don't,' Zoe said, putting Mac's lead back on. Worried she may have sounded curt, she added, 'Thanks for seeing us. You've had to work very late this evening.'

Patrick reached for the door to let her out, but stopped short of opening it. 'I enjoyed our chat at the Mackenzie barbeque, and Mac got on well with Peggy. I wonder if you'd like to come out for a walk with us over the weekend? Not a long one, of course. Even dachshunds with a full complement of legs don't need as much exercise as a dog Mac's size.'

Zoe's immediate reaction was to make an excuse, but wasn't that a bit silly? Mac did enjoy spending time with other dogs.

He took her silence as a no and opened the door. 'Another time, maybe. If Mac's eye is still weeping when the drops are finished, bring him back.'

'Yes,' Zoe said. 'To the walk, I mean.'

Patrick's face lit up. 'That's great.'

'Where will we go? I'm not good going up or down steep hills anymore.'

'Leave the route to me. Sunday morning suit you?'

'Alright. As long as I can drive. I'm most comfortable in my own vehicle these days.' It also meant she could control how long they stayed out.

'You come to me and we can go on from there.'

After agreeing on an early start to avoid the worst of the heat and Patrick giving her directions to his house just outside Duns, Zoe left him to do whatever vets do after taking surgery and went to the reception desk to settle her bill.

During the short drive home, she remained on the alert for that blue Fiesta, experiencing a moment of panic as she approached Westerlea and saw one driving along Main Street towards her. However, its occupant was a white-haired woman who looked unlikely to even know what aviator sunglasses were.

ELEVEN

Wellies? Zoe tapped into her mobile.

Kate replied immediately. *Yes & trousers. Do you own walking stick?*

No. Ground rough?

No. Brambles!

By the time Kate arrived at Keeper's Cottage on Friday morning, Zoe was beginning to regret agreeing to join her on another of her expeditions, this time to an abandoned graveyard. However, the day felt a little cooler and she didn't have to work, so providing they weren't out for long it might prove interesting. She just hoped not to be caught short like on a recent walk, when she'd had to hide behind a hedge to pee, all the time being stared at by Mac.

'Weren't you supposed to be going back up to Edinburgh today?' she asked Kate once they were in the kitchen.

'I need to solve the mystery you set me first,' Kate said. 'I've come up with a theory and today we're testing it out.'

'Before we do that, I need to tell you something.'

'What?'

'I've been looking into the eye colour issue, and I'm afraid I may be sending us on a wild-goose chase. Your client's great-great-grandfather could have had brown eyes when his parents had blue ones. It does happen, though not often. I can email you a link to the research I found, if you like.'

'Actually, I don't think you were wrong at all, but I'm not going to tell you my theory until we find the evidence I hope is in the graveyard.'

Zoe raised her eyebrows. 'So you're going to make me wander around without knowing what I'm looking for?'

'It'll be fun. I've got a flask of coffee and a packet of biscuits in the car.'

'I'll need more than that.'

'You're not playing the pregnancy card, are you? I'm trying to do what you tell me everyone should do — not treat you any differently despite the baby you're carrying.'

After raising her hands in mock submission, Zoe moved to the sink to fill her water bottle. A few minutes later, they were sitting in Kate's car, but instead of pulling away, Kate stared at the side of Zoe's head.

'What?' Zoe asked.

'Your earlobe's all red and swollen. Does it hurt?'

Zoe put her hand to her ear. The lobe felt hot and a little tender. 'A bit, yes. I'll bathe it when I get back.'

'I had to take my belly bar out every time I got pregnant because it kept on getting infected. But I don't suppose you have one of those.'

They both burst out laughing at the thought.

About twenty minutes later, Kate brought her car to a halt in front of a pair of intricately carved stone pillars, each of which supported a high metal gate. Zoe looked on as she took a pink backpack, two wooden walking-sticks and something large and flat, wrapped in a hessian sack, from the boot.

'What on earth's that?' Zoe asked, pointing at the sack.

Kate passed her a stick and put on the backpack. 'You'll see.'

One of the gates stood open, beckoning visitors to follow the track leading from it towards a band of trees.

'This is the start of the old Allankirk estate,' Kate said. 'The big house is long gone, as are the workers' cottages. All that's left are these gates and the graveyard. Hard to believe a couple of hundred people lived here in the early nineteenth century, isn't it?'

'What happened?' Zoe asked. 'Did they all just move away or was it something more sinister?'

'The laird decided he didn't want to look out on his workers anymore, so he built them a new settlement a few miles away and moved them there. We drove through it on the way here. Clarefield, remember? He named it after his wife.'

'I know where you mean.'

'Unfortunately, the cost of doing this was greater than he'd anticipated and it bankrupted him. He sold the big house to someone who in turn sold it on and it was never lived in again. In the 1920s, what remained of it was taken apart stone by stone.'

'That's so sad.'

'Don't you mean outrageous? Treating people like cattle, shunting them out of the way.'

'Into brand new houses. We might be outraged at the thought, but maybe for his workers it was a change for the better.'

'Hmm.' The expression on Kate's face told Zoe she wasn't convinced. 'Anyway, the graveyard isn't far but the path becomes a bit overgrown at one point. You must say if you start to get tired.'

Zoe waved the walking stick Kate had brought along for her. 'I will. Lead on.'

The path was at its widest until it reached the trees, when it started to taper until they could no longer walk side by side. As the height of the trees increased, the sunlight diminished and the path gave up all pretence of being anything but a narrow tunnel. For ten minutes, the only sound Zoe could hear was the scampering of small animals in the dense undergrowth; all birdsong had ceased. Just as she began to wonder if they would ever reach their destination, they stepped into a small clearing. She looked up at the blue sky and welcomed the heat of the sun on her face.

'The graveyard should be over there,' Kate said, pointing to their right.

'"Should be"? Have you never been here before?'

'No. You'll probably need your stick now. Come on.'

The final stage of their hike took them back in amongst trees, but these were more widely spaced than before. The soft ground, its surface littered with dead leaves and fallen pine-cones interspersed with patches of bright green nettles and creeping brambles, sunk under Zoe's feet. She swore as a nettle she'd pushed aside with her stick swung back and stung her calf just above the protection of her boots.

'Here it is,' Kate shouted.

Thank goodness. Zoe ducked her head to avoid a low-hanging branch and when she looked up again she saw Kate standing at a gap in an ivy-clad wall twice her height. Several piles of stones lying nearby, covered in moss and overrun by brambles, attested to this entrance not being man-made but the result of gradual decay.

They stared at the final resting place of many Allankirk residents. The graveyard was surrounded on all sides by the wall, except for an opening off to the right which must have been its original entrance. Because no trees grew inside, it was bathed in sunshine.

'It's not as overgrown as I would have expected,' Zoe said.

'It gets no regular maintenance, but a group of volunteers Auntie Joan belongs to cleared the worst of the vegetation in the spring.'

'Now are you going to tell me what we're looking for?'

Kate reached into the back pocket of her jeans and pulled out a small notebook. 'Remember I showed you the photocopy of the Criminal Register for 1861? When Adam and his parents—or, rather, the people I thought were his parents—were arrested, they gave their addresses as Clarefield. It wasn't long after the new village had been built so they had probably lived on the old Allankirk estate before then.'

'But whose gravestone are you hoping to find here?'

'We must look for a baby boy who died in about 1845, and Grace's sister.' Kate glanced down at the notebook. 'Her name was Lily. She would have died around the same time.'

'I don't suppose you know Lily's surname?'

'Sorry. She was likely married but I haven't been able to find a record of that yet.' Kate grinned. 'I know what you're thinking.'

'The words haystack and needle do spring to mind,' Zoe said, rubbing her leg where it had been stung.

'Let's look for half an hour. If we don't find anything by the end of that, I promise we can give up and go home. Here, I've brought some vital bits of equipment for you.' Kate slipped off her backpack and undid the zip to its main compartment, from which she took out a pair of gardening gloves and a dustpan brush. 'Give me a wave if you find anything interesting.'

As Zoe weaved between the gravestones, she found no statues of angels or intricately carved sarcophagi; the Allankirk graveyard wasn't inhabited by members of the gentry. This had been a burial ground for working people, their families' limited means probably stretched to commission even these simple tributes.

Unlike Westerlea's graveyard, scene of one funeral Zoe had attended the previous November and another she had deliberately stayed away from, the gravestones here may have started off in serried rows but they were now scattered. Hardly any still stood completely upright. Some were supported by large fieldstones placed at their base, one was propped up with a tree branch. Many had fallen over and been piled haphazardly on top of each other, while a number of them looked like oversized paving-stones, having lain on the ground for such a long time that the earth had risen around them. All were covered with lichen and moss, and some with ivy too.

Unable to bend down far enough to read any prone on the ground, Zoe nevertheless threw herself into a task which was far harder than she expected. Most of the inscriptions had lost their sharpness as the stones were eroded by rain and frost, and patches of green and yellow lichen also served to make them indistinct. She gently swept the brush Kate had given her over one of the larger headstones and managed to read the dates but the words on it still evaded her. She sighed and moved on to the next one.

Gradually, she started to make sense of what she saw, her eyes and brain adjusting to the faint, archaic lettering. Still no Lily or small child, though.

Sooner than she expected, she heard Kate call to her. 'Half-hour's up. Do you want to stop or carry on?'

'I'm happy to carry on if you are.'

'Excellent.'

Twenty minutes later, her back starting to ache, she had just decided to ask Kate if they could try again another day when she heard a shout.

'Come and see what I've found!'

Zoe spun round to see Kate waving frantically, brush in hand. She waved back and made her way between the gravestones to her.

'Ta-da!' Kate gestured at a flat-topped gravestone standing at a worrying angle next to her. 'Look at this.'

Zoe stared at the stone but couldn't make out the

writing on it. Kate lifted something out of the hessian sack she had carried from the car. 'This might help.' It was a plastic mirror, and Zoe watched, fascinated, as Kate held it at an angle, directing the bright sunlight across the gravestone and casting shadows in the indentations. All of a sudden, Zoe was able to read the inscription.

Lily Douglas
Beloved wife, mother and sister
Died December 1845 aged 31

'I'm pleased you've found her, although I still don't understand why she's so important.'

'I'll explain it all in a minute. But first, look at this one too.' Kate moved sideways to reveal a much smaller stone leaning against Lily's.

Zoe bent over as far as she could and squinted at it. 'Can you do your magic with the mirror for me? I'm struggling with this one too.'

'Even with the mirror I can't make out all the words either. But I got the important stuff – "infant son" and "1845".'

'That's the same year Lily died. So her son died too? How sad.'

'I think it's a wee bit more complicated than that. But I can see you rubbing your back, so let's sit down. I'll get the coffee out and explain.'

They walked over to a pair of stones which had lain on top of each other for so long they were held together by moss and ivy. Kate checked the stones' stability then motioned to Zoe to sit down. She pulled a flask and a small tin mug from her bag and while she concentrated on pouring their coffee, Zoe tried to work out how those two graves could help solve the puzzle she'd inadvertently set her friend.

Their eyes met as Kate passed Zoe the mug, filled to its brim with strong coffee, and a chocolate biscuit.

'Are you comfortable?'

'As much as I can be, sitting on a pile of gravestones.'

'Will I hold off telling you my theory until we get back to the car?'

'Certainly not. I've got this far. Tell away.'

'Okay. There's something you need to remember in all this.'

'What?'

'Adam appears to have been Grace and Archibald's only child. There's no record of him having any siblings, which was very unusual, given that people had nothing but the most rudimentary contraception back in the nineteenth century. And Grace was over forty when she gave birth to him.'

'Okay. And what's the significance of these facts?'

'I'll get to that. The reason I brought us here was I discovered Grace had a younger sister, Lily, who had also lived in Allankirk. I think that's her grave over there. As we can see, she died in 1845, which according to parish records is the year Grace's son Adam was born.'

Kate paused and looked at Zoe, who nodded to confirm she was with her so far. 'Even though I can't find a written record, we know Lily had a child, as her gravestone says *Beloved wife, mother and sister*. But if that child died at around the same time as she did, why wasn't he or she buried in the same grave? That's what usually happened. Her family was poor—they wouldn't have gone to the expense of a separate gravestone.'

'So you're saying the dead child wasn't Lily's?'

'Exactly. What if the child whose tiny gravestone this is was actually Grace and Archibald's son? That would have left Lily's baby with no mother and Grace grieving for her only child and unlikely to be able to have more because of her age. What better solution than for Grace and Archibald to informally adopt their nephew and bring him up as their own? They wouldn't have cared that he'd inherited his real father's brown eyes while theirs were blue.'

Zoe gave this some thought, then said, 'I can see your reasoning. But you mentioned the baby's father. Would he really have given away his son?'

'He probably looked upon it as a good thing. There was no way he could have cared for a young child and continued to work to keep a roof over their heads. Depending on when her own child died, Grace may even have still been lactating. Lily's surviving baby probably hadn't been weaned so she would have been able to take over feeding it.'

'This all sounds very plausible, but what proof do you have? You're making the limited facts at your disposal fit your theory, rather than vice versa.'

Kate ran a hand through her hair. 'Fair comment. My problem is that it wasn't compulsory in Scotland to register births, marriages and deaths until 1855. I've got a lot more work to do on this.'

'What about names? You're saying Grace and Archibald's son called Adam died and was replaced by a boy with brown eyes who had the same name. How likely is that?'

'Infant mortality was high back then. If a young child died, the next one born in that family would often be given the same name. So if Grace and Archibald adopted Lily's son, they could've simply renamed him after their dead son.'

'Oh.' Despite the heat of the day, Zoe shivered. 'Can we go now? I'm finding all this talk of dead babies a bit grim.'

Kate leapt to her feet. 'I'm so sorry. What was I thinking?'

'It's okay, I'm not upset but that's the problem. Because this all happened such a long time ago, we're talking about it in a detached way. For Grace, losing a sister and a son around the same time must have been devastating. If what you suggest really did take place, I hope she drew comfort from bringing up her sister's child.'

Zoe tried to rise from the gravestones she was sitting on but her legs were tired and her bump suddenly seemed far larger than ever before. She struggled to lift herself; Kate came over to help, chuckling. As she pulled Zoe to her feet she said, 'You'd best not sit on anything that low again, at least until the baby's here. My poorly back can't take it.'

'Luckily the only beanbag in Keeper's Cottage belongs to Mac.'

While Kate gathered her kit together, Zoe walked to the edge of the graveyard where a patch of wild flowers was growing. She picked a few, then returned to Lily's stone and laid the flowers in front of it. Leaning over, she touched the smaller, adjacent stone and whispered, 'They're for you as well, whoever you were.'

Shocked by how exhausted she felt by the time they got back to the car, she turned down Kate's offer of lunch at Tolbyres. It was a relief to let herself back into the cottage, enjoy the usual ecstatic welcome from Mac, whose eye was already looking less swollen, then release herself from jeans into a loose, sleeveless dress. Her earlobe hurt a lot now, so she took out her gold studs and placed them on the bedside table before lying down to ease her back. The next time she glanced at the clock, nearly an hour had passed.

Her mobile rang as she was debating whether to get up and eat something or turn over and go back to sleep.

'I'm sorry I haven't called before.' Andrew's voice sounded impassive, which Zoe knew to be an act.

'It's alright.' When her father stayed silent, she asked gently, 'Has something happened?'

'Helen's still with us, if that's what you mean. But I can't leave her now until . . . it's over.'

'I know. Don't worry about me. I just wish I could

do something to help.' Zoe had no personal experience of living through the final days of someone close with a terminal illness, although she had advised countless patients in the situation Andrew found himself. Today, though, she avoided giving out any of the advice she would normally offer; it felt banal and insincere.

'There's nothing anyone can do. I'm in the greenhouse, watering my tomatoes because it feels like that's all I'm good for.'

'Are you getting the practical help you need?'

'Friends are in and out all the time, with food and offers to sit with Helen, but she can't cope with visitors any more. She—' Andrew's voice broke. Zoe heard him take a deep breath. 'She had me go through her jewellery box yesterday, telling me who should get the things she hasn't already set aside for Nina. She even wants her favourite cousin to have the little watercolour she treated herself to when she sold her first book.'

She's a writer. With a jolt, Zoe realised she knew little about Helen beyond the fact she was Andrew's wife. 'I can see how upsetting this must be for you, but it means she's accepted what's happening to her.'

'You're right. I should be thankful, but all I feel is anger. She's only sixty, for God's sake. That's no age at all.'

'No, it isn't.'

'Oh, Zoe, I get so much comfort from knowing you're there and being able to talk to you.'

Before she could respond she heard another, muffled voice. Andrew spoke away from his phone. 'Tell him I'll be with him in a couple of minutes.'

'You have to go?' she asked when he said her name again.

'Doctor's here. I'm sorry. I was really calling to find out how you and the baby are.'

'We're both fine. Please, Andrew, ring me whenever you need to.'

102

'You'll have enough of listening to other people's problems in your job.'

Zoe's eyes prickled. 'You're not other people. You're my father.'

After they said their goodbyes, she opened the bedroom door and let Mac in. He jumped up on the bed and she lay down next to him and stroked his head. Any idea of getting back to sleep had vanished.

You're my father. Blurting this out to Andrew had taken her by surprise. Even as a young girl, she had never clung to a romantic notion of her absent parent, and growing older didn't change this. Self-aware enough to know that while she might have developed into a different person if she'd been brought up by two parents instead of one, she also had the insight to recognise this wouldn't necessarily have made her any happier. The sudden loss of her mother and moving away from everyone and everything she knew, to be brought up by her grandparents, had sown a seed of curiosity about the other side of her family but still hadn't brought on a longing for her father to appear on the scene.

This indifference to exploring her roots had been brought to an end by Gran and Grandad dying within six months of each other. She was already married to Russell by that time but their ill-fated relationship hadn't been enough to shield her from the realisation that she was alone. And so she had moved to the Borders a year ago, motivated in part by the opportunity this offered to search for her father. As it turned out, he had found her first.

Her stomach rumbled; she should have eaten lunch hours ago. As she got up, she knocked the bedside cabinet and winced at the pain which shot up her arm. That wrist would probably never totally recover from being fractured last November. Worse still, the jolt had caused one of her earrings to fall onto the carpet then bounce under the bed. She slowly lowered herself to her knees but couldn't reach the earring until she lay flat out.

Head on his paws, Mac stared as his owner returned to a kneeling position then braced her arms against the bed and pushed herself up. She imagined Kate's amused concern at this manoeuvre and how she would have rushed to help, despite the danger of hurting her own back. People are cumbersome things to lift.

About to return the earring to its mate, Zoe's hand hovered above the bedside table. Pulling the boy out of the river must have been hard work. He wasn't big but he literally would have been a dead weight, his wet clothes making him even heavier. The man who had retrieved him might have damaged himself doing it. Strained his back, maybe. Like that patient, what was his name? John Wilkie.

She dropped onto the bed, narrowly missing Mac's head. It came to her now what John Wilkie had said which hadn't felt right. He described the boy as having been beaten up before going into the water, but how could he possibly know this? The police were deliberately keeping all the boy's injuries secret, except for the damage to his hands.

He had to have seen him.

It all fitted. The timing, his vagueness about how he'd hurt himself, his interest in more information about the boy (although she had to admit he shared this last detail with nearly all yesterday's patients). Then again, wasn't she making a huge assumption, something she'd earlier accused Kate of doing? John Wilkie couldn't be a poacher, he seemed such a decent man. Poachers were thieves. And she'd heard it was big business these days, not an individual boosting his income with the occasional fish no one would miss.

'What do I know about people?' she asked Mac. He wagged his tail. 'Thanks for the vote of confidence, but you're impressed when I can open the fridge door. I don't want to make yet another huge mistake.'

As if her mention of the fridge had reminded him his last meal was hours ago, Mac jumped off the bed and made for the kitchen. Zoe got up more slowly and followed him.

TWELVE

In anticipation of their long walk the following day with Patrick, Zoe decided to take it easy on Saturday and just stroll to the village and back. She had run out of milk and dog biscuits, so her destination was the shop, now reopened after several months' hiatus.

Despite being virtually empty, the backpack Kate's children had given her for Christmas, the same as their mother's pink one but in a more subdued blue, felt hot against her back. After two slightly cooler days, the summer heat had returned with a vengeance. Halfway to Westerlea, she leaned against a tree trunk in the shade for a rest. Why hadn't she brought the car or at least come out earlier?

Reflecting the lifestyle of many of their customers, the shop's new owners had left a bowl of water on the ground just outside the front door. Zoe tied Mac up next to it and went inside. The familiar clanging of the bell took her back to earlier visits, although the layout had completely changed. Many of the chiller cabinets had been replaced with rows of wicker baskets containing fresh fruit and vegetables, and the rear wall now held a display of greeting cards and gift wrap, reminding Zoe of Kate's birthday next week.

The face behind the counter was new as well: a girl in her late teens with red hair and freckles. She smiled and nodded then returned to wielding her pricing gun. Zoe located the milk and biscuits for Mac without trouble, couldn't choose between two birthday cards so took them both, and sighed with disappointment at not being able to find the food she used to treat herself to when she needed cheering up.

'Can I help with anything?' the girl asked. Zoe saw now she wore a badge bearing her name: Kirsty.

'I don't suppose you'll be stocking taramasalata? I used to buy it here but I know you've changed things.'

Kirsty looked blank and shook her head. 'Sorry. But I've got a notebook here I'm supposed to write in when people ask for something we haven't got.' She reached under the counter. 'What was it again?'

Zoe spelled out the word and gave her name when asked for that too. Kirsty looked surprised. 'Oh. You're Doctor Moreland?'

'Yes.'

'Someone's been in this morning asking where you live.'

Zoe froze. 'Who?' she asked, her voice sounding far higher than normal.

Kirsty shrugged. 'Some bloke. I told him I didn't know you so I couldn't say.'

'Was he young or old? What did he look like?'

'Young, I think. He wore dark glasses and a hat.' Seeing the look on Zoe's face she tried to be more helpful, adding, 'Bought a bar of Galaxy and a packet of cheese and onion crisps.'

'But you didn't tell him anything?'

'Like I said, how could I? Anyway, an old lady was in here at the time and you know how they like to gossip. She told him.'

Zoe kept Mac on his lead as she strode home more quickly than she probably should have. Neither of the two cars which passed them on the road was a blue Fiesta but she still stared in at the drivers as they sped by, relieved to see long blonde hair on one and a short grey crop on the other. Like everyone these days, they wore sunglasses.

Her legs trembled as she unlocked the front door; after relocking it behind her she went around the house checking all the windows were secure as well. But instead of making her feel safer, completion of the task saw her anxiety ramp up further. Her heart began to pound uncontrollably and she felt dizzy. The next stage would be hyperventilation. She must avoid that or end up having a full-blown panic attack.

She forced herself to sit down, then concentrated on breathing steadily. Little by little, this worked; her heartbeat slowed and the room stopped tilting. Her mobile rang, still in the backpack where she'd thrown it down on the hall floor. She let the call go to voicemail.

Once it felt safe to do so, she slowly rose and went through to the kitchen for a cold drink, accompanied by a solicitous Mac. She leaned against the sink with her glass of water and tried to focus on what to eat. However, regaining control of her body had been simple compared with halting her anxiety about the situation she was in. Because, combined with being followed by the blue Fiesta and its furtive driver, only one conclusion could be drawn from what Kirsty had told her.

She was being stalked.

It was a measure of Zoe's anxiety that she forgot to check her mobile until late Saturday evening as she sat on the sofa with Mac and tried to concentrate on the BBC's latest Scandinavian crime drama. She live-paused the action to make sure she hadn't misread her log of missed calls. No mistake. The number which had phoned her earlier had been blocked, just like all those others. Oddly, this didn't unnerve her; if anything it was reassuring. If he was still phoning, maybe he wasn't planning a visit.

She grew weary and put her feet up, apologising to Mac as she coaxed him onto the floor, but ten minutes later she decided going to bed was preferable to waking on the sofa in a few hours' time with a back that ached even more than usual. Her bedroom felt stuffy, its window having been completely shut. Mac slipped past her and jumped on the bed. She let him stay.

She slept sporadically, waking frequently bathed in sweat and needing the loo, her dreams populated by strangers and, bizarrely, various wild animals which followed her around a city she didn't recognise. Giving in at five o'clock, she got up for a mug of tea and stood at the French windows smiling as she watched Mac sniff around the back garden until the kettle came to the boil. The next time she looked out, he was nowhere to be seen.

Her stomach lurched. She ran onto the patio, shouting his name. After a few seconds, Mac trotted back into view from behind a pile of earth, carrying something in his mouth. Even before he came close enough for her to prise the crisp packet from between his jaws, she knew its contents had been cheese-and-onion-flavoured.

THIRTEEN

Zoe was no stranger to living through prolonged periods of anxiety, of continually having a tight feeling across her chest and waking up panic-stricken several times in the night. Knowing these physical symptoms were the result of her body releasing stress hormones — adrenaline and cortisol, she could even name them — was no consolation, because now she had someone else to consider. The child inside her not only fed off the nutrients her body provided but would be affected by her emotions. As a mother-to-be, she had a duty to stay calm, to fight off the fear which sometimes threatened to engulf her.

Knowing she would feel better in the company of someone else and taking exercise rather than lounging on the sofa, she suppressed an urge to call Patrick and cancel their outing. At eight-thirty on Sunday morning, she and Mac got into the Jeep. The crisp packet Mac had found, in all likelihood dropped by a workman, now lay in the kitchen bin beneath the piece of buttered toast she'd tried to eat for breakfast. Out of sight, if not out of mind.

As they approached Duns, passing several walkers — with and without dogs — and a young woman on an elegant grey horse, everything felt so normal, except for the heat, that Zoe started to relax and enjoy the drive. Eventually, she took the sharp left turn on the bend Patrick had told her to look out for and drove along a narrow lane for a mile until she came to a row of cottages. Number four was at the far end, its front garden laid entirely to sun-faded lawn, in contrast to the other three which were bright with well-watered flowers and vegetables.

Shrill barking announced her arrival. When the front door opened, Peggy bounded out wearing a fetching turquoise harness.

Patrick, one foot booted, the other only wearing a sock, said, 'Come in, Zoe. We're nearly ready.' He led her through a narrow hall into a room on the left, every second footstep thumping on the bare floorboards, and indicated she should sit down on a faded two-seater sofa spread with a blue towel. As soon as she did so, Peggy jumped onto her lap, not in the least held back by a missing front leg. The dachshund looked and felt tiny compared with Mac, who was no colossus himself.

Having sat on a matching and similarly faded chair, Patrick concentrated on lacing up his boot while Zoe looked around the room. She saw no television, no ornaments, no pictures, but books lay on every surface, as well as filling floor-to-ceiling shelves across one wall. Three cardboard boxes stood in a corner and she wouldn't have minded betting they contained books too.

'I'm guessing you're a keen reader,' she said.

He looked up and grinned. 'You could say that. When I moved here I swore I'd operate a one-in, one-out policy but as you can see, it hasn't been a success.'

'I started using an e-reader to kid myself I was keeping mine under control.'

'Oh no, I could never do that. Love the feel of a book in my hands too much.'

'What do you read?'

'Practically anything, fiction and non-fiction, except for romance and religion.'

Zoe laughed. 'Come to think of it, I'm the same. Though I'd add science fiction to my list of least favourite genres. All those robots.'

Patrick rose and walked to one of the boxes. After

rummaging through its contents he pulled out a slim paperback. 'Try this, it may change your mind. Not a single robot, I promise.'

Zoe had never heard of *I Am Legend*, and her face must have conveyed her doubt that she would enjoy a novel which sported a cover depicting soft-focus zombies. 'I'll tell you a bit about it as we walk,' Patrick said. 'If I can't pique your curiosity, you don't even have to take it home with you. Deal?'

'Deal.'

As they left the room, Zoe paused to study two small photographs in pine frames standing on a cupboard. Both had a spaniel in the foreground, with the same overweight, middle-aged man slightly out of focus behind them. Judging by the facial resemblance, he had to be Patrick's father.

'I know it's weird to fill your house with photos of dead pets,' Patrick said. 'But those were two of the best dogs anyone could have had. As you can see, I've not always lived with a dachshund.'

'That's you?' Zoe asked, unable to keep the surprise out of her voice.

'I don't just keep those to commemorate Jack and Ziggy. They remind me of what I used to be too.' Not waiting for a response, he touched her elbow to propel her out of the room.

She had expected they would all pile into the Jeep and drive somewhere but this was evidently not what Patrick had in mind. 'You can let Mac out now,' he said. 'Although I recommend keeping him on his lead while we're on the road.'

'Where are we going?'

He pointed towards a clump of trees in the distance. 'Over there. We'll go at a steady pace but promise me you'll say if it starts to get too much.'

'I'll be fine,' Zoe said, opening the car door and releasing Mac from his harness. He ran around the lawn with Peggy then they both submitted to being put on their leads.

'I'm glad his eye's improved,' Patrick said.

They set off down the road, and just when Zoe was beginning to wonder if they would find anything to talk about other than how amusing their dogs were, Patrick began to tell her about the area's history. She was captivated by his description of how the Borders became a frontier land during the struggles between Scotland and England in the sixteenth century, as he pointed out the ruins of a fortified house in the distance which he'd take her to one day. He also drew her attention to wildlife she would probably have missed had she been alone, the most thrilling of which was a buzzard swooping down on its prey, although after the dogs were let off their leads such sightings vanished and she had to make do with an occasional fleeing hare.

'Do you plan to stay in Scotland, Zoe?'

'I can't think of a better place to bring up a child, can you?'

'I was brought here at the age of ten and it feels like home to me.' Patrick pointed at the ground ahead of them. 'Careful.'

Zoe sidestepped the entrance to a burrow, nearly hidden in the parched grass. 'I thought from your accent that you'd been born here.'

'No, I'm a Polish Irishman. Doesn't sound like it but Dunin's a Polish name, dates back to the twelfth century. You try to fit in when you're ten, so I quickly started to sound like my new friends.'

'Did you move here from Ireland or Poland?'

'Ireland. My parents met and married there. I can't remember being told we were coming to Scotland, just getting excited about travelling on a ferry for the first time. But what about you, Zoe? Why did you decide to relocate to the Borders? I think someone said you'd lived in Nottingham before.'

While Zoe had grown tired of this question last year, no one had asked it of her for several months. Despite this, her stock response came out as easily now as it used to. 'I lost my husband and needed a change of scene.'

Although usually enough to move the conversation along, this didn't work with Patrick. 'But why here?'

'Why not here?' Zoe replied, adding, 'Oh dear, I can't see the dogs.'

Stopping in his tracks, Patrick said, 'You really don't like talking about yourself, do you?'

'You're not the first to accuse me of that. Mac, where are you?'

Patrick opened his mouth to speak but Zoe never got to hear what he planned to say. At the first ring of his mobile, he pulled it from his pocket, checked who the caller was and said, 'Sorry, I need to take this.'

He moved a little way off and Zoe concentrated on scanning the terrain ahead, eventually spotting Mac running back in their direction, followed by Peggy. She looked at Patrick. If his face and the gestures he was making with his free hand were anything to go by, he was losing patience with whoever had called him. She caught his eye; he mouthed, 'Sorry,' and turned away.

She crouched down to give the dogs a biscuit each and persuade them to drink from Mac's portable bowl, not realising Patrick had returned until he cast a shadow over the ground in front of her. His expression told her their trip was coming to a premature end.

'I'm sorry, Zoe, I have to go back.'

'Of course. Are you on duty?' She knew he wasn't. That call had been personal.

'A friend needs help.'

'Oh dear.' She waited for him to say more but all he did was whistle for Peggy and put her on the lead. 'If you're in a hurry, why don't I stroll back with the dogs and you can go on ahead at your own speed?'

Patrick chewed his lip, obviously torn between wanting to leave and feeling obliged to stay with her. 'You're sure you'll be okay?'

'It's no further than I would normally walk on my own.'

He nodded and thrust Peggy's lead at her. 'Thanks.'

She watched him break into a slow jog and disappear back the way they'd come.

Patrick had done a good job of selling *I Am Legend* to her, so after lunch Zoe sat down to read it. Instead of boring her as she'd feared, the book had gripped her from the start, transporting her out of her own troubled world into a fictional, post-apocalyptic one. She was so engrossed that even though she knew Patrick would be coming round to collect Peggy, the sound of the doorbell made her jump.

'You don't know me well enough to recognise this as my contrite look,' he said, bowing his head between raised shoulders.

Unable to stop herself from smiling, Zoe stood aside. 'You'd better come in.'

Peggy rushed to greet her owner, followed by the obviously besotted Mac. 'Thanks for hanging on to her,' Patrick said. 'I should have told you where I hide my spare key.'

'She's been no trouble. In fact, having her here has made me seriously think I should get a companion for Mac. They've had a great time.'

'I'm always on the lookout for people wanting to give a dog a home but maybe you'd best wait a few months before making a firm decision.'

'You're probably right. Would you like a drink?'

'Thanks but no. I just came to take Peggy off your hands and apologise again for rushing off like that.'

'Is your friend okay?'

'I hope so. He's having a hard time at the moment.'

'He's lucky he can rely on you.'

A look passed over Patrick's face which Zoe found impossible to interpret. He was right: she didn't know him at all.

'To make up for my lack of gallantry, how about we go out for supper one evening?'

'Well, I . . .'

'Not a date. Please don't think I'm asking you out.' He winced. 'And please say that didn't sound as insulting to you as it did to me.'

She laughed. 'No offence taken. My dating days are over, for a while at least. Okay, you're on. As long as you promise not to run out on me this time.'

'In which case we'd best make it when I'm not on call. Can I check my schedule and get back to you about when exactly?'

After Patrick's departure, dragging the reluctant Peggy behind him, Zoe locked the front door and returned to her book. Any hope she had of staving off anxiety by reading was dashed when the house phone rang, sending her pulse racing. She lifted the handset with foreboding; relief flooded through her as she heard Paul's voice.

'My dear, I'm so sorry to disturb you on a Sunday but I've just heard from Walter and needed to talk to someone.'

'What's happened?'

'He says he's not coming back for another week.'

Biting back what she thought of his partner's disregard for others, Zoe said, 'We can manage without him for a bit longer, can't we? I'm still capable of doing some additional sessions.'

'Thank you, but I fear this is a problem which isn't going to go away.'

116

'What to do you mean?'

'Reading between the lines, I think we need to prepare ourselves for bad news. I suspect Walter's continued absence is because he's planning to return to Wales on a permanent basis.'

'Oh.' Not such bad news after all.

'I hoped bridges had been mended after that fuss last winter, but it would appear he thinks otherwise.'

'Are you sure of this, Paul? Has he actually said anything about leaving?'

'No, but we've worked together for a long time and I don't need to tell you that Walter's not one for hiding what's on his mind. Although I can't do anything at present, we must to be prepared, in order to safeguard the practice and look after our patients' interests.'

'How can I help?'

'I have to rush off to a meeting tomorrow lunchtime, so can we get together on Tuesday morning after surgery for a chat?'

'Of course.'

As she put the phone down, Zoe couldn't help smiling at Paul's parting words, counselling her not to worry about this development. Compared with everything else going on, although it would definitely have an impact on her life, Walter's possible departure posed no threat to her peace of mind. Indeed, it provided something welcome and new to consider: the prospect of becoming a partner in the Westerlea practice. It would mean putting down roots in a place she had friends — and family, now — but where some pretty awful things had happened. Was this what she wanted? And more importantly, did what she wanted actually matter any longer, now she had someone else to consider?

FOURTEEN

As usual, both Paul's and Zoe's Monday morning surgeries were packed out, so the time they spent together amounted only to passing in the corridor outside their consulting rooms and exchanging smiles. Paul had casually mentioned Walter's continued absence to the practice staff and nobody queried his assertion that things would get back to normal the following week, although Margaret's eyebrows had briefly risen at the news, as if she knew exactly what was going on.

Driving out of the health centre car park at lunchtime, Zoe stared off to the right, where she had noticed the blue Fiesta lying in wait for her just a few days ago. The space it had occupied was empty now, and more than a day had gone by since she received a silent call. She went straight home and felt secure enough to sit with her book outside, under the umbrella's shade, although only a few steps away from the French windows. She read and dozed the afternoon away until her mobile buzzed with an incoming text.

Fancy a visitor? Can't be till kids in bed tho. K
Lovely. See you later. Z

Kate arrived at Keeper's Cottage at eight-thirty, handing Zoe a small plastic box as soon as she stepped through the front door. 'Mum's been making tablet and wanted you to have some. She says you need to keep your energy up.'

Zoe grinned. 'I'm still not sure I can justify eating something made entirely from boiled sugar and condensed milk, but thank her for me, won't you?'

'Of course. Though you're forgetting there's butter in it too, which makes it practically a dairy product.'

'Like yoghurt, you mean?'

'Exactly.'

Having had her day's ration of caffeine, Zoe was relieved when her friend said all she wanted to drink was water. They took their glasses outside and sat in the relative cool of the evening. Mac stalked a moth; the cat wandered past on her way out for the night.

'So,' Zoe said. 'What's been happening?'

'Before I start ranting and forget,' Kate said, 'I'm having a birthday lunch at Mum and Dad's on Friday. It was supposed to be a secret but Mhairi blabbed. Please say you'll come.'

'I'd love to. What time do you want me? I could come early and lend a hand.'

'It's unlikely Mum'll let you do anything, but turn up when you like. We'll probably not sit down to eat before two.'

Zoe nodded. 'Alright, I'll look forward to it. Now, rant away.'

'I got to see my solicitor at last,' Kate said. 'And the bad news is although Ken's a good-for-nothing waste of space, unless I can prove him spending time with the children I've brought up single-handed since he buggered off will put them at risk, he has equal rights to me.'

'I feared that might be the case.'

Kate's cheeks reddened. 'How can it be fair?'

'Maybe in the long run it'll be for the best. If they get to know their father now, they won't feel the urge to seek him out in the future. And your children aren't stupid. Ken won't be able to hide his true character from them if they see him regularly.'

'So if your baby's father waltzed back into your life in a few years, you'd be okay with him having unlimited access to a child he's never met?'

'That's a low blow. Our situations are completely different.'

Kate slumped back in her chair. 'My solicitor suggested we use a family mediation service but I'm not sure I want strangers involved.'

'Ken might listen to someone he doesn't know.' And so might you.

Zoe worried for a moment she'd actually said this last thought out loud, because Kate stared at her, unblinking. Eventually, she asked, 'Are you alright?'

'I can't believe what I just said to you,' Kate said. 'I'm so caught up in my own little world that I forget other people have far more serious situations to deal with. Forgive me?'

'There's nothing to forgive. You're just upset.'

'When I got my first job I shared a flat with a friend called Tina. We'd get together every evening over a bottle of wine and compare notes about work and boyfriends. If things had gone badly, we'd console each other by chanting "But at least no one died".' Kate shook her head. 'When I think what happened to you, I realise how lucky I am, how little I have to complain about.'

'Things haven't exactly turned out as I planned, but I'm very happy now, honestly. And the support I get from you and your family has helped me reach that state.'

'Really?'

'Cross my heart.'

'What a lovely thing to say. Mum's so fond of you, I'm almost jealous.'

'You have no reason to be.'

'Just kidding. Although I do envy you one thing.'

'What?'

Kate looked wistful. 'I'd love to have another baby. Before it's too late.'

'I had no idea you felt like that. But you've got years left. You're younger than me.'

'Things are so up in the air with Erskine, I can't see even being able to try for one for a long time. Anyway, let's not go there. I've remembered something I wanted to ask you.'

'Ask away.' Zoe drank the last of her water.

'Would you like me to be your birthing partner? I've got practical experience and I'm not at all squeamish. Trust me, you don't want to go through it without someone there you can safely swear at.'

'I haven't given it much thought, to be honest.'

'You've not written a birth plan?'

'No.'

'Is that because you don't think you need one?'

'I've got a form somewhere to fill in. I just haven't found the time.'

'They do say doctors make the worst patients.' Kate got up from her seat. 'The offer's there, so think about it and let me know. In the meantime, see you on Friday.'

'Thank you. It's a kind offer and I'll probably take you up on it. Put my due date on your calendar. August—'

'—the eighteenth. I know.' Kate leaned over and hugged Zoe. 'Don't get up.'

Once alone, Zoe reflected on the arguments going on in her head both for and against becoming a practice partner. She had toyed with the idea of discussing it with Kate but at the last minute decided not to because Paul might be wrong about Walter planning to resign. Her uneasy truce with him would be well and truly broken if he thought she was hoping to replace him before he'd even chosen to leave.

The house phone started to ring, but by the time she reached it, the caller had rung off. She dialled 1471: number withheld. Which meant nothing. It could, after all, have simply been one of those annoying companies trying to sell her something she neither needed nor wanted.

121

FIFTEEN

Zoe sat down opposite Paul on Tuesday morning after surgery, noticing that his face remained hairless but the nick on his cheek suggested he'd not yet become used to the daily ritual of shaving. And there was something else different about him today. For the first time in the year she'd known him, the tie he wore wasn't tartan but floral. Although not the height of fashion, it was elegant, in subtle shades of green and coral silk. More like the kind of tie Erskine Mather wore.

There could be only one explanation for these recent changes in Paul's personal style: someone else had initiated them.

She smiled involuntarily. Following her eyes, Paul self-consciously touched the tie. 'Doesn't suit me, does it?'

'It's different to what you usually wear, but it's gorgeous, really.'

'I'd hate to think I was making a fool of myself.'

Aware he may not only be referring to the tie, Zoe said, 'If it feels right, trust your instincts.'

He picked up some pieces of paper, tapped them vertically against his desk to make a neat pile, then set them aside. 'If Walter does decide to leave,' he said, 'I'm not sure I want to carry on alone. Given my age.'

Zoe shrank back into her chair. How had she managed to misread the situation so badly? He's not looking for a new partner. He wants to retire. 'Oh.'

'It pains me to say this, but I'm not sure what else to do. Given your change in circumstances.'

'What do you mean?'

'I knew Walter was getting restless and would sooner or later want to quit our partnership. I'd hoped by then you would feel sufficiently settled to join me in his place, but now . . . '

When he failed to finish his sentence, Zoe asked, 'Do you mean now I'm pregnant?'

'Yes, dear. The timing's all wrong.'

If she'd been having this conversation with anyone else, Zoe would have accused them of sex discrimination, of making excuses for denying her a great career opportunity. However, she knew Paul better than that. He genuinely believed she couldn't make the huge commitment—which would be monetary as well as professional—to become his partner because she was expecting a baby. Instead of anger, she felt relief.

'It's only wrong if you think having a baby means I wouldn't make a good partner.'

'Of course I don't.'

Zoe reached across the desk and laid her hand gently on Paul's. 'In which case, if Walter takes off and you want me to replace him, I'm in.'

The next couple of days passed more quickly than Zoe expected, given her impatience for Walter to return from Wales and confirm or refute Paul's speculation that he planned to resign from the practice. However, the absence of any further silent calls or sightings of the blue Fiesta meant she could relax a little and busy herself preparing for the baby's arrival.

A distinctive green and white John Lewis van delivered the items she had ordered while up in Edinburgh with Kate. The unembellished wood furniture resembled adult-sized pieces in all but their scale and required no assembly. After the delivery men had left she unpacked everything and pushed it around on the laminate floor, then hung the curtains in different shades of coral which Kate had tried hard to dissuade her from buying and defiantly placed a matching cushion on the rocking chair.

She went into work on Thursday expecting to see John Wilkie. It was a week since he'd come in for help with his sore back, so the painkillers she'd prescribed would have run out by now. Despite trying to set aside her suspicion that he was the poacher who'd pulled the dead boy out of the Tweed, the more she thought about it, the more convinced she became. He must have taken to catching and selling fish as a way of making ends meet while out of work, and would do it rarely now he had a new job. Others might have turned a blind eye to a person in the river, but John's innate decency had compelled him to jump in and try to save the boy's life. Moreover, on finding he couldn't, he did the next best thing and immediately reported the body, enabling the police to launch their enquiry far sooner than if he'd told no one.

Who did she think she was kidding? Her patient had been committing a crime when he did what any right-minded person would have done and pulled the boy out of the river. And then, instead of sticking around to help the police by telling them what he'd seen, he ran away to save his own skin, stopping only to make an anonymous telephone call. A bad back was the least he deserved.

Recognising the truth probably lay between these two points of view did nothing to help Zoe decide on a course of action for when he eventually turned up at the health centre. His absence from Thursday's patient list brought a degree of relief, but on Friday morning she read his name and still had no idea what she was going to say as she led him into her consulting room. Apart from the obvious.

'How's your back, John? You appear to be walking more easily.'

'It's much improved, thanks, Doctor, though I haven't gone back to work yet. Any chance I could get more of those tablets?'

Zoe nodded and turned to her computer to print off a prescription. As she typed, she said casually, 'You'll soon be able to take up your hobbies again. You fish, don't you?'

'Not as often as I'd like. But how do you know that?' John took off his glasses and started to rub them with the bottom of his tee-shirt.

'I guessed.' She took a deep breath. 'Like I'm guessing you didn't hurt your back decorating but when you pulled that boy's body out of the river at Paxton.'

The silence between them lasted too long for his eventual response to be convincing. 'You're mistaken.'

'Am I?' Zoe held his gaze until he looked away.

'How did you work it out?' he mumbled.

By losing an earring under my bed. 'I put two and two together. Your bad back, your evasiveness when I asked how you'd done it, and the fact you knew the boy had been beaten up before he died. The police didn't release that information.'

John's face had gone bright red. 'I told the truth about doing up our daughter's bedroom,' he said. 'Trouble was, we didn't have enough money for what she wanted, so I thought, what's the harm in taking a couple of fish to sell? They'd not be missed.'

'The poaching's not important,' Zoe said. 'The police are only going to be interested in what you saw and heard, not why you were there.'

'The police? I can't go to the police.'

'John, you must. Don't you realise you may be able to help them catch whoever killed that poor boy?'

'I don't know who they were.'

'You said "they", so it wasn't just one person. You already know more than the police do.'

'I hid in the bushes when they drove onto the

bridge, so I didn't see them, just heard them talking in some foreign language. I thought they'd stopped for a smoke or to admire the view. It was a full moon.'

'How many of them were there?'

'Two, I think. They sounded like they were arguing about something, then it went quiet for a bit, and then I heard a loud splash.'

'Didn't that make you look out?'

'Not till I heard their vehicle start up.'

'So you saw them drive off?'

'And come back again.'

'They came back?'

'They'd come from the Scottish side and only crossed to the English side to turn round.'

'You have to tell the police.'

'I can't.'

'It doesn't matter what you were doing when you witnessed all this.'

'I don't care about being done for the poaching. Don't you understand? I waited till I was sure they'd gone for good before going to see what made the splash. If I'd done something straightaway, I might have saved him.' He put his head in his hands.

'The boy was already dead when they dropped him into the water,' Zoe said. 'There was nothing you could do.'

He wasn't listening to her. 'I never learned how to do mouth-to-mouth, so I put him on his side, thinking the water might run out of him, but it was too late.'

'John, they'd already killed him.'

He slowly lowered his hands. 'You mean it wasn't my fault he died?'

'It wasn't your fault he died.'

'Thank God.' He let out a long breath. 'I've felt so guilty.'

'Now will you go to the police? You may be able to help bring his killers to justice.'

'If I don't, will you tell them anyway?'

'No, I'm not allowed to do that because of patient confidentiality. What you say in here can go no further unless you say so.'

'I don't want them coming to my house.'

'I expect they'll agree to meet wherever you want.'

'Someone might see me going into a police station.'

'What about here?'

John considered this, then nodded. 'Later today, if possible. Let's get it over with.' He gave Zoe his mobile number and she promised to contact Sergeant Trent as soon as she finished taking surgery.

Half an hour later, a familiar voice answered Trent's phone. Not the man himself but his boss.

'Hello, Zoe. Dave's not working this morning because his wife has been taken to hospital. Can I help?'

'Oh no. Is she okay?'

'I'm afraid there's no news yet.' Mather said again, 'Can I help?'

Inexplicably tongue-tied, Zoe stumbled over words she'd practiced saying. 'I er, I have some information. About the dead boy in the river. Or rather, a patient of mine has.'

She imagined Mather sitting up in his chair as he replied, 'That's interesting. What has he or she told you?'

'He's agreed to tell you himself, although he took a bit of persuading.'

'In which case, thank you. How do I get in touch with him?'

'Because he's so wary of the police, I had to suggest you meet him here at the health centre. Would you be prepared to do that?'

'Is he wary because he's a poacher?'

'You know I can't tell you anything myself.'

'Alright. If he saw something to move this case along, I'll go wherever he asks.'

'I promise you, he has valuable information.'

'Did you agree when?'

'Five o'clock this afternoon, if you can make that.'

'I'll see you then. And thanks.'

'Won't you be at Kate's birthday lunch?' After picking her words so carefully to avoid revealing John Wilkie's identity by mistake, Zoe realised she'd put her foot in it as soon as she asked the question.

'No.' She could tell from his voice that Mather had no idea what she was talking about.

'Oh well, it must be just a family thing. I'll see you at five.'

SIXTEEN

After texting John with a carefully-worded message telling him to come to the health centre at five o'clock, Zoe went home for a change of clothes and to pick up Mac. The book about gravestones had arrived in the nick of time. Having forgotten to buy gift-wrap, she loosely wrapped it inside a vintage silk scarf she'd been saving to give Kate for Christmas and set off with Mac next to her on the passenger seat. When she arrived at Tolbyres Farm, she was glad to see just a handful of cars. Kate hadn't understated the size of the guest list this time.

The news she'd listened to on the way over had been full of a rumoured plan by the government to introduce a hosepipe ban across the UK if the weather didn't break soon, but Kate's parents were unlikely to allow the small matter of legislation to put their garden at risk if this happened. Even more flowers jostled for space in the herbaceous borders, the lawn was a darker, richer green than on Zoe's last visit, and the fragrance of lavender had been joined by that of roses.

She rounded the front corner of the house. A man's voice called out her name and she saw Douglas, Kate's brother, waving to her from the sitooterie. Zoe waved back and walked over to where the guests milled around a long table set for about twenty-five people. It was a family affair but she knew nearly everyone: Kate's aunts and uncles, cousins, nieces and nephews, and Kate's own children. Etta and Ranald Mackenzie were probably still in the kitchen with the birthday girl, putting finishing touches to what would undoubtedly be a huge and delicious spread of food.

Douglas hadn't attended his parents' recent barbecue owing to his wife having only recently given birth to their second son. In Kate's words, Hazel 'had a rough time of it', although she hadn't gone into details. Here now, Hazel sat apart from the crowd with her baby whose name Zoe had forgotten. Since her pregnancy started to show, she'd become resigned to people thrusting babies at her to admire or hold, so it was a relief when Hazel did no such thing. Indeed, she seemed to hug the baby closer to her breast as Zoe approached them.

'This is Hugo,' Douglas said proudly. 'He weighed in at over ten pounds when he was born.'

Unsure how best to respond to this, Zoe smiled and said, 'Gosh.'

The dress Hazel wore was creased and dowdy, in contrast to her son's smart if somewhat old-fashioned sailor suit with smocking across the chest. She avoided Zoe's gaze and said nothing. As if compensating for his wife's aloofness, Douglas started to relate exactly what had taken place during her long labour. To Zoe's relief, Kate appeared just as her brother had moved on to the birth itself and instructed everyone to take their seats, beckoning Zoe over to the chair beside her. Shortly afterwards, Etta and her younger sister who was known by everyone as Auntie Joan, appeared bearing trays of chicken drumsticks, slices of cold pork and rare beef and an enormous side of cooked salmon to join the bowls of rice, pasta, salad and potatoes already on the table.

The clamour accompanying their meal suggested more talking than eating was going on, yet after an hour, very little food remained. Mac sat for the entire meal at the children's end of the table, gulping down every scrap thrown to him. Zoe had consumed scarcely anything herself, which didn't escape Kate's attention.

'You don't eat enough for one, let alone two.'

'I had some salmon and salad. I'm saving myself for pudding.'

'You'd better eat lots of it. I'll be watching.'

Kate tried to get up and help her mother but was persuaded to sit down again as several volunteers made light work of clearing the table. They reappeared soon afterwards with trifle, bowls of strawberries and jugs of cream, followed by Etta's entrance bearing the cake. She placed it in front of Kate, whose face showed both delight and surprise at the three layers iced in different shades of pink and decorated with fondant flowers.

Generous slices of cake were being passed round the table when Zoe heard a mobile ring and saw Etta frown at Douglas as he reached into his breast pocket. As he blocked out the noise around him with one hand and holding the phone to his ear with the other, his expression became grim. He ended the call, went round to the other side of the table, and spoke into his father's ear. Ranald, who had been laughing at Mhairi's impatience for her portion of cake, got up. Etta followed her husband and son into the house.

A few minutes later, realising she needed the bathroom, Zoe went inside too. As she passed a window in the hall, she saw Ranald and Douglas drive off in the battered white pick-up which Kate had used to deliver logs to Keeper's Cottage during the winter. She went into the downstairs cloakroom and was surprised to see the door to the tall, slim cupboard she assumed held loo rolls and spare towels hanging open. It was empty.

Afterwards, she went to the kitchen in search of Etta, finding her there with Auntie Joan. They were making pots of tea and coffee and piling squares of tablet onto glass plates.

'Is everything alright?' Zoe asked.

'Douglas has just had a call to say a dog's been spotted worrying our sheep again,' Etta said. 'He's gone to see if they can deal with it once and for all.'

'If it's the one that chased Mac, they'll have to be careful if they try to catch it. It's huge and seemed completely out of control.'

'They'll not be trying to catch it,' Auntie Joan said. 'They've taken the shotgun.'

So that's what had been stored in the cupboard. 'Are they allowed to kill it? I'm not saying they shouldn't, of course.'

Etta took a jug of milk out of the fridge. 'As long as you can prove what it was doing and the police are notified straightaway.

'It's happened to us too,' Auntie Joan said. 'The dogs didn't actually kill any sheep but they caused several of our ewes to miscarry.'

'Here, Zoe, you can take this,' Etta said, glaring at her sister and thrusting the jug towards Zoe, who suspected the reference to miscarriage in front of a pregnant woman had caused her annoyance. She obediently carried the milk outside and sat down again.

'You haven't had any cake yet,' Kate said, reaching over to cut a piece big enough to last Zoe a week.

Most of the guests had left or were preparing to leave by four o'clock, several citing dogs to be walked or cows to be milked. Mac had joined Zoe where she sat answering Auntie Joan's questions about her preparations for the baby's arrival, until she spotted a familiar figure walking across the grass towards them: Patrick. His expression was grave.

'Would you mind if I borrowed Zoe for a few minutes?' He spoke very quietly, as if worried about being overheard.

'She's all yours,' Auntie Joan said, getting up. 'I should be in the kitchen helping Etta.'

'I've come to ask you to do something that's not very pleasant,' Patrick said.

'What?'

'Look at a dead dog. We need to know if it's the one you saw chasing Mac.'

'Sure,' Zoe said, sounding more poised than she felt. 'I don't want Mac coming with me, though, so let me leave him with someone.'

'You won't be long. It's just in the barn behind the house. But the children mustn't know.'

'I understand.'

A few minutes later, with Mac left in Etta's kitchen, Patrick led Zoe past her car and down a track to a large, green metal shed where several men were gathered around the Mackenzies' pick-up. As Zoe approached, they moved aside to reveal something lying in the back of the vehicle, covered by a tarpaulin.

Douglas stepped forward. 'Are you alright about doing this, Zoe?'

'Of course, if it helps.'

He pulled back the tarpaulin, though only far enough to show her the animal's head, neck and front legs, all of which were flecked with blood. Its teeth were bared, vicious yellow spikes which would have made short work of Mac if they'd got hold of him. And if this had been the dog that had chased him.

'This isn't the dog I saw.'

She heard murmurs of disappointment behind her.

'You're sure?' Douglas asked.

'Positive. It had a brown coat. This one's grey and it's much smaller.'

'Animals look different when they're dead,' Patrick said. 'I've known people not recognise their own pets.'

'While I'm not familiar with lots of different breeds, I know this one definitely isn't the same. As well as

133

the difference in overall size, its head is longer and thinner.'

When no one else tried to argue with her, she added, 'And it's wearing a collar. The other one didn't.'

'Pity it hasn't got a name-tag,' Douglas said. 'Then we could've involved the police, got them to pay an official visit to the owners.'

'What will happen to the body?' Zoe asked.

'I'll drive it back to the practice and check to see if it's been microchipped,' Patrick said. 'Though that seems unlikely. Then I'll record a few details in case its owners are traced, and have it disposed of.'

'And I'll call the knackerman.' With a grim expression, Kate's father came from behind Douglas and pulled the tarpaulin back over the dog.

'How many sheep did you lose?' Zoe asked.

'Three this time,' Ranald said. 'Vet's patched up a couple that weren't seriously hurt, though only time will tell if they'll survive the shock.'

Patrick took Zoe's arm. 'Let's go back to the house, shall we? Mrs Mackenzie offered me a cup of tea earlier and I think I'll take her up on the offer now.'

As they went into the hall, Zoe glanced at the grandfather clock Kate said her father wound up every Sunday evening without fail. The time was four forty-five.

She had arranged to meet Mather and John Wilkie at five.

SEVENTEEN

Zoe raced into the health centre car park just after five, having left Mac in Etta's care after promising Kate she would call round to Tolbyres Cottage later when she collected him. She saw only Paul's car and one other. Either Mather or John Wilkie was late.

She realised when she entered the building that neither of the men she had arranged to meet was there; the second car must belong to the cleaner, who was about to start hoovering the waiting room floor. Paul looked up from his desk when she put her head round his consulting room door, so she explained why she was there, suddenly concerned her arrangement should have been okayed with him first.

'If Walter were here, I suspect he would have had something to say about this,' Paul said. 'But it sounds to me like you've handled a tricky situation very well.'

'I couldn't think what else to do,' Zoe said. 'We can't force patients to do the right thing, can we?'

'How much easier our lives would be if we could, my dear. Let me know how it all turns out, won't you? And now, I think I hear one of your visitors at the front door.'

DCI Mather stood peering in through the glass. Even at the end of a hot day his ecru linen suit looked freshly pressed. How did he manage that?

'Sorry I'm late, Zoe. I've been talking to Dave Trent.'

'How's his wife?'

'She had to have an emergency caesarean.'

'Are they both alright?'

'Annie's doing fine now, but the baby's in an incubator.'

'Oh dear. Is he very tiny?'

'That's all I know at the moment.' Mather adjusted his already straight tie. 'I'll tell Dave you were asking. Now, where's this patient of yours?'

'He's not here yet.'

They both looked at the clock on the wall.

Twenty minutes of stilted conversation later, Zoe left Mather in her consulting room and went to the reception desk to call John Wilkie on his mobile and then his landline. No answer either time. She returned to the policeman to admit defeat.

'Can't say I'm surprised.'

'Well I am. He seemed to genuinely want to help.'

'Hardly anyone wants to help the police. We're used to it. Now will you tell me who he is so I can do it my way?'

Shaking her head, Zoe said, 'I wish I could, but . . .
'

'Patient confidentiality. I know.' Mather pulled a business card from his breast pocket. 'Thanks for trying. If you see him again, give him this, will you? And you can pass on my assurance that whatever he tells us, we won't prosecute him for poaching.'

'I'm not sure that's what he's worried about.'

Zoe let Mather out of the front door and relocked it. She checked Paul's office but only the cleaner was there, dusting the few empty surfaces he could find. Returning to the reception desk, she made a note of John Wilkie's address on a scrap of paper then closed the computer down.

The Wilkies' semi-detached home sat back from a stretch of road Zoe had travelled along many times on her way to Kelso. She pulled into the parking area on the opposite side of the road and crossed to a green front door beside which hung a basket of trailing ivy and geraniums. It opened before she had a chance to knock.

'I knew you wouldn't leave him be.' The woman stood guard over the entrance, her arms crossed, a hard expression on an otherwise attractive face. 'Whatever you say, he's not going to the police.'

'Please let me speak to John, Mrs Wilkie. I won't try to make him do anything he's not comfortable with.'

A voice came from inside the house. 'Let her in, Heather.'

Heather spun round and marched back along the hall. 'He's in there,' she said, pointing to her left but continuing deeper into the house. Zoe found John in the family's sitting room, sharing his black leather armchair with a tortoiseshell cat. When he made to lift the cat from his lap, she said, 'Please don't disturb her on my account.'

John invited her to sit down, then they both started to speak at once.

'Doctor, I —'

'John, you —'

He smiled apologetically; Zoe gestured at him to carry on.

'Doctor, I'm sorry I didn't turn up, but I have to consider my wife and child. Heather's very worried about what'll happen if I get involved.'

'I understand your reasoning, but that young lad was someone's child as well. Don't you think we should all do what we can to help catch the men who killed him?'

'I can't believe you're telling us we should help the police.' Zoe jumped at Heather's voice. She had silently entered the room and now stood with her back to a collection of framed photographs of wild birds. 'It didn't exactly turn out well for you last year.'

'This is nothing like what happened to me.'

'Oh no? Murderers are wicked people who'll stop at nothing to get away with their crimes. Can the police guarantee John would be safe if he came forward as a witness?'

'I can't speak for the police.'

'And yet you're here on their behalf.'

The ensuing silence was broken by a little girl bursting into the room. Aged about seven, she wore an orange summer dress and matching flip-flops.

'Daddy, you were s'posed to be having tea with me.'

'Sorry, sweetheart. I'll be there in a minute.'

The girl looked at Zoe. 'Who are you?'

'That's not very polite,' her father said. 'Come and say hello properly to Doctor Moreland.'

'Hello. You're having a baby.'

Zoe shot a smile at John to show she wasn't upset by his daughter's directness. 'You're right, I am. What's your name?'

'Ailsa Jane Wilkie.'

'Hello, Ailsa. I'm Zoe.'

'Daddy said you're a doctor. I've got a book about doctors.' Ailsa went over to a shelf, brought back a book with a picture of a mouse wearing a stethoscope on the cover and laid it on Zoe's lap.

'Doctor Moreland's got to go now,' Heather said.

Conditioned by being an only child to doing what grown-ups told her, Ailsa looked disappointed but returned the book to its shelf. Zoe got up and John rose too, put the cat on his chair, and escorted her to the front door.

'You probably think me an awful coward,' he said.

Zoe replied in what she hoped was a noncommittal tone. 'You must do what you think is for the best.'

She passed him Mather's card, and left.

EIGHTEEN

After apologising to Etta for being away so long and thanking her for looking after Mac, Zoe bundled the dog into her Jeep without bothering to strap him in and drove the short distance to Kate's house. Although called Tolbyres Cottage, it was on a much larger scale than her own home, having been created from a pair of semis originally built for farm workers. The conversion had never been finished, but she hardly noticed the two front doors, two staircases and wall jutting halfway across the sitting room any more.

As soon as she opened the Jeep's passenger door, Mac jumped down and rushed away, coming to an abrupt halt as he encountered the only enemy he'd made in his short life: a bantam cockerel named Clyde. Requiring no physical contact to assert his authority, the tiny chicken puffed out his chest and flapped his wings, which was enough to send Mac scurrying back to Zoe.

'Shoo, Clyde!' She waved her arms and Clyde retreated to the base of the pear tree where a brown hen nearly twice his size was enjoying the early evening sun. Never one to pass up an opportunity, he jumped on top of her, bounced up and down for a few seconds and jumped off again. The hen shook herself and resumed pecking at the ground.

Kate appeared on her doorstep in time to observe the cockerel's antics. 'That's what you could do with part of your field. Keep poultry. As you've seen, they're very entertaining.'

On the point of rejecting this idea, Zoe realised it might be worth considering. What was the point of bringing up a child in the country if you don't let them have a pet or two? 'Maybe. You'll have to tell me more about what it involves.'

'Frankie's the livestock expert these days. He'll show you.'

'He told me at your party that he's planning on keeping goats next.'

'He saw them at last year's Kelso Show. I hoped he would have forgotten about them by now.' Kate leaned back against the door to open it. 'Come away in. Do you want some more cake? You didn't finish the piece I gave you earlier.'

'Only if I get to say how big it is.'

During the winter, Zoe's favourite position in Kate's kitchen was leaning against the Aga, but it had been too hot to do that for quite some time. Even Bluto, the family's ginger cat, had been forced to abandon his preferred spot on the plate rack above the stove and now spent most of his time under the hedge surrounding Kate's back garden. The temperature was, if anything, higher than it had been at lunchtime. They walked through the house and out the back door.

'Have a seat,' Kate said. 'I'll bring you a glass of Mum's lemonade and a wee wedge of cake.'

'Thanks. It's very quiet—where is everybody?'

'They're staying at Richard's tonight. Because his children are being educated in a posh private school over the Border, they haven't broken up yet and couldn't come to my party. He and Charlotte are giving them their own do this evening.'

'Does that mean you'll have company later?'

Kate screwed up her face. 'I'm not sure if Erskine'll turn up. We had a bit of a tiff last time I saw him.'

141

'But it's your birthday.'

'He won't even remember.'

'Are things really so bad between you?'

'If I get started talking about it I might not be able to stop.'

'In which case, you'd better get our drinks first.'

Zoe leaned back on the seat and rubbed her side. As usual at this time of evening, the baby was working on his kick-boxing skills, but today she gained no pleasure from picturing those little arms and legs waving around inside her. Having well and truly messed up with John Wilkie, she now felt guilty at her relief that Mather was unlikely to show up at Kate's home.

Kate reappeared carrying a tray and wearing the pink scarf Zoe had given her as a birthday gift. 'Thank you so much for this. It's just my colour.'

'I hoped it would be.'

'And the book about gravestones looks fascinating.'

'You're the only person I know who'd appreciate it.'

'We've both been so busy, I haven't had a chance to tell you how useful our trip to the Allankirk graveyard was.'

'Have you solved the mystery?'

'As best as anyone could, given so many missing records. I'm pretty certain now that Adam was actually Grace and Archibald's nephew. He'd been born to Lily and I've managed to identify his real father and go back a generation. He came from a family of Northumberland farmers.'

'That's brilliant. Is your client pleased?'

'He doesn't know yet. I'm meeting him on Monday to get his agreement before going any further back.' As Zoe's mouth was full of birthday cake, Kate continued, 'Douglas told me the dog they shot wasn't the one you saw chasing Mac. Horrible to think there could be a whole pack of vicious dogs out there.'

'I'm glad he believed me. Some of the other men looked as though they didn't. But the dead dog was completely different to the one I saw.'

'Take no notice of them. You're a woman, and pregnant to boot. Secretly, they're a bit scared of you. Except for your friend the vet, of course.'

Zoe arched her eyebrows at this, unable to protest due to having taken another mouthful of cake.

'The more I see Patrick, the more I like him,' Kate said. 'Mum hasn't found out much about him before he came here, which is unusual, but she likes him too and her instincts are pretty sound. I just wish I'd listened to her about Ken.'

'She approves of your friend the policeman.'

'Whereas Dad can't see beyond the fact Erskine's been married.'

'Isn't the problem that he still is married?'

'Yes.' Kate ran her hands through her hair, making it stand on end more than ever. 'That's sort of what we argued about last weekend.'

'Calling time on a marriage is hard to do, though I don't need to tell you that.'

'They don't have children to consider. And now he thinks Laura's started seeing someone.'

'He can hardly blame her for that. You're back in his life, after all.'

'So why is she trying to hold on to him?'

'Is she?' Zoe asked. 'Are you sure it's not him dragging his heels?'

'You don't know what he's really like. No one does. Erskine likes to appear unemotional and totally in control, but it's just an act. The situation's causing him grief too.'

'Maybe so, but unlike you he has the power to do something about it.'

'You always see things in black and white, don't you?' Kate's voice remained calm but Zoe could tell she was getting defensive.

'I just don't want to see you get hurt. What exactly did you two argue about?'

'Remember I told you we were planning to go to Crieff Hydro next half-term? I wanted to make our reservation this week, although it's ages away yet, because they get very booked up. But even though he was the one who suggested it, Erskine simply won't commit to it now.'

'His job's probably to blame.'

'No, it's because his in-laws will be celebrating some major anniversary and Laura may want him to be there and pretend everything's hunky-dory for the rest of the family.'

Zoe reached for her glass of lemonade, playing for time. Her automatic response was to condemn Mather, who obviously had no intention of disentangling himself from his wife in the near future, but she didn't think Kate would react well to that. 'At least he's being honest with you,' she said eventually.

Kate nodded. 'He always has.'

She looked so downcast, so unlike her usual self, that had they been standing, Zoe would have given her a big hug. Instead, she reached over to her friend and laid a hand on her shoulder. 'Your mum taught me a great saying last winter. "If it's for you it won't go past you". Things probably seem overwhelming at the moment, but the situation will resolve itself.'

'I know. Don't waste any pity on me. I don't deserve it.'

'Let's change the subject, shall we?' Zoe searched for something to cheer Kate up. 'I've been thinking about your offer to be my birthing partner. If you're serious, will you come to an antenatal class with me?'

'Of course. I was going to suggest that myself. And then we can work on your birth plan.'

The ensuing conversation about babies and giving birth was a high price to pay, but at least Kate brightened up. And Zoe managed not to mention seeing Mather earlier in the day.

By nine o'clock, Mather had neither texted Kate nor turned up. Putting a brave face on what must be a hurtful situation, she insisted she was looking forward to an early night after a busy day, so Zoe took Mac home and they sat together for a while in their own back garden until being driven indoors by relentless mosquitoes.

She fetched her mobile and stared down at it. A week had passed since she last heard from Andrew. Did this mean his wife had died? It felt awful, not knowing. If Helen was gone, he would have too much to do, what with making funeral arrangements and holding his proper family together, to be able to call someone he'd only met six months earlier. Her finger hovered over his entry in her contacts list. Surely a brief, sympathetic text could do no harm?

Answering her own question, she sighed, tossed the phone to the other end of the sofa and went across to the bookcase to choose her next read. Its shelves looked dusty, and they felt gritty when she ran a hand along them. Her plans for a relaxing weekend evaporated as she walked around the cottage finding grime everywhere. Although the builders had done their best to minimise the mess they created, every room needed to be blitzed, and because the cupboard under the sink was shamefully bare of cleaning materials, she'd have to pay a visit to the shop in the morning.

Despite her worries about Kate and Mather, John Wilkie and the dead boy, her father and his wife, and her stalker, Zoe got the best night's sleep she'd had in a long time. She was sitting up in bed drinking a mug of tea and considering the soporific qualities of chocolate cake when Mac barked and rushed to the front door.

The perfectly-pressed jeans and short-sleeved shirt visible through the spy-hole gave away her unexpected visitor's identity. She unlocked the door and slid back the security chain to let Mather in, remembering the first time he'd turned up to see her, Sergeant Trent in tow.

'Do you have any news about the Trents' baby?' Zoe asked as he stepped over the threshold and bent down to pat Mac in that awkward manner shared by people who always want to wash their hands immediately after touching an animal.

'No change.'

'What can I do for you?'

'I'm on my way to Kate's and wanted to swing round to thank you.'

'Whatever for?'

'John Wilkie rang me last night. Couldn't have been long after you'd seen him.'

'That's a surprise. When I left him he was still adamant he wasn't going to talk to you. I wonder what changed his mind.'

'I have no idea.'

'Will what he saw help you?'

'I'll find out when I see him at eleven. That's why I'm about so early and why I must get round to Tolbyres as soon as possible.'

'Kate'll be pleased to see you, although she wasn't . . .' Zoe paused. Had Kate been involved with anyone else, she would have told him to stop messing around with her friend's affections. But she felt inhibited by the dealings she'd had with Mather in his professional capacity and the stern exterior she rarely saw behind, even on social occasions.

He finished her sentence for her. 'She wasn't very happy last night? No I don't suppose she would be.'

'Actually I was going to say she wasn't alone, because I spent most of the evening with her. It being her birthday.'

Mather flinched as if she'd slapped him. 'Point taken. I'll be on my way. I just wanted to say thanks.'

Zoe inclined her head. 'You're welcome.'

Apart from her trip to Westerlea's shop, from where she returned laden with a different cleaner for every type of surface, Zoe stayed at home over the weekend, only venturing out to walk Mac. As well as polishing, bleaching and scrubbing, she sorted cupboards, filled several boxes with unwanted books, DVDs and music CDs, and separated out clothes she would never wear again, even if she did get her figure back. When she first came to the Borders, Keeper's Cottage had been intended as a stopgap until she moved somewhere bigger. She still had packing cases in the garage full of things she'd lived a year without needing and decided this was as good a time as any to make a start on going through them. However, the first one she opened contained so many reminders of Russell and their marriage that she firmly closed it again. This was a task for another day.

Patrick rang on Saturday afternoon. He had checked his work schedule and wouldn't be responsible for taking out-of-hours calls from anxious pet owners the following Friday evening. They agreed Zoe would pick him up at seven.

'Bring Mac over if you like. He and Peggy can keep each other company while we're out.'

'He'll love that. Where are you planning to eat?'

'I haven't decided yet. Do you have any strong culinary dislikes?'

'Curries don't agree with me at present.'

'No danger of me taking you for one of those. I've not found anywhere down here that does a decent curry.'

NINETEEN

The smell of lemon polish and bleach still lingered in Keeper's Cottage when Zoe left for work on Monday morning, picking her way through the bags of belongings which littered the hall, waiting to be taken to the charity shop in Duns. The one chore she'd been unable to carry out was removing the thunder-bugs from inside several pictures hanging on her walls. She would wait until the summer was over to get those fixed professionally. Again the weather had turned muggy, yet the rain being welcomed in the west of the country was predicted to peter out before it reached the Borders. A hosepipe ban became more likely every day.

Margaret looked up as Zoe entered the reception area. After her usual cheery greeting, she said, 'Walter's back,' and indicated, with an uncharacteristic frown, the space on the desk next to her.

'I've got a big electric fan at home,' Zoe said. 'I can bring it in tomorrow, if you can wait.'

'That won't be necessary, thank you. My Hector's dropping one off from home any time now. It'll do until the situation's sorted out when Doctor Paul comes in this afternoon.'

Walter didn't stand a chance.

Feeling obliged to acknowledge her colleague's return after several weeks' absence, Zoe made her way to his consulting room and knocked gently on the door he kept shut at all times.

'Come!'

Walter continued to write as Zoe entered the room, giving her the opportunity to study his dark, wavy hair. Definitely dyed. Eventually, he looked up and acknowledged her presence with a nod.

Accustomed now to his scant regard for social niceties, she said, 'Welcome back. How was Wales?'

'I wasn't on holiday. There's a lot to do when someone dies.'

'Yes. I know.'

Anyone else who had taken on a newly-widowed employee a year ago would have been struck with embarrassment, apologised profusely for being untactful. Not Walter.

'How long until you go on maternity leave?'

'I could have gone at the beginning of June, but as long as I feel fit enough to work, I'll do so.' Zoe could almost see the struggle going on in his head. He wanted to be rid of her as soon as possible, yet at the same time he would resent the idea of her being paid to stay at home while the practice had to foot the bill for a locum. In the end, he nodded again and went back to his work. Zoe retreated to her own room.

The list of patients attending that morning's surgery was on her desk. She recognised many of the names, and one stood out. She'd not expected to see John Wilkie again so soon.

Anxious to hear what John had to say, she expected the first part of her surgery to feel like it would never end but she was pleased to find that wasn't the case. The day turned into one which reminded her why she'd made the move from working in a hospital to becoming a family doctor. Her patients this morning were courteous and friendly, their ailments varied. John's appointment came upon her before she realised it.

He walked with ease and met her gaze from the start. As he sat down, he pulled a box of tablets from his trouser pocket and placed them on Zoe's desk.

'I won't be needing these now, Doctor, thanks to you.'

'I'm glad to hear you're feeling so much better, but we always recommend taking the full course, to be sure the problem's completely resolved.'

He shook his head. 'You won't have heard, but I took your advice and rang DCI Mather. And before I even saw him, it was such a relief to be doing something that I felt one hundred percent better.'

'What changed your mind?'

'After you'd gone, Ailsa got out her doctor book again and sat on my lap while I read it with her. We'd bought it last year when she had to go into hospital for a small operation on her foot. One of the pictures shows a teddy bear having an injection and saying that although what a doctor does to you can sometimes be uncomfortable, they're only doing it for your own good. It made me realise I couldn't look my daughter in the eye again if I didn't do what you were suggesting and speak to the police.'

Zoe beamed at him, delighted her instincts had been right. He was a good man and had wanted all along to help but allowed himself to be swayed by his wife's fears. Little Ailsa had given him a way out.

'So you've met with the police now?' she asked.

'On Saturday morning. I was there for hours and remembered far more than I expected to, like the boy only having one hand bandaged when I found him in the water.'

'I believe they're trained in methods to improve witnesses' recall.'

'This afternoon they're taking me to the river to see if being back there jogs my memory about anything else. That's why I've not gone to work today.'

'You're doing a good thing,' Zoe said. 'When she's old enough to understand, Ailsa will be proud.'

'I hope so. Heather's still not happy about it.'

'She'll come round to the idea, I'm sure.'

John rose from his chair. 'Well, it's done now.'

As Zoe watched him leave, for all her satisfaction at an outcome she'd worked hard to bring about, she felt an inexplicable sense of foreboding.

Once surgery had finished, she worked through a pile of paperwork, checked the repeat prescription requests Margaret brought to her, and tidied out the drawers in her desk. This consulting room had been hers for a year, so she should probably give it a belated spring-clean as well. However, she decided to leave that until nearer the time a locum would be taking it over.

On her way out, she met Paul coming in.

'Hello, my dear. That's you done for the day? I hope you're going home to rest.'

'With a cold drink and a good book.'

'Excellent. I'm having a catch-up with Walter later.'

'Item one on your agenda is going to have to be who gets the big electric fan.'

'It won't be the first time I've had to act as practice referee.'

Zoe laughed and wished him luck. On stepping outside, she gasped at the heat: it felt like she'd opened an oven door. Despite what she'd told Paul, her intention had been to tackle some of the boxes in the garage but once home she decided she really would just sit in the shade and read.

She woke with a start when her book fell onto the ground. Four o'clock already. She'd slept for more than an hour. A good thing she was awake now, as the sun had moved round and the large umbrella stuck in the middle of the garden table no longer protected her bare legs from its rays. Wisely, Mac had repositioned himself while she slept but he wandered over, tail wagging, when he saw she was awake.

A text had come in while she slept. *Want to go to beach on Weds? K*

Maybe too hot for me. Refuse to wear bikini at present. Z

Have use of beach hut so no excuses.

It was no good arguing and anyway a trip to the seaside might be fun. *OK Pick you up @ 11. Will bring food. You bring drinks & dog.*

After going indoors for a glass of water and to replenish Mac's bowl, Zoe moved her sunbed and sat down again. She stared at her mobile. There had still been no word from Andrew. Maybe she could risk ringing him? He'd told her he didn't keep her number stored in his phone but had memorised it and deleted the record every time they spoke. If anyone else answered her call, there was no way they could know who she was.

She took a deep breath and pressed the keypad on her mobile. After a couple of rings a male voice which wasn't Andrew's said, 'Hello.'

'Sorry, wrong number.' Zoe broke off the connection and flung her mobile, as though it had become too hot to handle, into the chair next to her. She sat wishing she'd withheld her number and waiting for the person who'd answered — was it Andrew's son? — to call back.

The house phone rang instead.

TWENTY

The phone call late on Monday afternoon had been from Paul. He had sounded so vague about his meeting with Walter that Zoe suspected Walter was listening in as they spoke. All she'd been able to glean was that the partners met to discuss the future of the practice and her name had — not unexpectedly — come up. She had agreed to see them on Tuesday lunchtime. Now that time had arrived and she was walking towards the health centre's front door, her stomach churning in a way which couldn't be blamed on the baby.

The trouble with Walter was his unpredictability. During Zoe's first few months at the practice, he had sometimes lulled her into a false sense of security by behaving like a normal person, then out of the blue he would do something completely unexpected, like that time he accused her of passing on confidential information to the police. She and Paul had eventually discovered the root of his resentment towards her, but she could never relax around him and always felt he was teetering on the edge of a complete meltdown, when he would run through a litany of all her failings and end by telling her to get out and never come back.

Colin sat at the reception desk next to the fan Margaret had claimed while Walter was away. She must have won that particular tug of war; something else for Walter to be grumpy about. Zoe and Colin exchanged greetings and he cocked his head in the direction of Paul's office. 'I'm to tell you to join them in there as soon as you arrive.'

'Thanks.' Zoe took a deep breath and strode towards the closed door, hoping she looked more composed than she felt.

Paul responded to her knock immediately, telling her to come in. The first thing she noticed was the heat in the room; Paul had obviously given his own fan to Walter as a peace offering. It crossed her mind that if things got too difficult, she would be able to feign a convincing dizzy spell. Both men watched her sit down on the only available chair, which had been positioned uncomfortably close to Walter's.

'How are you, my dear?' Paul asked, as if weeks rather than hours had passed since he last saw her.

'I'm doing away, as I think the expression goes.'

Paul smiled while Walter, clutching a manila envelope, remained stony-faced.

'We're having this meeting,' Paul said, 'because I'm sad to say that Walter has decided to leave the practice and return to Wales for good.'

Unsure if she should feign surprise and determined not to express any false regret, Zoe settled on giving a brief nod.

'I've told Walter that you and I—at my instigation—briefly discussed this possibility, as I had an inkling it may be in the offing. And that you were interested in exploring the possibility of becoming—'

Walter held up a hand, stopping Paul mid-sentence. Zoe shifted in her seat, suddenly desperate to move away from his knee, which was nearly touching hers.

'It's not quite as simple as that.' Walter pulled a document out of the envelope he held and passed it to Paul. 'I've been reading the agreement we both signed when I joined the practice. It appears I have a say in who replaces me, and I recommend we cast our net wider than you're suggesting.'

Despite being clean-shaven now, Paul made the gesture bearded men often use to indicate deep thought, stroking his face with a hand as he read the clause which Walter had helpfully marked with a highlighter pen. Then he put the document down and said, 'Ah.'

Walter said, 'I have a friend, currently a salaried GP in another practice, who is very interested in moving here. He's been waiting for an opportunity like this.'

'You've already discussed it with him?' Paul asked.

'Indeed I have. The practice would be in a safe pair of hands if he became your junior partner.'

Zoe took a deep breath. If she couldn't stop her heart from racing, there would be no need to pretend to faint. Paul caught her eye and smiled. Was he trying to apologise or be reassuring?

She stood up, not as quickly as she would have liked, but at least she got both men's attention. 'It sounds like you two have a lot to discuss. I'll be in my room for a couple of hours, doing paperwork, then I'm off all day tomorrow.'

Avoiding Paul's gaze, Zoe turned and walked out. Half an hour later, as she was reflecting on how much she hated paperwork, Margaret arrived carrying a mug of herbal tea.

'I thought you might like this,' Margaret said.

'You're an angel, thank you.'

'They're still at it. I even heard raised voices, which isn't like Doctor Paul.'

'You know what's going on, don't you?'

Margaret sat down opposite Zoe and leaned across the desk. 'I'm only saying this because he'll not be here much longer,' she whispered. 'I've never liked that man. My Hector says the sooner he buggers off back to Wales, the better.'

'You hide your feelings very well. I'm afraid that after my first few weeks, when he made it obvious he didn't want me here, I couldn't be bothered anymore.'

'It's my job to get on with everyone.' Margaret patted Zoe's hand. 'But there are some of you I like more than others.'

Zoe was about to say how much she appreciated the older woman's kindness when the door swung wide open and Colin rushed in.

'Doctor Zoe, I need your help. My patient's collapsed.'

TWENTY-ONE

Kate arrived at Keeper's Cottage earlier on Wednesday morning than she and Zoe had agreed, eager to talk about events at the health centre the previous afternoon before she was even inside the front door. 'I heard about old Mrs Curtis. They're saying it was another heart attack and you tried to save her. Is that true?'

'I did try to save her, yes, but it would be wrong of me to tell you any more until the post mortem's done and her family's been told,' Zoe said.

'She hasn't got any family.'

'Even so, I can't discuss it. You should know that by now.'

Kate shrugged. 'It was worth a try.'

'Has anyone ever told you you're callous?'

'No, because I'm not. But I'm also not a hypocrite. She wasn't a very nice woman and I'm not going to pretend otherwise. I was more concerned about you when Mum told me what happened.'

Zoe thought back to the previous afternoon and how she'd rushed to the treatment room with Colin while Margaret called an ambulance. As soon as she saw Mrs Curtis she knew it was hopeless, but they went through the motions anyway, until the paramedics arrived and took over. 'I'm always sad to lose a patient but it was far worse for the other staff. However ill they are, people don't usually die while they're at the health centre.'

'I hadn't thought about that aspect of it.'

'Our newest receptionist was so upset, we had to send her home.' The arrival of the ambulance had also broken up the partners' meeting, with Paul rushing to help, followed more slowly by Walter.

This quietened Kate, giving Zoe enough time to put Mac on his lead and pick up a brightly coloured canvas bag she'd rescued the previous night from the sacks of charity shop donations which still stood in her hall. After grabbing a hat and putting on her sunglasses, she ushered Kate out of the house.

'Can we take the Jeep? I'm more comfortable in it these days.'

'As long as Mac accepts he's sitting in the back. It'll make a nice change not to drive.'

'You can be navigator. I don't know where we're going.'

'It won't take us long to get there. Which is good, because I'm gagging to ask your advice about something.'

The drive to Coldingham took them just over half an hour. Zoe thought she had been to the village once before but only on the way somewhere else, and she was in uncharted territory when Kate told her to take a right turn just before the pub. Soon they came out the other side of the village and Kate again pointed to a road off to the right.

The number of vehicles in the car park made Zoe fear the beach would be packed, but as they walked over the dunes she realised that like most visitor attractions in the Borders, Coldingham Bay had room to spare. Small groups of people were scattered across the sand but there was plenty of space between them even with the tide in. Mac whined and strained on his lead, and Zoe felt unexpectedly gripped by a desire to kick off her shoes, run across the sand and plunge into the sea.

'Gorgeous, isn't it?' Kate said.

'I had no idea this was so close to home. Why have you never brought me here before?'

158

'I don't think of you as an incomer anymore, so I assumed you knew about it.' Kate beckoned Zoe to follow her. 'Come on.'

As they walked along the beach, Kate explained that Auntie Joan had recently bought a beach hut, something she'd set her heart on several years previously but which rarely came up for sale. 'She says it needs work, but she'll wait till the autumn before getting someone in. It's dark green apparently, which she hates, but that should make it easy to find.'

True enough, the beach hut they were looking for stood out from the white, blue and turquoise ones. Kate unlocked the door and removed the window shutter. Inside, it resembled little more than a clean garden shed, with most of the floor space occupied by folded-up deckchairs, a windbreak, assorted buckets and spades, and a pair of semi-inflated lilos. A gas stove, a full mug-tree and a glass jar of sugar sat on top of a small cupboard positioned against the rear wall.

'I'm starving already. Must be all this sea air,' Kate said. 'Let's pull the seats out so we can reach the cupboard and find something to eat our lunch on.'

Zoe hoped to find a seat which offered her more support than the old-fashioned deckchairs but eventually had to admit defeat, cautiously lowering herself into one at its most upright setting. She put her foot through the loop of Mac's lead. Kate had suggested letting him run free but he'd never been to a beach before and might be too excited by the experience to come back, especially if he encountered people with food.

'You won't be getting out of that in a hurry,' Kate said, laughing. 'But there's no need for you to. Just stay there and I'll bring your lunch to you.'

She soon unearthed a foldaway table and set it down in front of Zoe, loading it with plates, glasses and more food than her backpack seemed capable of holding, then turning to Zoe's bag and bringing out its contents.

During all this, unable to maintain eye contact for them to carry on a conversation, Zoe sat back to enjoy the sea breeze which gently ruffled Mac's coat and admire the view of the horizon where an extraordinarily blue sky met sea just a few shades darker.

'Eat up,' Kate said as she finally sat in her own deckchair. 'We'll take a walk along the shoreline afterwards so don't hold back.'

Zoe helped herself to a slice of homemade game-pie, one of Etta's specialities. 'You and Erskine okay again?

'Aye. He said he'd seen you on Saturday morning and that you were a bit snarky with him. He also admitted he deserved it. You can judge how guilty a man feels by the size of the bouquet he gives you. Mine was huge.'

'I'm glad you've sorted yourselves out.'

'Till next time.' Kate frowned. 'You know I said I had something big to tell you?'

'You don't look very happy about it, whatever it is.'

'I need to handle this in a cool, calm and collected manner, so I'm hoping you'll tell me what to do.'

'Now you're being a tease.'

'You'll never guess who's got in touch with me via my website.'

'George Clooney thinks he may be descended from William Wallace?'

'I wish. No, here's the thing, I got an email from Mrs Mather yesterday. Though she goes by her maiden name, Laura Foxton.'

Zoe's mouth dropped open. 'Oh my God. Was it telling you to stay away from her husband?'

'That's what I expected, when I saw it sitting there in my inbox. Took me ages to pluck up the courage to open it. But it's actually just . . . strange. Here, see for yourself.' Kate reached into a side pocket of her backpack and pulled out a folded piece of paper.

Zoe scanned the message. 'It's rather businesslike, isn't it? "I think it would be in both our interests if we could discuss matters".'

'From what Erskine has said about her — and that's not much — she sounds a bit of a cold fish. Her email backs that up.'

'Which is a good thing, surely? You wouldn't want to deal with someone seething with resentment who starts sending you ranty emails.'

'At least that would have been understandable. This has freaked me out.'

'Presumably this means Erskine has told her about you? After all, she knows you're deaf.' Zoe read again from the email, '"Because you can't talk on the telephone I think our best option would be to meet in person".'

'I suppose so. He says he's always been honest with her, but I don't know what that means in practice.'

'How did he react to this?'

'You're the only person who knows so far.'

'Don't you think you should tell him about it?'

'I'd rather find out what she has to say first.'

'So you are going to meet her?'

'I'm swithering. What do you think I should do?'

'When have you ever taken notice of my advice?' Zoe smiled to let Kate knew she was only joking.

'There's a first time for everything. Really, I want to know what you think.'

'I'm not sure what I think. It's your decision.'

'I know.' Kate got up. 'Come on, let's go for a paddle.'

Ten minutes later they were walking barefoot along the water's edge, Mac trotting happily a few metres in front of them on his extending lead. Zoe couldn't remember the last time she'd felt sand beneath her feet.

'This is wonderful. I think I may come here a lot in the future,' she said.

'You could take up windsurfing,' Kate said. 'I'll sit on the beach and play with your baby. Which reminds me, have you heard the latest about Dave Trent's son?'

'No. Is he alright?'

'He's out of danger, though he'll be in an incubator for a while longer.'

'What a relief for his parents.'

'And Erskine. It means Dave's back at work.'

Zoe drew up and faced her friend head on. 'Speaking of whom, is all this fresh air helping you to decide how to answer Mrs Mather's email?'

'Not really. Should I agree to meet her without telling Erskine? It was obvious when we briefly got together last night that he has no idea she's been in touch with me.'

'If you refuse, what do you think she'll do?'

'I'm more worried about what her husband will do. If I tell him, he's bound to rush off and confront her, but if I don't and he finds out — he's a detective, after all — I'll be in trouble for keeping him in the dark.'

'Be honest, Kate, aren't you just a tiny bit curious about what she's like and why she wants to see you? I would be.'

'You're saying I should meet her without telling him?'

Zoe put her hands up. 'You can't expect me to comment on that aspect of it. My point is, if you don't see her, you'll never know what she wants. Maybe she's decided to be your friend.'

They both laughed at this idea, then turned to continue their walk along the beach. Back at the hut, Zoe opted to sit on a towel rather than risk the deckchair again, and a damp but happy Mac settled next to her.

Kate sat down opposite them. 'My other piece of news is I've lost a client and gained two new ones since we last met.'

162

'Wasn't the rugby-playing banker pleased with your brilliant deductions about his ancestors?'

'One of things you learn early on in this game is that clients have to be handled very carefully. They often have unrealistic expectations of what a genealogist is able to do, and they don't want to hear about any loose ends. Worse still are those who bring along their own preconceptions about what you're going to find, based on family lore or something Great-Aunt Ada once told them. So I explained in detail to Simon how I made the jump from the Criminal Register to what we found in the graveyard and the records I subsequently unearthed. I needed him to understand that my theory about his lineage on his father's side going across the border to Northumberland wasn't just a wild guess.' Kate paused to take a mouthful of lemonade.

'Was he displeased at the suggestion one of his ancestors had been a petty criminal?' Zoe asked.

'I couldn't tell what he thought. You know me, I'm pretty good at interpreting facial expressions and body language, but I found him almost impossible to read. He heard me out, nodded, then asked me to hand over the copies of documents I'd brought with me and email him the balance of my bill. He didn't even want the presentation copy of his family tree which I give every client. Either he wasn't interested or for some reason he was pretending not to be.'

'That's bizarre. He seemed very keen at the start, didn't he?'

'Maybe it's a case of buyer's remorse. He suddenly realised how much I'd had cost him and wished he'd kept hold of his money.'

'Does that happen often?'

'I don't usually meet clients face to face, so maybe more of them regret hiring me than I know.'

'You'd have gone out of business years ago if that was the case.'

'True. In fact, if you look on my website you'll see I've got a pageful of testimonials. And, perhaps more importantly, I've only ever not been paid in full once. The credit card I'd put the deposit through on was refused for the balance and the client—who'd given me an address in Alaska—never responded to emails or letters. I chalked it up to experience.'

Zoe shifted on the towel, ending up with her legs splayed out in front of her. This felt unladylike but extremely comfortable. 'So you'll do as he asked and then just get on with the next one?'

'I already have. Anyway, let's not talk about work. How's Patrick?'

'I've not seen him since your birthday. Why would I?'

'He mentioned you'd gone out walking together.'

'Our dogs get on well.'

Kate burst out laughing. 'That's priceless. You will tell me if your dogs decide to take their relationship to the next level, won't you?'

'Don't you think they deserve some privacy?' Zoe said, trying to keep a straight face.

Before they realised, it was time to leave. Despite a lavish layer of suntan lotion, Zoe's shoulders had started to redden and her back ached. It had been a lovely day but she felt relieved to be on her own again when Kate dropped her off at Keeper's Cottage.

Expecting to have been contacted by Paul by now, she dialled 1471 on the house phone to see if she'd missed any calls. She had, but the anodyne female voice informed her that whoever had rung just after two o'clock had withheld their number.

Another unwanted sales pitch for home improvements? Or was her stalker back?

TWENTY-TWO

Although he was seeing no patients on Thursday morning, Walter's door remained shut and Margaret reported relations had been frosty between the partners since their heated discussion on Tuesday. Paul wasn't due in until the afternoon, and in the absence of a phone call from him, Zoe wondered if she should stick around after surgery to see him. She even briefly considered barging into Walter's room and tackling him face to face about this latest discord which had at its heart his long-standing resentment of her.

In the end, she decided to wait for the men to work things out between them. Which wasn't like her at all. 'Having you to think about is changing me,' she whispered as she sat down and smoothed her white blouse over her bump.

Half an hour later, during a lull caused by two patients in a row failing to turn up, she checked her mobile and found a text had come in from Kate.

Meeting Mrs M tomorrow morn in Edinburgh. Wish me luck. K

Good luck. Let me know how you get on. Z

Again suppressing the urge to confront Walter, Zoe left the health centre around noon to go home. As soon as she walked into the hall and tripped over a pile of books she knew she could no longer put off going to the charity shop.

165

She took a call from Patrick just after loading the final bag into the Jeep.

'Hi, Zoe. I'm calling to check you're still on for our not-a-date tomorrow night.'

'Have you decided where we're going?'

'I thought we might try the Rowan Tree Inn. It closed last year but someone new's taken over and it's reopened as a small restaurant rather than a pub. Do you know it?'

'I've driven past it a few times.'

'I have to go through Westerlea to get there, so can you tolerate my driving for one night?'

'If you want. Though I'm off alcohol anyway so you might still prefer it if I picked you up.'

After a pause, Patrick said, 'No need. I'll be there for seven, if that suits you.'

'Alright.'

Weary of waiting for Kate, Paul and her father to get in touch, Zoe decided to get away for a few hours the next morning by taking Mac for a long walk somewhere further away from home. Tempted to go to Coldingham Bay again, she opted instead to drive to the Chain Bridge. Hadn't she told Sergeant Trent that Mac would enjoy walking alongside the river? Returning to where the boy's body had been pulled ashore didn't worry her. She had no fear of open spaces; experience had taught her that far greater dangers lurked indoors.

Surprised to find no parking spaces at nine-thirty on a Friday morning, she drove the Jeep onto the Chain Bridge, concentrating on negotiating those concrete bollards. When she looked up, the sight ahead made her gasp. The centre third of the bridge was heaped with flowers. Several wreaths and many bunches, some large but mostly small, had been placed on the wooden walkway, while still more had been tied to the web of metal struts. As she watched, a young woman approached these floral tributes and crouched down to add her own.

A vehicle's horn sounded, making Zoe jump. She held up her hand in acknowledgment and slowly drove across the rest of the bridge and through the second set of bollards, parking on the road behind several other cars.

Laying floral tributes to a young man they'd never met hadn't been enough for some visitors. They had also left cards, many of them made by children, and notes on pieces of paper which had started to curl in the sun. Zoe read several, felt her eyelids prickle and a lump rise in her throat, and resumed walking until she and Mac were back in Scotland. Going down the steps she had climbed up with Sergeant Trent, she felt relieved to be alone again, and stopped to blow her nose. Had it only been three weeks ago?

She took a drink of water and walked on, dragging Mac away from a smell he didn't want to leave. Even this close to the river, lack of rainfall had turned the grass yellow and the ground beneath it looked cracked and dry. She stopped to admire several butterflies feeding on a patch of wild flowers. Less welcome were the clouds of flies which occasionally collided with her.

Nearing the bench she had sat on while waiting for Trent, she heard a clamour of voices. Once past the bench, she saw the source of the noise. About a dozen people crowded around the stones Zoe had stepped over to reach the dead boy, one pointing upriver towards the Chain Bridge, another standing a little apart, taking photographs.

She turned on her heel and led Mac back the way they'd come. As they reached the Jeep, she took a call from Robbie Mackenzie who was polite but clearly put out that her solicitor hadn't yet returned some paperwork connected with her purchase of his field. She apologised and promised to chase it up, but when he rang off, she stood staring at her mobile, trying to figure out why such a minor transaction, for Robbie at least, seemed so important to him. From what his sister had said, money was no object to that branch of the Mackenzie clan.

Since coming to the Borders, Zoe hadn't been out on what could even loosely be termed a date. Her efforts to forget the closest she had come to one were usually successful, but that extraordinary night lingered stubbornly in her mind on Friday evening as she waited for Patrick to arrive. The feelings she'd had then were certainly not replicated now, but she was in the same house killing time once again before a man came to take her out for a meal. Agreeing to this had been a big mistake.

Her vague hope that history might repeat itself to the extent that he wouldn't turn up was dashed when she heard Mac barking. She looked out of the window. Patrick wore a blue-and-white striped shirt over a pair of jeans, instantly making Zoe feel overdressed in the silk maxi-skirt which still fitted her because it had an elasticated waist with its matching blouse unbuttoned as a jacket over a sleeveless tee-shirt.

As he leaned back into his car, she froze. Don't say he'd brought her flowers. Relief flooded through her when she saw Peggy jump down and scamper towards the cottage's front door.

Despite the informality of his clothes, Patrick had trimmed his beard and a pleasant lemony smell hung about him. They settled the dogs in the lounge, shutting the kitchen door to prevent Peggy from escaping through the cat-flap as she had nearly done on her earlier visit, and Patrick acquiesced to Zoe's insistence that they go in her Jeep.

Just before the track leading to Tolbyres Farm, a tractor flashed its lights at them and Zoe waved to its driver, Dod Affleck, the Tolbyres herdsman. From there, the journey to the Rowan Tree Inn took about half an hour, during which time they discovered a shared love of seventies rock music. In between singing along with The Steve Miller Band and Fleetwood Mac, they chatted about how much patients and pet-owners relied on the internet for information. Although good-naturedly trying to top each other's stories for absurdity, both were discreet when it came to identities. In such a small community there was probably a great deal of overlap between their customers.

Apart from Kate, Zoe found few people had the ability to raise more than a wry smile in her these days, so it felt good to laugh out loud at Patrick's imitation of the enraged owner of a Siamese cat who refused to believe her beloved pet's swollen tummy wasn't indication of a tumour but impregnation, most likely by a neighbour's moggy. He laughed too, then groaned.

'What's wrong?' Zoe asked.

'I've just realised that's probably an insensitive story to tell a heavily pregnant woman.'

'Oh please. I'm not the delicate flower everyone thinks I am. Didn't you hear me laughing?'

They arrived at their destination. Separated from the road by a stretch of grass and the inevitable rowan tree, the inn no longer looked sad and neglected as it had the previous times Zoe had driven past it. The front door sat open, as did the windows which for so long had been boarded up. The building's paintwork was fresh and bright, and a new sign hung from an ornate metal bracket.

After parking at the rear, Zoe and Patrick walked back towards the front entrance.

'Rowan trees are at their prettiest later in the year when they have berries,' Zoe said. 'I'm going to plant one in my garden once my building work's finished. Kate tells me it'll protect us from fairy spells.'

'There's a lot of folklore attached to them,' Patrick said. 'As well as warding off evil, did you know that rowan's traditionally used to make Maypoles? They're supposed to aid flirtation and romance.'

'You know some pretty unlikely facts for a vet.'

'You've seen my house. I read a lot. Can't help absorbing all sorts of stuff.'

They were taken to a table beside one of the open windows, a faint breeze ruffling the paper serviettes wedged into wine glasses which would remain unused as Zoe ordered a sparkling mineral water with ice and lemon and Patrick ordered a Becks Blue.

'I'm sorry, sir,' the waitress said. 'We don't sell alcohol-free beer, only low-alcohol.'

Patrick briefly looked as though he wanted to make a fuss, then said, 'In which case, you'd better make that a large bottle of mineral water.'

They both concentrated on reading the menu so by the time their water arrived they were ready to order their food. Zoe said she would only have a main course, the salmon with salad and new potatoes. Patrick looked stricken.

'That doesn't mean you can't have a starter,' she said.

'I'll probably not bother with a sweet.'

'In that case we'll be quits, as I probably will.'

He ordered stuffed mushrooms followed by a sirloin steak, medium rare, with garlic chips and roasted cherry tomatoes, and pulled a face as the waitress left. 'Couldn't have ordered a more blokeish meal, could I?'

'Eating out is the time to either go for the food you love or to try something you've never had before. I once met a man on holiday in Malta who had a T-bone steak every night for the two weeks he was there. His wife was embarrassed, but I could never understand why. He was doing what made him happy — isn't that what holidays are for?'

'Malta? You like to travel, then?'

'Not very widely. I've never been to America, though I guess in a few years' time I'll be under pressure to visit Florida. What about you?'

'I go to see relatives in Poland every now and then. And when I lived in Glasgow I travelled to back to Ireland a few times.'

'Did you train to be a vet in Glasgow?'

'No, I was in another line of business back then. Moved to Edinburgh and applied to study at the Dick Vet.'

Zoe tried and failed to suppress a smile. 'The Dick Vet?'

'Go on, laugh. Everyone else does.'

'Sorry. Childish of me.'

'It was established by a chap called William Dick in the early nineteenth century and is the best place in the country to study veterinary medicine. Being the butt of jokes for going there was worth it.'

'Do you hope to have your own practice one day?'

'One day. I should have by now probably, but I got waylaid.'

'By what?'

'My own stupidity. Oh good, here come my mushrooms.'

In between mouthfuls of his starter, Patrick threw out questions to Zoe about herself. At first she resisted giving him anything more than the bare details of her life, but his quiet persistence and genuine interest started to break down some of the barriers she habitually erected to keep people at arm's length. Rather than try to cram too many tables into the dining room, the Rowan Tree's owners had spaced them wide enough apart to offer a degree of privacy. She no longer held back over her life before she moved to Scotland, even telling him about Russell and some of the circumstances surrounding his death. Thankfully, because she would have shut him down very quickly if he had, Patrick knew better than to examine her about what had gone on since her arrival in the Borders. Like most people, he probably thought he knew it all anyway, thanks to the newspapers.

The Rowan Tree's service tipped over from speedy to hurried when their main courses arrived almost immediately after Patrick's empty starter plate had been taken away. By now, Zoe was feeling hungry, so she didn't mind, but she noticed him hesitate before picking up his knife and fork as though suppressing a comment.

The food was excellent and they ate at a relaxed pace, chatting as friends do, without any flirtatious undertones. Pregnancy had rendered Zoe asexual, at least as far as the rest of the world was concerned. She didn't know how this made her feel.

Patrick was mopping up the meat juices on his plate with the last of his chips when his phone rang. He took it from his shirt pocket, checked the screen and frowned. 'Once again, I have to take this. Sorry.' He got up. 'Won't be long.'

As he walked across the room, Zoe smiled apologetically at an elderly pair of fellow diners whose faces expressed annoyance at their quiet meal out being disturbed. She couldn't really blame them. Was this call from the same friend who had cut short their walk?

She checked her own mobile, which she had muted before leaving Keeper's Cottage, and felt no surprise that no one had texted or phoned her. Phone etiquette was still evolving, but being left alone at a restaurant table while the person who had invited her out took a call was starting to feel like a slight. She tried not to keep glancing at the station clock on the wall to see the minutes passing and hoped Patrick would be back soon, although she was tempted to visit the bathroom and let him think she'd got fed up and gone home if he returned while she was away.

He wore a pained expression when he came back. 'Zoe, I'm so sorry. That took longer than I thought it would.'

'As you keep reminding me, this isn't a date.'

'Even so, I care what you think of me.'

'Is everything okay or are you likely to get another call?'

'I hope not.'

Their plates had been cleared during Patrick's absence, and now the waitress brought the sweet menu. Zoe chose the lemon torte. Patrick, having missed out on his final chips, ordered biscuits and cheese. They chatted as they ate, mainly Patrick telling Zoe about various places in the Borders that he recommended she should visit, but the easy familiarity which had been developing between them had disappeared. Zoe started to feel tired and uncomfortable; the baby's persistent kicking didn't help. She opted for peppermint tea instead of coffee.

Patrick's phone sounded again, an incoming text this time. He checked his message and looked helplessly at Zoe.

'If you need to go, we can cancel our drinks,' she said, expecting him to argue.

'Thanks for being so understanding.' Patrick waved the waitress over and asked for the bill.

'I can't properly understand if you don't tell me what's going on,' Zoe said.

'It's someone else's problem and I'm trying to help them out. Sorry, but I can't go into details.'

She forced a smile. 'Now I know how Kate feels. She's always saying I'm too guarded about what I tell people.'

'Which gives me hope that our friendship can survive despite this evening being cut short, as I didn't think you were at all guarded while we were talking. I'll make this up to you, I promise.'

They travelled back towards Westerlea in silence. Zoe concentrated on driving while Patrick sent and received so many texts that she had to fight the urge to pull in, grab his mobile and throw it out of the window. They weren't far from the turning to Tolbyres Farm when a text came in. Patrick read it and said, 'Zoe, I can explain now.'

This had better be good.

'Alright,' she said.

'First of all, I need to tell you something about myself.'

Zoe glanced in her rear-view mirror and saw flashing lights bearing down on them. 'Sorry, it'll have to wait. I need to get out of the way of that fire engine.'

The road was narrow; at first glance she could see nowhere to go, then she spotted a gateway into a field. The gate was closed but there was enough room to pull up the Jeep in front of it. She indicated, veering off the road almost immediately. The fire engine sped past.

'Looks like someone else's Friday night has been ruined,' Patrick said.

Zoe threw him a rueful grin. 'That's put things into perspective.'

She checked for other vehicles and pulled back out into the road. The fire engine was still visible; it had slowed down ahead of them. Then it turned right.

'Oh crap, it's going to Tolbyres,' Patrick said.

Zoe put her foot down.

TWENTY-THREE

'The fire engine would never have got down here if we'd had rain recently,' Zoe said, as her Jeep lurched from side to side along the rough track leading to Tolbyres Farm. She could smell smoke now and from the look on his face, so could Patrick.

'Maybe it's a false alarm, or just something gone on fire in a barn,' he said.

As they rounded the bend, they saw his optimism had been misplaced.

Tolbyres Cottage was on fire.

Zoe brought the Jeep to an abrupt halt. She and Patrick looked in horror at the scene in front of them.

Smoke poured from every downstairs window of Kate's home. On the right of the building, the redundant front door which was always kept locked had burned away, its frame now a blackened portal into the blazing hallway. The sash of one window ignited and flames took hold of the dry wood which had only recently been repainted. Zoe thought about the waxed floorboards throughout the house, the wooden shelves piled high with books and magazines, and the revealed beams in the sitting room. The whole place was a tinderbox.

Unable to bear watching the destruction any longer, Zoe turned her attention to what was being done to bring the blaze under control. A firefighter wearing a mustard-coloured uniform and yellow helmet raised a panel on the fire engine's side and started to pull out a black hose. Another, in a white helmet, spoke a few words to him then strode off towards the house, the back of his jacket announcing that he was the Incident Commander. A third firefighter appeared carrying first aid equipment which he set down some distance away from the scene.

Behind the fire engine, the only two men on the scene not in uniform were grappling with each other. Patrick got out of the Jeep and ran to them. As Zoe watched him join the scuffle she realised what was happening: Dod Affleck was trying to prevent Douglas Mackenzie from running into his sister's house.

She made her way as fast as she could to the men. Despite now being outnumbered, Douglas obviously had no intention of giving in and continued struggling to get free. Even though its siren and flashing lights had been switched off, the vehicle's engine continued to run, so she had to shout to make herself heard. 'Stop it, all of you! Douglas, listen to me. Are the children in there?'

'No, they're staying with Mum and Dad tonight. But Kate is. She was going to have an early night and collect them in the morning.'

'Has anyone told the firefighters that she's deaf?'

Dod's jaw clenched. 'It was me who called to report the fire,' he said. 'But I was that upset, I wasnae thinking straight.'

'It's not too late,' Zoe said.

She dashed over to the firefighter who had been organising the first aid equipment and was now speaking into a hand-held radio. 'Excuse me,' she shouted. He looked up at her. 'There's something you need to know. My friend who lives here is deaf. She's in bed and could be sleeping through all this.'

'Do you know where her bedroom is?'

'At the back on the right of the building.'

Directly above the worst of the flames.

The fireman nodded, repeated what she had told him into the radio and listened to the response. Turning back to Zoe, he told her to stay where she was; the Incident Commander would come and speak to her. As if on cue, the man in the white helmet emerged from the side of Kate's house and hurried towards them.

'You're certain your friend is the only person in the building?' he said.

'Her children are with their grandparents, thank goodness. You've realised it isn't two houses any more, but just one?'

'I thought it was strange not to have a fence separating the gardens. Does that mean we should be able to reach your friend by going up the left-hand stairs?'

'Yes. There's a long corridor at the back and Kate's room is at the far end of it.'

'Good. Now please go and move your vehicle well back. Two more appliances will be here any minute.' He turned and strode towards the fire engine. As if on cue, Zoe heard sirens approaching.

She reversed the Jeep and steered it through an open gate into the field where Frankie's chicken shed stood. Clyde and his hens had been closed up for the night, although the poor creatures must have sensed something was wrong because she heard clucking and the frantic beating of wings as though they were trying to escape. Before she could make her way back to Patrick and the others, the sirens suddenly sounded much closer and two more fire engines swept into view, followed by a police car.

While the firefighters concentrated on Kate's house, three uniformed police officers set about cordoning off the site. Zoe remained behind the field's wooden fence and watched Douglas remonstrate with one of the officers about being made to move back. He finally gave in and came over to her.

Patrick joined them shortly afterwards. 'Why don't you go home, Zoe? The ambulance'll be here soon.'

'I'm not here because I'm a doctor. That's my best friend in there. I can't leave.'

He looked like he wanted to argue but at that moment they were distracted by the sight of Kate's remaining front door being smashed open with a red battering ram. Several firefighters wearing breathing apparatus charged inside and were instantly enveloped by smoke.

'I've a friend who's a retained fireman,' Patrick said. 'They're incredible. They'll get her out in no time.'

Having worked in a hospital and treated victims of smoke inhalation, Zoe didn't respond. She knew that in many house fires, deaths were due to people breathing in toxic gases like carbon monoxide rather than any burns they might suffer. Kate was in real danger, even if the flames hadn't yet reached her.

Overcome by the noise, the smells and fear for her friend, Zoe started to feel faint. She leaned against the fence for support and tried to lower herself to the ground in a controlled fashion, but her knees buckled and she fell sideways. Patrick, talking on his mobile again, didn't notice; however, Douglas and Dod came running. Dod pulled off his cotton sweater and helped her sit down on it.

Briefly distracted from watching the firefighters at work, they all jumped at a loud explosion followed by the sound of breaking glass. Once again Douglas tried to run towards his sister's house, and this time a policeman restrained him. Zoe looked up at the men standing over her. Their faces confirmed they were asking themselves the same questions she was: what had exploded and was it anywhere near Kate and her would-be rescuers?

She went to stand up, but Dod put a hand on her shoulder to restrain her. 'There's nothing any of us can do,' he said, looking grim. His phone rang. He answered and Zoe realised he was speaking to Kate's father, trying to stop him from coming over and reassuring him that the fire service had the situation under control. After agreeing to ring as soon as he knew anything, he ended the call.

'They must be frantic with worry,' Zoe said. 'They'll be able to hear all the commotion and see the smoke from across the field.'

'Douglas not answering his phone doesn't help. Scared them into thinking something had happened to him too. And the children are upset about the cat and Frankie's chickens.'

Patrick shouted, 'They're bringing her out.'

With Dod's help, Zoe struggled to her feet in time to see two firefighters materialise out of the smoke. They carried Kate between them over to the casualty area, where they gently laid her onto a tarpaulin and one of their colleagues clamped a mask attached to an oxygen tank over her face. Throughout all this, Kate remained motionless.

Please let her be alright.

A car drew up and seconds later a tall figure ran from it towards the group of firefighters taking care of Kate. Erskine Mather. Zoe felt overwhelmed by the urge to join him, but fought it down. Another person crowding round Kate would do no good at all.

'Where's that bloody ambulance?' Dod said.

'Those fire officers are as well trained as any paramedic,' Patrick said. Dod looked unconvinced, but at that moment they all heard another siren. As the ambulance appeared, lights flashing front and back, Zoe felt a hand on her arm. She looked round and saw Sergeant Trent.

'Hello, Doctor. I'm sorry to see you caught up in all this.'

'It's out of choice, Sergeant, although I feel useless just standing here. Can you find out how Kate is and let us know so we can tell her family? They're distraught, as you can imagine.'

'I'll see what I can do.'

The fire started to diminish under the onslaught of water coming from those enormous hoses. The air was hot, heavy with smoke and steam. Small pieces of charred paper and flecks of soot floated around Zoe's head as she watched Kate being loaded into the ambulance. Mather exchanged words with a green-clad paramedic and Trent, then climbed inside with her. Shortly afterwards, siren blaring, the ambulance set off for Borders General Hospital.

Trent spoke to one of the uniformed officers then came over to Zoe and the three men with her in the field.

'Is she going to be alright?' Douglas demanded.

Trent frowned, obviously unsure how much to share. 'This is Douglas Mackenzie, Kate's brother,' Zoe said.

'Sorry, I didn't realise. The fire hadn't reached her but she's inhaled a lot of smoke. They're giving her oxygen therapy and as soon as she reaches the BGH the doctors will assess her and decide what else she needs.'

'Is she conscious?'

Trent swallowed hard. 'No.'

'Hell.' Douglas put a hand to his head. 'I need to go and tell everyone, then arrange for Mum to get to the BGH. She'll want to be there when Sis wakes up.'

'What can I do to help?' Zoe asked.

'I . . . I don't know. I can't think straight.'

'Your Mum's got my number, so just call if you need anything, alright?'

Douglas nodded absentmindedly and started to walk away. After a few steps he stopped and looked back at Zoe. 'Would you come to the hospital? The worst part of when Dad had his stroke was we didn't understand what the doctors were telling us.'

'Of course I will.'

'Okay. See you there.'

'Do you think you should?' Patrick asked once Douglas was out of earshot.

'The Mackenzies have been good to me. I'll do whatever it takes to help them get through this.'

'Let me come with you.'

'No need for that, but it would be great if you could take Mac home with you. I don't know how long I'll be and he'll hate being left alone all night.'

'Okay, if you're sure that's what you want.'

Trent had been talking to Dod, taking notes as he listened to how the herdsman had spotted the fire and called it in. Now he said to Patrick, 'Before you go, can I take your details, sir?'

'Why?'

'It's routine to note down who's at the scene, that's all.'

Patrick looked set to argue, then must have thought better of it and reeled off his name and address. Zoe could tell from Trent's overly blank expression that he hadn't liked having to justify himself.

Before leaving, she looked back at Kate's house. The fire hoses were still trained on it but seemed to have brought the blaze under control. She could no longer see any flames, although plumes of thick smoke and clouds of steam still filled the night sky.

'I can't believe anyone would do that on purpose,' Patrick said.

Zoe turned to stare at him. 'What on earth makes you think it was arson?'

'I heard one of the fire officers say he could smell petrol at the front door.'

'You must be mistaken. Kate hasn't got any enemies.'

181

'Everyone's got enemies, Zoe. They just don't realise it.'

'That's a very jaundiced view of the world.'

Patrick shrugged and got into the Jeep.

TWENTY-FOUR

When Zoe dropped Patrick off at Keeper's Cottage, he again tried to make a case for accompanying her to the hospital but she wasn't going to be swayed.

'I have no idea how long I'll be, so looking after Mac is the best help you can give me at the moment. I'll phone you when there's anything to report.'

She put the Jeep into gear and drove away before he could argue further.

Despite it being a Friday night, the time when city-dwellers were out in force to celebrate the end of their working week, the Borders roads were nearly empty as Zoe travelled west towards Melrose. The baby, seemingly aware this evening was anything but ordinary, continued to somersault inside her far later than usual. Once on the Melrose bypass, the hospital within a couple of miles, Zoe attempted to distract herself from worrying about Kate by imagining her journey along this road in about six weeks' time, on the way to give birth. That was the thing about hospitals. They saw lives begin as well as end.

Oh, Kate, please be alright.

She parked the Jeep and hurried past the curved wall of the chapel, unable to stop herself from glancing into the two ambulances parked up outside the main entrance. They were both empty.

The Accident and Emergency Unit's front door swooshed open when she approached it, only requiring the briefest of pauses before she could continue along the short passage past the waiting room to reception.

The woman behind the glass looked up and asked, 'Can I help you?' She stared at Zoe's stomach, obviously wondering if the reason for this new arrival was pregnancy-related.

'I've come about a patient who will have recently been brought in by ambulance.'

'What's the name?'

'Kate Mackenzie.'

'You're a relative?'

'No.' The receptionist raised an eyebrow and Zoe hastily added, 'I'm her GP. My name is Doctor Moreland.'

'As I explained to the patient's family, the consultant is still with her.'

Zoe looked over at the only people in the waiting room, a young man holding a towel to his blood-streaked forehead and his female companion whose eyes were fixed on her mobile. 'Her family's here? I can't see them.'

'They may have to wait a while for news so we've put them in a separate room. I'll get someone to take you there.'

Zoe didn't have to wait long before being led to a small, windowless room where Etta and Douglas Mackenzie sat in silence. Etta's normally compliant grey hair flopped over her face, and her glowing skin which usually spoke of many hours spent gardening was drained of colour.

Kate's mother rushed to Zoe and hugged her. 'What has she done to deserve this? Everyone knows she's deaf.'

'She's in good hands here,' Zoe said.

'No one's told us anything, except that they're doing tests. We don't even know if she's woken up yet.' Etta choked back a sob.

'Can't you find out what's happening?' Douglas asked Zoe. 'They'll talk to you.'

184

'I've already tried. The receptionist genuinely doesn't know anything. I'm afraid we're going to have to wait for the consultant to come out. Can I get you both a drink while we wait?'

Etta shook her head. Douglas said, 'White coffee with sugar, please.'

A short corridor led from A&E to the hospital's main reception area, but as Zoe expected, the volunteer-run shop was closed for the night. The only people present shared a sofa, both apparently asleep. She passed the empty enquiries desk and another person, sitting at a table, came into view. He wore a heavily creased shirt and chinos with dark stains, and it took a while for her to realise she was looking at Erskine Mather. How could she have forgotten he'd been in the ambulance with Kate?

Their eyes met as she approached the table.

'Hello, Zoe.' Mather pulled out a chair for her.

'Hello. Kate's mum and brother are in the family room. Have you seen them?'

'I've been elsewhere.'

'You were allowed to stay with Kate?'

'No.' Mather's jaw clenched briefly. 'They wheeled her into the resuscitation room and I went to the chapel.'

'Oh.' Zoe failed to hide the surprise in her voice.

'Just for the peace and quiet.'

'Etta's desperate to hear how she is. Can you tell her anything that may help?'

He momentarily shut his eyes, as if replaying what must have been a terrible journey in the ambulance. 'Kate didn't regain consciousness. As far as the paramedics could see, she's suffered no burns but who knows how long she'd been breathing in smoke and fumes? Her breathing sounded terrible, like a low-pitched croak coming from the back of her throat. Then she went quiet and I thought this was a good sign until I saw how the paramedics reacted. Luckily we weren't far away by then, so I stayed clear while they wheeled her in as soon as the ambulance stopped.'

Zoe knew what Kate's silence in the ambulance indicated: her airway had become completely blocked. 'Oh no.'

'She's going to die, isn't she?'

'There's a team of experts doing their utmost to make sure she doesn't.' Zoe almost put a hand on his shoulder, probably would have if it had been anyone else. She sat in silence until he spoke again.

'You're right,' he said. 'I'm always telling people to trust the professionals to do their job.'

'Will you come and see Etta?'

'I'm not sure how warm a welcome I'd get from Kate's father.'

'He's not here. It's just Etta and Douglas at present. Knowing you were in the ambulance with Kate will help her. Trust me.'

They both stood up; a mobile rang. Mather reached inside his back pocket. 'It's Trent. I must speak to him.'

'I'll wait here.'

He nodded and moved away.

Zoe rummaged inside her bag and checked her own mobile. She looked again at Kate's text from the day before: *Meeting Mrs M tomorrow morn in Edinburgh.*

Did Mather still not know about this? In the circumstances, he needed to be told but she dreaded being the one to do this. There was no way Kate's rendezvous earlier today with his wife—however badly it had gone—could be connected with Tolbyres Cottage being set on fire, but it would come out. Better he learned it from her than from one of his officers.

She waited for Mather to finish his conversation with Sergeant Trent. He seemed angry at one point, his face reddening and his voice raised, although Zoe still couldn't make out what he was saying. Just as she'd decided to return to A&E on her own, he jabbed at the screen then slid the mobile back into his pocket.

He was still flushed when she met him halfway across the room. 'It was definitely arson,' he said. 'And the decree has come down from above that I'm not on the case, due my involvement with the family.'

'I can understand their reasoning.'

'Me too. I'd be the first to say it if anyone else was in a similar position.'

'But there's something I need to show you.' Zoe pulled out her mobile. 'Kate swore me to secrecy, but you have to know now.'

Mather quickly read the text. He didn't say anything but his expression changed to one of confusion.

'I know your wife can't possibly be connected to what's happened tonight, but I thought it better you found out they were meeting before one of your colleagues does.'

He continued to stare at Zoe's mobile. 'Why on earth did Kate do this? I told her I was sorting things out.'

'You've got it all wrong. This wasn't Kate's idea, it was your wife's. She emailed her and suggested they meet up.'

'You're certain of that?'

'Of course I'm sure. Kate had no reason to lie to me.'

'Sorry. I need to call Laura. Then I'll come and find you and Etta.'

Zoe nodded and made her way to the drinks machine on the first floor. As she walked back towards the family room with coffee for herself and Douglas, he met her at the double doors. 'We were wondering what had happened to you,' he said.

'I bumped into Erskine Mather.'

'Why's he still hanging around?'

Thinking it prudent not to respond, Zoe continued to the family room and sat down next to Etta. 'Erskine

Mather's here. Did you know he travelled over in the ambulance with Kate?'

Etta shook her head. 'No one told me that. Do you think she knew he was there?'

'I don't know. He's taking a phone call at the moment and then he's going to join us here, if it's alright with you.'

Douglas harrumphed his opposition but Etta managed a weak smile. 'I'm glad.' Her face fell. 'I nearly said no when Kate texted to ask if the bairns could stay with us for the night. They'd been so boisterous they'd given me a headache. I can't help thinking about what might have happened if I'd made them go home.'

'But you didn't, and they're safe.'

'I suppose we've got their father to thank for that.'

'What do you mean?'

'Didn't Kate tell you? They were with us because Ken was coming round to see her again. Ranald and I worried it would go badly and it did, apparently. I don't know the details but Kate was so upset she decided to have an early night and collect the bairns in the morning.'

'So Ken was at Tolbyres earlier in the evening?'

'Yes.' Etta stared at Zoe. 'You don't think he had anything to do with the fire, do you?'

'That's for the police to decide.'

'I can't imagine him wishing Kate any serious harm.'

Douglas leaned forward to join the conversation. 'I'd hoped we'd seen the last of him. Kate's better off without him and so are her children.'

'Nothing ever stays the same, Douglas,' Etta said.

Their conversation petered out. Zoe occasionally glanced at her mobile to keep track of the time and Etta sat bolt upright beside her, while Douglas slumped and fidgeted. He continually received texts and relayed messages of support to his mother from friends and family keen to help despite the late hour.

At around one in the morning, Mather arrived, accompanied by Trent. The presence of his sergeant, even though only one of them was officially investigating the fire at Kate's home, appeared to have restored his usual air of being in command, despite the state of his clothes.

'Hello, Etta. Have you heard yet how Kate is?'

Etta scrambled to her feet, although this didn't nearly bring her up to Mather's height. 'No. They won't even tell Zoe. Can you find out for us?'

'Better they spend time tending to her than talking to us, I think. But Sergeant Trent is here in an official capacity, so that may open some doors.'

Always able to interpret the most oblique of his boss's instructions, Trent left the room. Etta sat back down, making room for Mather to sit next to her, and Zoe listened to him tell her about the treatment Kate had received in the ambulance. She hadn't realised she was dozing until her mobile startled her by announcing an incoming text. To her surprise, Mather had gone.

The message was from her father. *Helen's died. I know you won't get this till morning but I needed to tell you. Will call when I can. A*

She muttered, 'Oh no,' under her breath, forgetting Etta had exceptionally good hearing for someone of her age.

'What's wrong, Zoe?'

'A friend's wife has passed away.'

'How sad. Was she young?'

'Only sixty. She had breast cancer.'

'Are they close friends?'

'Not really.'

'He must have wanted very badly to tell you, texting this late.'

'I don't suppose he'll be getting much sleep tonight. It probably helps, having something to do.'

'You'll know better than me, having lost your husband.'

Zoe bit her lip, unsure what to say. 'Has Kate told you about that?'

'No. I thought you'd come to it when you felt ready.'

'Now's hardly the time though.'

Etta covered Zoe's hand with one of her own and looked about to speak, when the door opened. Expecting to see Mather or Trent again, Zoe was surprised when a man wearing a navy blue tunic entered. His thick dark hair was cut in a boyish style and he looked familiar.

'You're Kate Mackenzie's family?' he asked.

Etta jumped to her feet. 'I'm her mother, this is her brother and her friend Zoe.'

'I'm Jacques Kerr, the A&E consultant. I've been looking after Kate since the paramedics brought her in.'

Zoe remembered him now, from her own visit to A&E after the car crash last winter.

'Is she going to be alright?' Douglas demanded.

The consultant's face remained impassive, the look Zoe tried to maintain when giving out bad news. Her heart sank.

TWENTY-FIVE

'Thankfully, the fire didn't reach Kate so she's suffered no burns,' Jacques Kerr said. 'But she inhaled a lot of smoke and was having difficulty breathing by the time the ambulance got here, so I've had to put in a surgical airway. She's now on a ventilator to get as much oxygen into her lungs as possible.'

Etta clutched at Zoe's arm as if to stop herself from collapsing. 'Is she awake? She'll be so frightened. You do know she's deaf, that she lip-reads, don't you?'

'The paramedics told us that as soon as they brought her in. She's unconscious at present because we're keeping her sedated. When the blood tests and chest X-rays indicate an improvement in her condition, we can lighten the sedation and she'll gradually wake up.'

'Has she been moved to Intensive Care?' Zoe asked.

'She will be shortly, but I thought you might all like to see her before then.'

'We can see her?' Etta said.

'Of course. I'll take you now.'

They followed the consultant out of the family room, Etta leaning heavily on her son's arm and Zoe bringing up the rear. Just before they entered the area on the other side of the door marked 'Resuscitation' through which Zoe had been wheeled several months earlier,

Jacques Kerr stopped and turned to them. 'She's connected to tubes and drips but Kate's still there underneath it all.'

Etta cried out in dismay when she saw Kate, rushed to her side and lifted her hand, taking care not to dislodge the drip running into it. Douglas hung back, staring at his sister on the trolley, her pink nightie all but covered by a pale blue blanket. Alongside the usual hospital smells, Zoe caught the tang of smoke. Despite years of seeing patients in similar situations, she was shocked by the sight of someone she cared for like this.

Monitors beeped, the ventilator hissed, no one spoke. They stood like that for what felt like minutes to Zoe but was probably only a few seconds, until a nurse broke up the tableau by bringing in a chair for Etta. The consultant then explained to Etta and Douglas what each of the machines surrounding Kate was doing for her. They nodded silently at this, until he pointed out the cricothyroidotomy.

Douglas, still standing well away from his sister, flinched. 'You had to cut a hole in her neck?'

'We would have intubated through her mouth but her airway had swollen badly from the heat and smoke.'

'But it'll come out soon?'

'When Kate's able to breathe unaided, yes.'

Etta stroked her daughter's face. Without looking up she said, 'Zoe, is there anything else we should know?'

'Only that Kate's in the best possible hands,' Zoe said. 'They have one-to-one nursing in the ICU, so she'll get all the attention she needs.'

'She'll be so frightened if she wakes up and no one's there to explain what's happened. Can't I stay with her?'

Zoe looked to the consultant for help.

'Once she's settled in the ICU someone will find you and take you up to see her,' he said.

It looked for a moment as if Etta was going to refuse to leave her daughter's side, but she slowly rose, bent over to kiss Kate's forehead and allowed Douglas to lead her away. Zoe hung back to speak to the consultant.

'You're a GP, aren't you?' he said. 'I remember seeing you here a few months ago.'

'Yes. I crashed my car. Nothing broken, thank goodness.'

'I do my best not to blind relatives with science, but from the look on your face, you want to know more than I told them.' He smiled. 'Go ahead and ask.'

'I've spoken to Kate's friend who travelled over in the ambulance with her. It sounds as though she stopped breathing before she got here and . . .'

'And you're worried about possible long term effects?'

Zoe nodded.

He looked her square in the face. 'I can't give you any guarantees. We'll only know when she wakes up.'

On her way to rejoin Etta and Douglas, Zoe found herself clinging to the fact he'd said 'when', not 'if'.

Nearly two hours passed before a nurse in a wine-coloured tunic came to take them up to Intensive Care, during which time Douglas had tried to persuade Zoe to go home and Richard had arrived, reporting that all three of Kate's children were asleep but Ranald was refusing to go to bed until he'd spoken to his wife.

In the lift, Etta again voiced her anxiety that Kate's deafness might be overlooked.

'We won't forget, I promise,' the nurse said.

Kate had been redressed in a hospital gown, her smoke-ridden pink nightie doubtless now consigned to a bin. She slept peacefully surrounded by even more equipment than she had been in A&E. Her mother sat down next to the bed and whispered, 'I'll not be far away, sweetheart. The doctors and nurses are going to care for you and I'll be back soon.' Looking up at Zoe, she said in her normal voice, 'Silly, aren't I? She couldn't hear me even if she was awake.'

Zoe left Borders General Hospital a little after four-thirty in the morning, refusing the offer of a lift back home from Douglas, who was returning to Tolbyres Farm while Richard took their mother to her friend in Melrose. The last time Zoe had stayed up all night was when she'd been working in a hospital herself several years before, but rather than fatigue, she felt charged with nervous energy as she walked to the Jeep. It was getting light. In fact, although she'd moved just a few hundred miles north, the Scottish skies barely seemed to go dark at present. Already vehicles were coming and going in the car park, but the roads were empty once she had driven a few miles. Now heading northeast, she had to grope for her sunglasses as the low sun blazed in through the windscreen.

Try as she might to dispel them, thoughts of Kate constantly bombarded her. Even forcing herself to reflect on the joy of seeing her baby in just a few weeks only served to remind her of their recent conversation when Kate confessed to wanting another child. And now Kate's own life hung in the balance, all her hopes and plans — and those of her family — put on hold.

A wave of exhaustion swept over Zoe. Her legs and arms felt weak and tears pricked at her eyes. She considered pulling over into a layby for a rest, but with Westerlea only a few miles away, she took a deep breath and drove on.

With no joyful greeting from Mac, the cottage felt empty and unwelcoming. Having consumed nothing more than a packet of crisps and several vending-machine coffees since her meal with Patrick, which felt like days ago, she made herself a piece of toast and a mug of tea then sat down with her mobile. She reread Andrew's brief text but put off responding until later. She did, though, text Patrick to tell him she was home and planned to sleep for a couple of hours, and to ask when she should collect Mac. Her mobile rang almost as soon as she'd hit send. It was still only five-thirty in the morning.

'What news on Kate?' Patrick asked.

'She's in Intensive Care, sedated and on a ventilator.'

'What do the doctors say?'

'They're being noncommittal.'

'How's the family coping?'

'They're pulling together, as they always do. Etta's refusing to go far, though no one's allowed to stay with Kate all the time, so Douglas has taken her round to a friend who lives in Melrose to be close at hand. The other brothers are on their way. I don't think they want Ranald to see her like that because he's so fragile himself, but they can't keep him away forever.'

'And what about you, Zoe, how are you?'

'I'll be fine. I'm just tired. And worried, of course.'

'Well, you needn't fret about Mac. He's okay here, more than okay, in fact. Why do you think I'm up so early? He and Peggy were chasing each other round the house at five o'clock.'

'Don't you have to work today?'

'I might have to pop out briefly but the dogs can be left alone for a couple of hours. Unless you're missing Mac so much you want me to bring him home?'

'I'm going back to the hospital later so it would suit me if he stayed with you for a bit longer, if you don't mind.'

'Do what you need to do. Just keep me informed, okay?'

'Thanks.'

She ended the call, wondered briefly what Patrick had been going to tell her last night just before the fire engine appeared behind them, then went to bed. When she lay down, her mind filled with images of Kate in her bed in the ICU and Etta sitting on a chair beside her.

Although she would never tell anyone this, Zoe feared the worst for her friend. Heart racing, she reached over for her book but she'd hardly read one page when her eyes started to close. The next thing she knew, the house phone was ringing and her bedside clock read eleven-fifteen.

She didn't rush to answer the phone but couldn't get back to sleep either, so a few minutes later she got up, put on the kettle and dialled 1471 to find out who had called. It was Paul's home number.

'Thank you for ringing back, my dear. You must have thought I was trying to avoid you. I wanted to put you in the picture about how things stand with Walter.'

He hadn't heard about Kate's fire. Zoe tried to stay calm but was embarrassed to end up almost crying down the phone as she told Paul of the previous night's events. When she finished speaking, he took so long to reply that she wondered if he was still there.

'How dreadful,' he said eventually. 'It puts my troubles with Walter into perspective. How is she this morning?'

'I haven't phoned the hospital yet and I'm not sure if they'd tell me anyway. I'll text Douglas in a minute.'

'Don't let me stop you from doing that. Would you like me to call you again later?'

'Thank you but a few more minutes won't make any difference. Have you managed to persuade Walter to stop his ridiculous vendetta against me? I really thought we'd sorted this out months ago.'

'Sadly not. If anything, he's even more entrenched. I'm kicking myself for not reading our agreement more carefully before I signed it.'

'So what are you going to do? Maybe I should step aside for this other doctor.'

'Certainly not! I've realised how much latitude I've given Walter over the years. He's not going to get away with being so self-centred any longer. I'm seeing my solicitor on Monday.'

Surprised to hear such fighting talk coming from Paul, Zoe wondered if the same influence which had caused him to shave off his beard and discard his tartan ties was now giving him the courage to stand up to his partner. 'Maybe then Walter will back down. He won't like spending money on his own legal advice.'

'That's what I'm hoping. Anyway, my dear, I'll get off the line and let you find out how your friend is. Do keep me in the picture, won't you?'

After saying goodbye and putting down the house phone, Zoe picked up her mobile again. Douglas had given her his number just before she left the hospital. She struggled with what to say, eventually settling for: *Any news? Z.*

The response came back almost immediately: *No change. Am back with Mum in Melrose, waiting to go in to see K.*

Do you want me to come over?

Would you bring Dad? He's threatening to drive himself.

Of course.

Thanks. Will call and tell him. No rush.

Seeing no point in hanging around, Zoe had showered and was ready to leave before a half-hour had passed, having also texted a brief, sympathetic response to her father's news. Despite keeping her windows up, she could smell smoke way before she took the turning down to Tolbyres Farm. She averted her eyes as she drove past Kate's ruined home and minutes later was walking down the side of the farmhouse.

A small figure ran up and threw arms around her waist. 'Take me to see Mummy too, Zoe. Pleeease.'

She stroked Mhairi's hair and said in a soft voice, 'I can't, sweetheart. I'm sorry.' Not knowing how much the children had been told, she held back from saying anything else.

197

Taking the little girl's hand, she went into the house and through to the kitchen. The atmosphere was quite the opposite of the usual hubbub: subdued and with no clamour of voices today. Auntie Joan had taken the place of her sister, transferring homemade biscuits from a tin to a dinner-plate set down next to a huge pot of coffee. Eva sat with Hazel, watching intently as baby Hugo gorged himself on milk from a bottle. There was no sign of Frankie.

Several men, most of whose faces were familiar although Zoe couldn't put names to them all, crowded round Kate's father at one end of the Mackenzies' oversized dining table. They spoke in hushed voices.

Mhairi dragged Zoe towards her grandfather. 'Granddad, Zoe's here. There's plenty of room in her car for me to come to the hospital too.'

Ranald Mackenzie shook his head. 'Auntie Charlotte's taking you all to play with your cousins, remember?'

At the sound of his wife's name, Richard looked over and nodded a sombre greeting to Zoe, who responded in kind. 'She'll be here soon,' he told Mhairi. 'Why don't you go and find your brother, make sure he's ready.'

'Can't. He's gone to see his chickens.'

Dod Affleck swore under his breath, jumped up from his seat and headed for the door.

'He was told not to,' Ranald said.

'But they can't stay in all day, they'll be too hot,' Mhairi said indignantly.

'Would you like a coffee, Zoe?' Auntie Joan asked.

'Thanks, but I'm not sure I've got time,' Zoe said, glancing at Kate's father.

'He was agitating to leave ten minutes ago but now he's sat down again you might have a bit of a wait.'

Zoe accepted the coffee but turned down a biscuit. As she took her first sip, Auntie Joan said, 'I've put a wee bag of clothes together for Etta. Would you take them over for her? I know Eleanor will be looking after her as best she can, but she can't be expected to clothe her as well.'

'Of course I will. Is anyone over there with her now?'

'Douglas came back briefly for a shower just after six, while Richard kept their mother company. Now they've swapped places again. Douglas —'

Auntie Joan broke off at the sound of a commotion just outside the kitchen. Everyone in the room turned towards the door as Ken stormed in, Dod following him with a pinched expression on his face.

'Did no one think to tell me what had happened?' Ken shouted. 'I come to visit my children and find my son standing alone outside his home which has burnt to the ground.'

Richard rose from his chair. 'We would have if we'd known how to get in touch with you. And thanks for your concern about my sister. She's in a coma in intensive care and we don't know when she'll wake up.'

'All the more reason you should be looking after the children. There's enough of you to do that. Yet when you eventually realise Frankie's missing, you send a farmhand after him. Jeez.'

The boy appeared at the doorway, his eyes red as if he'd been crying.

'I think you'll find Dod knows Frankie a hell of a lot better than you do,' Richard said.

Ken looked at Eva then Mhairi. 'Come and say hello to your daddy, girls.'

With no enthusiasm, his daughters approached and he threw his arms around them. 'You'll be all right now I'm here to look after you.'

Mhairi looked up at him. 'Can we still go to play at Auntie Charlotte's? They've got a new puppy.'

In the silence which followed, Ranald Mackenzie slowly rose from his seat and walked over to Zoe. 'I think I'd like to go and see my daughter now.'

Zoe nodded, linked her arm through his and escorted him to the Jeep.

TWENTY-SIX

Zoe and Ranald Mackenzie had travelled several miles before either of them spoke.

'How does Kate look?' Ranald asked, his voice wavering. 'The boys won't tell me anything except that she's asleep.'

'Which of course she is.' While wanting to minimise his distress, Zoe also thought he needed to know the truth. 'But she has a tube in her throat to help her breathe and she's connected to various drips and monitors. The equipment can look and sound scary, which is why it's best the children are kept away at the moment.'

'My family are treating me like a child. They think I'm so old and doddery that I can't cope with all this. What I can't cope with is the idea of my only daughter dying before I get to see her.'

Zoe had no idea how to respond.

Her passenger shifted in his seat to look at her. 'You youngsters don't like to even think about death, let alone discuss it. Maybe you're different, Zoe, being a doctor and having lost your husband. But I'm eighty-one. I've lived longer than two of my brothers and many friends, and I've learnt there are far worse things than dying. Can you imagine Kate wanting to be kept alive if she can't lead a normal life afterwards?'

Keeping her eyes on the road, Zoe said, 'No, I can't.'

'She nearly died when she had meningitis and lost her hearing. Did she tell you that?'

'No. We've only ever discussed her determination not to be defined by her disability, not what caused it. Though I know, of course.'

'That's Kate for you. She refused point blank to learn sign language, said she wanted to be able to communicate with everyone. We had to respect her wishes, although she found lip-reading very difficult at first.'

'Which is hard to believe, seeing how good she is at it.'

'She's always been determined. That's what'll get her through this now, if anything can.'

Ranald became lost in thought again, while Zoe concentrated on driving. As they passed the turning to the crematorium, her mobile told her a text had come in, but although anxious to see who it was from, she drove on.

'Don't you want to stop and see who that was?' Ranald asked.

'No, I'm sure they can wait another ten minutes.'

'Even Richard's youngest has a mobile.' His head-shaking led Zoe to assume he disapproved, but then he said, 'I wish there'd been mobiles when Kate was a teenager. It would've been much easier for her to stay in touch with her friends. And us.'

He sounded so forlorn, Zoe searched for a suitable response. To her surprise, she found herself saying, 'I met an old friend of yours recently. Andrew Balfour.'

Her passenger's face was blank for a moment then he said, 'The agricultural engineer? Used to live in Kelso?'

'That's right. He's retired to Dumfries and Galloway now.'

'I remember having some enjoyable sessions in the beer tent at the Kelso Show with him. Quite popular with the ladies, was Andy.'

'Oh.'

'Sorry. Ignore this old man's ramblings. '

'I'm surprised, that's all, though I don't know him well.'

'How did you two meet?'

Zoe was searching for an answer which wasn't an outright lie when she saw the sign for the hospital. 'Here we are,' she said, indicating left.

A few minutes later, they walked in silence towards the main hospital building, Zoe making a conscious effort to slow her pace so Ranald could keep up with her. She scanned the cafe as they passed through it and saw two men huddled at the far end with their backs to her: Erskine Mather and Sergeant Trent.

Kate's father hadn't noticed them and Zoe was undecided what to do. She wanted to catch up with the policemen but she also knew the relationship between Mather and Ranald Mackenzie was cool at best. It would be best to get Ranald up to the ICU and come back down alone, although by then they may be gone.

Her quandary was solved by the men getting up to leave and Trent looking over and spotting her. He came straight across to them, although Mather uncharacteristically hung back. He wore cleaner clothes than the last time Zoe saw him, but the red eyes staring out from his pallid face suggested he'd still got hardly any sleep.

Zoe introduced Ranald to Trent.

'I'm part of the team trying to find out who set fire to your daughter's house,' Trent said. 'I'll not delay your visit, but perhaps I could come and speak to you at Tolbyres Farm later this afternoon?'

'You would be very welcome and of course we'll do everything we can to help your investigation.' Ranald moved off, dipping his head slightly in Mather's direction. The policeman responded with the same gesture.

'I could do with talking to you as well, Doctor Moreland,' Trent said.

'Are you staying here for a while?' Zoe asked.

'I can, if you'd like me to.'

'In which case I'll see Kate's father up to the ICU then come straight back down.'

Zoe caught up with Ranald and they took the lift to the hospital's second floor. Douglas was standing outside the ICU, vigorously tapping a text into his phone. He embraced Zoe and briefly gripped his father's upper arms, the closest she'd ever seen the Mackenzies come to a man hug.

'How is she?' Ranald asked.

'Still no change. Mum's choosing to see that as positive but I'm not so sure.' Douglas looking searchingly at Zoe, as though she could settle who was right. She was saved from having to respond by Ranald asking, 'Can't we go in?'

Etta sat in the same position as when Zoe had last seen her, holding one of Kate's hands between both of her own. When her husband entered the room, she rose to give him a peck on the cheek then motioned to him to take her seat. Instead of sitting, Ranald stood staring down at his daughter. As if aware of his gaze, Kate suddenly got agitated, moving her limbs and rolling her head from side to side.

'Is she in pain?' he asked.

The nurse standing on the other side of Kate's bed shook his head. 'No, she's sedated, she can't feel a thing. She's just a bit restless.'

Ranald sat down; Etta smiled at Zoe and moved to stand beside her husband.

A few minutes later, Zoe slipped out of Kate's room and headed back downstairs. She didn't expect to be away long. After all, she knew nothing about who could have set Tolbyres Cottage on fire.

Sergeant Trent looked sweaty and tired, the can of Diet Coke and empty Galaxy wrapper on the table in front of him suggesting he'd gone in search of a pick-me-up while he waited for her to return. He offered to fetch her a drink but she shook her head. 'Mather's gone home?' she asked.

'I hope so. He went back earlier for a nap and to change his clothes but wasn't gone long.'

'Has he been able to see Kate?'

'He knows one of the ICU doctors, so they let him in for half an hour before the family got here. He didn't think her menfolk would welcome his presence.'

'Kate's the baby of the family. The boys and her father are very protective of her. What your boss doesn't know is how hostile they'd be towards her ex-husband if he turned up.'

'Is he likely to? I need to speak with him as well.'

'Ken made an unwelcome appearance at Tolbyres Farm just as we were leaving. I doubt he'll still be there but he won't go far. If he genuinely wants to get to know his children again, this is the ideal opportunity.'

'Have Mr Simons and Ms Mackenzie —'

'Please call her Kate, Sergeant. Ms Mackenzie sounds too formal. Like . . . like she's dead.'

'I'm sorry. Have he and Kate remained on good terms since they parted? I believe Mr Simons lives out of the area and rarely visits.'

'I'd be lying if I said Kate harbours any affection for him. She was happy he stayed away and now he's moving to Northumberland and demanding time with the children, she's turned to her solicitor for help. Not that he could possibly have tried to kill her because of this.'

Trent made no response. He must hear such assertions all the time, many of them destined to be proven misguided. She wondered why she'd even said it and tried to compensate by asking, 'Is there anything else I can help you with, Sergeant?'

'The DCI told me about your text from Kate saying she was going to Edinburgh to meet his wife. Mrs Mather says they parted on good terms, but apart from you, no one even knew about their arrangement, let alone can tell me what happened.'

'No one can think she's involved in the fire, surely?'

'It's only on the telly that the police choose one suspect and go all out to prove their case against them. In real life we have to pursue every line of enquiry.'

'It must be hard for your boss, not being able to take part in the investigation.'

'Aye, though he's still supposed to be working alongside the Major Investigation Team trying to find out what happened to the boy who was fished out of the Tweed. I've been taken off that and put on the Tolbyres arson. Nasty business, arson. Setting a fire and running away's right cowardly, in my opinion.'

'What can I do to help?'

'Unfortunately, Kate held all her work records on a laptop which was badly damaged in the fire. We've got experts looking to see what, if anything, they can retrieve from its hard drive but seeing as you're a friend, I wondered if you can tell me anything about the people she's currently working for.'

'I know who she's just finished working for, if that's any use.'

'It may be.'

'His name's Simon something.' Zoe closed her eyes, visualising the John Lewis restaurant and Kate's client pushing back his chair and getting up to leave. Still unable to summon up his surname, she shook her head in annoyance. 'Sorry. It'll come to me. But in the meantime, would you like me to give you a description?'

Trent's eyes widened. 'You've seen him? When?'

'Kate introduced us, though I was only briefly in his company. We went shopping in Edinburgh and she had a meeting with him in John Lewis.'

'When exactly was this?'

'A fortnight ago last Wednesday.'

'And what you do remember about him?'

'He's mid-twenties, I'd guess, and built like a rugby player.'

'Big, like?' Trent raised a hand about six inches above his head.

'No, about your height, but with wide shoulders, huge thighs and a nose which looked as if it's been broken at least once. He works at the RBS head office, something in IT.'

'It was definitely RBS?'

'I'm pretty sure. I remember Kate telling me about the complex the bank had built on the outskirts of Edinburgh, how it's bigger and has more shops and restaurants than a lot of Borders towns.'

'Sounds like Gogarburn all right. Did she ever go there to see him?'

'I don't think so. She mostly used email, for obvious reasons. And texts. Have you found her mobile? She kept it with her all the time, to stay in touch with her family.'

'It may be in her bedroom but that's too dangerous to access at present. Not long after the fire crew got her out, part of the floor collapsed.'

Zoe tried to shut her mind to a vision of Kate in bed, sleeping soundly under the Laura Ashley duvet she'd recently bought off eBay for a fraction of its normal price, then plunging through the floor into the room below. Her mouth was dry and she struggled to swallow.

'Sorry, I wasn't thinking,' Trent said, peering anxiously at her.

Zoe massaged the back of her neck, suddenly feeling exhausted. 'This makes no sense, Sergeant. Why on earth would he want to harm Kate? Failing to track down all his relatives is hardly grounds for murder.'

'Is that what she did? Fail, I mean.'

'It's quite complicated, but Kate found proof—not even proof really, just a possibility—that a few generations back on his father's side, one of her client's ancestors hadn't been born to the couple who gave him their name and brought him up. She came up with a hypothesis about this ancestor's real parentage, but before she could do any more work on it, Simon pulled the plug, didn't want her to continue.'

'Did he give a reason?'

'She thought it was probably financial.'

'But he didn't tell her that?'

'People rarely admit they can't afford something, do they?'

Trent sat quietly staring at his notes then asked, 'Any progress with his surname yet?'

Zoe thought again but the more she concentrated, the more elusive it became. 'I'm pretty sure it's also the name of a place. Not very helpful, am I?'

'Scottish? English? Somewhere you've been recently?'

She let out an exasperated sigh. 'It'll probably come to me as soon as you've gone.'

'Text me if it does. And that applies to anything else you remember which could be useful.' Trent stood up. 'If you're returning to the ICU I'll go up with you. The baby unit's on the same floor.'

'Oh God, Sergeant, I forgot to ask how your son is. Please forgive me.'

'Understandable, in the circumstances. He's doing well, thank you, although it'll be a while before we can take him home. My wife spends a lot of time here.'

'What have you called him?'

'Daniel. After my wife's late father.'

'That's nice. I have no idea what I'm going to call mine.'

'It'll be obvious as soon as he or she appears. Until we saw him, Daniel was going to be Frederick after my father.' Trent held Zoe's gaze. 'Look after yourself, Doctor

Moreland. I wouldn't wish what we're going through on anyone.'

They got out of the lift on the second floor and went in opposite directions. A wave of panic surged through Zoe as she entered the ICU and found the Mackenzies standing outside Kate's room, Etta in tears, Ranald leaning heavily on his stick, and Douglas a distance away from them, staring out of the window.

'Oh my God, what's happened?'

TWENTY-SEVEN

Douglas came over from the window. 'An alarm went off and the nurse asked us to leave. She said something about a blocked tube.'

'Oh Zoe, I'm so frightened,' Etta said in a shrill voice.

'It sounds like the tube in Kate's neck which is helping her breathe may have got blocked,' Zoe said, making a conscious effort to keep her tone as light as possible. 'That happens sometimes, but the ventilator sounds an alarm if it does, so the nursing staff know to clear it. I'm sure there's nothing to worry about.'

'I hope you're right,' Douglas said.

Zoe hoped so too.

Douglas returned to window-gazing and Zoe had just persuaded his parents to sit down when a nurse emerged from Kate's room. 'Your daughter's comfortable again now,' she told Etta cheerfully. 'Come away in.'

Zoe caught Douglas's arm as he followed his parents back into Kate's room. 'Auntie Joan gave me some clothes for your mother. They're still in the Jeep. Will I bring them up?'

'No need for you to do that. I'll come down when you go and put them straight into my car. I'm dropping Mum back round at Eleanor's for a few hours and taking Dad home. Thanks for driving him over, by the way.'

'I was happy to help. Has he told you Ken turned up at Tolbyres earlier?'

'Richard texted me while you were on your way here. As soon as you and Dad had left, he made sure Ken got the message he wasn't welcome, though not before the stupid idiot had promised to bring the children to see their mother.'

'I don't think that's a good idea.'

Douglas grimaced. 'Don't worry. It's not going to happen. There is some good news, though.'

'What?'

'While he was out checking on his chickens, Frankie spotted the cat. Bluto's spooked and refusing to be caught at the moment, but at least he's alive.'

Forty minutes later, Zoe's mobile started to ring as she drove home from the hospital for the second time in less than twenty-four hours. Whereas six months ago she would have wrested it out of her bag with one hand in order to answer the call, that sort of risk didn't seem worth taking now, so she let it go to voicemail. She debated whether to travel straight on to pick up Mac from Patrick's house but decided against this. The later she went for him, the more likely Patrick was to have given the dogs an afternoon walk, so she wouldn't have to.

When she reached home, she discovered the call had been from her father. Kicking off her sandals, she collapsed onto the sofa and listened to his message again. No mistake, for the first time ever, he'd asked her to phone him back. This probably wasn't just because he no longer had to hide her existence from his wife. She remembered when Russell died; once the news first got out, she had been inundated with calls from kindly souls—many of whom she hardly knew—offering their condolences, wanting to know when the funeral was going to be held, and asking if they could do anything to help. Death brought compassion from many directions, and the rest of Andrew's family would be unsurprised by his speaking with someone they had never met.

Several unanswered rings forced her to consider whether to leave a message or not, but she was saved from making a decision by Andrew's voice. 'Hello, Zoe. Thanks for calling me back.'

'How are you? And the family?'

'We're coping in our own ways. Nina's baking cakes and making sandwiches for every visitor who appears at our door. Ewan only comes out of his room for meals, but at least he's here, he hasn't disappeared off with his mates again.'

'And you? Are you tending your tomatoes and walking your Border collie?'

'You already know me so well.' Zoe heard genuine pleasure in his voice. 'We braced ourselves for Helen's death for so long but now it's happened, I still can't believe she's dead, even though I've held her body in my arms.'

Struggling to find a response which wouldn't sound trite, Zoe said, 'I looked her up on Amazon. She wrote an amazing amount of books. You must be proud at what she achieved.'

'Her books used to be very popular, although these days young people seem to spend more time playing games on their phones. But her early readers are now passing on her stories to their own children. Only last summer she appeared at a local book festival and the tickets sold out. We hoped she'd be able to go again this year . . .'

Andrew's voice trailed off and Zoe found herself trotting out the phrase everyone used when dealing with the recently bereaved. 'Is there anything I can do?'

'The funeral's probably going to be next Friday. I wish you could attend, but I don't suppose that's a good idea.'

'I can't blend into a crowd at the moment. You'd keep on being asked who the pregnant woman is, and it wouldn't be the best time to break it to them.'

'You're right.'

'Was Helen able to tell you what she wanted to happen? I get the impression she was a very organised lady.'

'She chose everything, down to the hymns and the outfit to be buried in. I can't be doing with a lot of fuss, but her religion was important to her, and the local minister's a friend.'

'In my experience, even if one doesn't have a faith, a farewell of some sort is an important part of the grieving process. Earlier this year I attended an elderly patient's funeral at a natural burial site in a wood. There was no ceremony as such, but it gave comfort to his family and friends.'

'In a wood? I like that idea.'

'It's a beautiful place. They use sheep to keep the grass down, not machinery.'

'Even better.' Andrew sighed. 'Anyway, how are you, Zoe? Is my grandchild still kicking at all hours?'

'We're both fine. Less than six weeks to go now.'

'I'm looking forward to meeting him or her.'

'Me too.'

After a pause, Andrew said, 'I've just seen the news for the first time in days. I hope none of your patients were involved in that awful fire near you.'

He evidently expected her answer to be in the negative, but Zoe couldn't lie. 'I'm afraid the house where it happened belongs to the Mackenzies. And Kate was in it at the time.'

'Dear me. Is she alright?'

'She's in intensive care at Borders General Hospital. You know she's deaf, don't you? She was in bed when the fire started, and didn't wake up. The firemen got her out before the flames reached her, but she's inhaled a lot of smoke and fumes.'

'What a dreadful thing to happen. Was it an accident?'

'No one knows for sure yet.'

'I can't imagine what poor Ranald and his wife are going through. Keep me informed, will you?'

'Of course.'

Their conversation ended shortly afterwards with a promise to meet up as soon as they could. To stop herself from fretting over things she couldn't influence, Zoe turned her attention to her laptop. She hadn't checked for emails in days and hardly needed to now, as more had been trapped by her spam filter than had made their way to her inbox. The genuine ones comprised a couple of promotions from book publishers, notification of reduced fares from a railway company whose line she had never travelled on, and a Google alert. She hesitated before opening the latter, unsure if she wanted to see what had triggered it.

Initially distraught at the online article Frankie Mackenzie had uncovered about her, she had decided the best way of dealing with such occurrences was to stay informed and set up an alert herself. The first two hits had been about another Zoe Moreland who lived in Canada, but today's was definitely about her and the events surrounding the discovery of Ara's body on the side of the River Tweed, again on the ScotlandsNews.Scot website.

Beneath the headline DOES THIS MAN HOLD KEY TO TWEED KILLING? was a photograph, obviously taken with a very long lens, of the slope down to the river she herself had negotiated a few weeks earlier. Walking up it were John Wilkie and Mather, followed by several other men and women, some of them in police uniform.

Bloody hell. Mrs Wilkie was going to be furious.

Zoe read the article under the photograph, shaking her head at every jibe and innuendo.

The investigation into the death of the youth found on the banks of the River Tweed near Paxton in the Scottish Borders has so far proved unsuccessful. A spokesman for Police

Scotland confirmed yesterday that several lines of enquiry are being pursued, yet was unable to reassure the public that the killer among them will be apprehended soon. However, in an unexplained operation, a man was escorted to the body dump site yesterday, where he spent several hours with officers. Although Police Scotland refused to name him, the man is known locally as John Wilkie, aged 40, from Westerlea. Mr Wilkie is the second resident of that village who appears to be involved with the police investigation. On the day the body was discovered, Doctor Zoe Moreland, who gained notoriety last year when she became embroiled in the so-called Body in the Bonfire murder case, was seen on the Border Union Bridge from which it is believed the dead boy was thrown.

That final sentence made Zoe want to hurl her laptop against a wall. Instead, she closed it with a shaking hand and placed it down on the sofa beside her with exaggerated care. Kate had said the website was new, and thus far no one had mentioned seeing the earlier photograph of her on the Chain Bridge, so it obviously didn't get many visitors. She had no reason to make a big deal of this.

She leaned back and closed her eyes, only to be disturbed what felt like a few seconds later by her mobile ringing. She looked at who the caller was before answering and noticed the time. She'd napped for half an hour.

'Are you home now?' Patrick asked.

'Yes, sorry. I should've been over to collect Mac but I fell asleep on the sofa.'

'You still sound drowsy. Sorry for waking you. I mainly wanted to know if there's any news about Kate.'

'When I left the hospital she was still sedated. She won't be brought out of it until the doctors are confident she can breathe on her own, and then it'll take a while. She'll be weaned off the sedative very slowly.'

'But that's definitely going to happen, yes?'

Zoe rubbed at her eyes before answering. They felt gritty. 'I wish I knew for sure, but I don't.'

Patrick swore then remained silent for a while before asking, 'Do you want to stay for a bite to eat when you pick up Mac? I've taken a bolognaise sauce out of the freezer, which I can chuck over some pasta.'

'Thank you but no. I'm going to get a very early night. I'll be over soon.'

'Sure.'

Twenty minutes later, Zoe sat in Patrick's lounge while Mac and Peggy fought for her attention, Mac by rolling on his back to demand a tummy-rub, Peggy by jumping up on the sofa then worming her way onto Zoe's lap. In acknowledgement of Peggy's victory, Mac resigned himself to lying on the floor across his owner's feet.

Patrick appeared with two glasses of sparkling water. 'I've got something to show you,' he said as he put the glasses down on a small coffee table. Worried that he'd found the ScotlandsNews site, Zoe smiled in relief when he picked up a newspaper folded open at an inside page and passed it to her.

The photograph had been touched up to remove the bruises, but there was no hiding that the subject was dead. Zoe's light-headedness came on so suddenly that the glass slid out of her hand, bounced off the sofa and landed on the floor. Mac jumped up as he was sprayed with water.

216

TWENTY-EIGHT

Zoe apologised again to Patrick as he mopped up the mess she'd caused.

'It was my fault. I didn't think seeing his photo would upset you.'

'I wouldn't have expected it to either. After all, I saw his poor body after he'd been pulled out of the Tweed. Have I broken your glass?'

'It's cracked, but don't worry about that. I'm more concerned about you.'

'I'm fine now, really.'

'You look exhausted. Did you get any sleep last night?'

'Not a lot. I'll catch up tonight.' Zoe sat up straight and grabbed a cushion to put behind her back for support. 'Anyway, what does the Scotsman article say? Have they found out who the boy was?'

'No, quite the opposite. The police have released this photo as part of an appeal for help in identifying him. It's gone nationwide and they're consulting with Interpol too, apparently.' Patrick pushed his untouched glass of water towards Zoe and watched solemnly as she carefully lifted it to drink. 'It must be an almost impossible task, solving a murder when all you have to go on is an unidentified body.'

'He's someone's child. Finding out who he is and letting his family know what happened to him feels more important than catching his killer.'

'I'm not sure if I agree with you. Maybe his parents think he's here enjoying a better life than he could have got back home. What good will it do to tell them otherwise?'

'Wouldn't you want to know the truth?'

'I'm not a parent so maybe that disqualifies me from giving an informed opinion. But I think I'd rather live on in blissful ignorance.'

'We'll have to agree to differ,' Zoe said, sliding Peggy — who hadn't stirred when she dropped the glass — onto the seat beside her. 'Thanks for looking after Mac. And for our meal at the Rowan Tree, which feels like weeks ago.'

'Let's do it again, once things have calmed down.'

'Yes, let's.'

Back at Keeper's Cottage, after a supper of buttered toast followed by ice cream, Zoe went to bed and managed almost a full night's sleep, waking at five. As her mind once again flooded with everything she'd dropped off trying not to think about, she suddenly remembered Kate's client's name. Telford. His name was Simon Telford. She sat up, grabbed her mobile and dashed off a text to Sergeant Trent, to which she got an immediate response: *Thank you Doctor*. She hoped she hadn't woken him.

After rising at six and walking Mac at seven-thirty, she looked around for something to keep her busy until it was time to call the Mackenzies and find out how Kate was doing. Maybe today was the day for tackling those boxes in her garage?

Two hours later, dripping with sweat and having filled several more bin bags with clothes, bedding, kitchen utensils and ornaments she no longer had space to display, she went back into the house and called Tolbyres

Farm. Auntie Joan answered but passed her on to Douglas, who had telephoned the ICU first thing.

'The nurse said Sis had a comfortable night and her blood gases have improved. That sounds good but what does it actually mean?'

'As a result of breathing in such a lot of smoke, Kate had too much carbon monoxide in her blood and too little oxygen. It means the treatment to correct this is working. They'll also be regularly checking her lungs too. When it looks like she may be able to breathe on her own, they'll try taking her off the ventilator.' Not wanting to raise his hopes too much, Zoe added, 'She's got a long way to go still, of course.'

'I've just rung Mum. She's staying in Melrose, refuses to come home yet but maybe it's for the best. Eleanor's making sure she eats and sleeps, and she isn't rushing around here trying to look after the rest of us.'

'How's your Dad?'

'Not good. The children aren't the only ones who need to stay away from the hospital until Kate's awake. Robbie and Richard are going over this afternoon and we got no argument from Dad when we suggested he didn't go with them.'

'It sounds like Kate will have plenty of visitors, so I'll stay away too. But let me know if there's any change in her condition, won't you?'

'I'll call you later.' Douglas sounded as if he was about to end the call when he added, 'Zoe, do you know what the police are doing to catch whoever did this?'

'Not exactly. But I know they'll be doing their best.'

'You spoke to that sergeant at the hospital, didn't you?'

'Sergeant Trent, yes. He was asking me if I knew anything about Kate's recent clients. You know they found her computer but it had been damaged in the fire?'

'Yes. And they can't find her mobile either.'

'I know it's hard, Douglas, but we just have to trust them to do their job.'

'Erskine Mather can't be much help. Every time I go to the hospital, he's there too, pretending he's been sitting in the cafe all the time when I'm pretty certain they've let him go in and see Sis.'

'He's not allowed to work on her case. Because of their relationship.'

Douglas muttered something Zoe couldn't catch, then repeated his promise to call her later and rang off. She returned to the garage, but her heart was no longer in the task, as the image of Kate lying in the ICU surrounded by equipment kept forcing its way into her mind. She'd done enough. It was time to lose herself in a good book.

She and Mac had just got back from their afternoon walk when Douglas rang, this time sounding much more upbeat. 'They're going to start reducing Kate's sedation tomorrow,' he said. 'We may be able to talk to her by visiting time, although they've warned us she'll likely drift in and out of consciousness.'

'That's brilliant news,' Zoe said.

'Mum's still worried the doctors and nurses will forget she's deaf and she'll be scared when she wakes up and can't hear what they're saying.'

'I'm sure they're used to dealing with people with hearing difficulties.'

'That's what I said. Mum tried to persuade them to let her stay there all the time but they wouldn't agree.'

'Sometimes a person coming out of sedation can get quite agitated, which relatives find distressing. The staff are doing what's best for you all.'

'You know Mum. We may have grown up and left home but she still wants to look after us.'

'I bet you'll be like that with your children too.'

Douglas gave a short laugh, sounding more like his old self. 'You're probably right. As will you.'

Zoe made a face at this. It was strange enough to think she'd soon have one child. The idea she might go on to have more was unimaginable at present.

They agreed Douglas would phone after visiting his sister the following day. If all went well, Zoe might be able to see Kate herself on Tuesday.

Monday morning brought several cases of sunburn and an outbreak of food poisoning, probably as the result of undercooked burgers at a barbecue, to Zoe's surgery. She also had to deal with patients' curiosity about the Tolbyres fire, although most of the sympathy expressed towards 'the Mackenzie girl' sounded genuine enough. Glad when it was over, she escaped to the kitchen for a coffee, having checked first that Walter remained in his room. Until the partnership situation was resolved, she had no intention of spending any time alone with him.

Margaret joined her shortly afterwards. 'Thank goodness for the school holidays,' she said, ushering Zoe away from the kettle and making their coffee herself. 'We'd be even busier if this wasn't the time Scottish parents take advantage of our schools breaking up before English ones.'

Zoe's puzzlement must have shown on her face because Margaret rushed to add, 'Prices go up as soon as schools south of the Border finish. You'll know all about this in a few years.'

'I suppose I will. Though I can't imagine ever going abroad with a small child. I've been seated next to some on flights before now, wishing I wasn't.'

Margaret frowned. 'Here's me havering on about nothing while you must be so worried about your friend. How is she?'

'Improving, although she's still in Intensive Care.'

'What a terrible thing to happen. My Hector was only saying the other day that all the dry weather will lead to an outbreak of fires, but this wasn't an accident, was it?'

'The police are treating it as arson.'

'Who would do such a wicked thing? From what I hear it was only good fortune her bairns weren't at home too.'

'I have absolutely no idea, Margaret. Her family's devastated, as you can imagine. And mystified.'

'They say her ex-husband is back on the scene. Not that I set any store by rumours, of course.'

'Ken's moving back up from London, but he's got a new family now so I can't see why he'd want to harm Kate. And anyway, he wasn't to know his three children weren't in the house with her.'

'Maybe it was a prank that went wrong.' Margaret didn't sound convinced by this theory and neither was Zoe. She felt relieved when the older woman turned to the subject of babies. Anything was preferable to remembering Kate's blazing house.

After an hour spent doing paperwork, Zoe went home, had a nap, took Mac for a short walk then checked the ScotlandsNews website for anything more about the investigation into the boy's death. She found nothing, and no report on the Tolbyres fire either. Most of the space for Borders news was given over to the Common Riding festivals.

At six-thirty, she imagined Etta Mackenzie resuming her vigil beside Kate's bed in the ICU, and when her mobile rang just before eight, she assumed it was Douglas calling to give her an update on his sister's condition. Trent's name coming up surprised her. What did he want?

'Are you ever off duty, Sergeant?'

'It doesn't feel like it these days, Doctor. Thanks for your text this morning. Very useful it was.'

'Did you find Kate's client?'

'Will you be at the health centre tomorrow morning?'

'No, I'm not working till the afternoon.'

'In which case, may I come and see you at home, say around ten-thirty?'

Zoe paused before answering, giving the policeman an opportunity to say why he wanted to see her, but he waited her out. In the end, she said, 'Of course, anything to help,' and their conversation ended.

Trent arrived so on the dot of ten-thirty on Tuesday that Zoe suspected he'd been sitting in his car up the road, waiting for the right time to pull into her driveway. She watched from the window as he straightened his tie, picked up a jacket and put it back again, and pulled out a slim laptop.

Mac raced outside barking as she opened the door to let the policeman in. Having established he'd prefer a cold drink over a hot one, she led him through the kitchen out onto the patio and invited him to choose a seat while she fetched a jug of water and two glasses.

'They're starting to reduce Kate's sedation today.'

'So the DCI mentioned. That's great news.' Trent reached down for his case. 'I'm here today because I'd like you to look at some photographs for me.'

'Of what?'

He lay his laptop on the table between them, under the shade of the umbrella. 'I need to know if any of these men is the person you described meeting in the John Lewis restaurant and who Kate Mackenzie introduced to you as Simon Telford. If you recognise him, please tell me.'

'Alright.' Zoe stared at the screen as a series of six men appeared in front of a grey background. They looked forward initially, then turned their heads from left to right. None of them was Kate's client.

'He's not there,' Zoe said.

'The procedure is that I have to show you a second time.'

Zoe watched again, then said, 'You can make me look at them all day, Sergeant, but he's not there.'

'So it would surprise you to learn that one of these gentlemen is the Simon Telford who works for RBS at Gogarburn? In fact he's the only Telford they employ in the whole of the UK.'

'You're kidding. Which one?'

Trent pointed at the screen. 'The final one.'

Zoe stared at the laptop, shaking her head. 'Their hair's the same colour and they're both in their twenties, but that's where the similarity ends. I doubt this chap has ever held a rugby ball let alone broken his nose in a game.'

'He also says he's never employed a genealogist to trace his family tree, although he thinks a few generations ago his ancestors may have lived in the Borders.'

'So what do you do now?'

'Naturally, we've asked him a few questions, just to be sure. He's proved he was in London on a training course at the time you met the man claiming to be him in Edinburgh, and I have someone checking that on Friday he really was away visiting his family in Bearsden.'

'Forgive my ignorance, Sergeant, but where's Bearsden?'

'Posh part of Glasgow.'

'This doesn't make sense. Why steal someone's identity just to commission their family tree?'

'Does Kate only work for people who want their own family's ancestors uncovered?'

'I have no idea, though I assume so. It's quite a personal thing, isn't it? And not cheap. He doesn't have a brother, does he?'

'We thought about that and the answer's no. Just a sister.'

'Only a lot of Kate's clients get it done as a gift for someone else in the family, and of course they have to provide a certain amount of information for her to get started, like parents' or grandparents' names and dates of birth. It would help if we could find out what the bogus Simon told Kate when he gave her the job.'

'Unfortunately that information's lost with everything else.'

'Is anyone in the family famous?'

'You think the chap you met could be a journalist trying to dig up some dirt? It's a stretch.'

'A stretch?' Zoe felt her face begin to smart. 'Actually, the idea of someone trying to kill my best friend, a woman without a mean bone in her body, is completely un-bloody-believable!'

Trent jerked back in his chair.

'Sorry.' She brushed a few stray hairs off her face. 'I'm too involved to look at this dispassionately.'

'You have every right to feel that way,' Trent said. 'Which is why I'm reporting to another DCI on this case. You're not the only one whose emotions are running high.'

'At least you're not putting it down to my hormones.'

'Learnt my lesson the other day.'

They exchanged smiles and Trent closed up his laptop.

'So now you have two impossible cases in the Borders,' Zoe said. 'A murder where you can't identify the victim let alone his killers, and an arson attack by a man who isn't who he said he was.'

'I can't remember a victim remaining unidentified for ever. Trouble is, the public expect us to solve cases as quickly as they do on the TV. Real-life policing takes time.'

'It's human nature not to want to wait for anything. I have the same problem with patients who decide a week's course of medication I give them isn't working after two days. And if—'

Trent's mobile started to ring.

Whoever the caller was, the policeman's expression told Zoe he hadn't expected to hear from them. He stood up, said, 'Could I ask you to hold on for a moment?' then shot an apologetic look at Zoe and started to walk down her garden. She busied herself clearing away their glasses, frustrated at not being able to hear even one side of the conversation. Just before ending the call, Trent extended his arm to look at his watch. Whoever the caller was, he'd made an appointment to meet them.

'I'm going to have to go,' Trent said when he returned to the patio.

'Something exciting's happened?'

'Interesting, anyway.'

'But you can't tell me what it is.'

'Sorry, no.' He picked up the laptop. 'But I can tell you this. If the person who just rang me is genuine, one of our impossible cases is starting to look a lot more promising.'

TWENTY-NINE

Margaret waved energetically to Zoe from behind the reception desk. 'Guess what! Doctor Hopkins has taken himself off to Wales again. And he didn't look too pleased about having to go.'

'Wasn't he in this morning?' Zoe asked.

'Yes, but I took a call for him during surgery. The man had a Welsh accent, asked for Walter to ring him back as soon as he could. Not long after I passed on the message he rushed out, hardly taking the time to tell me you'll be covering for him.'

'First I've heard of it.'

Margaret tutted. 'I thought that might be the case. What a way to behave.'

'We won't have to endure him for much longer.'

'Unless his plans have fallen through.'

Zoe put on an exaggerated look of horror, making Margaret chuckle. 'Away with you, Doctor. If anyone saw us they'd think we come to work to have a good time.'

Smiling, Zoe walked along the corridor to her room, where she found a pile of insurance forms Walter must have dumped on her desk before rushing off. She looked up when she heard a light knock on her door a few minutes later.

'Hello, my dear. What news on your friend Kate?' Paul moved across the room and sat down. His cheek bore another small cut.

'They're starting to bring her out of sedation.'

'That's excellent news.'

'Unfortunately, it's not that simple. She stopped breathing in the ambulance, I don't know how long for.'

'Are you worried there may be lasting damage?'

'I'm trying not to think about that possibility.' Zoe took a deep breath. 'Anyway, I hear Walter's gone to Wales again. Do you know why?'

Paul shook his head. 'I got a text from him saying he'd be back by the weekend and you'd cover for him. I assumed he'd spoken to you.'

'I only heard when I got in a few minutes ago. What a charming way to treat his colleagues. I probably shouldn't say this, but I can't wait till he goes for good.'

'Few here will disagree with you, although we need to keep a united front for our patients.'

'I know. What did your solicitor say about challenging the partnership agreement?'

'First of all, he gave me the telling-off I deserved for not consulting him before I signed it, then he warned me it's couched in such ill-defined terms that Walter's reasonable say in who becomes the next partner could mean anything. And finally, he suggested I offer Walter a sum of money to relinquish his influence. This could be a cheaper option than challenging him legally.'

'Are you going to do that?'

'What, reward his underhandedness? I don't think so.'

Paul looked and sounded uncharacteristically fierce; Zoe didn't know how to respond. A year or even only six months ago he would never have stood up to Walter like this. Whoever was encouraging him to adopt a hard line, she'd like to meet her.

Unfortunately, he seemed to take Zoe's silence for disapproval. 'Or am I the one being unreasonable?'

'Far from it. I'm just sorry this situation has arisen because of me. Have you met the doctor Walter wants to take over from him? He might be perfect for the practice.'

'Zoe, my dear, you're the one who's perfect for the practice. And you're already here. This isn't your fault.'

After another hour of paperwork, Zoe went home, gave Mac a short walk and settled down with Patrick's book, eager to stay awake long enough to finish it. Her peace was interrupted by the arrival of two texts. In the first, Andrew confirmed his wife's funeral was to be held on Friday and repeated his wish that Zoe could be there although he knew this was impossible. The second came from Douglas, saying the doctors had started to reduce Kate's sedation but she hadn't woken during the first of their mother's twice-daily visits.

Mac's barks woke her from an unintentional nap in the late afternoon. She thought he was agitating to go out for another walk but snapped awake when she looked blearily out of the front window.

Erskine Mather's faltering steps into the hall, the dark circles under his eyes, and the sweat patches at his armpits told Zoe he wasn't there on official police business. She stared at him in shock, until he said, 'Sorry for just turning up but I didn't know where else to go.'

Zoe's legs threatened to buckle under her. 'Has something happened to Kate?'

'She's no worse, if that's what you mean.'

Zoe briefly closed her eyes. Thank goodness. 'Let's get a drink and sit down outside.'

Conscious of repeating what she'd done that morning with Sergeant Trent, she led Mather through the cottage and out of the French windows. 'Tea, coffee, juice or something stronger?' she asked.

'Coffee's probably best. I've already had a couple of whiskies.'

If she needed proof of Mather's desperation, this was it. With Scotland's alcohol limit for drivers lower than anywhere else in the UK, he'd risked his job coming here. What was going on?

Mather threw himself into one of the garden chairs and stared towards the field while Zoe went back inside, returning a few minutes later with a cafetiere of strong coffee and a jug of milk. She sat down and waited for him to break the silence.

'See this?' he said eventually, pointing at his pink-and-cream striped shirt. 'Kate bought it for me a few weeks ago. I haven't worn it before but I thought it would be nice if it could be one of the first things she saw when she woke up. I went back to the ICU not long after her mother left. She was starting to stir, so I sat holding her hand, ready to shove my ugly mug in front of her as soon as she regained consciousness, to let her read my lips while I explained why she was there.'

'What happened?' Zoe asked gently.

'Her eyes gradually opened, she looked at me, and then all hell broke out. She started to thrash about, tried to pull the drip out of her arm and the tube from her neck. It was like she was having a fit. Alarms went off and they asked me leave. I think they were planning to sedate her again.'

'That's awful, though it's not unusual. She'll have been very frightened, especially as not being able to hear would hinder her working out where she was. She may have been trying to speak, but the tube in her throat would prevent her from even doing that.'

'She didn't seem to recognise me.'

'Coming out of an induced coma can be like waking up from a bad dream, feeling disoriented, unable to tell what's real and what isn't.' Zoe poured out their coffee and put a cup in front of Mather. He ignored it. 'This isn't unusual,' she repeated.

'It's is all my fault,' Mather said.

'You're not suggesting your wife had something to do with setting the fire, are you?'

'No, of course not. But what you don't know is Kate texted me after Ken had left on Friday evening, asking me to go round. Even though I knew she was upset, I said no, because I had too much work on. I've always got too much bloody work on.' He put his head in his hands.

Zoe took a sip of coffee and said nothing. Mac wandered up to her, tail wagging, and leant against her leg with a contented sigh.

After a short time, Mather lifted his head and breathed out noisily through his mouth. 'Sorry for getting emotional.'

'I've seen worse.'

'Yes, I suppose you have.' He lifted his coffee then put it down again, untouched. 'My wife liked Kate, you know. Despite the strange situation.'

'I'm not surprised.'

'She said she asked to meet her because even though our marriage has ended, she wanted to make sure I'd be happy. Does that sound genuine to you?'

'Yes it does.'

'I'm not sure if a man would think like that.'

'Probably not.'

'Has anyone told you what a good listener you are, Zoe?'

'A couple of people, yes.'

'You've made me feel a lot better.'

'I'm pleased you felt able to come to me.'

'I've not got many friends, probably because I've let work consume me. And a man of my age can't keep running to his mother—not that mine's ever home these days, anyway.'

Zoe remembered meeting the tall, elegant Bette Mather last November. 'So she's keeping well?'

'Extremely well, thanks. It's as though surviving the stroke has given her a new lease of life.'

'Some people react like that to serious illness. They realise how precious life is and resolve to make the most of it.'

'Kate'll be like that when she wakes up, won't she?' Mather managed a brief smile. 'Though she already does her best to enjoy life.'

'Which can be exhausting for the rest of us, but I wouldn't want her to change.'

'I'm the one who's going to have to change. I threw away what we had the first time and won't risk doing it again.'

'Are you sure that's what she would want?'

'I'm not saying I'm giving up my job. But Dave Trent manages to combine a successful marriage with police work, so it is possible.' He sighed. 'I'm getting ahead of myself, aren't I? Kate's lying in Intensive Care and I'm talking about getting married.'

'Just make certain she's properly awake before you propose.'

Mather threw back his coffee in one go and rose abruptly from the garden chair. 'Thanks, Zoe.'

'What are you planning to do now?'

'Go home, get changed then head back to the BGH to see Kate *and* her family. I'm going to stop sneaking around when no one else is there.'

'Are you okay to drive?'

'After that coffee, I should be.'

'I make it strong, I know. But are you sure?'

'I'll be fine.'

When they reached the front door, he said, 'I'm glad to see you have a chain and spy-hole now.'

Zoe patted her stomach. 'It's not just me anymore. The new windows are more secure too.'

They embraced awkwardly, then Mather left.

Zoe waited for the inevitable call from Douglas expressing concern about his sister's condition. When it came, she didn't mention Mather's visit but repeated her reassurance about Kate's reaction to coming out of sedation being entirely normal. If only she could feel as confident as she tried to sound.

THIRTY

Wednesday was usually Zoe's day off, but Walter's renewed absence meant she took his morning surgery, much to the surprise of his patients. One middle-aged man refused to confide in her why he was there and left red-faced, but most of the others seemed pleased with the change. According to Margaret, who failed to suppress a smile when delivering the news, Walter's sudden rush back to Wales had been caused by the buyer of his mother's house threatening to pull out at the last moment, putting the purchase of his intended new home in jeopardy too.

'Maybe he'll decide to stay in the Borders after all,' Zoe had said, forcing a laugh.

As soon as the last patient had left her consulting room, Margaret rushed in, too excited even to knock. 'They've arrested someone for setting the Tolbyres fire,' she announced. 'My Hector's just heard it on Radio Borders.'

'Really? They seemed nowhere near finding him when I saw Sergeant Trent yesterday morning.'

Margaret looked down at her mobile. 'Hector says it's a twenty-seven-year-old man. They've not released any other details.'

Was it the bogus Simon Telford? That phone call Trent received while he was with Zoe must have been more useful than he'd let on. Her mobile buzzed from inside her bag, which she'd thrust into its usual place under the desk. She bent down and groaned when she couldn't reach it. Surely the baby hadn't grown that much in the space of one night? She slid her foot through the bag's handle and pulled it closer, while Margaret watched with an amused look on her face but made no comment.

The text was from Douglas: *Have you heard news? They've got arsonist.*

'Your phone will be red hot for a while,' Margaret said. 'I'll leave you to it. See you before you go home.'

As soon as Zoe had replied to Douglas's text, asking how Kate was today, another message came in, from Patrick this time: *News reporting arsonist arrested. Did you know?*

Just heard. Great news.

Douglas phoned instead of texting back. 'Do you know who it is they've arrested? I've left a message for Sergeant Trent but he's not rung me back yet.'

'I'm sure the police will tell you when they know they've got the right person.'

'At least it's not Ken. They've questioned him but he hasn't been arrested.'

'That's a relief. How's Kate?'

'The doctors are going to start reducing her sedation again tomorrow. This time they've agreed Mum can stay with her, so she'll see a familiar face as she's coming to.'

'Excellent. Believe it or not, the fact she has a tube in her throat is good news. It's far more comfortable than being intubated through the mouth and having to wear a mask. The only problem is she won't be able to speak.'

'They warned us about that and showed us the whiteboard she'll be given to write on. It looked far too small to cope with everything Sis'll want to say.'

Once Douglas had rung off, Zoe was struck by a compulsion to get in touch with Sergeant Trent. She knew she mustn't, but felt driven to find out if the man arrested was indeed Kate's mysterious client. Would the police get to the bottom of why he'd set fire to Kate's house? In many ways this was the worst part of the whole affair, trying to imagine how Kate had provoked such hatred in another person that he would try to kill her.

She decided to leave all her non-urgent paperwork until tomorrow, and go home; suddenly an afternoon with no company except Mac seemed inviting. Twenty minutes later, as she stood up to leave, her mobile buzzed again with a text. It was from her father. *Heard news re Mackenzie firesetter. Hope she's recovering. A*

Once back at Keeper's Cottage, Zoe scoured all the news websites she could find, including ScotlandsNews.Scot, in the hope of learning more about the arrest made by Police Scotland in connection with Kate's fire. The only additional information she could glean told her the unnamed man came from the Edinburgh area. Still fighting the urge to call Sergeant Trent, she went out to the garage to distract herself with more clearing out of redundant possessions. Even then, she could think of little else, her mobile sitting on top of a box, goading her.

At last a call came from a constable wanting to make an appointment for Trent to see her. But not until Friday morning.

'I'm surprised you're no' on maternity leave by now, hen,' Thursday morning's final patient said. Mr Griffiths' grin, which suggested he thought he was being helpful, disintegrated as he was overtaken by another coughing fit. He took out a grey handkerchief and spat into it. Zoe felt sure she saw blood.

'I'm going to refer you to a consultant in respiratory medicine at the BGH,' she said firmly. The old man didn't argue. He had become less combative in his recent visits, as if he knew it wasn't pollen he should be worrying about.

He had a point, though. She could no longer kid herself that being this big wasn't exhausting and problematic. Earlier, she'd struggled to reach the far side of a patient's chest when he lay on the couch without her bump leaning up against him, which had embarrassed both of them. However, the situation with Walter made her regular attendance at the health centre vital, and anyway, what would she do if she gave up work now? Keeper's Cottage was nearly ready for its new occupant, and she needed work to keep her mind off other things. Her anxiety about Kate wasn't uppermost in her mind when she had patients to deal with, and she'd almost managed to forget her stalker. There had been no sign of him for more than a fortnight. Perhaps he'd lost interest in her.

As Thursday wore on and she received no word about Kate's condition, Zoe's earlier anxiety returned with a vengeance. Even if Etta hadn't remained with Kate all day, Douglas had usually phoned by now to give her an update. She tried to stay positive but couldn't help remembering one of her patients from years ago who had raced upstairs to save his children when their home caught fire. Rescued by firefighters in an embrace with his two daughters who were already dead, he suffered respiratory failure on the way to the hospital and was later found to be brain-damaged. He died of pneumonia a few months later. Tragedies happen. The Mackenzies had no immunity against them just because they were nice people.

She carried her mobile everywhere she went, but in the end it was the house phone that rang. In her rush to answer it, she almost tripped over the cat.

'Hello, Zoe.'

'Etta, what news?'

'They . . . they think she's going to be alright.' Kate's mother sounded close to tears. 'She started getting agitated again and we feared the worst but then she woke up enough for me to tell her what had happened. She seemed to understand. She can't speak—of course you know that—but she nodded and gave me one of her lovely smiles before going back to sleep.'

Zoe felt like crying with relief too. 'Oh Etta, I'm so glad. Thanks for letting me know.'

'I've come home to tell Ranald the news and spend a night in my own bed. One of the boys will take me back over tomorrow.'

'If no one's told Erskine Mather yet, would you mind if I did?'

'He was there. Last night he came to find me and we had a long talk. What's happened to Kate has made him realise how important she is to him. I've told Ranald we must get used to treating him like a member of this family.'

'I'm pleased,' Zoe said.

'We're not going to take the children over until the air-pipe in Kate's neck has been removed. The girls may be scared by it.'

'Unlike Frankie, who'd be fascinated and want to check the other patients to see if they had them too.'

Etta laughed. 'The minute she's properly awake, I'm sure Kate will want to see you.'

'I'll be over there as soon as you tell me she's ready for visitors.'

Zoe was about to draw the conversation to a close when Etta asked, 'Are you in tomorrow? Joan's been baking non-stop since I went away. We have far too much, so I'll send someone over with a few bits and pieces.'

'Thank you, that would be lovely, but I've got a visitor in the morning and have to work in the afternoon.'

'Tomorrow evening, then. I expect you could do with some more eggs too.'

After she got off the phone, Zoe sat for a while on the patio. She stared up at the darkening sky, letting the news that Kate was going to be alright sink in.

THIRTY-ONE

Unlike his previous visit, Sergeant Trent was late arriving at Keeper's Cottage on Friday morning. Not very late but enough to make Zoe, who was anxious to hear about the man who'd been arrested, look out of her window for him every few minutes. When he eventually arrived, she was surprised to see Constable Geddes get out of the car too.

She let them in. Mac ignored Trent and went straight to the young constable, following him through the house. After declining coffee, Trent held up his briefcase. 'We have another video identification parade for you to look at, Doctor.'

'Am I more likely to recognise someone this time, Sergeant?'

Putting on a stern face, Trent said, 'You know I can't answer that. Come on, Geddes, you're here to learn so why don't you have a go at setting it up?'

The first subject Zoe was shown bore a close resemblance to the man she had been introduced to in John Lewis. His large-featured face suggested a well-built body, and his nose bulged about halfway down, suggesting it had once been broken. The second was less like him, his lips far too thin.

She knew who the third man was as soon as his head and shoulders came into view.

'That's him,' she said, pointing at the laptop's screen.

Geddes glanced at his superior, who nodded. 'Where have you seen this person before?' the constable asked.

'He's the man who I was introduced to by Kate Mackenzie in John Lewis. She believed him to be Simon Telford, and she was researching his family tree.'

Geddes beamed and went to close the laptop. Trent put out a hand. 'Steady on. We must show the witness the rest of the video, remember?'

Zoe shot a sympathetic smile at the young policeman, then watched the screen in silence as she was shown another two men. The entire process was then repeated, and again she said, 'That's the man I believed to be Simon Telford,' as the third image came up.

Trent shut the laptop. 'You can take this back out to the car now,' he told Geddes. 'And check in, make sure there are no messages.'

Geddes looked ready to argue but nodded when Trent gave him a hard stare and left the room, Mac trailing behind him.

'So you've got him?' Zoe said as soon as they were alone.

'Aye. This was just a formality. He's already admitted doing it, and has been charged with fire-raising on the strength of the other evidence against him.'

'Such as?'

'He'd decanted petrol from his car into a washing-up liquid bottle which we found thrown into a hedge not far from the scene. This had his fingerprints on it, and the residue of fuel left inside was analysed and proven to match the petrol which started the fire. Better still, a drip of the same mix of fuel was found on the bottom of a pair of his trousers.'

'Has he said why he did it?'

Trent chewed his lip, evidently debating with himself how much more he should tell her. She gave him a beseeching look. 'Please.'

'Well . . . he's actually named Trevor Kennedy, and it was the real Simon Telford's father who put us onto him. Trevor is also his son.'

Zoe gasped. 'Oh my God. But Simon doesn't know about him?'

'No one does, apparently. The boy's mother had a brief fling with her boss and Trevor was the result. Mr Telford has never publicly acknowledged him and it would appear Trevor's become obsessed with making him do so.'

'He thought getting a family tree would do the trick?'

'It sounds misguided to us but to Trevor it made perfect sense. Simon's mother is English, whereas his own is a Scot. In Trevor's mixed-up mind, a family tree demonstrating he was continuing his father's Celtic heritage would trump Simon being the legitimate but half-English son.'

'No wonder he was so upset when Kate discovered the likelihood that only a few generations back his father's family was English too. But I'll never understand how he believed he was justified in trying to kill Kate because of it.'

'He says he was just angry and hitting out at her property. He never intended to hurt anyone.'

Zoe snorted. 'It was only luck the children weren't there too.'

'He swears he knocked on the door and when there was no reply—'

'—she's deaf, for goodness' sake!'

'You're right, but he claims that when there was no reply, he assumed no one was home.' Seeing the expression on Zoe's face, Trent added, 'It's all bollocks, of course, and he'll be going away for a long time, but that's his story and he's sticking to it. Ironically, in a way his plan's worked, because his father's the one who's paying for his fancy solicitor.'

'Have you told the Mackenzies? They'll feel a lot better if they know the person responsible has actually admitted he did it.'

Trent didn't get a chance to answer Zoe's question because Constable Geddes rushed back into the room. 'I'm sorry, Doctor, but your dog's got out. He's headed off down the road.'

'Oh no,' Zoe said, pushing herself up out of her chair.

'Don't just stand there, son,' Trent said. 'Who left the door open, eh? Get after him.'

'It's not a busy road but cars do tend to speed along it,' Zoe said.

'Don't you worry, we'll bring him back,' Trent said. He followed Geddes out of the house. By the time Zoe had walked the short distance to the road and looked up and down it in both directions, there was no sign of either Mac or his pursuers. He'd only done this once before, but today was a lesson: she'd have to put up a front fence and gate before long, to be sure of keeping both her dog and her child safe.

She heard someone call her name and turned to see Trent coming back towards Keeper's Cottage followed by Geddes, who clung on to Mac's collar. She went to meet them.

'There's a dead badger on the side of the road up there,' Geddes said. 'He must've smelt it.'

'Bad boy,' Zoe scolded, bending towards the dog then recoiling. 'Ugh!'

'Aye, he was rolling on it,' Geddes said. 'They do that.'

Persuading Mac to walk into the shower and stay there while she sprayed him down proved problematic, especially as just water did nothing to remove the stink of dead badger from his coat. In the end, Zoe had to use some of her own shampoo on him. Her dress clung to her stomach by the time she'd rinsed off the final suds, and the parts of her which had managed to stay dry were then drenched when Mac shook himself as soon as she released him.

They both went outside to sit in the sun, though it soon proved too hot and they sought out the shade, Mac under a bush, Zoe under the umbrella. The next time she looked at her mobile it was gone noon. Helen's funeral would be underway now. She wondered how Andrew was bearing up.

Paul had insisted on taking both surgeries that day. 'Things have quietened down now, with people going away on holiday. Rest up while you have the chance.' She had only half-heartedly argued with him, and was pleased to be able to spend the afternoon reading and ordering a few baby basics online.

Early in the evening, Dod Affleck arrived with a box of food from Etta. He also delivered the news that Kate had started to complain about being bored, so Etta had suggested Zoe might like to visit her the next day.

'It must be hard for her to just lie in bed,' Zoe said. 'I'll look out some books to take over.'

'She's never been one to do nothing,' Dod said. 'She was up a stepladder painting her kitchen less than a week after little Mhairi arrived. Mind, that could be something to do with the numpty she married.'

'Has Ken been back since he turned up the day after the fire?'

'Aye, twice, but auld man Mackenzie wasn't going to let him take the bairns off the farm, so he just sat outside wi'em.'

After Dod left, Zoe sorted through Etta's box of goodies. She put the plain sponge straight into the freezer, on top of half a dozen fruit scones. The bag of tablet and plastic box of shortbread went into a cupboard, and the fridge was the only place to keep eggs in the current heat. It wasn't until she cut herself a wedge of chocolate cake with frosted icing and glanced down, expecting to see Mac looking pleadingly up at her, that she realised he wasn't there. She called for him but he didn't come running as usual.

Trying to keep control of her rising panic, she searched all over the house for the dog, then in the garden. The gate was still firmly shut, but a short distance from it she spotted a hole in the ground, disappearing under the wire fence. Mac had found the siren call of the dead badger so irresistible that he'd spent most of the afternoon digging his way out. And she hadn't even noticed.

Still wearing her flip flops, she rushed out to the road. There was no sign of Mac but she knew from this morning which direction he would have gone in. She found him a few minutes later, too busy rolling around on the badger's carcase at the side of the road to realise she was there until she grabbed his collar. A cloud of flies flew up as she pulled the dog from his new plaything, then settled back down on it.

Regretting she'd left through the side gate and hadn't picked up a lead from the hall, she dragged Mac along the road. They were both going to need a second shower.

She heard a car's engine and looked up in time to see the blue Fiesta veer onto the grass verge on her side of the road.

It was heading straight for her.

Zoe didn't react at first. Her brain couldn't accept what she was seeing, that the car wasn't slowing down or changing direction. By the time she grasped the situation, it was close enough for her to recognise the driver. He wore a red hoodie today but the dark glasses were the same.

She couldn't run in her flip flops, and anyway, where would she run to? There were no gateways along this stretch of road.

The Fiesta passed the entrance to Keeper's Cottage. It swerved off the verge back onto the road, but only momentarily. Then it resumed its course, as though aiming for her.

Zoe released her grip on Mac's collar. As she'd hoped, he immediately turned and started to run back towards the dead badger. Towards safety.

She put one hand on her stomach and thrust the other in front of her, fingers splayed, pleading with the driver to stop.

The car kept on coming.

She threw herself backwards into the hedge with as much force as she could muster.

THIRTY-TWO

The car swerved away from Zoe at the last moment.

Jammed into the hedge, too scared to move, to breathe even, she heard a squeal of brakes and felt of rush of air as it passed close by. Then it accelerated away.

Sprawled against the hedge, her body supported by twisted brambles, branches, twigs and stems, she remained immobile for what felt like several minutes. At some point she started to breathe again. And began to feel the scratches, scrapes and stings, not just on her bare arms and legs but through the thin cotton of her dress.

The only means of escape was to twist her body sideways, plunge a hand further into the hedge until it found a slim but firm tree trunk and push against it. The hedge gave her up begrudgingly; she could feel small rivulets of blood coursing down her shoulders and back. But eventually she was free.

She looked down the road and froze.

The Fiesta sat idling just before the first bend.

Was the driver watching, planning to come back for her?

She glanced towards Keeper's Cottage. He'd have to turn round or reverse—either way she should be able to make it back home before he reached her. She'd already lost one flip flop in the hedge, so she kicked off the other one and prepared to run. But before she did, the car started to move forward.

It didn't stop.

Zoe watched until the car was out of sight, then stumbled along the road to Keeper's Cottage, looking back over her shoulder every few seconds. She threw herself inside, slammed the front door shut and leant against it, struggling to bring her breathing under control. Although she hadn't worn them for months, her wellies stood in the hall; she pulled them on, grabbed her keys and Mac's lead, and went out to the Jeep. Shaking so much that she struggled to find reverse gear, she eventually drove out onto the road and headed towards where the dead badger lay. Finding Mac there, once again rolling around on the rotting corpse, was one of the best sights she'd ever seen.

She made the dog sit on an old jacket that had been on the back seat, then drove home, where Mac got his second shower of the day. After towelling him down, she removed her blood-streaked dress, pulled several leaves from her hair and got under the water herself, gasping at what felt like a thousand pins being simultaneously driven into her body. Once the water ran clear, she stepped out of the shower, wrapped herself in a towel and went to sit on the patio. Her hand shook slightly as she raised it to brush her hair.

Had someone just tried to kill her?

THIRTY-THREE

Saturday felt marginally cooler than the norm that summer, making it almost tolerable for Zoe to wear a long-sleeved blouse and her faithful maxi-skirt in the hope of avoiding awkward questions from Kate about the state of her arms and legs. She had slept badly, her scratches and stings smarting and her heart racing as soon as she went to bed, but managed to drop off around two in the morning once she'd resolved to speak with Mather about the Fiesta and its malevolent driver. She hoped her visit to the hospital would coincide with one of his own, because if forced to seek him out, she would probably lose her nerve. Apart from her slight injuries, which proved nothing except she'd fallen out with a hedge, she had no evidence it wasn't all in her mind.

She settled Mac in the kitchen, checked all the doors and windows, then set off for Melrose in the Jeep, wishing for the first time that she drove a smaller, less conspicuous vehicle. The journey was an ordeal. Hyper-alert for any sign of the blue Fiesta, she frequently checked her rear-view mirror, at one point pulling into a layby to allow a suspect car to pass. Its driver was an elderly woman. On arrival at the hospital, she parked as close to the entrance as possible, and jumped back onto the pavement as another small blue car approached, scolding herself when she realised it wasn't even a Fiesta. A young man coming up from behind asked if she was alright and insisted on taking her arm and escorting her into the main building.

She only became aware of how much emotion she was suppressing when tears nearly came as Kate greeted her in a low, hoarse voice with, 'You've got enormous. How many weeks was I unconscious for?'

Zoe forced a laugh and gave her friend a hug, which was complicated by her bump and Kate still being on an intravenous drip. She pulled back and asked, 'When did they take the tube out of your throat?'

'This morning. They're moving me into a normal ward as soon as they can find a bed.'

'You're looking great.'

'Erskine tells me my voice is now deep and sexy.'

'He's been here already, has he?'

'He'll be back later. Do you need to —' Kate started to cough. Zoe passed her some water and waited.

While she caught her breath, Kate pointed at Zoe's hand. As soon as she could speak, she said, 'What happened?'

'I had a fight with the old rose bush by the fence. It won.' Zoe pulled her sleeves down as far as they would go.

'Don't you think it's time to start taking it easy? You've given up work now, haven't you?'

'Things have got complicated. Walter's resigned.'

'There's not many will be sad to hear that, but his timing's crap. He's done it on purpose, hasn't he?'

Trying to ignore a sting on her left shoulder demanding to be scratched, Zoe said, 'Probably. But I'm not here to bore you with my problems. Have they said when you can come home?' Kate didn't answer. Thinking she hadn't spoken clearly enough, Zoe repeated her question.

'I know what you said.' Kate squeezed her eyes shut but a tear trickled down one cheek.

'Oh my God, I'm sorry.' Zoe grabbed Kate's hand and squeezed it. When her friend opened her eyes, she repeated, 'I'm so sorry. I didn't stop to think what a stupid question that was.'

'The loss adjuster went to see the house on Thursday. It's very badly damaged, not just from the smoke and flames but the water they used to put the fire out. We're going to have to pull it down and build a new one. I don't have a home anymore.'

'But you're safe. And so are the children.'

'And Bluto. That's cats for you — they look after themselves. Last thing I remember, he was curled up on the bed beside me.'

'Really? You have no memory of the fire or coming to the hospital?'

'I remember being pissed off with Ken being so stubborn, texting Mum to ask her to keep the bairns, then taking myself upstairs for an early night. Next thing I know, I'm waking up here with tubes coming out of everywhere and Mum leaning over the bed, telling me to stay calm.'

'You must have been scared.'

'I was. They told me I woke up before but made such a fuss I had to be put under again. I can't remember any of it.'

'That often happens.'

'What, me making a fuss?' Kate's attempt at a laugh came out as a low rumble in her throat then another cough. After sipping more water, she lay back on her pillow.

Zoe asked, 'Have the children been over to see you yet?'

'They're coming this evening. And Dad. Frankie's going to be disappointed to have missed seeing me breathe through a tube coming out of my throat. I got Erskine to take a photo for him.'

'Everyone's been terribly worried about you.'

'I know. It's unbelievable someone would put me and my family through all this just to avoid paying a bill.'

'I thought he did it because he was angry at what you'd discovered about his family.'

'There's that too. But I still think it's more likely he didn't want to pay me.'

'At least it sounds as if he he's going to plead guilty so you won't have to go through a trial.' The itch in Zoe's shoulder flared up again and without thinking she slipped a hand inside her blouse to scratch it. 'He must have been convincing to have fooled you.'

'The only thing a bit off about him was the complicated story he told me when I asked for a deposit. He said a friend owed him money so rather than putting it into his own account then paying me out of that, he'd asked him to pay me direct. Should've rung alarm bells, I suppose, but let's face it, as long as a bank transfer happens, who cares whose name's on it?'

'But it was from his own account, presumably?'

'Aye, his real name's . . .' Kate screwed up her face. 'You'd think I'd be able to remember what the man who nearly killed me is called, wouldn't you? Erskine did tell me but it doesn't seem to have sunk in.'

'You've been through a lot. Give it time.'

'As usual, you're right. Anyway, how are you? You seem a bit on edge. Has coming here brought it home to you that you're going to be giving birth in the not too distant future?'

To avoid any further grilling, Zoe agreed this was probably the case. The two women chatted a little more, but Kate spoke increasingly less; Zoe could tell she was tiring. And still no sign of Mather.

'I've brought you a couple of books,' Zoe said, reaching down into her bag.

Kate asked, 'What's happened to your back? You're bleeding.'

Zoe twisted round to look at the shoulder which had been itching and saw blood had soaked through the white cotton of her blouse. 'Just another scratch from the rose,' she said. 'It's nothing.'

'How did it scratch you there? Were you gardening topless?'

'I was wearing a not very sensible dress.'

'Doesn't sound like you.' Kate lifted her water again but continued to look at Zoe over the top of it.

Zoe searched for something to say to fill the silence but was saved by the arrival of Douglas Mackenzie. He greeted her warmly and bent over to kiss his sister.

'Here, have my chair,' Zoe said, rising. 'I must go now.'

'Not on my account, I hope,' Douglas said.

'I've got lots to do at home.' Zoe turned to Kate. 'It's been great to see you looking so well. I'll come back on Monday, if you like.'

'I'll get Mum to phone you with which ward they move me to. And take care of yourself.' Kate gave Zoe a stern look.

Placing the strap of her bag over the opposite shoulder to the one where it usually rode, in an attempt to hide the blood on her blouse, Zoe left the ICU. She took the stairs down, rather than the lift, in the vain hope that she would bump into Mather on his way up. Walking out of the hospital's entrance, she resolved to phone him. Or maybe Sergeant Trent.

THIRTY-FOUR

The summer heat returned with a vengeance on Sunday, bringing with it a humidity which suggested the rain that Scotland's west coast was now enjoying might get as far as the Borders this time. Zoe decided to walk Mac somewhere they were unlikely to encounter people, so she could wear a sleeveless top and get some air on her poor, scratched arms. She also felt safer driving a distance from Keeper's Cottage before going anywhere on foot.

If challenged, she couldn't have explained her reluctance to tell the police about the Fiesta nearly running her over, but she also knew she mustn't put it off any longer. When they got back from their walk, she'd definitely text Mather or Trent. The police could do nothing because she still hadn't managed to memorise more of the car's registration than its first letter, but if anything bad happened to her, at least they'd have some clues as to who they were looking for. With this happy thought, she fastened Mac into his car harness and allowed herself to become distracted by the idea that in a few weeks' time she would be doing almost the same thing with a baby. She'd need a car seat: yet another big-ticket item to research and order.

They took the road east, as though travelling to Berwick-upon-Tweed, but soon went left onto a narrow lane Zoe had passed many times but never driven down. She had no idea if it led to the landmark she was aiming for, but they had plenty of time and a large bottle of water, so it would be interesting to find out. Although their destination quickly came into sight, reaching it seemed to take an age, as the lane zigzagged erratically, following the contours of the fields it served. At one point, she could see Westerlea again. They hadn't travelled far.

After parking the Jeep on the verge to allow other vehicles room to pass, she got out and looked across at the field opposite. When she'd mentioned taking this excursion weeks ago, Kate warned her she might not be able to walk across the field if the grass hadn't yet been cut, but several large stacks of bales told her it had. And at the rear of the field was the building Zoe had come to see.

She stood admiring the stone dovecote which, according to Historic Scotland's website, dated back to the mid-eighteenth century. A cylindrical tower topped with a conical roof, it also had a wooden door which stood partly open. If that wasn't an invitation to explore, what was?

She let Mac run free as they walked across the grass field until he'd twice chased after hares, only returning after she nearly shouted herself hoarse. He wasn't happy to be constrained; the closer they got to the dovecote, the more he tugged on his lead and growled.

'I don't know what's got into you these days,' Zoe said, pulling him up short once again before letting him walk on, as she'd learnt in their dog obedience class. She stopped a few metres away from the dovecote to appreciate the stonework. It looked in far better condition than she would have expected for something built so long ago to stand in a field. Above the bleached wood of the door—which could surely not be original—was what looked like a picture frame made out of carved stone. She wondered if this had once held some sort of plaque, perhaps attesting to who had owned the dovecote or the exact date it was built.

She jerked on Mac's lead but now he refused to move. 'Come on, we're just going to take a quick peek inside.' After being fed a biscuit, the dog reluctantly allowed himself to be led towards the dovecot.

Several pigeons suddenly flew out of the roof, making them both jump. Zoe took a deep breath and dragged Mac the final couple of metres to the door which hung ajar, one of its hinges broken. She squeezed inside.

Temporarily blinded by moving out of bright sunlight into gloom, she heard the snarl before she could see anything.

THIRTY-FIVE

The animal snarled again, took a step towards Zoe, then evidently thought better of leaving its feast unattended and returned to the hare's carcase. Rooted to the spot less than six feet away, Zoe stared at the dog which had chased Mac into the field of rape. As her eyes adjusted to the murky interior of the dovecote, she took in the stringy mixture of drool and blood dripping from its jaw, the scars along its body and the ragged-edged ear.

Mac whined. The other dog raised its head again.

Not much remained of the hare.

Silently telling herself to stay calm, Zoe stepped backwards, all the time watching the dog. As soon as she felt the heat of the sun on her back, she spun round, gathered up Mac's lead and started to run—as well as a heavily pregnant woman can run—back towards the Jeep. As luck had it, the ground was firm and flat, and she'd worn lightweight trainers rather than cumbersome boots today. She allowed herself to glance back once and saw no sign of the dog, but this was almost her undoing. The dip in the ground had been deep enough to trip her up if she hadn't spotted it seconds before she ran into it. With visions of falling down, an ankle broken and goodness knows what harm done to the baby, she slowed her pace.

They had both scrambled into the Jeep and Zoe had locked the doors before she looked again towards the dovecote. The lure of the dead hare had been so great that the dog was only now slinking out into the sunshine, where it raised its head to sniff the air and loped off across the field towards a densely wooded area. She sighed with relief but continued to watch until the dog disappeared among the trees before allowing herself to lean back, heart still thumping, and reach for the bottle of water. Her hand shook as she unscrewed the top. After drinking her fill, she poured some into the plastic bowl which currently lived in the Jeep and Mac lapped it up.

Back at Keeper's Cottage, she couldn't stop thinking about the dog, while at the same time wondering why it had disturbed her so much, given what else was going on in her life. Unable to settle, she fetched the tatty ordnance survey map which had been left in the cottage by an earlier occupant. Several of its folds were torn, so she spread it out carefully on the kitchen table and traced with her finger the route she and Mac had taken that morning. Eventually, she found a small circle which must be the dovecote, enabling her to determine the direction in which the dog had run off. With rising excitement she saw the patch of woodland it had gone into was marked on the map as having a track running through it. And that track led to a sizeable, unnamed building. The dog had to belong to someone, even if they weren't looking after it properly. Could this be where it lived when it wasn't out hunting for food?

Her first thought was to contact one of Kate's brothers, because the Mackenzies had an interest in tracing whoever was allowing their dogs to roam and attack livestock. However, the family was still dealing with the aftermath of the fire, looking after Kate's children and sorting out what was to happen to Tolbyres Cottage. Also, she wasn't entirely sure she wanted to see the situation addressed with a shotgun.

She decided to phone Patrick.

'In my experience, people who keep vicious dogs often turn out to be of a similar nature,' he said. 'Have you considered telling the police?'

'They've got more serious stuff to deal with, like tracking down whoever killed the boy found near the Chain Bridge. What if I'm wrong? I just want to check out the house on the map. The dog may not have even gone there.'

Patrick sighed. 'If I don't come with you, you'll do it anyway, won't you?'

'You didn't see the dog. It looked half-starved. Who knows what it'll attack next. I don't feel happy walking Mac, knowing it's still going about.'

'Okay, you've convinced me. I'll come over after lunch.'

Zoe opened the fridge and saw a block of cheese and the eggs Etta had sent over. 'I can get us a bite to eat, if you like.'

'Thanks, but I need to see someone first. I can be with you by two.'

A few minutes later, Zoe was whisking up some of the eggs to make an omelette when her mobile rang. It was her father. Once they had exchanged greetings, she asked, 'How is everyone after yesterday?'

'Nina's a bit weepy. I don't think she'd truly accepted her mother was gone until now. And Ewan's . . . still being Ewan. He didn't even wait till our guests had all gone before dashing away to his friend's house. Texted me to say he was staying over. He's not back yet.'

'Are you sure his friend isn't a girl? It would explain why he spends so much time there. He *is* sixteen.'

'That hadn't occurred to me, but you could be right.'

'And what about you, Andrew? How are you bearing up?'

'Yesterday was hard but comforting as well, if that makes sense.'

'It does.'

'So many people turned up. Helen's agent and the woman who used to be her editor came together all the way from London.' Andrew's voice still sounded flat, as though he was reporting on matters which didn't concern him, but Zoe recognised this as an attempt to bottle up his own grief, to hide it away like a guilty secret. 'We shared lots of stories about her. I can remember hearing people laugh once we were back at the house and thinking Helen would have so liked to have been there. Silly, really.'

'Not at all.'

'I was actually phoning to see how you were, Zoe. And to ask you an important question.'

'Ask away.'

'I want to tell Nina and Ewan about you once we're all three here together with no one else around. Would you mind?'

'Of course not. But are you sure you don't want to wait a little longer?'

'Why? The last few months have been a terrible strain, and not just because of Helen's illness. I don't like sneaking around, seeing and speaking to you in secret, not being able to tell people I'm soon to be a grandfather.'

'You don't think you'll be adding to your other children's grief?'

'They've just lost their mother. Nothing can be worse than that.'

'It's your choice. I only have to tell Kate and her mum and it'll be all over this side of the Borders, so I'll wait to hear from you before saying anything to them. But promise me one thing.'

'What?' Andrew asked.

'Tell them the absolute truth about when you met Mum, because sooner or later the sequence of events will become clear to them and they'll hate you for lying.'

'That's good advice. Thank you.'

After ending the call, Zoe put her omelette mix into the fridge and cut herself a piece of chocolate cake instead. This time, Mac was at her heels, ready to catch a tiny piece when she threw it to him.

She had just changed into trousers which didn't fasten properly and the lightest long-sleeved tee-shirt she could find, when Patrick arrived. He looked her up and down. 'Are you really going to do this?'

'Oh for goodness' sake. I've got more than a month to go and first babies are always late anyway.'

'Steady on. I wasn't referring to you being pregnant. It's mighty hot out there and you're after going to search for a dangerous dog.'

Zoe put a hand to her brow. 'I'm sorry. I've dragged you into this, so the least I can do is be polite.'

'Apology accepted. Do you want to show me where we're going?'

They went through to the kitchen and she pointed at the map. 'Here's the dovecot—'

'Doocot.'

She nodded. 'Here's the *doocot*, that's the woodland where the dog disappeared, and here's what looks like a house on the other side of the wood.'

'I've driven past the doocot before, but I had no idea there was a house in there. I wonder who owns it?'

'Let's go and find out.'

As they walked into the hall, Patrick said, 'We'll take my car. If we find the dog, I may need something out of the boot.'

They retraced the route Zoe had taken earlier in the day, halting at the same field to plan the next stage of their expedition. 'According to the map,' Patrick said, 'we should be able to get into the woods just past the bend up ahead.'

They found the entrance easily, but it was closed off with a gate.

'Shit.'

Patrick adopted a look of mock horror at Zoe's language, then laughed. 'Don't be downhearted. I've not met a gate yet I couldn't get through.'

He jumped out of his car, crossed to the gate and leaned over the left-hand end of it. Then he pushed it open.

'See?' he said, getting back in the car. 'You give up far too easily.'

Zoe pulled a face at him.

Entering the trees brought a slight relief from the heat of the sun beating down on them. The track meandered and Patrick's car shuddered as it travelled along deep gouges in what would have been mud a few months ago. At one point it forked off to the left but they continued in the direction shown on the map.

'What have you done to your arms?' Patrick asked.

Zoe looked down; she hadn't realised that in the heat she'd pulled up her sleeves. 'Had a fight with a rose bush.'

'Looks like it won. They can be pretty nasty.'

'Careful of the pheasant ahead. You know how silly they are.'

He slowed the car down and they followed the pheasant for a while as it weaved back and forth, unable to decide where it wanted to go. Shortly after it disappeared from sight, they broke out of the wood into brilliant sunshine. The track stretched ahead of them, intersected about a hundred metres away by another gate, then arched round to the right, coming to an end in front of a large house.

They drove up to the gate and Patrick parked on the grass at the side of track. He got out, but unlike last time, returned shortly afterwards, leaving the gate still closed. He leaned into Zoe's window. 'There's a padlocked chain which I could get through with my bolt cutters. Or should we respect the owners' obvious wish for privacy?'

'You carry around bolt cutters in your car?'

'How else would I disentangle a sheep from a piece of barbed wire fence or get a ring out of a bull's swollen nose?'

Zoe put a hand to her ear. 'Listen. If I'm not mistaken, that's a dog barking.'

'It's not coming any closer so it must be tied up,' Patrick said.

The gate bore a black metal letterbox and an engraved wooden sign which had seen better days announcing the house up ahead was called Oakbank. Zoe stuck her fingers into the letterbox. 'Empty. I wonder if that means the owner's at home?'

'There's only one way to find out.' Patrick placed a foot on the gate's lowest rail.

'Sorry, but you'll need to help me.'

He looked along the gate to the wire fence connected to it. 'Might be easier to get you over that.'

'It may be lower than this gate but in case you haven't noticed, it's got barbed wire along the top. Do you want me to leap it, like a hurdler? Or maybe you'll stand on one strand and lift another till me and my bump can squeeze through.'

'Do you think you can climb the gate?'

'I have no doubt I can. It's more a matter of whether I should.'

'Only you can decide that, Zoe.'

'I know. It'll help if you're already on the other side.'

'Guaranteeing you a soft landing if you fall, you mean?'

'I might need you to steady me. It's easy to get wobbly halfway over a gate at the best of times but especially now my centre of gravity has changed somewhat.'

They both climbed the gate without mishap although as Zoe reached the ground on the other side she hoped the still-barking dog would remain tied up. She didn't fancy her chances of scrambling back over in a hurry.

'What will we say if the owners are in?' she asked.

'Let's take a look at the dog first. If it's the one you've seen going about, I'll introduce myself to whoever's at home and explain it's in danger of being shot if they don't keep it under control.'

'And if it's another dog entirely?'

'I'll ask if they've seen one on the loose and apologise for climbing over their gate.'

Zoe stopped in her tracks. 'An apology won't be necessary. Look.' A roofless outbuilding stood on their left, in front of which, straining to be free of the chain it had been tied up with, was the dog she'd seen earlier in the dovecote.

'You recognise it?' Patrick asked.

'That's definitely the one.'

The dog's barking got more frantic as they approached the ramshackle shed it was attached to. Several times it withdrew slightly then ran at them, only to be roughly yanked back by its chain. They stopped well away from its furthest reach but still Zoe stood poised to flee in case it managed to liberate itself.

'Looks like he's been in a fight or two,' Patrick said. He took a step closer. The dog's barking became even more frantic.

Zoe grabbed his arm. 'Careful.'

'I'm trying to get a better view of what that is over there.' He pointed at something on the ground at the base of the shed. 'I think it's another chain.'

'So the dog the Mackenzies shot came from here too.'

'Seems likely, yes. Which makes me even more nervous of meeting whoever lives in this house. One vicious, half-starved dog is bad enough, but what sort of person keeps two?'

'One with something to hide.'

'Are you sure you want to carry on?' Patrick asked. 'We've found the dog and it's being kept in unsuitable conditions, as we suspected. Let's go back and report it to the SSPCA if you don't want to trouble the police. They have more powers than you'd expect.'

Although glad he'd been the one to suggest a retreat, Zoe shook her head. Trying to keep her voice light, she said, 'We can't go back. If they're at home, they must have heard this racket and seen us by now.'

As they walked on, the rough track became a gravel drive. The size and shape of the house reminded Zoe of Tolbyres Farm, with its stone walls and small-paned windows, but unlike the Mackenzies' home, which had seamlessly incorporated its outbuildings into extra living space, an earlier owner here had built a single-storey, flat-roofed extension which would forever look tacked on. The lawn couldn't have seen a mower for at least a year, and the contents of the flowerbeds flopped and trailed across a cracked, concrete path.

Patrick said, 'There's no sign of a vehicle and still no one's come out to see why their dog's barking. This place looks deserted to me, but I suppose you want to knock on the door to be sure.'

At first, the front door seemed unexceptional: stained wood bearing a brass knob and a Yale lock, with a fanlight above. But as they drew close, Patrick whistled under his breath. 'Someone's security conscious. Look at that.' He pointed to the sturdy chrome clasp secured to the doorframe with a large padlock.

Zoe stood back to take in the entire front of the house. 'Not very welcoming is it? As far as I can see, all the curtains are closed, upstairs and downstairs. And if I'm not mistaken, there's newspaper stuck over the fanlight.'

'Maybe it's not lived in at the moment.'

'You're forgetting the dog. Someone's put him back on his chain since our encounter in the dovecote.'

'Doocot. And you're right. But they're obviously not here now.'

A brief movement at one of the upper windows caught Zoe's eye. She blinked, sure she was imagining things, but there it was again, a slight tremor in the curtains, as though someone had opened them a fraction to look out. She returned to Patrick's side and said, 'We're being watched.'

'You've seen someone? Where?'

'The curtain at that window moved.' She pointed.

'Are you sure?'

'I wasn't the first time, but it's happened twice now. There's someone in there.'

They both stared upwards. Just as Zoe convinced herself she really had imagined seeing something, the curtain at another window moved slightly. This time, Patrick saw it too.

'There must be another door at the back,' he said. 'I'll scoot round and see.'

'Good idea,' Zoe said. While he was gone, she pressed her face against the glass of each of the windows on either side of the door, searching for any gaps in their curtains. When this proved unsuccessful, she pulled at the sashes, trying to open them and failing at that too.

When Patrick returned he said, 'It's the same story at the back. Door padlocked and every curtain pulled. Looks like they're doing some major DIY inside, judging by the piles of rubble and broken plasterboard in the garden.'

'Did you try the windows?'

'They're locked too. Are you thinking what I'm thinking?'

Zoe nodded. 'The owners of this house aren't trying to keep unwanted visitors out. They're trying to keep someone in.'

THIRTY-SIX

When Patrick returned to the car without a word, Zoe knew what he'd bring back with him. She smiled her approval as he raised his bolt cutters in salute.

'I've watched enough TV crime shows to know we're about to break the law, even if we were the police,' he said, placing the bolt cutters' blades on either side of the padlock. 'You're a doctor, I'm a vet. Are you sure you want me to do this?'

She looked towards the gate, reassuring herself they had no witnesses. 'There's something not right here. We can't just walk away.'

He brought his arms together. The padlock snapped off but when he grasped the door handle and pulled, it still didn't move.

Zoe groaned. 'We'd make crap burglars. Forgot about the Yale lock, didn't we?'

'Not me.' Patrick pulled out his wallet. 'It's never a good idea to use a credit card for this. They're too easily damaged and what a rigmarole you have to go through to get them replaced.' He produced a piece of plastic slightly larger than a credit card, bent it out of shape and jiggled it around between the door and frame.

'You're not telling me you regularly have to do *this* as part of your job?'

He didn't answer but a minute or so later, he grunted with satisfaction and pushed the door open. 'Normally I'd let a lady go in ahead of me, but these aren't normal circumstances.'

Zoe followed him into a long, narrow hallway, its floor covered in a typical Victorian mosaic of brown, blue and cream tiles. Every door leading off it was shut. They stood silent, listening, but could hear no sound. However, another of their senses was flooded.

Zoe wrinkled her nose. 'That smell reminds me of making house-calls to elderly patients who kept equally elderly cats. And the plug-in air freshener over there isn't up to the task.'

'You smell cat's pee,' Patrick said, grasping the handle of the first door on their left. 'I think it's something else.'

'What?'

'I'm still hoping I'm wrong.'

They cautiously entered the room. It was a small lounge, sparsely furnished with a scruffy sofa, two mismatched chairs and a coffee table. No television, no books or even shelves, no framed photographs. Another air-freshener pumped out a different fragrance to the one in the hall, but the same underlying odour hung in the air, albeit more faintly.

'Not exactly homely,' Zoe said. 'Do you think we're getting this out of proportion? Perhaps an old person is living upstairs, unable to get down to the ground floor, and the high security is to keep them safe.'

'No, I don't think that.' Patrick turned round and fixed her with a serious expression. 'I want you to go back to the car, Zoe. Now.'

'Why? What aren't you telling me?'

'If I'm right, something very serious is happening here.'

'But what?'

'Please, just go back to the car.'

'Climbing over that gate on my own probably represents a greater danger than anything we could find in this house,' she said, striding out of the room towards the far end of the hall.

Footsteps sounded on bare floorboards directly above them.

Zoe jumped. Patrick caught up with her. 'At least let me go first,' he said. She moved aside to let him pass.

As he opened the door at the end of the hall, they were blasted with a much higher dose of the disagreeable smell. Zoe put a hand over her nose. She felt nauseous, like during the early days of her pregnancy. 'Not cats.'

'No,' Patrick said. 'Look.'

They stared into a space which had once been divided into separate rooms but was now open-plan due to the rudimentary removal of several internal walls. Shattered pieces of plasterboard clinging onto jagged-edged bricks hung from the ceiling and electric cables dangled. A dog-legged staircase rose to the floor above, its wooden bannisters missing most of the carved spindles and its carpet showing little of the original colour under ground-in dirt. Over in the far corner, next to what Zoe guessed was the house's back door, a coat-rack of brass hooks mounted on dark wood remained, incongruous and forlornly empty.

The floor, stripped back to concrete, was scattered with a thin layer of dark brown crumbs which got thicker on the right-hand side of the room and culminated in a mound of the same material against one wall. Zoe's uncertainty about what this could be was resolved when she spotted the stacks of empty plant pots. It was compost.

'What the hell's been going on here?' she said.

'It's a cannabis farm,' Patrick replied. 'This must be where they do the potting up. I saw a bundle of plastic compost bags when I tried the back door, but they didn't register at the time.'

'How do you know so much?'

'My boss sent me along to a presentation the police did a few years ago alerting people in the countryside, like landowners and those of us in jobs which take us out and about, to the signs of large-scale cannabis growing. It was more interesting than I expected.'

'So where are the actual plants? I can't believe the smell can linger this much if they've already been taken away.'

Patrick pointed towards the ceiling.

Zoe started to make for the staircase but he called her back. 'We must stay together and get the police here as soon as possible.' He pulled his mobile from his shirt pocket. 'Crap, I've can't get a signal. We need to go outside.'

'But what about the person upstairs? Shouldn't we find out if they're okay?'

'We'll let the police do that. Our priority is to get them here before whoever's responsible for this comes back. Come on.' Patrick grabbed Zoe's arm as if preparing to drag her out of the house if she didn't come willingly, but his apprehension was contagious. She needed no encouragement to move towards the front door as quickly as he did.

As they neared it, they heard the dog barking. Patrick darted into the sparsely-furnished room they'd seen on the way in and Zoe heard him swear before running back into the hall. 'There's a Range Rover at the gate.'

'What can we do?' Zoe's words came out in a shrill voice she hardly recognised.

They both looked at the door, still half open as they'd left it. Whoever was in the Range Rover wouldn't have to travel far up the drive to know the house had been broken into. Patrick rushed over, reached for his bolt cutters which he'd left outside and pulled them in, then shut the door. He slid across an old bolt at the top as well. 'That won't hold them off for long.'

'Let me try to call the police with my mobile. I'm on a different network to you. I may get a signal.'

'Okay. I'll scout around for another way out or somewhere to hide.'

'Be careful. We still don't know who's upstairs.'

Patrick ran back towards the potting area. Zoe's mobile showed a measly single bar but it was enough; with trembling fingers, she started to dial 999, but stopped after the second nine. If she spoke directly with Mather or Trent, wouldn't that produce a quicker response? There would be no having to give her own details and waiting to be transferred to the police. She took a deep breath and called Trent.

He answered on the third ring and sounded relaxed. 'Doctor Moreland, hello. How are you?'

'Sergeant, this isn't a social call. I'm in danger and need urgent help.'

She imagined Trent sitting up straight, grabbing a notepad. 'Where are you?'

'I'm with Patrick Dunin, the vet. We've found a cannabis factory. And the people who own it have come back.'

'Give me the address.'

Zoe's throat constricted. She had no idea where they were.

'Doctor, are you still there? Zoe?'

'The house is called Oakbank but I don't know the address. I can tell you how we got here from Keeper's Cottage. It isn't far.'

She could hear muffled voices, as though Trent had put his hand over his phone and was talking to someone else, then he said, 'Alright, do that.'

Closing her eyes to concentrate, Zoe recalled the map on her kitchen table, her finger tracing the route to the house in the trees. She started to describe how to reach it, then stopped abruptly at the sound of running feet above her, followed by a bump and a shout.

Again, Trent asked, 'Are you still there?'

'Patrick's looking for a way out and I'm worried what's happened to him.' She started moving away from the front door.

'Stay with me, Zoe! Someone'll be there as soon as possible but keep talking to me.'

'I have to see if Patrick's okay.' She arrived at the foot of the stairs, took the phone away from her ear, and listened. At first there was silence, then another shout. Was that Patrick's voice? She heard more hurried footsteps pass overhead, going towards the stairs.

At first, she saw only a pair of legs wearing blue denim taking the stairs two at a time. As they reached the bottom of the first flight and turned the corner, the rest of their owner came into view.

Zoe gasped and stepped back in bewilderment.

She had seen this boy before. Or rather, his dead body. On a large, flat stone by the side of the River Tweed.

THIRTY-SEVEN

On seeing Zoe, the boy came to an abrupt halt halfway down the second flight of stairs. His legs were running so fast that he had to grab hold of the banister to stop.

They stared at each other in silence.

Of course this wasn't the boy who'd been thrown from the Chain Bridge. Although he had the same jet-black hair and wore similar clothes, this one was even younger, twelve at the most. His arms were streaked with grime and his knuckles gleamed white through the dirt as he continued to grip the banister with his left hand. He shook uncontrollably.

'It's okay,' Zoe said, trying to summon a smile to reassure him. 'We're here to help you.'

'I don't think he understands English,' Patrick said from the top of the stairs.

The boy glanced round, his face contorted with fear, then pitched himself down the few remaining stairs. Zoe tried to stop him but he barged past, knocking her mobile out of her hand. The noise it made as it hit the concrete floor was drowned out by banging.

Someone was trying to come in.

The boy skidded to a stop. He looked back at Zoe then at the door, as if trying to decide where the greatest danger lay.

A dull thud suggested the person outside was now throwing their full weight at the door.

'Zoe,' Patrick called. 'Come up here to me. We need to hide.'

'We can't leave the boy on his own.'

'They're expecting to find him. We're the ones in danger.'

'I've called the police. They should be here soon.'

'We can't rely on that.'

Patrick appeared at the bend on the stairs and beckoned to her. She started to climb towards him, picking up speed at another thump on the door. The old bolt could give way at any time.

Damp heat hit her as she neared the first floor, and as she took the final stair, intense light coming from the rooms off the landing made her blink. Patrick opened his mouth to speak but he was interrupted by a noise below them.

'What's that?' Zoe asked.

'They gave up on the front door and simply went round to the back. I've got no idea if there's anywhere to hide up here but we have to keep out of their way until the police arrive. Come on.'

Zoe followed him into the first room on their right and gasped at what she saw. Just like downstairs, several walls had been removed from adjoining rooms to create one huge space where industrial-sized lamps suspended from the ceiling blazed with light which was intensified by curved metal shades and walls lined with reflective plastic. Below the lamps sat row upon row of plants about a metre high, their foliage buffeted by the breeze from electric fans which were scattered around the room. Above all this hung a huge white pipe resembling an oversized tumble-drier hose.

'Don't touch anything. Especially that.' Patrick pointed to a board hanging off the wall into which about twenty power cables were plugged. The cables then snaked around the room, some running along the floor, others looping through the air. 'They've bypassed the electricity meter. This place is a death trap.'

They dashed between the rows of plants, passing a Winnie the Pooh mural, but aside from the clutter of equipment, there was no furniture, no en suite bathroom, nowhere to hide. The noise from the fans and the extractor meant they couldn't hear anyone approaching, so Zoe kept looking back. When she collided with a hanging cable, Patrick took her hand. 'Let's try the rooms on the other side.'

A cursory glance told them the other rooms were a mirror image of where they'd come from, only with smaller plants. Back on the landing, they spotted a door bearing the picture of an old-fashioned bath.

'There's one place which must have a lock,' Zoe said.

Getting inside the bathroom was a struggle; the door would only open a few inches. Watching Patrick squeeze himself through the narrow gap, Zoe doubted she and her bump would fit, but she breathed in and they did. She nearly tripped over the obstruction, a grubby single mattress lying on the floor parallel to the bath. Next to it lay a plate and a plastic knife and fork. The room stank.

'They're making him eat and sleep in here?' she said.

'He's their prisoner, kept to tend to the plants. They don't care about the conditions he works and lives in.' Patrick manoeuvred around Zoe and the mattress to secure the door. Unfortunately, although it still had its lock, the key was nowhere to be seen.

'Get in the bath and sit down,' he instructed. Zoe hesitated, saw the expression on his face and obeyed. This freed up enough space for him to fold the mattress in half and lay it in front of the door. They both looked around for something else to add to this inadequate blockade, but apart from an empty soap dispenser and a filthy hand-towel, the room was empty.

Patrick tried to open the window. It was painted shut.

'What did you do with the bolt cutters?' Zoe asked.

'I put them down while I was trying to persuade the boy to come out onto the landing. Big mistake, eh?'

'The police'll be here soon.' Zoe felt water from one of the taps dripping down her back, which was a good thing, given the oppressive heat in the room. Her mouth felt dry, but she feared turning the tap fully on would attract unwanted attention.

Patrick didn't reply. He leaned against the wall, hands jammed in his armpits. Despite his outward composure, his reluctance to look Zoe in the eye told her the truth. He was scared too.

The moment of reckoning came swiftly but in an unexpected form. Instead of someone trying to knock down the door to reach them, they heard a gentle knock and a quiet 'Hello'. Paradoxically, this was all the more frightening. Zoe put a protective arm across her stomach.

'Hello, you in there.' The voice was deep and heavily accented, probably Eastern European. 'Why don't you come out? We won't hurt you.'

Zoe closed her eyes and wished Trent's men would hurry up and get there. She reached into her pocket for her phone then remembered it lay on the floor downstairs.

The nice-guy act was quickly dropped. 'We have guns.'

Patrick mouthed to Zoe, 'You stay there. Okay?'

She shook her head.

He frowned and patted his stomach.

She frowned back at him, signalling she didn't need reminding her priority had to be the baby.

Patrick pulled at the mattress, stepped round it and opened the door just enough to get out. He closed the door behind him.

'Tell the woman to come out too.'

'What woman?'

'You think I'm stupid?'

The boy must have told his captors who had breached their security. Given his young age and experience in this house, how could he know to trust Patrick and Zoe?

She climbed out of the bath, struggled briefly with the mattress and went out onto the landing.

Instead of two men controlling Patrick by pointing guns at him, she was met by the sight of him pinned up against the wall by one man holding a vicious-looking knife to his throat. She glowered at Patrick's skinny captor, who kept running his tongue round his lips as if trying to reach the silver studs protruding from his cheeks. He stared at her stomach. This would usually make her squirm, but now she sensed her condition could be useful. Surely no criminal, however ruthless, would hurt a pregnant woman?

Cheek-studs jabbed the tip of his knife into Patrick's flesh, producing a small trickle of blood. 'What sort of man brings his pregnant wife to nose around someone else's house?' he said.

Zoe tried not to stare at the crude tattoos which decorated the thumb, every finger and the back of the hand holding the knife, or at the sinews standing out on Patrick's neck as he strained to evade it. 'I'm not his wife,' she said.

'Police, then?'

'No. We came here because of the dog.'

'The dog?'

'The one outside. It chased mine. We were trying to find out who owned it.'

The man's jeering laughter surprised Zoe and scared her even more. 'You British and your animals.'

'I've called the police. They'll be here soon.'

'I don't think so. There's no mobile signal in this fucking place.'

She didn't argue. Forcing herself to adopt a look of defeat wasn't difficult: she wondered if Trent's non-appearance meant she'd got the house name wrong, or maybe that it alone hadn't been enough for the police to trace where she'd been calling from.

Cheek-studs' tongue continued to work round his lips. Zoe could see the predicament he was in and hoped Patrick would take comfort from it as well. Because, despite the knife, he was one man faced with keeping two prisoners under control for an indefinite period of time. His misplaced gloating about the lack of mobile coverage meant he had no way of contacting anyone to get help and judging by his agitation, he was less confident his associates were going to turn up soon than she was about the police.

They were deadlocked.

Unless, of course, he got jittery and decided he had nothing to lose by killing Patrick with one thrust of his blade then dealing with her in the same fashion.

'Come here.'

She hesitated, weighing up not wanting to upset him against her disinclination to move into range of his knife.

A small groan escaped from Patrick as the blade pricked his flesh again. He looked pale, his eyes half-closed.

'I have only to move my knife a little more and your friend is dead.' Cheek-studs flashed a humourless grin at Zoe. 'Unless he faints first, in which case he has only himself to blame.'

She took a step forward.

'Good girl. A little closer.'

Glancing towards the stairs, Zoe thought she saw something move at the doorway to the children's room.

She forced herself to look away and move nearer Cheek-studs. If the police were here, she didn't want to alert him.

If he stretched out his arm now, he could thrust the knife into her baby.

Involuntarily, she moved her hands towards her stomach.

'Arms behind your back.'

She complied without comment, feeling even more vulnerable. What was he planning?

Risking another brief look along the landing, she saw nothing this time. It had been wishful thinking.

'I have a sister who is pregnant,' their captor said. 'She has far longer to go than you, but even now she would do anything—anything!—to protect the child inside her. I truly believe that if given the choice between her own life and her baby's, she would die before seeing it harmed. That is what being a mother is all about, yes?'

Zoe nodded.

'And even if you aren't the baby's father, you don't want to be responsible for its death, do you?'

Patrick, unable to move his head, raised his right hand very slightly.

'Now we've all agreed on this important matter,' Cheek-studs said, looking pleased with himself, 'I'm going to move a little but you will both stay still. Understood?'

Zoe nodded again. Patrick opened his eyes momentarily then shut them. His left leg started to shake with the effort of staying calm while a knife was millimetres away from slicing into his carotid artery.

In a single, swift movement, Cheek-studs reached across Zoe's body and seized her upper arm. Now she realised what he planned to do. With no idea of the relationship between her and Patrick, whether one would be prepared to sacrifice the other to save themselves, he planned to use the baby inside her to ensure complete submission from them both.

Which meant very soon he would transfer his razor-sharp knife from Patrick's neck to her stomach.

She felt dizzy with fear.

Several things happened next.

Cheek-studs lowered the hand holding the knife from Patrick's neck towards Zoe's stomach.

Patrick shouted, 'Zoe, get back!' He propelled himself off the wall he'd been leaning against, kicked out at Cheek-studs' legs, and pushed at the arm holding the knife.

Zoe twisted away from the men. The grip on her arm intensified. She felt herself being pulled down and struggled to stay on her feet. Just when she thought she was going to collapse, Cheek-studs released her. She stumbled backwards, nearly fell through a doorway, and grasped the wooden frame to keep herself upright. All she could hear was panting and grunting.

When she turned around, Patrick was down on one knee, both hands clasped round one of Cheek-studs' wrists, holding it a few inches above the floor and trying to make him drop the knife. His opponent leaned into him, his free arm pressed against Patrick's neck. Each man strained to overcome the other but neither had an advantage.

Zoe ran into one of the growing rooms, searching for something she could use as a weapon. She'd hoped to find Patrick's bolt cutters but they were nowhere to be seen. Despite the removal of several walls, not a single brick or lump of plaster remained, unlike downstairs. A desk-fan would have been ideal but the electric fans here were on stands, making them too unwieldy.

Bending down, she had to half-close her eyes to protect them from the intense light coming from the lamp suspended directly above. The naked bulb also emitted a searing heat, and as she broke off a plant near its base and picked up its pot, a horrific image flashed into her head.

She knew how the dead boy's hands had been so badly burned.

When she got back to the landing, both men were on their knees, the knife seesawing between them as they struggled for control of it. As she approached them, Patrick toppled over. Cheek-studs, sensing victory, jumped on top of him. The knife flashed through the air.

Zoe bellowed, 'Get off him!' and brought the plant pot down on Cheek-studs' head with as much force as she could muster. He grunted, fell onto his side and lay still, legs drawn up, his right arm under him.

Patrick sat up. 'The knife, where's the knife?'

'Are you okay?'

'Yes, but we need to find the knife.'

She pointed over his shoulder to where the knife stuck up from the wooden floor.

Patrick let out the low whistle Zoe now recognised as his response to any surprise or shock. 'That was close. Thank you.'

She leaned over to help him up.

Moments later, Cheek-studs raised himself and slashed at Patrick's leg with something in his right hand.

He had a second knife.

THIRTY-EIGHT

The knife sliced through Patrick's jeans into the back of his thigh. He cried out and fell against Zoe. She struggled to support his weight, wanted to lower him to the floor but saw the knife rise again. Although Cheek-studs was still on his knees, Patrick was well within his reach.

Zoe clutched Patrick and staggered back, trying to help him get out of range of the knife. The second blow struck his other leg. This time he made no sound but instantly became too heavy for her to hold. He slipped to the floor.

Cheek-studs rose to his feet.

'You don't have to do this,' Zoe cried.

He responded by roughly shoving her to one side. She landed on the floor, then watched in horror as he bent over and lifted Patrick's head, readying himself to slit the vet's throat. Unable to do anything to save Patrick, Zoe turned away.

That was when she saw the boy.

He came up silently behind Cheek-studs and brought Patrick's bolt cutters crashing down on the man's head.

Cheek-studs pitched sideways on to the floor. Although he was still breathing, blood oozed from a wound behind his left ear. He wasn't going to get up a second time.

Zoe crawled over to Patrick, pulled off her tee-shirt and pressed it against his legs to stem the bleeding. She found herself crying.

And then she heard sirens.

'I'm sorry we had to let your attacker go to hospital first,' Trent said to Patrick, who lay on a stretcher waiting to be wheeled into the second ambulance when it arrived. 'I have to go by what the paramedics tell me. His condition's life-threatening.'

'It's okay,' Patrick whispered. 'There's no way I would've wanted to travel in the same ambulance as him, even with one of your officers there too.'

Trent turned to Zoe. 'You're going to the BGH as well, I hope, Doctor.'

'Only to keep Patrick company. The paramedics have checked me out. I'm fine.' Zoe pulled the blanket she'd been given closer around her shoulders. Despite the heat of the day, she felt cold. The blanket also hid her maternity bra and the mound of flesh between it and her trousers.

The boy had kept hold of the bolt cutters and remained standing over the unconscious man until the first police officer appeared at the top of the stairs. Then he'd dropped them and run into the bathroom. He was sitting on the grass now, being examined by the female paramedic who had coaxed him out.

'He saved our lives,' Zoe said, nodding in the boy's direction. 'What's going to happen to him?'

'You probably saved his life too,' Trent said. 'It must have occurred to you that the boy your poacher friend fished out of the Tweed is almost certainly connected with what's been going on here.'

Unwilling to mention the shock she'd received on seeing him for the first time, she said, 'I did wonder.'

'We'll get an interpreter in so we can ask the laddie some questions. He's obviously a victim, but he also

281

may be able to help us track down those responsible for his enslavement and the first boy's death.'

'Will he be returned to his family?'

'If they can be found. I've just spoken with a colleague from our special unit which investigates human trafficking. He said the boy's most likely Vietnamese, brought to the UK by one criminal gang and sold on to another to be their gardener here.'

'Gardener?' Zoe frowned. 'What a benign term for a child locked in a house with little food and hundreds of cannabis plants to tend.'

'Trust me, Doctor, I'm not making light of what he's suffered. And the worst of it is, his masters probably had other plans for him in the future, like forcing him into prostitution.'

Zoe looked again at the boy, felt the urge to go over and put her arms round him. 'Poor little thing. I wonder if he knew the boy who died.'

'If he did, he's possibly the only chance we have of identifying him.'

A second ambulance appeared out of the trees and sped through the gate, which had been left open for the continuous stream of police vehicles which followed hard on the heels of Trent and his colleagues.

'I'll have someone drive you home when you're finished at the hospital,' Trent said. 'We need to take formal statements from you both but that can wait.'

'Thank you.'

'There's just one more thing, Doctor.'

'What?'

'I'd rather you didn't visit Kate Mackenzie while you're there.'

'Why ever not? She'll never forgive me if she hears about what's happened today from someone else.'

Trent gestured towards the house. 'Because this property belongs to her brother Robert.'

THIRTY-NINE

Still protesting there was nothing wrong with her, on arriving at Borders General Hospital Zoe was taken to a cubicle in A&E where a middle-aged nurse carried out a range of checks on both her and the baby. A bruise had started to come up where Cheek-studs had grabbed her arm when Patrick attacked him, but everything else was normal, even her blood pressure.

'I should arrange for you to have an ultrasound,' the nurse said.

'There's no need, honestly,' Zoe said. 'I've had a nasty experience but I'm fine. And judging by how much he's bouncing around at present, my baby is too.'

The nurse peered at her over the top of a pair of pink-rimmed spectacles Kate would have been delighted to wear. 'Seeing as you're a doctor yourself, I'm not going to argue. But you do know what to look out for, don't you?'

Zoe quoted what she would have told any woman in her care: 'Vaginal bleeding, leaking fluid, abdominal pains or a decline in the baby's movement.'

'Alright, you pass,' the nurse said with a grin. She handed Zoe a carrier bag. 'There's a police officer waiting outside to take you home. She asked me to give you this before you leave.'

Zoe peered inside the bag and saw her mobile, seemingly undamaged apart from a cracked screen, and an oversized white tee-shirt. She pulled on the tee-shirt and walked out to the hospital corridor. A tall, red-haired police officer approached, introduced herself as Constable Reid and offered Zoe a wheelchair.

'Thanks but I can walk just fine.'

'News has got out there's been an incident,' Reid said. 'A few reporters are hanging about at the front door.'

'How did they find out so quickly?'

'It's impossible to keep anything quiet these days. I'll go first, you follow. Don't say anything.'

'Don't worry, I won't.'

Trying to look as though a police officer was walking ahead of her merely by chance, Zoe felt the colour rush to her face as the small group of men and women standing outside the hospital's main entrance ran towards them. The neutral expression she had adopted before stepping out of A&E vanished when someone called her name; she turned and saw the photographer who'd snapped her that day on the Chain Bridge. She glared at him. He smirked and raised his camera.

Zoe shouted, 'Leave me alone.' The only response she got was the sound of cameras taking her photograph.

The damage done, Reid took Zoe by the arm and led her towards the car park. By the time they reached the police car, Zoe's legs were trembling. She fell onto the front passenger seat with a groan. 'I lost my cool there. Sorry.'

'No you didn't. Losing your cool would have been telling them to fuck off.' Reid put the car into gear and concentrated on getting them away from the hospital.

As they'd agreed in the ambulance, Patrick phoned Zoe when he got home, which was a couple of hours after Reid dropped her off at Keeper's Cottage.

'How are you?' she asked.

'Walking like Kenneth More playing Douglas Bader but glad to be alive. What about you?'

'As long as I don't dwell on what might have happened if the boy hadn't found your bolt cutters, I'm okay. It was a relief to walk in here and be swamped with affection from the dogs.'

'Would you mind bringing Peggy over here later? The police haven't brought my car back yet and I don't think I could drive it anyway.'

'Are you sure you don't want her to stay here with us for a couple of days? She and Mac are still having a great time.'

'It'll do me good to take some short walks. And although she might not be missing me, I miss her.'

'We'll see you in about half an hour,' Zoe said.

After grabbing scones and bread out of the freezer, a few pieces of shortbread and tablet, and half a dozen eggs, she herded the dogs into the Jeep and made the short journey to Patrick's home. He came to the front door to meet them, wearing a pair of blue pyjamas.

When Zoe got closer, she could see the pain etched in his face. Even bending down to pat Peggy caused him to wince, and for once he didn't pick the dog up to give her a cuddle. In spite of this, he lightly touched Zoe's shoulder and said, 'I'm sorry.'

'Whatever for? I roped you into going there and you ended up with stitches up the back of both legs. I'm the one who should be apologising.'

'If only I'd left you in the car. When I realised what we'd found, we could've driven off and called the police from a safe distance.'

'Let's agree that we both messed up and leave it at that. Alright?'

'Alright.'

Zoe followed Patrick indoors. Just before they reached his sitting room, he stopped walking and leant against the wall.

'You're obviously in a lot of pain.'

'The injection the doctor gave me in A&E has worn off.'

'Didn't they also give you some medication to help you get through the next few days?'

Patrick winced and stared at the floor. 'I can't take them,' he said eventually.

'Why ever not?'

Still he wouldn't look her in the eye. 'There's a lot you don't know about me, Zoe.'

'Are you going to explain what you're talking about?'

He raised his head, took a deep breath and said, 'I can't take any drugs because I'm a recovering alcoholic.'

'Oh.'

'I've never abused pills, but I know I could very easily become addicted to painkillers so I avoid them. This is a bit worse than a headache, though.'

She said nothing.

'I've shocked you into silence, haven't I?'

'No, I was simply hearing you out. I'm a doctor, remember. I don't shock easily.'

'Doesn't mean to say you want an addict for a friend.'

'You don't know what I want.'

'I know the closest you've ever come to substance abuse is singing along with *The Joker* in your car.'

'Just because I can't recognise the smell of weed doesn't mean I'm some sort of goody two-shoes!' Zoe didn't realise how loudly she'd spoken until she saw Mac slink off down the hall, his tail down. 'Oh God, Patrick, I'm sorry. Let me help you get to your seat and we can talk about this.'

His jaw clenched. 'I can't even sit down.'

'In which case let me help you find a position you can manage.'

To head off any further argument, she took hold of his arm and they walked together to the sofa, where she instructed him to lie face down. He complied, though not without protest. 'I feel ridiculous. And useless.'

'And less likely to keel over, I hope.'

He propped himself up on his elbows and nodded.

'May I see the pills the hospital gave you?' Zoe asked. 'Or have you thrown them down the toilet?'

'They're in that box over there,' Patrick said, pointing.

She found the packet underneath a layer of battered paperback thrillers. 'These would definitely make you feel more comfortable. I can help make sure you stick to the prescribed dose.'

'I won't risk it. Trust me, I'm not being a martyr. There's a very real danger they could trigger a relapse. If you look in the bathroom, you'll see I even use alcohol-free mouthwash.'

'And there's nothing I can say to convince you otherwise?'

'No.'

'In which case, I'm going to stay here and look after you.'

'Why would you do that? You're not my doctor.'

'I'm your friend. It's what friends do. And to be honest, I don't feel like being alone tonight.'

'After what happened today, Zoe, someone should be looking after you.'

'If it makes you feel better, let's say we're taking care of each other.'

'You must think me very weak.'

'No, quite the opposite, actually.' She fetched a cushion from the armchair and tucked it behind his shoulder. 'Will I get us a bite of supper? You'll feel better if you have something to eat.'

'Depends if you like ham and cheese. I haven't got much else in.'

'Lucky I brought a few bits and pieces with me, in that case.'

Zoe cobbled together a light meal which Patrick was able to eat without having to sit up. They chatted and ate and, later, napped, Zoe in the armchair using a small box of books as a footstool, Patrick face down on the sofa. His bladder forced him up at around three in the morning, after which she made mugs of tea and talked to distract him from the pain in his legs. They both spoke of intensely private things, Zoe about what had happened to her since coming to the Borders, including meeting Andrew for the first time, and Patrick about being saved from an uncertain future by Alcoholics Anonymous.

'I'm guessing that the friend who keeps calling you at inconvenient times is another AA member,' Zoe said.

'Yes. I'm his sponsor. It's the first time I've done this and I don't want to screw it up.'

'It's a big responsibility but you seem to be devoting a lot of time and effort to him.'

'Sorry I couldn't tell you before, even when he was interrupting our outings. I probably shouldn't have said anything now, but you're a doctor, after all.'

They dropped off again around five o'clock, and Zoe woke with a start at seven-thirty, glad to have been rescued by the dogs' whines from a bad dream in which she couldn't staunch the blood coming from Patrick's legs. She looked over at the sofa, relieved to see him sleeping peacefully, and rose to let the dogs out. While Mac and Peggy ran around the small garden at the back of the house, she stood admiring the view and thinking about the events of the previous day. By rights, she should be suffering from shock, but all she felt was relief that the baby was unharmed. Near misses no longer mattered; the only important thing was what actually happened.

Peggy ruined Zoe's plan to let Patrick sleep on by racing back indoors and jumping up to lick his face. He stirred, groaned, and put a hand down to stroke the small dog.

'I'll make you a cup of tea,' Zoe said. While she stood in the kitchen waiting for the kettle to boil, she heard the toilet flush and when she turned round with their mugs of tea she saw Patrick standing at the door. His hair and beard looked unkempt and his clothes were rumpled, but at least he was standing up straight, which he hadn't been able to do the previous evening.

'Hello,' she said. 'How are you feeling?'

'The pain's subsided a lot, though my legs have stiffened up during the night. Thanks for keeping me company. I don't know how I would've coped on my own. How much sleep did you get in the chair?'

'It was more comfortable than I expected. But I'll have to go home soon. Today's Monday, remember? I'm taking a surgery at ten.'

'Don't suppose I'll be able to work for a couple of days. Getting anywhere's going to be the tricky part.'

Zoe walked through to the lounge, Patrick following. 'Do you think you can sit up to drink your tea?' she asked.

'I'll try.' He perched on the edge of the sofa and grimaced. 'Ouch. But I couldn't do this last night, so it's already an improvement.'

'You might not manage to walk Peggy today, so I'll come back after work and take her out with Mac, if you like.'

'Maybe I should argue with you, but I'm not going to. Do you want to leave Mac here till then? It'll take the pressure off me having to amuse Peggy.'

'Okay, it's a deal. I can make you some toast before I go, if you like?'

'No, but you could feed the dogs. I don't know about yours, but mine won't settle for a minute if she doesn't get her breakfast on time.'

Zoe's mobile rang just as she was putting two bowls of dogfood down on the kitchen floor and telling Mac not to steal Peggy's. The call came from the Mackenzies' landline.

'Thank goodness you're alright,' Etta said. 'Erskine told us yesterday evening what had happened and when I couldn't get hold of you at Keeper's Cottage last night or this morning I was starting to worry. I suppose you had an early night and you're walking the dog now.'

'I'm fine, really, although it was a horrible experience. Did you know poor Patrick was injured?'

'That's another reason I wanted to speak to you. We haven't got his home number.'

'I have his mobile.' Zoe called the number up and read it out to Etta.

'Thank you. Were you planning to go and see Kate today?'

'I'd like to.'

'She's not in Intensive Care any longer, thank goodness. With luck they'll let her out in a couple of days. In the meantime . . .' Etta's voice trailed off.

'You'd rather I didn't mention finding the cannabis factory?'

'Sergeant Trent told you the house belongs to Robert, didn't he?'

'Only because he didn't want me to blurt something out before he got to speak to Robbie about it. Has he done that now?'

'No, he can't.' Etta's voice wavered.

'Why not?' Zoe asked, dreading the answer.

'They've gone away on a last-minute holiday, and Robert's not answering his mobile. He's probably turned it off to be sure of getting some peace and quiet.'

From what Zoe had heard from Kate and seen for herself, Robbie wasn't the sort of person to cut himself off from work, no matter where he went. But she could hear the worry in his mother's voice, so she said, 'I'm sure you're right.'

'Robert would never have knowingly allowed one of his properties to be used for drugs, but unfortunately Erskine says they can't confirm this with the man who attacked you because he hasn't woken up yet.'

Zoe hadn't watched or listened to the news since getting home from the hospital. 'I didn't know he was so badly injured.'

'He deserved whatever you and Patrick did to him. You were defending yourselves.'

The hand Zoe was extending towards her mug of tea froze in mid-air. Was that what people believed had happened? 'I . . . I can't really talk about it.'

'Of course. I'm sorry for even mentioning it. Are you sure you're feeling well enough to drive over to the BGH yet again?'

'You know me, never happier than when I'm behind the wheel of a car.'

Etta Mackenzie rang off after urging Zoe to start taking it easy now the baby's birth was just a few weeks away. Zoe leaned back in the chair and groaned.

'What's wrong?' Patrick asked.

'The good news is you'll get a call soon from the Mackenzies and Etta's almost certain to send round more food than you can eat in a week.'

'And the bad news?'

'The man from the house hasn't regained consciousness.'

'Should we care what happens to him?'

'People have assumed you and I were the ones who hurt him.'

'The police know otherwise.'

'Yes, but they're not saying publicly what happened, presumably because there's a young person involved.'

'He was going to kill us. I don't mind if the world and his wife think I was the one who hit that criminal on the head. Even if he dies.'

'I do,' Zoe said.

It took a few seconds for Patrick's puzzled expression to change to one of embarrassment. He must have remembered their exchange of confidences during the night. 'I'm sorry. I wasn't thinking.'

'It's alright. The truth'll come out soon enough and people will know I'm not some sort of avenging angel.' She got up. 'I'd best be going. I'll need to shower before I go to work. Are you sure you can manage on your own till I get back?'

'I'll probably have to go back to lying on my stomach but that's no great hardship.'

'Consider yourself lucky you're not heavily pregnant.'

Zoe's forlorn hope that her involvement in the previous day's newsworthy events hadn't got out was dashed as soon as she entered the health centre. Margaret rushed from behind the reception desk to hug her. 'I'm so glad you're alright. Doctor Paul wasn't sure if you'd be coming in today but I knew you would've told us by now if you couldn't.'

'Thanks, I'm fine. Just a little shaken.'

'How's Patrick?'

Despite Margaret's fondness for animals, her husband's allergies meant the couple were unable to keep any pets, something she often reflected sadly on when hearing about Mac's latest exploit. 'I didn't know you knew him,' Zoe said. 'He's not a patient here, is he?'

'He's a friend of Hector's. I've never met him.'

292

'Well, you can tell Hector that Patrick is going to be okay. He's at home, though he was injured and won't be able to work for a few days.'

'He was lucky you were there to look after him.'

'I'm not sure if he'd agree with you. I got us into that situation.'

'Now you mustn't blame yourself, Doctor Zoe. There are some nasty people going about, even in the Borders, aren't there?'

'You're right, unfortunately.'

'They said on the news this morning a whole gang of criminals was working out of that house.'

'We only saw one of them. Which was enough.'

'My Hector says it'll be the Russian mafia behind it.'

'I wouldn't know about that. Anyway, have you got a busy morning lined up for me?'

'There's one less patient than there should be. We've just had notification that Mr Griffiths was taken into the BGH last night.'

'Oh dear.' Zoe remembered the elderly man's persistent cough and wondered if she should have done more. 'Let me know when you hear how he is, won't you?'

'I will. And Doctor Paul said to tell you he'd be in before you finish surgery because he needs to see you.'

Zoe moved off towards her consulting room, wondering if the Walter situation had been resolved at last. An hour later, halfway through surgery, she remembered a saying Russell used to trot out if she came home complaining about having had a rotten day: 'Sometimes you eat the bear and sometimes the bear eats you.' The bear definitely had the upper hand today. Every patient so far had been uncooperative if not downright stroppy, expecting Zoe to identify and offer instant relief from whatever troubled them and blaming her if this didn't happen. One young man had launched into a tirade against the NHS for being kept waiting for three minutes past his appointment time, while a mother of six-month-old twins had accused Zoe of thinking she knew it all because she was pregnant herself.

Realising tiredness, an aching back and the after-effects of the previous day's shocks were all contributing to a lower than usual tolerance for bad behaviour, she used the ten minutes which would have been Mr Griffiths' appointment to do her breathing exercises. When the time came to collect the next patient, she felt more able to cope, although this didn't stop her from wishing the whole thing was over and she could go home.

Home? Fat chance. She had to go back to check on Patrick, walk the dogs, then drive over to the hospital. Again. If Etta hadn't phoned and Kate hadn't been expecting her visit, she would have cried off. Still, Kate would be out in a few days, and things could get back to normal.

She scolded herself as soon as she had this thought. Kate's life wouldn't be back to normal for a long time. The least she could do was willingly visit her friend in hospital.

Paul appeared at her door soon after her final patient had left.

'My dear, how are you feeling?' he asked as he entered the room. 'Should you even be at work?'

'I'm fine, although if I'd known what a demanding bunch this morning's patients were going to be, I might have been tempted to stay at home.'

'Some days are like that. And then you'll find another surgery is filled with the most charming people who hang on your every word and apologise to you if their prescriptions didn't work.'

Zoe slumped back in her chair and stared at the ceiling.

Paul reached across the desk and patted her hand. 'If you don't mind me saying, you look exhausted.'

'I stayed over to look after Patrick last night. Slept in his armchair.'

'Was he badly hurt? The news is still very sketchy about what actually went on. They seem more interested in reporting the street value of the drugs you found.'

Zoe gave him a brief outline of the previous day's events in a matter-of-fact fashion, even though her heart started racing as she got to the part where they were at the mercy of Cheek-studs. 'It remains to be seen if that boy is connected with the dead boy pulled from the Tweed, although I can't believe he isn't. I really want to see that particular mystery solved.'

'I had no idea how much danger you'd been in. The man unconscious in hospital is the one who attacked you?'

'Yes. I refuse to think about what would have happened if the boy hadn't taken a swing at him with Patrick's bolt cutters. Anyway, he did, and we're all safe.'

'Where is he now?'

'With Children's Services, I expect. It's not like the police have arrested him. He's a victim too, poor little thing.'

Paul nodded but said nothing, giving Zoe the opportunity to change the subject. 'Any developments in the Walter situation?' she asked.

'That's one of the reasons I wanted to speak to you. He called me last night at home to say he's backing down from his demands, as long as we don't expect him to work out any notice.'

Tears welled up in Zoe's eyes. She told herself they had a lot to do with the events of the past twenty-four hours. Or maybe for the first time she was allowing herself to admit how much she wanted the practice partnership.

'Oh dear,' Paul said. 'Have you changed your mind? Maybe I should have checked first before springing this on you.'

'Not in the slightest. I'm happy. And relieved.' Zoe took a tissue out of the box she kept on her desk for patients and dabbed at her eyes. 'I have no idea why I'm crying.'

'You need to go home and get some rest.'

'I can't. I said I'd check on Patrick once I've finished here, and then I have to go over to the BGH to visit Kate. She's out of Intensive Care, thank goodness.'

Pulling his chair closer to the desk between them, Paul said, 'I'm just a silly old man but I'm a doctor too. And if you were my patient I would sign you off work with immediate effect. You're doing far too much, not to mention the shock you received yesterday. Zoe, you must slow down—for both your sakes.'

'I know. But now Walter's gone, I can't possibly stop working yet. And I feel fine, honestly.'

'That's the other thing I had to tell you. I've found a locum to cover your maternity leave. She can start as soon as we need her and stay till you're ready to come back.'

Embarrassed at the tears which started to course down her cheeks again, Zoe smiled, unable to speak.

FORTY

Once it kicked in, the Jeep's air-conditioning kept Zoe blissfully cool as she drove to Borders General Hospital on Monday afternoon. She and Patrick had agreed it was far too hot for both her and the dogs to go out walking in the middle of the day, so she had left Mac panting on the floor next to Peggy after promising to exercise them both when she returned. Patrick had regained some of his colour but still moved awkwardly, although he'd felt well enough to prepare them ham sandwiches for lunch.

Looking for ways to stave off the boredom of a journey she had taken several times in the past ten days, she tried to retrace Constable Reid's cross-country route the previous day. At one point she thought she'd lost her way, but then recognised what the policewoman had told her was Hume Castle, an imposing ruin high up on a hill surrounded by a cornfield edged with poppies. What cheerful, resilient little flowers they were.

Although it wasn't yet time to make the disclosure, she practiced different ways of breaking the news to Kate about meeting and getting to know Andrew. Her friend would initially be resentful of being kept in the dark about something so important, but Kate's affection for her own family and her reliance upon them for support meant any pique would quickly be replaced by happiness for Zoe. And intense curiosity, of course.

Today's scenic route felt a lot slower but actually only added five minutes onto her journey. With the summer holiday season well underway, the car park was a lot emptier than usual and she found a space immediately, albeit nowhere near any shade. At the hospital's automatic doors, she became aware of flashing lights approaching but forced herself not to turn and stare at the ambulance bearing another poor soul whose life had suddenly taken a turn for the worse.

Kate sat up in bed wearing a pink nightie, a small plaster at her throat the only visible evidence of the experiences she had recently lived through. 'Here's my friend I was telling you about,' she said to an elderly woman in the next bed. Her voice still sounded gravelly, making Zoe want to clear her own throat.

They hugged.

'How are you feeling?' Zoe asked.

'Fine, thanks, but what's going on at home?' Kate replied. 'Mum was in a peculiar mood last night when she visited. I knew something was up, though of course she denied it.'

Reaching to the back of her head to check her new barrette hadn't worked loose, Zoe said, 'I've not seen her. I expect she's just tired with all the worry and travelling over here every day.'

'You're fiddling with your hair. You do that when you can't think what to say. What on earth's going on?'

Zoe was spared having to answer this question by Kate looking past her and asking another one. 'And what's *he* doing here?'

Zoe turned around and saw Sergeant Trent coming towards them. His shirt was stained with sweat and he looked worried. After greeting them, he said, 'Doctor Moreland, I'm glad to find you here. Your mobile must be switched off.'

'I always mute it in a hospital.'

'Sorry for interrupting your visit, but I need you to come with me.'

'What's happened?'

'We'll talk about it outside.'

'Okay. I'll be back soon, Kate.'

Trent opened his mouth as if to argue with that statement, but stopped himself. Zoe's heart pounded as she followed him into the corridor. She felt no better when he took her arm and started to lead her towards the stairs.

'What's going on, Sergeant? I won't let you frogmarch me out of the building without an explanation.'

'My orders are to get you home as soon as possible.'

She planted her feet firmly at the top of the stairs and grabbed hold of the bannister, confident he wouldn't pull her and risk sending her tumbling headfirst to the landing below.

'You're scaring me. What's happened?'

'If I agree to tell you, will you keep moving?'

The low pitch of his voice and the gravest look she'd ever seen on his face stopped her from arguing further. 'Alright,' she said, releasing her hand from the bannister and taking the first stair down.

'I have some bad news.'

'Has the man who attacked us died? Can't say I'd be too upset about that.'

'No.'

'What then?'

'John Wilkie's dead.'

They were halfway down the stairs now. Zoe halted, felt Trent tighten his grip on her arm to urge her on. They reached the ground floor before she could find her voice.

'Did someone kill him?'

Trent murmured something about avoiding the main entrance and guided her off to their right, towards A&E.

'He was knocked down by a car as he crossed the road outside his home.'

'On purpose?'

As they rounded the corner opposite the A&E reception, Trent slowed down and swore under his breath. Constable Reid and a woman were walking towards them, the woman sobbing into a large handkerchief.

Trent pulled Zoe out of their way. Just as Reid and her charge drew level with them, the woman lifted her face from the handkerchief. She locked eyes with Zoe and bared her teeth.

'This is all your fault!' Heather Wilkie shouted. 'You made him go to the police and you got him killed!'

FORTY-ONE

Trent insisted on driving the Jeep back to Keeper's Cottage. At first, he tried to make conversation, but although Zoe expressed pleasure at hearing how well his premature son was doing, he eventually got the message her mind was elsewhere and shut up.

Heather Wilkie was right. Zoe had persuaded her husband to tell the police what he'd seen and heard that morning the boy had been thrown off the Chain Bridge, and because of this, his identity had been revealed online. The owners of all those cannabis plants which were currently being destroyed by the police must have mistakenly linked him with yesterday's raid on the house in the woods. They'd killed him because of her meddling. Another little girl would grow up without a father.

Even the baby's kicks, which had started up as they pulled out of the hospital grounds, felt like reprimands. Stupid, stupid, stupid.

The drive home took forever.

Zoe broke the silence as she unlocked her front door. 'What about Patrick? He could be in danger too.'

'He's taken care of,' Trent said.

'My dog's still with him. Can't I at least go over and fetch Mac?'

'I'll have someone bring him to you.'

'What about releasing the news that John wasn't with us when we found the cannabis factory, that it had nothing to do with him? If they know they've killed the wrong man, they might think twice about hurting anyone else.' Even as she said this, Zoe knew how naive it sounded, and Trent was kind enough not to respond, instead insisting on entering Keeper's Cottage before her. As she followed him inside, the little house felt unwelcoming without Mac bounding up to greet them.

While Trent checked all the rooms, his mobile clamped to his ear as he made arrangements to be collected, Zoe went through to the kitchen and poured them both some water from a jug in the fridge.

'I'd normally invite you out onto the patio, but I don't suppose you'd recommend that at present,' she said, passing the policeman his glass. They sat down on opposite sides of the kitchen table.

'Just for a few days. I know you're ex-directory but it's hard to keep someone's home address a secret any more. Especially round here, where everyone knows everyone else.'

Zoe nodded in agreement. The young man in the Fiesta — her stalker — had managed to track her down. She tried to remember if she'd first noticed him following her before or after being pictured on the ScotlandsNews website.

'I can tell by your face I've struck a chord,' Trent said. 'Have you had any unwelcome visitors here recently?'

'I'm sure he's nothing to do with the cannabis factory.'

'Who are you talking about?'

It was a relief to tell Trent about being followed by the Fiesta and the silent calls coming in on both the cottage phone and her mobile. When Zoe described how matters had escalated to her stalker driving his car at her, Trent jumped up and stood with his back to the sink, staring at her blouse as if trying to see through it. Zoe self-consciously crossed her arms.

'Sorry,' he said, turning pink. 'I was remembering finding you yesterday with your shirt off. I wondered what had caused all those scratches but didn't like to ask. Why didn't you tell anyone about this?'

'I felt stupid, not taking the car's number down and besides, I've not seen him since.'

Trent strode over to the French windows and looked outside. Although his face was hidden from her, Zoe could see his fists were clenched.

'Don't get angry with me,' she said. 'Be honest, what would you have done if I'd made a complaint? Told me to be careful and get his number next time, that's what.'

He turned to face her. 'I would have expected after the events of last winter . . .'

'It's because of what happened then that I didn't want to involve you. I promised myself I wasn't going to let such a horrendous experience make me live the rest of my life in fear.'

Trent opened his mouth to speak and closed it again, frowning.

Zoe held up a hand. 'I know what you're thinking and in the light of *your* recent experience, I can't blame you. But I'd never do anything to put my baby at risk. Had I known what was happening in that house, we wouldn't have gone near it. I thought we were simply dealing with a stray dog.'

'We don't have the manpower to post someone at your gate, but I'll arrange for a car to drive by here regularly. Promise me you'll get in touch immediately if you see anything or anybody suspicious.'

'Of course I will.'

A knock on the front door made Zoe jump. 'I'll go,' Trent said.

Seconds later, Mac bounded into the kitchen and rushed to Zoe's side. She leaned over to hug him. 'You'll look after me, won't you?' she murmured.

303

'Are you sure you don't want us to take you to Tolbyres Farm?' Trent said as he re-entered the room. 'We can wait for you to pack a few things.'

'Etta's got enough lodgers with Kate's children there, and Kate herself is coming out of hospital shortly. I'll be fine here. My new windows and doors are so secure they actually met with your boss's approval last time he visited.'

'Do you plan on going into the health centre tomorrow?'

'No, Paul insisted I take the day off even before this happened. He's found a locum to cover for me when I'm on maternity leave and he's pulling her in straightaway. Who knows, if she fits in, maybe I can finish work in time to catch up with all the things I'm supposed to do before the baby arrives.'

Trent nodded his approval at this. 'I must go,' he said. 'You've got my number, so call me if you're at all worried, okay?'

'I can't live the rest of my life looking over my shoulder.'

'I know.'

Despite all the things she had to do, Zoe couldn't settle to any task after Trent left, and ended up reading and snacking on tablet for most of the evening. Mac wandered around, confused at not getting his early-evening walk and probably missing Peggy's company too. She felt mean and foolish locking the French windows during his occasional tours of the garden, forcing him to bark to be let back in.

Keeper's Cottage became hotter and more stuffy as the evening wore on. Zoe usually threw all the windows wide open to take advantage of the cooler air, risking the arrival of moths and other flying insects, but tonight she was wary of other, more dangerous, visitors. When her bedtime eventually arrived, she fetched the

304

electric fan, glad now she hadn't taken it to the health centre, and succeeded in falling asleep with it on.

At five the next morning, her bladder having forced her to get up several times during the night, she rose and went through to the kitchen to make a cup of tea, briefly opening the French windows to let Mac out. Despite the early hour, the air still felt heavy and humid. She locked up again as soon as the dog came back in.

Guilt continued to overwhelm her: for causing John Wilkie's death, for leading Patrick into danger, and for risking, albeit unknowingly, her child's life. She couldn't even look Mac in the eye, knowing he wasn't going to get a walk for what might turn out to be days. Only the needs of the baby inside her made eating possible, and she kept going back in her mind to that morning on the banks of the River Tweed. None of this would have happened if she'd stuck to doing her paperwork and made the police officer wait for Paul.

Another bout of tears decided her: the only way to stop falling apart was to stay busy. She went online to research car seats. She'd just decided to delay ordering one until she could ask Kate's advice, when an email came in notifying her of the imminent delivery of some earlier purchases. These included a crib-set in a cheery farmyard design, which reminded her of another task she could undertake now she had time. She'd bought it to match some stencils she'd found months ago, so why not decorate the second bedroom's walls with cows, chickens, ducks and pigs now? Who cared if it was still only seven-thirty in the morning?

Stencilling turned out to be both easier and messier than she expected, so she donned the chef's apron Margaret had given her for Christmas, even though it no longer fitted in every direction and she had to wear it folded over and tied round her middle, like the old-fashioned waist pinny her grandmother had favoured. Stopping regularly for cold drinks to cool down and stave off dehydration in the oppressive heat, she worked on. She was poised to add one final brown hen when the doorbell rang and Mac barked.

She placed the can of spray adhesive on the hall table and wiped her hands on the apron. Her stomach churned as she looked through the front door's spyhole but the familiar sight of a hi-vis waistcoat and baseball cap, both bearing the Royal Mail logo, brought a surge of relief. She didn't recognise the face under the cap but Donald the postie had mentioned he was going on holiday soon.

Mac danced excitedly round her feet as she opened the front door, so she bent over to hold him by the collar. The postie moved towards her, holding up a small package.

'Thank you,' Zoe said, reaching out for it.

The postie grinned.

And grabbed her by the wrist.

FORTY-TWO

The man's grip on Zoe's wrist made her wince. 'What do you think you're doing?' she demanded, letting go of Mac's collar and trying to pull herself free. He dropped the package on the ground, grabbed her other arm and despite Zoe's struggles, propelled her backwards until they were both standing in the hall. Mac, realising something wasn't right, started to bark in a tone quite unlike the one he used to greet visitors. The man kicked out, his booted foot landing a blow against the dog's leg, making him yelp.

'Leave him alone!' Zoe shouted.

Mac snarled and backed off as the fake postie aimed another kick at him.

'Fucking dog,' the man said in a heavily accented voice. 'Fuck off.' He leaned against the door with one shoulder, slamming it shut with Mac outside.

'Who are you?' Zoe asked. Already she knew the answer didn't matter. He had come here to kill her. She could hear Mac still barking on the other side of the door, desperate to get in to defend her. She was completely alone.

Her captor brought her two arms together and held both wrists with one large hand. She briefly wondered if this was her chance to break free. Then she saw him remove a gun from his waistband and point it at her.

'Do not try to get away, okay?'

'Okay.'

'That's sensible.' He released her arms. 'Now lock the door so we aren't interrupted, okay?'

Zoe's legs shook as she walked the few steps to the front door, lifted the handle to engage the high-security lock and reached for the key. What was he going to do to her? Perhaps he intended to make her death look like a robbery gone wrong, or an extreme sex attack. As the narrow hall seemed to close in around her, it took all her self-control not to sink to the floor and curl up into a ball in the corner.

The baby started to kick. He was usually inactive at this time of day but the stress hormones coursing through her body must be affecting him too. He was telling Zoe she couldn't just give up.

When she turned round she saw the man had removed the Royal Mail baseball cap and thrown it on the floor. She stared at his head, at the crescent-shaped scar just above his right ear. This was the man who'd taken Ara into the Duns chemist.

She put a hand behind her back.

'What are you doing?' the man demanded.

'I need to undo my apron.'

'What?'

'This.' Zoe brought one of her hands forward and looped her thumb under the striped material. 'It's cutting into me.'

The man grunted. Before he could tell her not to, she pulled the bow loose and dragged the apron away from her bump.

He stared at her stomach and swore. He used an unfamiliar language, but she recognised the explosive and venomous words for what they were. He must have thought she was overweight under the bulky apron, not pregnant, but now he knew better. And unlike Cheek-studs, this seemed to matter to him.

'Not long to go now.' She forced a smile and patted her bump.

The gun pointing at her didn't waver as the man took his mobile from his back pocket and hit a number programmed in it. The call was answered promptly. He spoke again in his own language, giving the person on the other end little time to respond and becoming increasingly agitated. Throughout the conversation, his eyes didn't leave Zoe's stomach.

With a shake of his head, he rang off.

'Didn't tell you I was pregnant, did they?'

'Shut up.'

'You may have found murdering a defenceless boy and throwing him in the Tweed easy, but imagine how you'll feel if you do the same to me,' Zoe said. 'My child is nearly ready to be born, so you'd be killing two of us. A woman and a tiny baby. I don't think you want to do that.'

'Shut up, okay.' The gun started to wobble. She was getting to him.

'Or is nothing out of bounds to the likes of you? Nobody indispensable?'

'I didn't kill that boy.'

'If not you, one of your friends. While you stood by and did nothing to stop it.'

'No!' The fingers of his free hand worried at the scar on his head. 'We found him already dead. He killed himself.'

'Oh come on. I know about the injuries he suffered. What happened? Did you hurt him so badly that he couldn't work and was no more use to you?'

'I never touched him. He put a metal fork into the electric.'

Zoe remembered the power cables trailing along the floor upstairs in the cannabis factory, coming together in makeshift extension boards, and Patrick's warning not to touch anything. Then her mind filled with the image of the dead boy on a flat stone beside the River Tweed, his arms stretched out in front of him, one hand bandaged while the other, although just as badly injured, was not. She and the police assumed the second bandage had come off in the water, but what if he'd removed it himself, in order to grasp a piece of metal and thrust it into one of those lethal power-points? Enslaved and abused, had his life had become so intolerable that this was his only remaining option?

The idea appalled her more than thinking someone had murdered him.

'We only took him away from the house,' the man said.

'That's alright then.' Zoe wanted to cling to the anger she felt on behalf of the dead boy, hoping it would give her the courage to put into action the desperate plan she'd come up with as she'd stood by the front door. Because there would be no last-minute rescue this time. She only person who could save her child.

They stood in the hall just feet apart, the man still pointing his gun at her, Zoe still holding her apron.

Mac's barks had stopped.

The man raised his gun, aiming it above Zoe's stomach.

The bell rang, causing the man to glance involuntarily at the door.

Zoe flicked at the gun with her apron. She'd hoped to knock it from the man's hand, but instead the limp material simply hung off the barrel. Lunging towards the hall table, she grabbed the can of adhesive and sprayed it in her aggressor's face.

He yelled and dropped the gun.

She rushed to the door and yanked at the handle, having only pretended to lock it. Dashed outside, slamming the door closed behind her. Ran a few metres towards the road.

Straight into the arms of a young man wearing a red hoodie and aviator sunglasses.

FORTY-THREE

Zoe screamed, less in fear than in rage. This was so unfair. She tried to shove her stalker aside but he clung on to her. He seemed a lot younger up close, with a smattering of acne across his forehead and round his mouth, and smelled of cigarettes.

'What's happening?' he asked. 'Are you looking for your dog? He's alright. I found him running loose on the road and put him in my car for safety.'

Too distressed to speak, Zoe waved her hand back towards the house.

He released her. 'Please don't be frightened. I know you have every right to be, and angry too, but I've come to explain.'

Out of the corner of her eye, Zoe saw the front door open. She had no idea who this new arrival was but his obvious bewilderment told her he had nothing to do with the danger which now faced them both. She grabbed a handful of his red top and pulled at it, dragging him away from the house. 'We need to leave. Now.'

But it was already too late.

'Come back here!' In spite of continuing to wipe at his reddened eyes with one hand, the fake postie held the gun steady with the other.

Zoe felt the young man beside her take a step back as he realised the situation he'd wandered into.

'In there or out here, it's all the same. You're going to shoot me whatever I do,' she shouted. Now the adrenaline rush which had given her the impetus to flee had abated, her legs felt like jelly again.

A quiet voice behind her said, 'Do what he says but walk towards the garage, not directly at him.'

Her mind raced. How was that going to help? And who was he, this young man who at their last encounter had nearly driven his car into her? All the same, she did as she was told, staring into the half-closed and still weeping eyes of the man with the gun. He seemed not to grasp what an indirect route she was taking until he had to adjust his position to keep his weapon trained on her.

'Where are you going? I said come here, okay.' He flicked the gun sideways as if to influence Zoe's course.

And at that moment, a flash of red streaked past her, landing on the gunman. He fell backwards, the younger man on top of him.

The gun went off.

FORTY-FOUR

Zoe didn't move, didn't even dare breathe. The two men lay, the younger uppermost, at the entrance to Keeper's Cottage, both equally still. Which of them had been shot?

She watched her hoodie-wearing stalker roll off the man he'd thrown himself at, and felt a surge of relief when he rose to his knees and called over to her. 'He must have hit his head on your doorstep. Could wake up at any minute. Have you got a piece of rope I can tie him up with?'

Eyes closed, mouth lolling open, the man who had come to kill her no longer looked a threat, but Zoe stood well back as she stared down at him. She shook her head, unable to speak.

'Well something else, then. Anything.'

She edged past the prone figure, not taking her eyes off him until she was inside the hall, where the spray adhesive and her apron lay on the floor. Rope? Who the hell keeps rope in their house? She was about to go to the kitchen and start looking for an alternative when she spotted Mac's retractable lead hanging up with the coats.

'Will this do?' she asked, returning to the doorway and holding it out.

He took it from her and pulled out several metres. 'Perfect.'

This probably wasn't the time to ask, but she had to know. As he turned the gunman over, she said, 'Who are you? Why have you been following me?'

He peered up at her through the thick, wavy hair which obscured half his face. 'I'm Ewan. Ewan Balfour.'

'What? You're Andrew's son?'

'Yes. And I'm sorry for everything I've put you through. I —'

The gunman groaned and began to move. Ewan knelt on his back, struggling to bring the other man's wrists together, but he had regained consciousness enough to fight back, rocking from side to side and kicking up his heels. Gasping with the effort of keeping him restrained, Ewan said, 'Zoe, can you grab his legs for me?'

She stepped outside, knelt and put a hand round each of the gunman's ankles and pressed them into the ground. Had he been fully conscious, she doubted this would have subdued him, but he immediately calmed down, enabling Ewan to tie his wrists together.

'I'll hogtie him,' he said, holding the lead's plastic handle and unreeling another length. He climbed off the gunman and Zoe relaxed her hold of the ankles to move out of his way.

The gunman rolled onto his side and kicked out, hitting her stomach with his foot.

Thrown sideways by the blow, Zoe shrieked in pain and shock. She lay in the foetal position on the ground, clutching her stomach to comfort and protect her baby. 'Please be alright,' she whispered. 'We've come this far.' Dimly aware of the struggle going on next to her between the two men, she pushed herself further away from them as someone's limb crashed against her back. She knew Ewan needed her help but she couldn't risk any further injury to her child.

Her foot hit something.

The gun.

Zoe had never held a gun before. It felt heavy and unwieldy, and she had no idea if it had a safety catch let alone if this was on or off. She hoped she wouldn't need to find out.

She struggled to her knees. 'I've got your gun.'

Ewan lay in the same position she'd been in seconds ago, trying to protect himself from the vicious kicks the gunman, hands still tied behind his back and dangling the dog lead, was inflicting on him.

She staggered to her feet.

'I've got your gun,' she repeated, more loudly this time. 'And I'll use it if you don't leave him alone.'

Ewan's attacker froze. He slowly turned to face her, his eyes bulging and his breath rasping. 'I should have shot you as soon as I arrived, baby or no baby.'

'Lie down on your front,' Zoe said, making a conscious effort not to move the gun to emphasise her point. The astonishment she felt as the man obeyed without further comment was replaced by fear as the dull ache she'd felt earlier in her back suddenly got a lot worse and was joined by a searing pain in her abdomen.

She looked down and saw a clear liquid tinged with red coursing down both her legs. Her waters had broken. Her fear was joined by anger; she wasn't ready, emotionally or physically for this. Her baby needed another month in the peace and comfort of her womb, but instead was being forced to arrive early. If the man to blame for this moved an inch, the temptation to pull the gun's trigger would be overwhelming.

She took a deep breath and said, 'Ewan, please get up.' Her voice sounded as shaky as her legs felt.

Ewan groaned then slowly rose, grimacing as he tried to straighten his back. Rubbing his ribs, he moved towards the figure on the ground and while Zoe stood with the gun trained on its owner, he pulled the dog lead tight and tied the gunman's ankles too. For good measure, he wrapped the rest of the lead around the metal boot scraper set into a lump of stone and secured it with several knots. 'He's going nowhere now.'

Zoe carried the gun indoors and dropped it onto the hall table.

She wanted to phone for help, from the police to deal with the gunman and an ambulance to save her baby, but first she had to get to the bathroom. Two steps along the hall, she fell to her knees.

'Zoe, did he hurt you?' Ewan raced to her side and started to help her up.

'Please, let me stay here. The phone's in the kitchen, off to the left. You need to dial 999 and ask for the police and an ambulance. Tell them a pregnant woman has gone into labour a month prematurely. Then you can bring me a towel.'

Ewan closed the front door to block out the noise of the gunman shouting obscenities in English and his own language. He knelt down next to Zoe. 'They said the ambulance'll be about twenty minutes. Can I do anything?'

'If they take longer than that, your lambing experience might be needed.' Despite the pain she was in, Zoe laughed at the look of horror on his face. 'Just talk,' she said. 'Explain why you were stalking me.'

'I wasn't *stalking* you. I thought you and Dad were having an affair. Why else would he meet you in secret and delete all your texts as soon as he'd read them? Mum was sick and I hated him for betraying her. So I wanted to find out about you.'

'Did you think my baby was his too?'

'Why wouldn't I?'

'That must've made things worse, given you cause to hate me even more.'

'But I didn't plan to hurt you. I'd never do something like that.'

'You drove straight at me.'

'No way!' Ewan shook his head violently. 'I lost control of the car. It belongs to a friend's mum, she never drives it, so he's been letting me use it. The brakes aren't brilliant.' He met Zoe's gaze. 'I didn't mean to hurt you. Please believe me.'

He looked genuinely remorseful. And so young. With this thought, Zoe remembered something his father — *their* father — had told her. 'Hold on. You're only sixteen. You shouldn't even be driving.'

'Granddad taught me when I was twelve. He used to let me drive the Land Rover all over his farm. It's not hard.'

A wave of pain put paid to Zoe's response. She gripped Ewan's hand and tried to breathe steadily. As it subsided, she forced herself to keep on talking. 'When did Andrew tell you about me?'

'Last night. I couldn't believe it at first.'

'I presume he doesn't know you're here now.'

'No. I had to get away and think. And then I realised I had to come and explain. You won't tell him what I did, will you?'

'We won't be able to keep your presence here quiet. And the police won't let you drive home, once they know how old you are.'

'Do they have to know?'

'Don't worry, I'm sure saving my life today will mean they'll turn a blind eye to how you got here. And — ' Zoe gasped as she fought to deal with another contraction. When the pain lessened, she continued, 'And I won't mention last week's near accident to Andrew if you don't.'

'I'm sorry, Zoe.'

'I'm sorry too, about how your father keeping me secret has made the distress of losing your mum so much worse. But you must understand why he did it. He did it out of love, to save her from any more pain.'

'He wasn't thinking about me and Nina, though, was he?'

'Maybe not, which is something you'll have to forgive him for. Promise you'll at least try to do that.'

Ewan shrugged. 'He's my dad. Guess I have to.'

'He's mine as well. Which makes you my little brother, so I won't tell him about you smoking, either.'

They continued to sit side by side on the floor, silent except for Zoe's intakes of breath each time a new contraction arrived, until they heard the wail of sirens out on the road.

Ewan got up. 'I'll go and meet them.' He took one step outside the door and looked back at Zoe. 'You'll never guess what's happened.'

'Oh God, what now? Has the gunman escaped?'

'No, he's still here but he's getting wet. It's raining. Isn't that great? It's raining at last.'

FORTY-FIVE

The organ started up again and everyone stood for *All Things Bright and Beautiful*. This had been Zoe's favourite hymn when she was a child, but instead of singing along, she allowed her mind to drift as she looked at the people around her, most of whom rarely entered Westerlea church under normal circumstances but had attended the Sunday service to be here for her baby's blessing.

Kate stood with her arm looped through Erskine Mather's, all the better to show off the pale pink sapphire engagement ring he'd surprised her with during a recent weekend away, turning every now and then to check her children were behaving. Only an occasional cough into a tissue hinted at the lasting damage the fire had caused to her lungs, and which the doctors had said might reduce over time but would never entirely disappear. Zoe knew this worried Kate's parents; she regularly spotted Etta's frowns on observing her daughter resort to an inhaler to help with bouts of breathlessness. But at least Ranald and Etta had been spared the ordeal of seeing their youngest son face prosecution for involvement with the people who'd been running a cannabis factory in one of his properties. In Kate's words, the police recognised Robbie had 'behaved like a dickhead not a criminal' in settling one of his gambling debts by lending out his house for the summer, no questions asked.

The authorities were continuing their efforts to trace the family of Ara, the boy who had chosen to die rather than remain enslaved in the cannabis factory. The boy who saved Zoe and Patrick had been reunited with his parents, while Cheek-studs died without regaining consciousness and no one had claimed his body either. The gunman sent to kill Zoe had made a detailed confession, leading to several arrests and Trent's reassurance there would be no further attempts on her life.

Paul caught Zoe's eye and smiled. She'd been delighted to grant his shy request to bring a guest, because even Margaret had been unable to discover the identity of the person responsible for giving him a new zest for life and encouraging him to relinquish his beard and tartan ties. When he arrived at the church accompanied by Bette Mather, who wore a perfectly coordinated outfit of grey jersey dress and winter coat topped with a colourful scarf, Zoe and Margaret had looked at each other with satisfaction. The lack of surprise in Kate's demeanour as she approached her future mother-in-law and greeted her with genuine affection meant she must have known about this relationship for some time. Zoe felt in awe of her friend's uncharacteristic ability to keep such a big secret.

She gazed down at the sleeping child in her arms, perfect in every way despite arriving a month early. During the terrifying episode at Keeper's Cottage, she had feared neither she nor her baby would live to get properly acquainted with their family, yet Andrew, Ewan and Nina had been her first visitors in the maternity ward. Kate had arrived soon afterwards, her disappointment at having missed out on being Zoe's birth partner trounced by glee when she was introduced to the three strangers.

All Things Bright and Beautiful ended, snapping Zoe back into the present. After a few more words from the minister, the ceremony was over and everyone made their way out into the winter sunshine. Rocking the baby who was now awake, Zoe thanked the minister and invited him to join them for the celebration lunch the Mackenzies had insisted on hosting. She was imagining Auntie Joan putting the finishing touches to the piles of food which would now be sitting on the kitchen table at Tolbyres Farm, when she heard a familiar bark. Patrick stood a little way off with Mac and Peggy straining on their leads. She waved and Patrick waved back.

So did one of two figures standing at the church gate.

Zoe stared.

Sergeant Trent remained still as the second man pulled off his knitted hat, revealing a bald head.

Zoe no longer heard the chattering around her, and was unaware of walking down the path until she found herself at the gate. Trent had moved a short distance away.

'Hello, Neil.'

'Hello, Zoe.'

'I wondered when we'd see you again.'

'I was never far away. You got my postcards?'

'Yes.'

His eyes were fixed on the baby. 'Hope you don't mind me just turning up.'

'I've called her Poppy. Hope you're alright with that.'

'She's beautiful. I'd like to get to know her.' He glanced over at Trent. 'When I have more time.'

Zoe nodded. 'We're not going anywhere. This is our home.'

She turned and walked back up the path to the church.

THE END

THANK YOU FOR READING

If you have enjoyed this novel, please consider leaving a review on Amazon or Goodreads. Reviews are important because they help other readers choose which book to buy next. They also increase a book's visibility, helping authors by boosting our sales and making it more likely that we can continue writing books for you to enjoy.

Due to the wonders of modern technology, you can also contact me direct to tell me what you thought of *Too Soon a Death*:

Tweet me: I'm **@JanetOKane**

Post on my Facebook author page:
https://www.facebook.com/JanetOKaneAuthor

Email me via my blog: **www.janetokane.blogspot.co.uk**

If you haven't already done so, you may like to read my first Borders Mystery, *No Stranger to Death*, which introduces Doctor Zoe Moreland, Kate Mackenzie and Erskine Mather. Both Borders Mysteries are available as ebooks and paperbacks.

ACKNOWLEDGEMENTS

I'd like to thank the following for the help I received in writing *Too Soon a Death*: Nigel Adams, Keith Hall, Ruaraidh Hamilton, Lisa Hartley-Elliott, Yvonne Johnston, Phil O'Kane, and the many Facebook friends who shared some of the mysteries of pregnancy with me. If you live in the Scottish Borders and thought you recognised a couple of the characters, you were right: George Romanes and Jacques Kerr not only advised me but also kindly agreed to appear as themselves. Any factual errors in this book are mine.

I and my book have also benefited greatly from the professional services of Jessica Bell, who designed the lovely cover; Julia Gibbs, whose proofreading has saved me many blushes; and Jo Harrison from Writer's Block Admin Services who once again has taken on some of this self-published author's essential IT tasks.

AUTHOR'S NOTE

Although I created the imaginary village of Westerlea as the backdrop for the main events in this book, many of the Borders locations I describe are real. The Union Chain Bridge, is an historically important yet relatively unknown structure linking Scotland and England. It was the first vehicular bridge of its type in the UK and remains in use, although its continued survival is now threatened. A campaign to have the bridge fully restored in time for its bicentenary in 2020 has been started. You can find out more about the Union Chain Bridge at **http://www.unionbridgefriends.com**.

52065183R00199

Made in the USA
Charleston, SC
09 February 2016